LABAN'S WILL

Albert Lebowitz

Random House New York

LABAN'S

WILL

FOR

NAOMI

LABAN'S WILL

1

Rachel Laban, a captive audience, played a childhood fantasy in earnest. She imagined she was in Leah's placid skin and destined, for the day at least, to play Leah's part in the scheme of things. While she loved her twin dearly, more than life, and might be willing to give up a kidney for her, it was disheartening to feel like her. She sat like a lamb in the courtroom, waiting for Laban's case to begin, when she should have been home with Bernie and Leah, thumbing her nose at Laban, exploring the curves (named Beatrice) he had thrown them. She sat in the first row behind the railing that separated the American public from its trials. The lawyers sat at two long tables before a tiered dais, waiting for the judge.

With Rachel in the front row, some distance away, was a cluster of six ancient colored people. They were so neat it was painful, the four men moist in black suits and the two women stiff in cotton dresses. She smiled at them but no one was interested or relaxed enough to smile back. Some were Laban's and some the other lawyer's, and disloyal though it might be, it made absolutely no difference to her which was which. What did matter was her difficulty in telling one from the other; she could die having to admit it even to herself. The men had caps of woolly gray hair the texture of S.O.S. scouring pads and the women were simply sacks of coal. One man, she finally noticed by severe concentration, was tall and hollowed at the chest, one was round as a potbellied stove; she fought to make the leap of segregation. She frowned. Laban segregated as easily as he breathed. He knew everybody's name and their children's diseases.

The beefy-faced man sitting at a desk against a side wall

banged a gavel and motioned everyone up. "Circuit Court, Division Five, now in session, Honorable George Brutsche, Judge." The judge, a slightly built, strong-nosed man of roughly Laban's age, dressed in a milky blue suit, shuffled to his chair with his head averted from the courtroom. He sat down and threw his shoulders back, and his eyes stared bold as brass. A king off and on his throne, or Sir Laurence Olivier off and on the stage.

"Good morning, gentlemen," he said. "Mr. Rogers"—to the clerk sitting below him. "Call the docket."

The clerk called out some cases and told the judge they were continued to another date. Then *Jones et al. versus Gray's Estate* was called, and Laban and the other lawyer said they were ready.

"Would you care to make an opening statement?" said the judge.

"We would, your Honor," said the other lawyer, and Laban nodded.

"You may proceed," the judge said, and picked up a pencil.

Rachel tried to listen but the lawyer was dull and pedantic and not at all good-looking. He was young enough but had a square face with rimless glasses and he took at least three baths a day. According to Laban he was a very good lawyer in nonjury cases like this one but terrible before a jury, and she knew why. A judge had to listen. She had nothing else to do so she concentrated on Jackson Schwartz, sitting with a yellow note pad behind Laban at the lawyers' table. He interested her. He didn't go with his name. And he hadn't come into the office at all that morning; Laban was ready to skin him alive. "Where the hell is Schwartz?" he'd said to Miss Trilby, running out of his office at nine-thirty. "What does he think he's pulling?"

"He's at court to make sure of the witnesses," said Miss Trilby, hands fluttering in rhythm with an internal, atonal symphony. Rachel marked her gestures as another of her tics to describe to Leah. The tremor in Miss Trilby's voice didn't really belong to her because it reminded Rachel of the giggle in Beatrice's voice.

"That boy's got a lot to learn. He's got one job, to make sure of *me*," said Laban. "Get ready," he added to Rachel, who was sitting like a waif in the lobby and making Miss Trilby nervous.

She hadn't really met Jackson Schwartz. At the courtroom he was waiting outside in the hall; Laban said, "My daughter," and pulled him aside. Rachel got an impression of white teeth trying to make the best of Laban's rudeness. "Everything tied together?" said Laban. "The people from the Negro Y? The police report? Our clients?"

"Yes, sir," said Jackson.

"Okay. Now listen, white boy, you're in the office at nine o'clock sharp every workday unless I say otherwise or you're out on your ass. Got that?"

"I just thought . . ."

"Don't think. Let's go." He turned to Rachel. "Baby, I'll show you where to sit. Have a ball while your old man works his tail off."

Eying Jackson Schwartz, Rachel figured that he had changed his name from Gerhard von Bruno or Jan Metterling. He had soft, blond wavy hair, plastic blue eyes and regular features, and was good-looking even though his face had a slightly lopsided shape. It went awry downward from his cheekbones, not enough to kill his looks, but enough to make it possible he had her Jewish or some other crazy blood in him. He was tallish with nice shoulders, a slim waist, and she liked the way his neck glided into his collar. If he had only stood up to Laban in the hall she would have notified Laban, I want him delivered to me at nine o'clock sharp for a trip to Niagara Falls, just like you and Beatrice.

The other lawyer finished and Laban made his opening speech. Even as a stranger she would have sat up and listened; even the clerks with boredom laced into their faces paid attention. Laban did have a way with an audience.

"Your Honor. Plaintiff's attorney has stated the facts so fairly that if this weren't an adversary proceeding I'd pack up and go home. If you have the facts on your side, who needs a lawyer? My client may be a ghost but he's certainly not an angel, which is what they're asking us to believe. Only an angel would move into an apartment next to total strangers and say to them, Why, folks, I love you to death. You just take care of little old buttercup me and I'll leave you twenty-five thousand dollars, truly I will. Mr.

Bowen, our dearly departed, lived for ten years at the Y and had any number of cronies—they're right here in the courtroom— who'd give him the shirts off their backs, and do they say he promised them anything? No, sir. And why did he move out of the Y? Because it closed up and that was the only reason. This was no sickly, feeble old man. He was the picture of health until the day he dropped dead on the sidewalk. He paid cash on the barrelhead and asked nothing for nothing. A good, God-fearing man, but an angel? No. No. And let's just say, which I don't, that these people made him a few meals, cleaned his apartment with a few swipes of a broom. Eight thousand dollars a month they're asking. Your Honor, I ask *you*. When people try to pick eight thousand dollars a month off a dead man's eyes, are we prevent- ing fraud? I'd say we're fostering it. It's up to these plaintiffs to eliminate the slightest smidgeon of a doubt they aren't pushing in here because Mr. Bowen's dead and buried. He can't get up—al- though God knows he's probably trying—and shake that finger of his which he worked to the bone on the B&O and say, Now, folks, I thought you were my *friends* and here you are, not doing right by me at all."

Rachel couldn't believe that the other lawyer wouldn't get up once to complain, not even about his clients taking money off a dead man's eyes. Laban was getting away with murder while that man sat without saying a word. And then when Laban sat down, the other lawyer had the nerve to wink. The sight of the bland, scrubbed face winking a cold eye behind rimless glasses made Rachel furious. She wanted to go up to the opaque face and slap it hard and say, You're no better than Laban. You have just as much fun playing with people's lives as he does. She admitted she wanted Laban's blood. She wanted him hit with more than a wink, wanted him carved up by the leader of the rival mob. She didn't expect the lawyer to hate Laban for loving his job, but he should at least let him know he'd been in a fight. She resolved to have nothing more to do with lawyers; she would never, never marry one. Having made her decision, she walked out of the courtroom, leaving Laban to win by himself.

Ever since she was a little girl, Leah Laban had had a dark secret. She admired her father without reservation. No matter how many times Bernie or Rachel or even her now dead mother said he was a silly man—no matter how silly he actually seemed—she never wavered. Since her attitude was a secret, she learned to hide it, and the cost to her was that she suppressed every natural instinct to imitate Laban, to frolic in public herself. She went underground and lived like a brown nut inside her body; and since communication was the imperative around the house, words flew like ticker-tape confetti about her head, stuffing her eyes and ears and mouth. Words became fictions and she sealed herself into what she regarded as reality. Her mind became her world, and since she sought a direct connection, she was prepared to sacrifice her body bit by bit; it stood in the way. A machine, it existed to serve her by fair means or foul—to have no other god before her.

She divorced herself from the responsibility for her physical needs. She satisfied the needs of the machine by letting other people abuse it as they would and, meanwhile, she stored up memories of the abuse. The more obedient her body was to the will of others, the less she expected to give of her person, and the freer she thought she became. Her faith, if she had one, was that the only morality of her flesh was the defense of her mind. She let the drone of a body speak for her, act for her, punish and be punished for her, while she remained, so she believed, inviolate. She worked at the paradox that to be true to herself she must play false to everyone. She remained firm-lipped through Laban's divertissements. She had been a docile, obedient, grave child and remained so as a girl of twenty.

Meanwhile, the secret had clouded and mushroomed into a contempt for human life—her own, certainly her brother's and sister's, even her beloved father's. She was unaware it had moved beyond her control. She believed, instead, that she was filled with a hoard of treasure with which she could toy. At will. In private.

Leah went to the door of the basement room and pulled it open. "Here it is," she said. "Laban's made me warden."

Bernie took inventory behind his horn-rimmed glasses and elastic face. Against the east wall, which was roughly under the front wall of the house, were two double-decker bunks with mattresses, pillows and blankets. Next to these was a desk, then a wire bookstand loaded with a Bible, Shakespeare's plays and an old set of the World Encyclopedia. On top of the desk was a survival handbook. Against the north wall was a bookcase, and on its shelves was a series of jars filled with water. Next to that, on the floor, were a thermos jug, a Coleman lamp, a bedpan, a giant garbage can with its lid attached by a chain, two smaller cans with lids, a metal tool box and two shovels. The west wall had a bureau and two wooden chairs and a square mirror hanging over the bureau. At the south wall were two buckets of sand, three buckets of water, a hand fire-extinguisher, a coiled garden hose tied together with rope, and a ladder.

Bernie pulled out the center desk-drawer: two transistor radios and two extra batteries, pads of paper, several ballpoint pens, pencils, envelopes held together by a band of adhesive paper, a roll of stamps. The other drawers contained a first-aid kit, tooth-paste tubes, toothbrushes, soap, four safety razors with packs of Schick stainless steel blades, a package of tongue depressors, a package of splints, three flashlights, ten flashlight batteries, kitchen knives, forks, spoons. He opened the bureau: blankets, towels, eight rolls of toilet paper, candles, five cartons of Kent cigarettes, ten boxes of stove matches, paper plates, cups and napkins, three can and bottle openers, four pocketknives. In the bottom drawer were neatly folded old newspapers.

Bernie faced Leah. "Stamps. Is that everything?"

Leah shook her head. She pointed to the closet and Bernie opened it. Built-in shelves were jammed with canned goods and packaged foods, chocolate bars, cartons of Coca-Cola, bottles of bourbon; on the floor were several pairs of blue jeans and blue denim work shirts, dozens of jockey shorts and two pairs of knee-length rubber boots.

"Everything?" he said.

"Yes."

Bernie sat on a wooden chair and crossed one leg high over the other. "He makes me feel old. It's as though to maintain his energy he has to drain off everybody else's. This convinces me. Laban will never die. He, not the Kremlin, will bury us with those shovels, not only us but the seven children he'll have by Beatrice. How can you stand it?"

"What?"

"Him."

"He's our father and I love him."

Bernie stood up and twirled on his heel, leaving a skid mark on the asphalt tile. "This is a monster's room, dedicated to the proposition that all men are created evil."

"Lots of people have survival shelters. If anything happened you'd want a place to hide."

"I knew something was missing. Where's the shotgun? How's he going to keep out all the poor slobs who didn't provide? The little children crying outside the door?"

"He'd share what he has. You can't complain that Laban's selfish."

"Money, honey, just money, and you can't buy generosity. Damn right I think he's selfish. I'm begging you. Come away before it's too late. He'll suck you dry into an old maid. Blood is his money in the bank."

"I forgot to show you something," said Leah. "It's outside." She led him up the steps and out the door at the landing. Sandbags were piled against the basement windows. "See? He's thought of everything."

"He's a genius. It's a privilege to have such a man for a father."

"I'm glad you realize it," said Leah.

"Leah," said Bernie, screwing up his pale eyebrows, "he's a nut. He's got squirrels gnawing at his brain. Grow up, will you? I wouldn't set foot in this cage again if it weren't for you, and neither would Rachel. We came back from school just for you, expecting the worst and finding it twice as bad. You're nothing but a servant around here; is that what you call the good life?"

"I have a very good life," said Leah.

"All he does is make life a big joke: his children, the hydrogen bomb, our mother's dying—everything's a big joke. He thinks it's a laugh-riot that his daughter washes his dishes while his sexy new wife polishes her fingernails."

"You don't understand," said Leah. "I want to keep house. Laban offered to get help but I wouldn't let him."

Bernie kicked one of the sandbags. "Where's Mommy today?"

"Is that what you've decided to call her? She's in her room. She doesn't usually get up before noon."

"Yes, sir. The dream life. Sleep late, rise from cocoon of bed to cradle of bath, moon over *McCall's*, while number-one girl Leah prepares breakfast and lays out fancy underthings. Dress in silk, have hair fixed, shop at small elegant stores, whisk home for nap while Miss Leah prepares dinner. Afterward, perhaps a little piano and song with adoring family gathered around. Then little roll in hay with sugar daddy, twenty years older maybe but still sassy, and all that sugar, and so to sleep. Do you realize she's twice as close to our ages as his?"

"Yes. Isn't Laban lucky?"

"Plenty. He's lucky he can't see the handwriting on the wall."

"What does that mean?"

"I'll give you a tip. She's a whore. She likes anything in pants."

"Even you?"

"By all means me."

"You're in the wrong tradition. You're just a nice Jewish boy."

"I may surprise you," said Bernie. "I'll admit you surprised me.

I didn't realize you'd become so pro-Laban. Don't forget, I can remember when. Or is it anti-Bernie? You know, I had a vision of myself coming back as a faithful Saint Bernard with a keg around my neck, saying, Don't worry, little sister, I'll save you from a worse fate than death. Who'd believe you prefer slavery to freedom?"

"I wouldn't call anyone tied up in knots free."

Bernie broke into a sad smile. "You've gotten tough. Where did you get so tough?" He was handsomer when he smiled—which was not often, even sadly.

"You live and learn," she said.

As they went inside to the living room, Bernie said, "Before you bring home a new baby you should prepare your other children. How much preparation did we get?"

"I'm not a child, you're not a child, Rachel's not a child, and Beatrice is not a baby."

"Answer, don't conjugate me."

"Laban doesn't owe us explanations. He's not our father confessor. How much explaining have you done about Barbara Sloan?"

"How did you find out about her?"

"Rachel told me."

"I'll thank her to keep her fat mouth shut about my affairs. That was classified information. But I can't blame her. She assumed she was talking to a fellow prisoner, not the warden."

"You count too much on words. I don't care if you're sleeping with Rachel's roommate and I wouldn't dream of telling Laban. Not that he would mind."

"Mind? He'd slap me on the back and wink. I'd tell him in a minute if I thought he'd mind. I bet he hands out free rubbers to your boy friends."

"You know perfectly well I'm a virgin."

"Sure you are. So is Beatrice."

"It may surprise you to know that you can't embarrass me."

"Where's your sunbonnet?"

"That's amusing. You're the provincial. You're the kind of brother who'd shoot my lovers first and ask questions afterward."

"For Christ's sake, go out with gentiles. Be forbidden fruit. Be dark-eyed, sensual, passionate."

"Why? To satisfy your sense of outrage? I'd rather cling to my roots, to my father and his father. You walk around with the weight of the family tree on your shoulders. That's why you're round-shouldered."

"Laban is some Jew. He doesn't lay gentiles, he marries them. Besides which, he's hedonistic, amoral and unloving. Even if I weren't his son I'd be his enemy because he *is* the enemy."

"Out of billions of people in the world. What right have you to judge? You're what you say Laban is, which he isn't, and you're unforgiving besides." She fought against irritation. She must never lose control. Her body was a mechanical toy that must dance only to her tune.

"My right is that I'm his son. I'll tell you what. If he'd let me once cut him up a little, I might love him. Defeated enemies become buddies all the time. We can't do enough for the Japanese and Germans. Laban gives me marbles but you don't see him letting me win any."

"Win them by yourself. Charity begins at home."

"You said it. And I'm his prize charity patient and you make me sick. Stop trying to be a ward healer and ride with us the hell out of here."

Beatrice, wearing a soft gray terry-cloth bathrobe and fluffy mules, wandered in and sat down in a thronelike chair, curled against its high straight back. A flap of her robe fell away and showed, before she pulled it back, that she had nothing on underneath. She wriggled on the chair and exposed a part of one breast. Bernie, staring intently, said, "Pull yourself together, Mom. You look as though you've had a hard day."

Beatrice cleared her throat. "I didn't sleep well. Do you have a cigarette?"

Bernie offered one. He leaned over her with his lighter. "You've got beautiful eyes," he said.

"Why, thank you," said Beatrice. She puffed at the cigarette. "I've promised your father to give it up. He's going to buy me one of those cute little pipes for women."

"You've got beautiful lungs," said Bernie. "You shouldn't smoke so much, Mom. It might affect your lungs."

Beatrice had a friendly but nervous laugh. "You're making fun of me; you're just like your father."

"Have you had breakfast?" said Leah. "I'd be glad to fix something."

"Would you? You're such a darling. You're spoiling me."

"Bacon and eggs?"

Beatrice made a face. "No, I'm getting too fat. Toast and coffee, if it isn't too much trouble. Don't you think I'm getting fat, Bernie?" She stood up, a tall, ample woman, and for a moment it looked as though she were going to open her robe for inspection, but she merely turned around.

"Mom," said Bernie, as though he had a mouthful of food, "you're built like a brick shithouse."

Beatrice looked at Leah. "He's naughty, isn't he? We should spank him and send him to his room."

"He's all bark and no bite," said Leah. "A dog without any teeth."

"Woof without warp," said Bernie.

Beatrice laughed. "Bernie," she said, "I want your advice about something—whether you think it would please your father."

"Like you said, Laban and I are peas in a pod. Please me, please him."

"I've decided to become a member of the Jewish faith. Don't you think he'd like that?"

"A member of the Jewish faith," said Bernie. "How about that? That's really great. How are you going to do it? Go to a rabbi? Take a *schwitz* bath? You'd knock them dead at Hebrew Union College. Don't you know, poor Mumsey, Jews are born, not made?"

"That's not so. What about all the movie queens?" said Beatrice, rolling names off her tongue with relish. "They became Jews."

"You're right," said Bernie. "I forgot. You know how they did it? You want to know?"

"Yes."

He put an arm around her shoulders and whispered in her ear. "Circumcision."

She jumped from under his arm, breasts swinging. "That's revolting. It really is."

"What's the matter?" said Bernie. "Can't you take a joke? Like father, like son."

"Your father would never be capable of saying a thing like that."

"It's the modern generation for you. The age of the sick comedian. Join us. You're too young to be my mother anyway. Let's be friends instead."

"I'd be your friend if you let me."

"Good," Bernie said and placed a hand on her breast. Looking him in the eye, Beatrice removed his hand and covered up. Without a word, mules flapping, she walked into the kitchen.

"You like that sort of thing, don't you?" said Leah.

"She asked for it. Don't tell me I took advantage of her."

"Not at all. I'd say the advantage was all hers." Leah walked over to Bernie and stood almost touching him. His eyes, amoebae, swelled behind his glasses. "Try me," she said and pulled his hand to her breast.

He jerked his arm away. "What are you trying to pull?" he said.

She dug her hand inside his belt. He pushed her back with the heels of his hands on her shoulders. "Stop it," he said. "It's not funny. I'm telling you. Get out of this house."

Laughter spread inside her but she didn't waste any of it. She let it flow into her mind and screwed the lid on tight behind it. She examined him gravely. "I told you," she said. "Your bark is worse than your bite." And she went into the kitchen to serve Beatrice.

The alarm sounded like a woodpecker with a muffled beak and Rachel, lying on her stomach with her face in the pillow, reached down with one hand to jostle Barbara, her roommate, in the lower bunk. Barbara would sleepwalk to the bureau, punch the clock and stagger back to bed for fifteen minutes. Rachel's hand brushed the thick wool of a rug and she rolled wild eyeballs to see who had abducted her during the night; all at sea, she realized she was home and that she had to get up because she'd decided, lawyer or no lawyer, she wanted to see a little more of Jackson Schwartz. She had run away, had gotten as far as the East Coast, but Laban's long legal arm had pulled her back. A lie. She had returned of her own free will for the summer. The way to beat down a revolting child was to provide her with no enemy troops. She was free as a bird—free, anyway, as a trained falcon that sweeps skyward with the speed of light and passes laboring astronauts right and left but has to obey the built-in voice of habit that says, Come back, little sparrow. She got out of bed quietly—Leah was still asleep in the twin bed—and went to the window. There it lay, her street, the one like no other because she had grown up on it, and in the morning sunlight, in all its pride, it refused to yield to her. All clean, neat, happy streets wanted to be alike. She tried to trigger her own chubby five- or ten- or fifteen-year-old legs into dashing across, she cocked her blooming arm for the throw of an old tennis or jacks ball; all she could do at twenty was nod her head.

She went to the bathroom. The hot-water faucet in the sink was leaking a splinter of water. With old petulance she turned the handle fiercely and the leak faltered to a drip. She was horrified that the maneuver still made her see red, made her want to rage at Leah, Would you please try with the hot water, at least *try?* How many times must I tell you? And then she would climb all over Laban to call the plumber and he would say, Sure, baby, and never would. Rachel swore that this time would be different. She was no longer a child at the mercy of adults; she would call the plumber herself and this would be one of the many changes around here. She caught herself up, suddenly aware of being trapped in a house haunted by infancy. There was more to family life than leaking faucets. As she foamed toothpaste at the mouth, facing the mad dog in the mirror, she was fascinated by the placidity of her eyes. She could have sworn they were Leah's, and she looked around to make sure. Identical eyes and voices, and what significant was left for the individual? Rachel curled her Crest-laden lips in defiance at the loss of identity. At least if she ever needed a kidney Leah would supply it—or would she? Not as important as the fact that *she* stood ready for Leah any time, any time at all.

Leah pushed open the door. "Aren't you through yet? I've been waiting."

"You know what I found when I came in here? Try to guess."

"A water bug."

"Worse. Much much worse."

"I can't imagine."

"The hot-water faucet was leaking. It's depressing to know you can leave a place for nine months and have it exactly the same when you get back."

"It's a comfort," said Leah. "All your possessions preserved intact for your homecoming. Laban, me, the faucet."

Rachel rinsed her mouth and moved away from the sink. "Why don't you ever go downtown with Laban?"

"Because I don't want to. I don't like tall buildings."

"Once before you die don't you want to see Laban's office,

meet the people he works with? Aren't you curious to see what
Miss Trilby looks like?"

"How do you know I haven't? Not only that, but I carry his
brief case to court and answer telephones during Miss Trilby's
lunch period."

Rachel stared. "You do?"

"No. I told you, I don't like tall buildings."

"You don't like anything," Rachel said, and slammed the door
behind her. Right away she was back on the defensive. What she
had meant to say was that the last thing in the world she wanted
to curry was Laban's favor. As she decided on her ice-blue dress
with a square bodice, shoulder straps, and an accordion skirt that
made her waist small, she mouthed the words, I love you, Father,
and they sounded hollow. I hate you, Father, she whispered
aloud, and it echoed in a wind tunnel. She saw him lying in an
open coffin at a do-it-yourself funeral chapel, sobered by em-
balming fluid; she would still be waiting for him to show his
hand, that same hand throwing bits of heart, like flowers, to roped
crowds.

She put on stockings and high-heeled black pumps and poked
her head into the bathroom. Leah wasn't there. Downstairs
Rachel found Laban sitting at the dining-room table surrounded
by a cup of coffee, the morning newspaper and the smell of
bacon and eggs. He was wearing a gray silk gabardine suit; gold
cuff links gleamed. He looked like an expensive lawyer, an Abraham Lincoln with a corporate practice. Rachel pushed the swinging door inward to the kitchen and discovered Leah, still in her
pajamas, making breakfast. If she saw Leah doing one more
wifely act she'd pull out the silverware drawer and crash it to the
floor, she'd pull the refrigerator plug, blow out the pilot light on
the stove. She'd take an axe to the place and let them know
prohibitions were back. She turned and sat down across from
Laban. Her foot found the floor buzzer, which sounded in the
kitchen. "For crying out loud," she yelled, "where's the food?
I'm starved."

Without lifting his eyes from the newspaper, Laban pounded

on the table with the handle of a spoon, punctuating each bang with a "Chow, chow, chow, chow." He was being a prison riot all by himself and she had herself to blame. Leah, a mother moving calmly through the disordered nursery, brought in a platter and sat down.

After breakfast, at which neither Bernie nor Beatrice showed up and Leah waited table like a slave, Laban drove Rachel downtown in his new car. It was a long, black, shiny thing, a gangster's car, and she said that she'd liked his convertible better.

"I'll tell you about that," he said. "It was air-conditioned, which didn't bother me in the winter time. You know, you don't think about it when it's cold; you don't need it and it doesn't need you. But the warm weather comes. I put the top down because it's a convertible, and then I put on the air conditioning because it's there and so I put the top up. That car drove *me*. So I tried leaving the top down with the air conditioning on and I could hear that air-conditioner grumble. I can't take lack of function. A beautiful piece of equipment that can work only when another piece can't. So I got this idea. I'd get a hardtop car with air conditioning, and windows with something to do. No idle equipment breeding mischief. Knock on the glass." She did. "Know what it is?" She shook her head. "Bulletproof. That window's got a reason. I told them at the agency every president needs a bulletproof car."

"What are you president of?"

"They asked me that," he said. "I'm president of the West End Improvement Association."

Rachel rapped her knuckles on the window. "Laban, we're safe from tigers."

"Better safe than sorry, right?"

He was describing changes in the city as they turned the circle in front of the university and drove east. "Every month, baby, a new project. Luxury motels, multiple-rise apartment buildings, office buildings. You won't believe it when I show you the river front. For years the city was dying on its feet and now it's dancing in the streets. And I'll tell you who's behind it: the dark men. Don't let anybody kid you with baloney about progress. It's the dark men. They're taking over. Tomorrow the world."

Rachel examined the crags and lines in her father's sunburned face. Really, he could be maddening, and it didn't matter if he was teasing or testing. It was too easy to imagine him dropping the same remarks into a racially mixed party at school and for the same reasons a boy combined radicals in his first chemistry set— to see what would happen. "That's not funny," she said. "I don't care who you want to act like, except a member of the Birch Society. There are some subjects you just can't joke about."

"Wrong," he said. "There's nothing you can't joke about, baby, and that's the truth. But you misunderstood me. I'm not criticizing the Negroes. I'm giving them credit. I'm proud of them. It goes to show the sacred cow the Negro's become. You can't praise him without getting mauled."

"Some praise."

"Sure. We wouldn't even be putting up a tent if the white boys weren't being pushed out. They drive for hours to get to work, so they figure, Before the city's defaulted, let's build it back up for ourselves. Let's turn the lights on again all over the world. Otherwise what will we have? Taxation without representation. Black man supremacy. Block busting. Police brutality to the palefaces. Reservation of the right to serve who they please."

"It'd serve us right. We'd know what the Negro's felt for hundreds of years."

"Who says no? *Quid pro quo*. That's what I said. We owe progress to the Negroes and I envy them their hunger. Fat cats sit on their asses and let the place go to the dogs. I'd rather be hungry than fat any time. You live longer." He jerked his head to the left. "Look there. A luxury apartment building and a deluxe motel going up. A new Catholic headquarters next to the church."

The Catholic building looked like a stack of pancakes. "It's ugly," she said.

"It's progress, and progress isn't ugly."

"Is it beautiful to rape forests, reserve Indians, club Negroes, raise billboards instead of flowers?"

"Baby, you can't see the forest for the trees. When you make omelets you break eggs."

"And then eat the omelet and are left with nothing. For that you killed the chicken."

He laughed. "That's why it crosses the road, to become good eggs."

Their conversation had become monkey business, as usual, and there was no profit for her in continuing. She was faced with the law of diminishing returns. Just let him talk, say anything he wanted, prove the world was full of hot air; he would not needle her into further gummy dialectic. With his lawyer mind he was too good at it. Here they were, with her held captive in a moving car, prattling, and their togetherness was as casual as if they belonged to a car pool.

"That minstrel show I tried. Why did you run out on me? It was great," said Laban. "Uncle Toms trying to screw each other out of an estate. A big argument for integration: they behaved just like white folks."

"I told you, Laban, I hate that kind of talk. What are you trying to prove?"

"I've already proved it. I gave them one hundred percent. I won for them. And I treated them right. You don't treat a person right if you ignore what he is. It's too late to think, Human being first and Negro second. Too late. I think, Negro, what you want, man? I supported the Public Accommodations Bill, the Fair Housing Act—helped draft them in fact. One of the circuit judges is Negro; I endorsed him to the Governor. White supremacy, baby, is part of the black man's history and don't you forget it. You don't help by sweeping it under the rug; you just make the black man dirty."

Rachel wouldn't look at him. She wanted to crawl into the safety of the rug he was talking about. He was treating her like a juror who needed just a little convincing. As if she were the one who was prejudiced for believing that prejudice, even within oneself, should be fought. He stripped her of the dignity of her convictions, and all just for the sake of argument.

At the parking lot Laban stopped inside the exit to razz the Negro attendant, calling him Tommy boy, asking him how he ever got to be a car jockey with cotton-picking hands and getting back the information that the car would be greased and oiled and ready to go after ambulances. "Tommy boy, this is Rachel, my daughter." Rachel stuck out her hand. Tommy looked at it, at Laban, grinned, wiped his hand on his overalls and shook hands. His hand was warm and limp. "Take care of that car, baby," said Laban.

"Yes, *suh*," said Tommy and as they watched he gunned the motor and the wheels squealed as he drove off.

As they walked the block to his office Laban said, "What did you think of Schwartz?"

"Who?"

"Jackson Schwartz, my new boy. You met him in the courthouse. What did you think of him?"

"I didn't think anything of him. I don't know him."

"Good-looking?"

"I don't remember."

Laban grinned. "He's *damned* good-looking. Want me to invite him to lunch with us?"

Rachel shrugged.

"Well, I can't. I sent him out of town on a deposition."

"I don't know what's wrong with you," said Rachel. "You're so silly."

"Listen, baby, I know that Schwartz. He's on the make. He'd like nothing better than to marry the boss's daughter. Let him sweat a little bit before he grabs for the brass ring."

"Just like that," said Rachel. "You think that little of me, forgetting what you think of your Jackson Schwartz."

"This boy's good and don't you forget it. He'd wrap you up in a pretty pink ribbon. Let him sweat."

"For your information, a lawyer is the last man on earth I'd marry."

"That's my baby," said Laban.

Inside the building, while they waited for the elevator, Laban passed the time of day with a polite Negro starter, who was dressed in a blue uniform with braid on the sleeves and shiny gold buttons. Laban did not introduce her and she asked him why.

"Because he's a horse's ass."

"Then why did you talk to him?"

"I can talk to a horse's ass, but that doesn't mean I'll introduce him to my daughter."

He made a face and stopped at a water fountain outside his office. As he bent over she noticed that his hair was thinning on top in the shape and size of a demitasse saucer. She felt triumphant, as if she'd put it there. Laban was growing old before her eyes and she was his Delilah by the cut of her irritation. She was as surprised as Delilah must have been that her scissors were actually sharp enough.

Once the excitement of going to Laban's office had been unbearable. She'd gotten sick and coughed until she was red in the face, and Miss Trilby had rushed out for a paper cup of water. Miss Trilby was pink and white then, with soft, tail-wagging brown eyes. Now, still unmarried, still in Laban's service, she had a network of wrinkles skimming a face that was turning muddy like lace or book pages. For Miss Trilby's sake Rachel wished she could still get red and confused, as if she were once more a child. It wasn't fair how many women were being used up to satisfy Laban.

Leah sat alone in the house, matching Laban's socks. The kitchen was quiet and dark, with the blinds drawn against the sun. For dinner she had decided on beef tenderloin and Bernie's favorite for dessert, French vanilla ice cream with orange slices and

Cointreau. Laban had announced that hamburger menus were over after thirty straight days, that he had never intended to run through the entire three hundred sixty-five recipes in the hamburger book. He had proved his point, he said: whatever they said about bread, man *could* survive on hamburger. She picked up the book and examined the cartoon of a round little man in a yeasty chef's cap carrying a smoking pot; she put it away in a drawer.

Laban wore ribbed, clocked anklets with elastic bands on top, and she enjoyed wrapping them inside each other into silken snails; they were a family of pets. When she had finished sorting she took them upstairs to Laban's bedroom and put them away in a bureau. She ruffled the fur of one of Beatrice's stuffed animals, a kitten with a red ribbon around its white neck, that lay on the oversized double bed.

The front door slammed and she went downstairs. It was Bernie, sweating; his white T-shirt had moons under the arms. "It's lousy," he said. "You know what I've been doing?"

"Running away from home."

"I wish I could. I've been crapping around the neighborhood staring at the houses and realizing they haven't changed by one brick since I was born. Hitler, Hiroshima, Martin Luther King, Eddie, Liz, Debbie, Richard, Khrushchev, and not a brick has changed. I feel like quick-setting mortar mashed in between."

"You should be happy that home is the place that doesn't change, that there is a place like home. You should learn to enjoy things."

"Things. You've got enough love of things for all of us. You'll be sitting on top of your furniture weaving quilts when the bomb drops."

"I hope so. And where will you be?"

He shook his head and sat down, swinging one wiry, impatient leg over the other. "Who cares?"

She noticed a hole in his sweat sock just above the shoe and made a note to darn it. "Do you ever think of mother?"

"You. Watch your language. You preach bloody revolt. Mother is dead, long live Mother. Sticks and stones hurt my bones but Mother can never hurt me. I'm supposed to wilt. Here, I'll kiss the ground she walked on. Our poor Mama, parked in storage, and Daddy nuzzling sweet, wholesome living flesh."

"Laban loved her very much. If he didn't he wouldn't have needed to remarry so soon."

"Is that the party line? Where's the party? Don't lay flowers, lay her successor on her fresh grave. Show respect, keep busy. Your mind works like clothes in a washing machine: soapy, watery, twisted, but getting all cleaned up and ready for use."

"Why bother with me then?"

"To straighten you out. Look at you. Look at your red hands and snarled hair. You're a college girl, not a middle-aged house-keeper. Forget *things* and think about life before it's too late. You're wasting away."

"In our father's house are many mansions."

"All his, none yours. You know what a nun is? A creature of habit."

Leah nodded. "You go to such extremes. You push and prod as though the meaning of life is to push and prod."

"And what is the meaning of your life?"

She made sure of her answer. She didn't propose to be trapped in words. "Not to look for meanings. I suppose that's too measly for you."

"You're right, it *is* too measly. On that philosophy I'd shoot myself."

"I won't. That's a worry you needn't have."

"Leah, I swear. If you don't get out you'll wake up one morning wishing you were dead."

"That's another worry you needn't have."

Bernie walked over to the bookshelves, stabbed at a book and went upstairs. She went to the window and raised the blinds so that the afternoon sun filled the room. She opened the window and was cradled in warmth. The air was filled with chirping and a large bluejay sat stockily on a branch of the pin oak. While she was standing at the window Beatrice drove up and parked at the curb. As she walked toward the house Leah noticed that she had dyed her blond hair an orange-brown.

Laban turned on his pen flashlight. "I'm going to shine this in your right eye, baby," he said, "and I want you to concentrate on it. I'm going to start counting and when I reach five you're going to fall asleep. Understand?"

Beatrice lay loosely on the couch, wearing her new orange hair and a brown knit wool dress that clung to her torso like caramel melted on apples. She nodded. Laban's idea of a hypnotic voice was to string each word out as if he were trying to teach an aphasia victim to speak. "One. Your eyes are getting tired and heavy as you concentrate on the light. There is no other place in the world but the light and you are looking deeply into the light. Two. The light goes on and on, deeper and deeper, brighter and brighter, and your eyes are getting heavier and heavier so you can hardly keep the lids up and soon I'll let you drop them but now you've got to look at that old light which is brighter and brighter. Three. Your eyelids are so tired and heavy they weigh a ton and you keep them up only because you're looking so hard at the light, you've got to look at the light which is brighter and brighter and fills up your whole big blue eyeball which is very, very tired. Soon you'll be able to close your eyes and rest but now you are looking with all your might at the light which is going deeper and deeper into your baby-blue eye and you can't see anything but the light. Four. Your eyelids are so heavy you want to put up your hands and pull them down like blankets but you can't because I won't let you because you've got to look at the light until I tell you to close your eyes which I'll do in just a minute because your eyes are so heavy and filled with light and in just a second, baby, I'll tell you to close your eyes and you'll feel sleepy and full like you had a big meal and now I'm going to let you close your eyes. When I say five next time you'll close your eyes. Now. Five."

Beatrice closed her eyes.

"Fine, baby, fine. You've earned the right to be tired and you're very tired and you want to curl up you're so sleepy and you're feeling so relaxed you could die and all you can hear or want to hear is my voice because I'm going to let you sleep.

You're getting ready to sleep but first you see inside your own right eye and you see a soft red spot that looks like velvet and it's red and soft and restful and about the size of a soft velvet nickel and you see it and you'll nod your head to tell me that you see it." Beatrice, eyelids folded over her eyes, hands clasped at her middle, nodded. "Fine, baby, very good. Now the red velvet spot disappears and instead you see a purple velvet spot just the same size and when I tell you the red spot is gone just like that it's gone and you see the purple spot which is even softer and more velvety and you're nodding to tell me that you see the purple spot and that it's beautiful and very restful." Beatrice nodded. "Swell, baby. You're so relaxed your legs and arms feel like mush and you're getting more and more relaxed and peaceful and contented and the purple spot disappears and you see the darkest grassiest green spot you ever saw and you sink into it and rest on it because it grows into a soft feathery green bed and you nod because you see the bed [nod] and now it's gone and you see a brown velvet spot and you sink into the brown spot and it spreads into an oversized bed and you nod because you're in the soft brown bed [nod] and you're sleeping and you're peaceful and happy and contented and asleep."

Laban stopped talking and leaned over Beatrice. She lay perfectly still except for a slight rise and fall of breast. Laban said, "Baby, you can't open your eyes. You just can't. I'm going to count to three and when I do you'll try to open your eyes but you just won't be able to. One. Two. Three." Her eyelids quivered but did not open.

"I'm going to count to three again and this time you'll open your eyes but when I snap my fingers you'll close them again. One. Two. Three." Beatrice opened her eyes. Laban snapped his fingers and she closed her eyes. Laban turned. "Okay," he said. "What do you want to ask her?"

"If she's faking," said Rachel.

"Are you faking?"

"No."

"Ask her to cry," said Bernie.

"Baby, I'll count to four and then you'll cry. One. Two.

Three. Four." Tears rolled out from under her closed lids.

Rachel said, "Laban."

"Ask her why she dyed her hair," said Bernie.

"Why did you dye your hair?"

"I want to be Jewish. I want to look Jewish and blonds don't look so Jewish."

"Anti-Semite," said Bernie.

"Why do you want to be Jewish?" said Laban.

"Because my Laban is Jewish."

"Some Jewish," said Bernie. "Ask her if she loves her husband."

"Do you love your Laban?"

"Yes."

"Her husband's family."

"Do you love Leah?"

"Yes."

"Rachel?"

"Yes."

"Bernie?"

"Yes."

"Is there anybody in the world she doesn't love?" Bernie asked his sisters. "I think she needs a lie detector test."

"Is there anybody in the world you don't love?" said Laban.

"I don't know," said Beatrice.

"If she loves Leah why does she let her do all the cooking?" said Bernie.

"If you love Leah why do you let her do all the cooking?"

"Because I'm a terrible cook. I'd make a mess of things."

"If she loves her husband why doesn't she want to cook for him?"

"If you love your Laban why don't you want to cook for him?"

"I would if he wanted me to, but I'm a bad cook and Leah is wonderful."

"The perfect, gentle wife," said Bernie. "Ask her if she thinks she's the perfect wife."

"Do you think you're perfect for Laban?"

"No. I think he's too good for me. I don't know what I've done to deserve him."

"Sex, Mom. How many times a week does she sleep with her husband?"

"Stop it, Bernie," said Rachel.

"How many times a week do you have intercourse with Laban?" said Laban.

"As often as he likes."

"How often does he like?" said Bernie.

"How often does he like?" said Laban.

"Stop it, Laban," said Rachel.

"Often," Beatrice said.

"Ask her how many other men besides her husband she's slept with," said Bernie.

"On advice of counsel," said Laban, "the witness refuses to answer any further questions. Baby, when I count to three you're going upstairs to wash the dye out of your hair. When I clap my hands twice you'll wake up and not remember any of this. One. Two. Three."

Beatrice opened her eyes, smiled, stretched and got up. She started upstairs. "Come on," said Laban, and they trailed after her.

Beatrice went into the bathroom and wrapped a towel around her shoulders. She filled the washbasin with hot water and shampooed her hair. They watched the suds foam. She seemed oblivious to spectators. Laban got a bath towel and wrapped it around her head. He scrubbed away and examined the results. Her hair was as orange as ever. He clapped his hands twice. Beatrice saw herself in the mirror and turned to Laban. "Do you like my hair?" she said. "The color?"

"It's fine," Laban said, and patted her shoulder.

"It's fine," said Bernie, "but why did you do it? I thought blonds were the only ones who had more fun."

"I don't know," said Beatrice. "It just came over me. Are you sure you like it?" she said to Laban.

"Sure I'm sure."

The telephone rang and Leah went to answer it. Oddly, since

she got very few calls, it was for her. "Leah?" a male voice said.

"Yes."

"This is Jackson Schwartz."

"Jackson Schwartz."

"Yes. I work for your father. Don't you remember? We met in the courthouse the other day."

Leah smiled. A case of mistaken identity.

"Oh, yes," she said.

"I wondered if you're not busy, if you'd care to go to dinner with me Saturday night?"

It was impossible, because who would make dinner for the family? "I'd like that," said Leah. "What time?"

"Would six-thirty be all right?"

"Fine."

"I look forward to seeing you then."

"Yes. Good-bye."

"Good-bye, Leah."

"Look," said Bernie after Beatrice left to brush her hair. "Listen to me for once. You can't take her to a rabbi. It's impossible, a fraud."

"What fraud? Who fraud?" said Laban. "She wants to be a Jew. In all Christian humility she wants to be a Jew. She isn't an Arab spying on Yiddish secrets. Let her be a Jew."

"Not her fraud. Yours. She wants to be what she thinks you are—we are."

"What are we? What would Hitler call us?"

"It's what we call ourselves that matters—or rather, what we think of ourselves. Why can't you be honest and tell her you were born a Jew and died to Jewishness?"

"Listen, baby, I don't know about you, but I'm a Jew. Your grandfather and grandmother were Jews. Besides, it's irrelevant. If my wife wants to convert, she converts."

"Nobody converts to Judaism. You know it and I know it."

"What's to know? It's all in the mind, and Beatrice has got it in her mind."

"Jews are born before they can be made."

Laban shook his head. "Baby, I love you like a son."

"Thank you," said Bernie. "With your love what else do I need? I'll try again. Judaism isn't just a religion. It's a community project. The community comes first, then the religion. The community is the Jews and the Jews are its religion."

"My son the rabbi," said Laban. "Tell me, boy, you Jewish? You don't look Jewish."

"I'm twice the Jew you are," said Bernie, "and I'd hate to become half a man like you."

"Where's your *t'fillin* and *yamulke?* Where's your community?"

"That's how much you know. The community is in my interest, in my frame of mind. Something you wouldn't understand. A little matter of conviction."

"I've been figuring by your figures," said Laban. "If you were half the man your papa is you'd be a quarter of a man."

Bernie drew a deep breath. "Screw it. If you want to dress Beatrice up like Sarah or Rebecca and parade her in the synagogue, be my guest."

"Now that we've got that settled," said Laban, "I'll get us some drinks. I've got something to tell everybody. Leah, get Beatrice. I've got an important announcement to make." He went toward the kitchen.

"Well," Rachel said to Leah. "Who was it on the phone?"

Leah called from the foot of the stairs, "Beatrice, Laban wants to see you. Could you come down?"

"Who was it?" said Rachel.

"It was for me."

"So who was it? Or won't you tell me any more?"

"Someone named Jackson Schwartz. He asked me to dinner."

Rachel jerked her head. "I didn't know you knew him. When did you meet him?"

"I didn't know you knew him."

"I don't. I just saw him once, downtown with Laban. Have you gone out with him before?"

"No."

"Where did you meet him? I thought you never went downtown. Did Laban invite him here?"

"I've never met him. It's a blind date."

Rachel stared. "Don't you see? It's a mistake. He wanted me."

"He asked for me. No mistake."

"He doesn't even know you."

"Why fuss?" said Leah. "I thought you told me you'd never go out with a lawyer."

"Did I say that?" said Rachel. "I guess I did." She shrugged. "Easy come, easy go."

Rachel watched Laban with half an eye. The rest of her was turned toward Leah. She still couldn't believe that Leah was serious. To take advantage of a mistake—this wasn't the sister she knew. What it came down to was a filthy practical joke, the kind twins pulled in comic strips where people were always asking, How can you tell yourselves apart? This was what living too long with Laban did to a person. She really didn't care about Jackson Schwartz; to hell with Jackson Schwartz. She didn't even know him. But she cared a lot about Leah and what was happening to her character.

Laban unfolded a blue-backed document. "This," he said, "is Laban's will."

"Is that your important announcement?" said Bernie.

"That's right. I want to read you my will to let you know

where you all stand. Then, if I'm done away with you'll know who stands to profit. You may not realize it, but I'm a wealthy man, and it's very important how I leave my money."

"Don't you know," said Bernie, "that your family loves you for yourself alone? Right, Mom? The money can go to the Salvation Army for all we care."

"I'll read the will. I, William Laban, of sound mind and disposing memory . . ."

Rachel stopped listening. She swam in the legal jargon as if it were amniotic fluid and she couldn't wait to break out into the open. The question of money was a terrible bore and Laban should have enough sense to realize it. But he couldn't resist a classic scene: the family gathered around while the lawyer, preferably with mutton-chop whiskers (Laban stroked his chin) and a thin, precise voice, laid down the law of property rights. Laban finished reading (and tapped his knee with a finger). "To summarize," he said. "Beatrice, as widow, is entitled to a third of my estate. The rest, after a bequest of twenty thousand to my faithful and devoted secretary Miss Trilby, goes to Bernie. Rachel and Leah get nothing."

"What are you trying to pull, the law of primogeniture?" said Bernie. "I don't think and I never did think you're funny."

"I'm not trying to be funny. This is a serious matter of money. I asked myself, Which of my children is the most deserving? Leah? I never hear an unkind word. She works like a mule seeing to my bodily comforts. The only dough she asks for is to make bread. So I say to myself, This baby is out for the bundle; why else would she be acting so contrary to nature? Nothing for Leah. Rachel? Rachel acts like I'm a hot potato in her mouth that she doesn't know whether to spit out or swallow. I call that mealy-mouthed, so nothing for Rachel. That leaves Bernie. Bernie's got no use for me in his brave new world and tells me so every chance he gets. Here's an honest man with guts, a chip ready to knock off the old block, and that's why I'm leaving my money to my son Bernie."

"I saw that movie," said Rachel. "It was lousy."

"Nevertheless," said Laban. "This is my last will and testament." He went to the bookshelves next to the fireplace. "I'll keep it here where it's handy," he said, taking out a fat book and inserting the will in its pages. "For your information, the book is"—he examined the title—"*A History of the Jewish People.*"

Rachel stared glumly at the bookshelf. The will depended for its life on Laban's death, and watching Laban sip his drink and enjoy his little scene, she had a sense of the fragility of the veins guiding blood to his heart. One sharp incision and the edifice of Laban's life, built over half a century, would collapse. One day he would die, and that wasn't a joke. He couldn't laugh his way into immortality and he would be unprepared for the seriousness of death.

Beatrice was sitting on the couch under her wet orange hair, smiling vaguely, and Rachel thought, irrational in anger, The merry widow.

"Baby," said Laban to Beatrice, "how do we get that dye out?"

"There's no quick cure," said Rachel. "I've seen the girls in the dorm try everything. She'll just have to let it streak out."

"I like her hair orange," said Bernie. "It makes her look Jewish."

"That's right, I forgot," said Laban. "Tomorrow we call the rabbi." He looked at Bernie. "Unless you've got a better idea."

"Sure I have. She wants to be a Jew like you, not a rabbinical, kosher-dish kind but a real, live, up-to-date, down-to-earth Jew like you."

"So?"

"So I'll teach her. I volunteer. First the Old Testament as moral philosophy and literature. A bible for the humanities. An ethical tour of Abraham, Sarah and Hagar, Absalom, Amnon and Tamar, David, Uriah and Bathsheba. Then a short snappy survey of pogroms. You can't tell a Jew without your pogroms. Finally the rise of the American Jew in Hollywood, Miami and New York."

"I accept your offer," said Laban gravely. "I put my wife's religious education in your hands. Let's shake on it."

Bernie regarded Laban's hand as if it were a silver dollar on the sidewalk he wanted to pick up but remembered another one somebody had cemented to the pavement. Nevertheless he shook hands. "If it's all right with Beatrice," he said, and she, watching Laban, nodded quickly.

The telephone rang and Rachel ran off to answer it. If it was Jackson Schwartz she'd straighten him out soon enough. But it was a Mrs. Schmidt for Laban.

Leah watched Mrs. Margery Schmidt sob into her handkerchief while Laban kneaded her shoulder. She was in her late twenties and had shapely legs and bosom and soft, blooming skin. She was blond, blue-eyed and, despite too much jaw, pretty. Laban had asked everybody but Leah to leave, and he insisted she stay. "I want you to hear this baby's problem. I want your opinion," he'd said. The girl had come into the house, sat down in the living room without a word and started crying.

"I'm sorry, I'm sorry," said Mrs. Schmidt. "It's getting me down. That filthy Charlie."

"Relax. Take it easy. The meter isn't running."

"But how could he do it to her if he loves her? He says he loves her and yet he does this to her."

"Do you think he loves her?"

"I don't know. I suppose. I've always thought so, but how could he and still put her away?"

"What does he say?"

"That it's for her own good, that the psychiatrist says it's the only thing to do."

"What's the psychiatrist's name? Have you talked to him?"

"Dr. Wanderscheid. Of course I've talked to him. As soon as I talked to Charlie I wanted to go to the hospital to see Grace, that's my mother, and Charlie said I'd have to talk to Dr. Wanderscheid."

"I've heard of him. He's got a decent reputation. What'd he say?"

"He said absolutely no visitors. It would worsen her condition. I'd get her all upset, he said. And after I've flown fifteen hundred miles to see her. Can they do this?"

"No, baby. This is the U.S.A. Nobody can be put away without a court order. How long has she been there?"

"Five days, I think. Yes, I'm sure of it. She wrote me three days ago and she was already in for two. She *begged* me to get her out. You should read the letter."

"You're right. You got it with you?"

"No. It's in my suitcase. I'm sorry I forgot it. I'm so muddled."

"Mail it tonight to my office. Now pay attention. Did the doctor say he committed her or that she went voluntarily?"

"He said she went voluntarily, but she couldn't have. Don't I know my own mother? She's saner than you or I."

Laban grinned. "Leave us out of it. If she went in voluntarily all she has to do is sign a request for release. If she didn't, somebody had to sign her in under medical certification that she was in danger of hurting herself or others. Do you think Wanderscheid did that?"

"I don't know. Nobody tells me anything and they won't let me see her. I even tried going to the hospital but they refused to let me talk to Grace without Dr. Wanderscheid's consent."

"Okay. The thing for me to do is call Wanderscheid, right? I'll be right back." And he went to the telephone in the dining room.

Mrs. Schmidt wiped her eyes. She stopped crying and smiled at Leah. "I think your father's wonderful. He takes such an interest in other people's problems."

Mrs. Schmidt tugged at her skirt, which was hiked up to the middle of her thighs over her beautiful nylon-cased legs. "I've got only one mother, after all," she said. "And I think the world of her. I hate to interfere between her and my stepfather but what else can I do? What would you do if your stepfather tried to lock your mother up as a loony?"

"I don't have a stepfather."

"But what if you did?"

"I think I'd let my father handle it."

Mrs. Schmidt frowned and shook her head. "My father's dead and Grace is helpless. You know, one of those Billie Burke people. So it's up to me. I'd never have suspected Charlie was capable of doing such a thing. It goes to show how you never really know about people. You should see how he treated her, like she'd melt or something if he wasn't careful, and here he puts her in a loony bin. He said she was so depressed she threatened to kill herself. That's a laugh. Don't I know my own mother? She smiles all day long and never had a care in the world."

Leah said, "I'm sure my father will help you."

Laban came back and stood with his hands on his hips. "Did you know your Mom took an overdose of sleeping pills? She almost died, the doc said."

"She couldn't have. It's a lie."

"You think the doc's lying? What reason would he have?"

"He's Charlie's doctor, isn't he? Charlie hired him. Anyway, maybe Charlie told him and he'd rather believe him than Grace. I tell you, Grace just isn't the type. Wait until you meet her." Mrs. Schmidt stared at Laban. "Are you going to help me or not? You sound more on their side than mine."

"Don't worry," said Laban. "I never bite the hand that feeds me. I've just got to know what I'm up against. He said she was a voluntary patient and I asked whether that meant she signed herself in, and he said not exactly, that Charlie signed her in on his advice."

"You see?" said Mrs. Schmidt. "There's something terrible going on. I know it."

"I asked Wanderscheid if he had signed a medical certificate that she was dangerous to herself or others, and he got huffy and said that wasn't necessary when the husband signed her in, that it was nobody's business but the husband's and that Mrs. Schmidt should go back where she came from and stop bothering her mother. He said you could only do your mother harm."

"You see?" said Mrs. Schmidt. "They're trying to throw away the key. Poor Grace." She started weeping again.

"All right," said Laban. "Stop crying and I'll tell you what we're going to do." She stopped crying. "The law allows the hospital to keep her ten days if there's medical certification. As far as I can make out there isn't. So they've got to release her. I'll call the hospital director tomorrow first thing in the morning and tell him I want answers, that I want him to set up a meeting with Charlie, Wanderscheid, you and me. If he won't I'll get a writ of habeas corpus and we'll get your mom out that way. Okay? Just one thing. What if she's really sick and needs to be in the hospital? What if we got her out and she cuts her wrists? You ready for that? It'd be on your head."

"Grace is not sick. She is not crazy. I know my mother," said Mrs. Schmidt. "If she gets out can I take her home with me away from Charlie?"

"Is she free, white and twenty-one?" said Laban. "She comes and goes as she pleases."

"What if Charlie won't let her go?"

"What's he going to do, chain her to the bed? Listen, he can't stop her. Go home, get a good night's sleep and I'll call you in the morning. Where you staying, at a hotel?"

"No. At . . . at Charlie's. He insisted that I stay there."

Laban smiled. "Charlie must be a nice guy."

"He is. He and I have always gotten along very well. That's why I can't understand all this."

"You want to stay on there?"

"I don't care, but if you think I should I'll go to a hotel."

"Listen, baby," said Laban. "You like to stay at Charlie's, you stay at Charlie's. Just tell me why he's doing this to your mother."

"I'm not sure. He keeps saying it's for her own good and that's all he'll tell me."

"What'd Grace say in her letter?"

Mrs. Schmidt hesitated.

"Come on, come on."

"She didn't put it in so many words, but I think Charlie's having an affair."

"So he gets his wife out of the way on a phony mental rap? Why doesn't he divorce her? Any money involved?"

"Charlie has money but he doesn't care about that. I think he's afraid of what people would think. He comes from an old-fashioned family."

"A crazy wife, yes; a divorced wife, no. You know what I think? I think your Grace needs to be in that hospital, that Charlie's doing the best he can for his wife and that he's got a tiptop psychiatrist. But if you want her out I'll get her out. Now. Am I still your lawyer and do you still want me to get her out?"

"Mrs. Schmidt's lips quivered. "Why are you being so mean? You've got no right."

"Baby, you buy my services, not me. Am I in the case or not?"

"Yes," said Mrs. Schmidt. "I want my mother out."

"Okay. Send me that letter and give me your telephone number. I'll call tomorrow. By the way, the doc tells me you've got it in for psychiatrists."

"I knew he'd bring that up."

"He said you called him a lousy headshrinker."

"He got me mad. That has nothing to do with my mother. She is not sick."

"Right. It's all in the mind. I'll call you tomorrow. You got a way home?"

"Yes. Charlie lent me his car."

"Good old Charlie. Good night, baby. Sleep tight and don't worry about a thing."

"Good night. Good night, Miss Laban."

"Good night, Mrs. Schmidt."

Laban let her out the front door and came back to Leah. "What do you think?"

"About what?"

"What's with this 'what'? The case."

"I have no opinion."

"Form one. Give your old man some advice. Show him you care. It's about time you raised the shades around here and let the world in."

"It's cooler this way."

"Play it hot for a change. That call was from Jackson Schwartz, wasn't it?"

"Yes."

"Going out with him?"

"Yes."

"All right. Should I take this case?"

"I thought you already had."

"I can still get out. A psychiatrist says she needs to be in the hospital. The husband sounds like Christ. My client believes this doctor wears a painted mask and rattles bones."

"It's up to you, Laban."

"No. I'm trying to tell you it's up to you. What's my duty? I don't think they put her in legally, so I can get her out. A potential suicide walking the streets. What should I do?"

"Couldn't you have her examined by another psychiatrist?"

"Sure I could but that would take time, and more, who knows what he'd say? My client wants her out now so she can save her poor mama from a fate worse than death."

"You should do what you think is right."

"No, baby. I'm going to do what *you* think is right. You can't get off the hook."

"Mrs. Schmidt came to you for help. If you can help her legally, I suppose you should. That's your job."

"What if it isn't right? Legal but not right. A paradox. Would that be right?"

"You're not a priest. You're not even a judge."

Laban smacked his lips on her forehead. "That's for sure. I'm not even a judge. That's the way to talk to Jackson Schwartz. Go get him. Eat him up."

He left her alone in the living room. She got up and turned off the lamp and sat with her hands folded in her lap. The darkness felt like the inside of a sealed parcel-post box weighed and addressed and ready for shipment. It was very peaceful.

When she finally went upstairs to bed, Bernie, in his pajamas, met her at the head of the stairs. "Hey," he whispered, "who was the doll?"

Rachel went with Laban to the hospital only because this time she was truly mad at him and wanted an opportunity to show it. Otherwise she'd be damned before she let him drag her around any more. Not that she could ever get involved with a boy who'd ask parental permission to date her, but she had the right to make that decision. Laban and his sense of humor were out on a limb that she was set to cut off and see how much he liked being the straight man. Jackson had asked Laban and Laban had said, "Not at all. Call her. Her name's Leah." Very funny. Laban couldn't wait to tell her, as if he expected her to laugh about it. And when she'd said grimly, "But he meant *me*; he's never met Leah," Laban said, "I know. Schwartz is a meatball looking for tomatoes and lettuce."

She wouldn't care, really she wouldn't, if he were doing it for Leah, but he wasn't. She and Leah were cute little tricks coming and going through the false bottom of a magician's box just so Laban could say, Hey, rube, to Jackson Schwartz, who deserved whatever he got. The very first chance she had at the hospital she'd spill a glass of water on Laban, tie his shoelaces together, strap him in a bed in the mental ward with a sign on his door, Do not open until Christmas.

At the front desk they were told to go to a conference room on the first floor. When they got there a man seated at a long mahogany table stood up and bobbed his head. He was large and fleshy and had a wrinkled, anxious face the color of the pearl-gray walls. "Charlie?" said Laban, coming forward with his hand out.

"Yes, sir," said Charlie, looking away as he shook hands.

"Charlie, I'm Laban, Mrs. Schmidt's attorney, and this is my secretary, Miss Rachel. Charlie, I'm going to give it to you straight. Why'd you want to put your wife away in a place like this? A nice boy like you."

Charlie got his hand back, not without effort. "You'll have to talk to the doctor. I'm just trying to do the right thing."

"Sure you are," said Laban. "But you know these medicine men." He tapped his temple. "They can twist anything and make it look screwy. You tell me. What did Grace do that was so crazy? Now that you've had a chance to think, just what was it?"

"She makes up things and then worries herself to death about them. I tell you she's got me half nuts."

"See?" said Laban with a wink. "Next thing you know that doc of yours'll have you in here. See how easy it is? What exactly does she make up?"

"Everything. She thinks a one-eyed man is hiding in the television set and if she turns it on he'll shoot her right through the glass. She wakes me up in the middle of the night and says, Charlie, hear that? He's trying to get out. You've got to save me. So I gotta go downstairs and turn the set on and tell her, Everything's okay, I saw his eye. He's still in there."

Laban patted Charlie on the shoulder. "Listen, baby. What about the other woman?"

"What other woman? What do you mean?"

"We've got evidence, Charlie. Going out every night to all hours leaving your wife to face the television set alone. The man at the gas station asking her where was the other woman who gassed up the car. Lipstick, Charlie, on the collar."

"Did she tell you that? It's her lipstick, nobody but hers. There isn't any other woman. Sure I go out sometimes at night. You know where? Bowling or to a movie. You've got no idea what it's been like."

"It's not too late to patch things up," said Laban. "It's an old story. You made a couple of mistakes. Forgive and forget, that's the ticket. I'll talk to your wife. I'll explain the whole thing. How a man gets fouled up. Charlie, two wrongs don't make a right. Making your wife out a nut is not the way."

Charlie sat down at the table with his head in his hands. "Margery sure picked a good one," he said, and Rachel couldn't have agreed more. Laban was such a bully. He was treating Charlie like a little boy he'd waylaid after school and grabbed by the collar. Listen, Charlie, bring me your big sister after school tomorrow if you know what's good for you. She should say something to Charlie, at least tell him she wasn't Laban's secretary but his daughter. But if she were truly honest she'd get up and walk out, because she had no business being there. Laban could find plenty of other claques, whose hands weren't blistered. The worst part of her position was that, not being a professional of any sort, she was afraid to interfere. Laban was about his official duties and however unfair his tactics seemed he was covered by his lawyer's mystique, even to her.

Two men came in, one gravely, the other all smiles. The serious one practically rolled in, he was so fat, and Rachel, looking for ball bearings, saw that his feet were encased in tiny, polished black shoes with tasseled laces. His legs swelled against the dark blue of his trousers and his short arms swung at his sides like flippers. His bald head was yellow, round and huge, and his features swam around his face as in a cartoonist's conception of futuristic man. The other was tall and smooth with silver-gray hair and neatly pressed features. He looked like Cary Grant in his later years playing the role of a psychiatrist who had just discovered one of his patients was Audrey Hepburn. Naturally with the perversity of nature the moon man turned out to be Dr. Wanderscheid and Cary Grant was Mr. Flaker, the hospital director.

After introductions, in which Laban once again identified her as his secretary and she remained mute under the increasing weight of deception, they sat around the big table and Laban opened his brief case. He handed her a stenographic tablet and pencil. She crossed her legs and flipped back the cardboard cover to the first lined page, the pencil poised in her right hand. Even if a thing wasn't worth doing, it was worth doing well. She scribbled busily. *My name is Rachel Laban. I am twenty years old. I have brown eyes and hair and in some of the very best circles am considered pretty. I have a twin sister Leah who washes dishes, a brother Bernie who's out to make the world safer, and a father who's out to make the world over into his image. P.S. I have a stepmother, Beatrice.*

"We really don't need to have notes taken of our conversation," Mr. Flaker said through his smiling teeth. "I thought we'd just have an informal get-together and try to iron the situation out. I'm sure we can come to an amicable understanding."

"No danger, baby," said Laban. "Don't mind my secretary. She's just along for the ride. She thinks of herself as Della Street. Just a clean, wholesome kid, so don't say anything dirty."

Mr. Flaker watched Rachel writing. "Well. I suppose Dr. Wanderscheid should begin."

"Hold on," said Laban. "We're not all here yet. You people are in a rut. You keep ignoring Mrs. Schmidt like she's some kind of bug crawling from the woodwork. Mrs. Schmidt is Grace's daughter and has a right to be here whether you think so or not. I wouldn't be here if it weren't for her."

A good lead in, wrote Rachel. *Now somebody have the nerve to take it up.* But no one did, so Rachel wrote, *Who needs you, Laban?* "You're perfectly right," said Mr. Flaker. He looked at his watch. "Does she know the time of the meeting?"

"I told her. She'll be here. Maybe she can't find the room."

"I'll check at the desk," said Mr. Flaker. He started out and paused. "How will I recognize her?"

"You can't miss," said Laban, "if you're half the man I think you are. Right, Charlie?"

"She's very pretty," said Charlie.

"You aren't just kidding," said Laban. "A girl like that you find in the dark."

Flaker left. Dr. Wanderscheid, the overhead light shining on his aged-in-the-wood dome, hadn't yet said a single word. "How long you been practicing, Doc?" said Laban.

The doctor folded his little hands on top of the table and smiled. Someone must have told him once that when he smiled he displayed the inscrutability of a Zen master. Rachel thought he looked more like Warner Oland playing Charlie Chan. She wrote, *Dr. Wanderscheid needs number-one boy. Interviews applicants from ten to twelve P.M. on quarter-moon nights. Must know how to handle sword cane.* "Isn't that," said Dr. Wanderscheid, "what you lawyers call a leading question?"

"Just making conversation Doc," said Laban. "I know better than to try to trap a man like you. What color underwear you like? You wear an undershirt? Do you think we really can afford to quit hydrogen bomb testing? What I mean, Doc, you being a psychiatrist and all, do you think God really exists?"

"I think we should wait for the others," said Dr. Wanderscheid. He looked at his watch. "However, I don't have much time."

"How much time you need? A nod or shake of the head, how much time does that take? A big talent, Doc, to be judge and jury both. We lawyers don't have that much guts."

"You have an interesting mind, Mr. Laban," said Dr. Wanderscheid.

"Sure I do. I'll make a deal. How about trading Grace's mind for mine? Take me instead of her."

"Very interesting," said the doctor, allowing himself a smile, and Rachel wrote from memories of Bible class, *And there came out of the pit locusts on the earth, and it was commanded them they shouldn't hurt the grass of the earth or any green thing or any tree, but only those men who didn't have the seal of God in their foreheads.*

Mrs. Schmidt came in, with Mr. Flaker close behind. She was wearing a pale green grass-of-the-earth dress of patterned silk, and a gold band was clipped to her wrist. Charlie jumped up as if she had thrown the switch on a little shock treatment. Dr. Wanderscheid, squat as a Buddha, didn't budge. Laban went to Mrs. Schmidt and led her forward with a sheltering arm around her shoulders.

When they had settled down, Dr. Wanderscheid said, "May we begin?"

"By all means," said Laban. "They wanted to start without you," he stage-whispered to Mrs. Schmidt, "but of course I wouldn't let them."

"In my opinion," said Dr. Wanderscheid, "Mrs. Grace Kohler is in serious need of psychiatric help. Hospitalization is imperative in order to protect her from outside influences during this critical stage. Otherwise she may very well do harm to herself or someone she loves. I cannot stress this too deeply."

"What is she supposed to have, Doc?"

"She is a paranoiac schizophrenic in the elementary stages. I am hopeful that a great deal of good can be derived from treatment at this time. Perhaps, in a few days, she may be able to have visitors."

"And on what do you base your diagnosis?"

"On my observations of the patient."

"And what did you observe?"

"She is highly distraught and suspicious without cause. She makes highly emotional charges without any accompanying emotional affect. It's as though her mind, the right hand, doesn't know what her emotions, the left hand, are doing."

"What is she suspicious of?"

"Her husband is the main object of her obsessive concern. She accuses him of infidelity, apparently without grounds. She blames him for not protecting her from imaginary enemies."

Laban leaned forward on his elbow. "What if her suspicions are well founded, Doc? What if Charlie's playing around? What then?"

"It wouldn't matter. It's the division of reason from intellect that is the basic problem."

"I tell you what, Doc. Why don't we let Mrs. Schmidt go up

and visit a little to satisfy herself that what you say is true? Then maybe we can all go home sadder and wiser."

The doctor shook his head. "I cannot permit that, in the best interest of the patient."

"You absolutely refuse to let this fine young woman visit her mother?"

"That is correct. I refuse to give my permission." Dr. Wanderscheid looked at his watch and then at Mr. Flaker. "I have an appointment," he said. "I must beg to be excused."

"Don't beg," said Laban. "If there's one thing I can't stand it's a begging psychiatrist. Before you go, Doc, did you ever hear of suits for false imprisonment?"

The doctor stood up and nodded pleasantly. "I am used to attempts at intimidation."

"You've got me wrong," said Laban. "I'm not testing your guts. I can see you've got plenty of that. I'm trying out your knowledge of the law. Do you consider Grace a voluntary or involuntary patient?"

The doctor rubbed his hands together and said good-bye. He nodded to everyone in a quick series and started out. Rachel wrote, *The doctor washed his hands of the situation and left Laban with the dirty linen.*

Laban seemed quite pleased with himself. He turned on Mr. Flaker, who was staring at Dr. Wanderscheid's unwieldy retreating back. "You see, baby? You never know who your friends are. Imagine his walking out and leaving you holding the bag. So I ask you, Is Grace a voluntary or involuntary patient?"

Mr. Flaker smiled anxiously. *As if,* Rachel wrote, *he inserted the key in the lock of his front door, went in, turned on the lights and found three men in tight double-breasted suits drinking beer in his living room.* "Really," he said. "Do you have to make a record of our conversation?"

"Come on, Flaker. No more wiggle-waggle. Is she voluntary or not?"

"Mr. Kohler here, her husband, signed her in. I'd say she's a voluntary patient, wouldn't you?"

"You know better than that, baby. That makes her involuntary, right?"

"I suppose so, yes."

"Now we're getting somewhere. If she's involuntary we need a medical certification that she's in danger of hurting herself or others. Do we have that? Did Dr. Wanderscheid or any other doctor certify her?"

"We didn't think it was necessary. Mr. Kohler . . ."

"Forget Mr. Kohler."

Mr. Flaker looked at Charlie. "Could you get Dr. Wanderscheid to make the certification right away?"

Charlie wriggled in his chair. "I guess so."

"Too late," said Laban, beaming at Mr. Flaker. "You know what we've got here? A case of false imprisonment. I'll give you one more chance. You get Grace down here right now, ready to go, and we'll forget the whole thing. Otherwise I'm applying for a writ of habeas corpus and then I'm filing a suit for false imprisonment against Charlie, Wanderscheid, you and the hospital. All of you in one bundle. Yes or no. Right now."

Mr. Flaker was perspiring. He patted his forehead with his handkerchief. "Dr. Wanderscheid is the physician in attendance. We can't let her go without his permission. It's against the regulations."

"Habeas corpus, baby. False imprisonment. Big publicity. Be smart. The rules be damned, full speed ahead. This is the law."

Rachel could see Mr. Flaker making up his handsome mind, and she made up her mind never to marry a good-looking hospital director. "I'm sorry, Mr. Kohler," he said formally to Charlie. "I don't believe, under the circumstances, that the hospital should get involved in this matter. I'm going upstairs to tell them to get your wife ready for release. She'll be downstairs in a few minutes. I'm sorry. She'll have to be admitted properly."

"That's my baby," said Laban. "I'm proud of you. You're a real hospital administrator." Unsmiling, broad shoulders back, head up, Mr. Flaker walked out.

Mrs. Schmidt ran to Laban and kissed him on the mouth.

Laban didn't resist. "Mr. Laban, you're absolutely wonderful. I can't wait for Grace to meet you. She'll be so grateful. Charlie, come outside. I want to talk to you."

Left alone with Laban, Rachel wrote, *You may not know it, Mr. Laban, but I haven't begun to fight.*

"Tell me, baby," said Laban. "What the hell you writing? You scared the pants off Flaker."

"Just doodling."

"Okay. You've been great. If you weren't a laywoman I'd split the fee with you."

"Thanks for nothing," she said.

"Enough," said Laban. "Doodle no more. Wait here for me. I've got to take a leak."

Alone at last, wrote Rachel. *I must have a plan. Every man needs a poltergeist. I could follow him down the hall and lock him in the bathroom. I've got a key; I could get into his car and drive away without him. I could print on several pages of this book Laban is a staphylococcus, and tack them to bulletin boards around the hospital.*

A nurse, white, starched and broad-based, came in and looked around her arched nose. "Mr. Laban?"

"No," said Rachel happily. "I'm his secretary."

"I see," said the nurse, and Rachel wrote, *Icy and I deserve it.* "Mr. Flaker wishes Mr. Laban to know that Mrs. Kohler will be brought down ready for discharge within five minutes. He must pick her up on his own responsibility at Mr. Flaker's office, which is at the other end of the hall on this floor. Room One Thirty-five."

"Room One Thirty-five. I'll tell him. Thank you very much, Nurse," said Rachel, and she had her plan. She ran into the hall and found Mrs. Schmidt backing Charlie against a wall with the thrust of breast and jaw. She was talking passionately and shaking her head, and Charlie had tears in his eyes. "You won't understand," he said. "She's a sick woman."

"I'll make her well. I tell you what. I won't take her away. I'll stay with you until she's well."

"You can't do that. You'd only make her worse."

"Charlie. You can say that to me after what you've done to her?"

"Let her make up her own mind. Don't browbeat her."

"Fair enough," said Mrs. Schmidt. "Let her make up her own mind. I'm glad you admit she's still got one."

"Sorry to interrupt," said Rachel, "but the nurse told me they're sending Mrs. Kohler down in a few minutes. You're to wait for her in the front lobby."

"Wonderful," said Mrs. Schmidt. She hooked Charlie's arm and drove him forward. "Your father's simply marvelous. It must be exciting to be his secretary."

"Yes. Very. Godspeed." She went back to the conference room and was so excited she couldn't sit down.

In a few minutes Laban came back, grinning. "You know anything about men's toilet habits, baby?" he said.

"Sure," said Rachel. "They stand and girls sit."

"They always wash their hands after they take a leak. That's screwy. Here are your nice, clean private parts, protected from dirt by two layers of clothing, being handled by dirty old hands. From now on I wash my hands before, not after, like a doctor before an operation."

"Why don't you wear rubber gloves?" said Rachel. "A nurse was in here looking for you. She says they're ready to release Mrs. Kohler in your custody. You're to go up to the waiting room on the fourth floor right away and you're to come alone."

Laban rubbed his hands. "How about that? What about ransom money? Okay. Wait here. If I'm not back in five minutes call the F.B.I."

"Sure," said Rachel. She waited until Laban left before she walked down the corridor to Room 135. Mr. Flaker was sitting with a small, round woman who had bulging, shiny eyes. "Mr. Flaker," Rachel said, "Mr. Laban got your message and says he'll be by in a few minutes."

"This is Mr. Laban's secretary, Mrs. Kohler," said Mr. Flaker.

Mrs. Kohler's eyes rolled on their stalks. "I can't wait to meet Mr. Laban. I owe him my life."

"He's humbly grateful to have been of service," Rachel said, and backed out of the office. She went to Laban's car in the parking lot and rapped on the bulletproof glass to make sure it was in place. For all she knew Laban had a pistol with telescopic sights in his brief case. She drove away in a fit of giggles but halfway home suffered a fit of depression. It was well and good to fight fire with fire but on the other hand if you lay down with dogs you got up with fleas. She decided her mood required a bit of instant catharsis so she pulled over to the curb and wrote *I'm sorry, Laban* fifty times.

Leah brushed her long, massive hair longer than was necessary because she loved the prick of boar bristles against her scalp, just as she'd lingered in the bathtub stroking the soft, warm water and moving the enameled surface of the soap over her skin, lathering her breasts until the nipples protruded like berries in clusters of white blossoms, and finally massaging herself with a bath towel. By the time she got dressed, Jackson Schwartz had been waiting more than half an hour, and he was reading a magazine when she came into the living room. He put it down and stood up with a smile. "Hello, Leah," he said.

"Hello."

He was tall and well formed, with broad shoulders and a slim waist, and he wore a light gray suit and a pale blue striped tie. When he hesitated in front of her, she extended her hand and he took it. She lingered with the dry, cool feel of his palm, smooth as a tree surface shorn of bark. "Shall we go?" she said.

"All right." As they walked toward the door he looked back up the stairs.

"Laban isn't here, or I'd have him greet you."

His fair skin turned dark with blood. "I wasn't planning on that."

"Rachel's upstairs if you'd like to see her. You met her downtown."

"Yes, I did." He paused. "I guess we'd better go if it's all right with you. We're a little late, though I think they'll hold our reservation."

"Whatever you say."

He wriggled his shoulders as they went outside. "It's interesting that you call your father Laban."

"We've always called him that. It's what my mother called him."

He opened the car door for her. It was a Volkswagen and when he got in behind the steering wheel his head almost touched the roof. "You're tall," she said.

"Six feet three."

"Why did you get a Volkswagen?"

He turned red again as he started the engine. "It was a good buy. A friend of mine sold it to me and I couldn't afford to pass it up."

"Doesn't Laban pay you very much?"

"I didn't mean that. Mr. Laban is a very generous boss. I get more than most guys at my stage of the game. I have no complaints. I consider myself very lucky to be working for him. He's one of the few truly great lawyers I've met."

"I'm glad to hear you say so. Some people consider him a little odd."

"They don't really know him. He's colorful and a lot of people are jealous of his originality."

He had a deep, full, rich television voice. She found it pleasant to listen to the sound. "I love my father, but you don't have to be careful of what you say to me about him. I never betray a confidence. At least I don't think so." She reflected a moment. "Laban can't be all good."

"Touché," he said. "I guess I deserve that. But he's really great. Let's see. He never lets you forget he's boss, and he lets you know it when you've made a mistake. But I can't exactly say that's a fault. I prefer it, as a matter of fact. You know the score. Some of the guys get invited to the senior partner's house for dinner, or to lunch at the club, and they think they're getting a junior partnership, but nothing comes of it. With your father it's strictly business."

"You have a lovely voice. I love to hear you talk. Did you go into law because of the way you sound?"

Jackson laughed, a staccato, high-pitched sound very unlike his speaking tone. "You're making fun of me but I don't mind."

"I'm sorry if you think so. It's not true. I don't make fun of people. Why did you go into the law?"

"I've never thought about it that much. It just seemed to be the right thing for me to do."

"When did you first decide? When you were a little boy, or in high school, college?"

"College, I think. Being on the debating squad might have had something to do with it."

"You see? The sound of your voice after all."

"Well, this may sound corny, but I felt a lawyer has a chance to help other people in trouble, that he plays a significant part in the administration of justice and the preservation of our way of life. It's easy to call a lawyer a shyster and an ambulance chaser but when you get down to it lawyers make the difference between democracy and a police state. The only person you can turn to when the police get rough is a lawyer."

"Are you a criminal lawyer?"

His hands were long-fingered, the nails carefully trimmed and manicured. They rested lightly on the steering wheel. "No. Your father doesn't handle criminal cases, but I guess I don't have to tell you."

"Yes, you do. I know very little about Laban's work. If you're concerned with protecting people why don't you work for a criminal lawyer?"

"That's a good question, but there's a lot more to law than representing persons accused of crime. Actually criminal law is only one course of many taken in law school and it's really the simplest in terms of legal study. There's also taxation, equity, torts, probate, trusts, real estate, labor, administrative, corporate law—all sorts of things that we do in your father's office. When he thinks of law the layman thinks of criminal law because of what he sees on television, but it's a very small part. And all phases of law consist of protecting the individual from the state or other individuals—unless, of course, you work for the government."

"You like being a lawyer?"

"Very much. It's very satisfying."

"Don't you ever want to do something with your hands?"

He looked at the steering wheel. "My hands?"

"Build bridges, or mousetraps, or grow flowers and potatoes. Law seems so unreal. You can't see it, feel it, smell or taste it. Man made it up. Don't you ever wonder whether you truly exist in the middle of all the words?"

Jackson shifted his shoulders and brushed her arm with his. The impact was firm and solid and she moved into it but he veered away. He slowly nodded his head. "Very interesting. Most people would say that law is about the most real thing imaginable. You know, not like painting or music or philosophy, but *really* real. Without law we'd be back living in the jungle."

"That's true, the last part. Remove the fantasy and you're left with the fact. Trees are a fact. Moss is a fact. Lions and tigers are facts. Jungles would exist even if man never did, but law is man's own creature and dies with him."

"You can sure tell you're Mr. Laban's daughter," said Jackson. "That's why he's such a great lawyer. He can always come up with an original point of view."

"It's hardly original," murmured Leah. She eyed his thigh, admired the long sweep of curve from waist to knee. She placed her hand on the round, full part of his upper leg and rubbed. It had the texture of a worn tennis ball until the muscle stiffened beneath her touch and then she might have been petting a cocker spaniel. After a moment his hand came down and covered hers and she pulled away.

"You have a nice body," she said.

"Don't pull your punches, do you? You come right out with what's on you mind."

"Don't you?"

"Are you kidding? You think I want to spend my life in jail?"

"I see my mind as a garden with weeds in it. The weeds are thoughts about people. They grow despite me, and the sooner I pull them up and throw them out the better my garden grows."

"I don't understand what you mean. Don't you like people?"

"I don't like to think about them."

Jackson hesitated. "You put your hand on my leg. That wasn't talk."

"It certainly wasn't. I told you, I like your body."

"Okay, then. I like yours too," Jackson said, and put his arm around her neck. She removed it. "You're on the track but going in the wrong direction. You didn't want my body but the idea of it. Nevertheless, it's a beginning."

He whistled. "You're a very unusual girl."

She fingered his arm muscle, bunched from holding the wheel. "I do like the feel of you," she said.

When they arrived at the Lawyers' Club for dinner, Schwartz insisted on letting her off while he found a parking lot, although she said she would prefer to go with him. The truth was that the downtown world of concrete, bricks and glass, the shower of blinking lights, the haughty stares of poised mannequins in windows and the haughtier glances of living polished flesh in jewels disturbed her. It was as though all the illusions she had banished on pain of death had regrouped in the form of a giant vacuum cleaner and sucked her up. Nothing penetrated the Good Housekeeping Seal—not a bird, insect, tree, blade of grass. The earth had vanished somewhere below the murderous thrust of man-driven vehicles.

She edged through a revolving door into a red-carpeted lobby of bare gold-braceleted arms and nylon legs, and found a vacant leather chair. She crouched and waited, feeling like an animal at bay, a nonferocious, butter-skinned animal with no teeth or claws. If she were attacked her only defense would be to lie on the floor with her legs in the air and her throat bared. Men passed in silk gabardine suits and their cuff links winked wickedly golden under the soft amber lights. Several eyed her. She stared back hungrily, trying to ferret out their edibility in a sprouting of teeth from her gums. Nobody stopped to talk to her; if one had she would have screamed. By the time Jackson returned she was curled on the chair with her legs tucked beneath her and her arms hugging her chest. He smiled. "You look just like a little girl."

She opened like a chrysalis at the timidity of his tone. "I missed you. It was lonely here."

"I'm sorry I took so long. I couldn't find an empty lot."

"There are no empty lots here. Only a cluttering of stone and steel pressing out of shape."

"I found one a couple of blocks away. Aren't you glad now you didn't come with me?" They went up in a high-speed elevator. "You'll enjoy the view. The whole city's spread out in front of you."

They stepped out onto a thick brown carpet and Leah dropped to her knees while Jackson and the elevator girl stared. She heard a muffled laugh as the door clanged shut and the elevator whined downward. She pressed her palms against the carpet and felt it respond to her touch. Jackson raised her up with an urgent hand at her elbow. "Leah, what are you doing? Somebody will see you."

"It looked so soft I couldn't believe it was real. Didn't you ever pinch yourself to prove you were there?"

"No. Where would I be?"

Jackson was looking around the restaurant with jerks of his head. It was deserted except for a maître d'hôtel, who was rushing forward. "Excuse me, miss, but I saw you fall. Did you hurt yourself?"

"You're mistaken. I didn't fall. I wanted to feel your carpet."

"Look," said Jackson, "I'm Mr. Schwartz. I made a reservation for two."

"Of course, Mr. Schwartz. Right this way, please." He led them through the dimly lit, empty room to a table next to a window and held their chairs while they sat down. A galaxy of city lights sparkled outside in the dark. "Would you care for a drink before you order?"

"Yes," said Jackson. "What do you want, Leah?"

"Whatever you order is fine."

"Two martinis, very, *very* dry, with a twist of lemon. No olives. Remember, easy on the vermouth."

"Yes, sir, two martinis."

Jackson leaned forward. "Leah, I want you to know that I have as big a sense of humor as the next guy, but are you trying to make a fool out of me? If so, just say so. I can take a hint. I want you to know that I like you very much but if you think I'm just a joke, just say so."

"I've told you what I think—that you have a very nice body. I have no idea whether you're a joke."

"Please, cut it out with the body. It makes me uncomfortable. That business with the carpet—didn't you realize it might embarrass me?"

"No. You're not responsible for what I do. Why should I embarrass you?"

He turned red. "We're together, remember? While we're together we reflect on each other."

"You think too much about too little," said Leah. "I touched the carpet because I wanted to touch the carpet. I touched you for the same reason. Listen, do something for me."

Their drinks arrived and Jackson took a big swallow. "If I can. But I'm afraid I don't have your devil-may-care attitude about things. Maybe I should, but I don't."

"Describe me."

"What do you mean?"

"Look at me and tell me what you see."

"I see a pretty girl."

"Pretend you're talking to a friend and he wants to know exactly what I look like."

"All right, I'll try. Remember I'm just a lawyer. You're about five feet four inches tall, brown hair and eyes, full eyebrows. Your features are regular. Your eyes are large, bright and well spaced. Your lips are full and your chin is broad and I don't think you smile very much. At least I can't remember what your smile makes you look like. You've got a nice build."

Leah nodded. "That's the way to talk."

Jackson finished his martini and ordered another. "To be honest, I don't see why. But if you want me to I'll certainly keep trying. Tell me, do you do this with all your dates?"

"I don't know what you mean by what I'm doing. Describe the room."

Jackson turned. "It's dark and lit by candles in glass containers on the tables. The waiters are dressed in black trousers and fancy checked red vests. The drapes are made out of the same checked red stuff. The walls are paneled with polished wood that looks like oak and there are a lot of murky portraits of old English hanging judges in their robes and long snobbish noses. They look like they've got the whole world by the tail." Jackson laughed. "This is nutty but I'm getting the hang of it."

Leah shook her head. "I'm afraid not. You were telling what you thought of the room. You made up a room."

"You might say I was trying to introduce hearsay as evidence," said Jackson, good-humored over his drink.

"You very well might."

"Jackson signaled a waiter, who came over immediately. "Another round, waiter, and some dinner menus."

"Yes, sir."

The large menu was printed on stiff cardboard in Old English letters. There was a great variety and Leah hesitated, running her eye over sirloin, filet mignon, prime rib of beef, steamed lobster, beef Stroganoff with wild rice, lobster Newberg, calves' liver, roast duck; she had settled on beef Stroganoff when Jackson said, "The prime rib is great. That's what I'd recommend," and she said, "That would be fine."

He said to the waiter, "We'll have the prime rib, rare, baked potatoes with sour cream, and mixed salad with Roquefort dressing. Coffee later." She would have preferred French dressing but said nothing.

"Say," said Jackson, "look who just came in." She turned,

heart beating, somehow certain it was Laban. But it was some-body she'd never seen before, a medium-sized, slim young man with a large head. "Hey, Creve," Jackson called. "Over here."

The man looked, hesitated and walked over to the table. "Hello, Jackson. Nice to see you."

"Creve, I'd like you to meet Leah Laban. She's William Laban's daughter. Leah, this is my old roommate from law school, Charles Crevecoeur. Sit down, Creve, and have a drink with us. This guy's terrible. I've been after him for months to go to lunch and he's always too busy."

"I haven't met your father but I've certainly heard of him," said Crevecoeur. Seen close up, it was not so much that his head was large as that he wore a shaggy, curly mop of black hair. His face peeked, soft-eyed and puckered, from the tangle. His voice was muffled and low and she had difficulty making out the words. "You have a nice name," she said, as he continued to stand. "Charles Crevecoeur."

"Creve's family is one of the oldest in the city," said Jackson. "That's how nice his name is. Come on, Creve, sit down and I'll buy you a martini. I won't take no for an answer." He hooked a finger at the waiter, and Crevecoeur sat down next to Leah and lit a cigarette.

"Jackson is about the only person left who counts my ances-tors," he said. "They lived in an unbroken line of genteel poverty. Not one businessman among them to pump in some social status. The proof is that not one street or school is named after them."

"That's too bad since it's such a lovely name," said Leah.

"Creve is going to change all that pretty damn quick. He's with the biggest firm in town. Did you know he ranked our law-school class?"

Crevecoeur shook his head and picked up his martini. His fingers, long, slender, graceful, were stained with nicotine, and the nails were bitten. "If I'm so smart why ain't I rich?" he said, smiling at Leah.

"Just a matter of time, that's all it is," said Jackson.

"Time is money," said Crevecoeur.

"I'll drink to that," said Jackson. His face was perspiring and his eyes were moist.

Crevecoeur quickly drained his glass and stood up. "Miss Laban, it was a pleasure meeting you."

"Stick around and have dinner with us," said Jackson. "I haven't seen you in a coon's age."

"I'd like to, but no, thanks. I'm meeting someone here for dinner."

"A date? You? I don't believe it. Do you know this guy went through law school without taking out a single girl?"

"That's right. I like the married kind. As a matter of fact I'm meeting Mr. Terryhill."

Jackson whistled. "Mr. Number One. Terryhill, Ronson, Blair and Wessler, that's Creve's firm. What did I tell you? Onward and Upward, huh?"

"I'd better get a table," said Crevecoeur. "Good-bye, Miss Laban." And he walked away.

Jackson watched him go. "A real nice guy," he said. "One of the best. But what a character. Imagine going to dinner with your boss looking like a bum. He gets away with murder and don't tell me it isn't his family connections."

Leah was sitting next to the wall. She turned and faced a huge portrait of a white-wigged, black-robed figure with a sharp, pointed nose and cold eyes, enclosed in an ornately carved frame. She fingered the whorls and dips of the wood and moved inward toward the paint. It was smooth and repellent as a fish's scale and she quickly withdrew her hand as Jackson said with his high laugh, "Want me to describe it for you?"

She stared at him until he looked away. "I know your secret," she said.

"What do you mean? What secret?"

"That you haven't any."

Although for some time Rachel had suspected that certain truths are not self-evident, such as that men are created equal or that they are endowed with rights or even reason, of one truth she had become sure: Beatrice and she, jointly and severally (to quote Laban) were the two worst cooks in creation, and if that mealy (Rachel's own adjective) Jackson Schwartz kept wining and dining Leah twice a week, Wednesdays and Saturdays, drastic measures would have to be taken, such as hiring a professional cook—which should have been done long ago in any event—or going out to dinner themselves. Maybe Laban could put the screws on Jackson Schwartz. See here, punk, baby, you can't root in my daughter's garden until after nine P.M., and that's an order. All Rachel had to do was suggest this and Laban would raise Schwartz's salary to cover dinner for two every night. For some incomprehensible Labanic reason, all systems were go for Jackson Schwartz's wooing of Leah. Rachel had seen and heard enough of him to rocket him off into some lost orbit, convicted of capital crimes: he lacked a sense of humor and was a bore, and there is no bore like a handsome one. She couldn't imagine what Leah and he talked about.

Tonight Leah was safely home in the kitchen, the roast leg of lamb was ready, and Laban had yelled from the head of the stairs that Beatrice and he were making their entrance. This was meant for Leah, to make sure they were all in the audience, and she came out of the kitchen, wiping her hands on her apron.

Laban was on costumes. He had already been Li'l Abner to

Beatrice's Daisy Mae, Wyatt Earp to her Calamity Jane, Sir Launcelot to Guinevere; the night before, dripping with sweat, they were Babylonian, wrapped in fringed, tasseled wool shawls of brilliant reds, greens, blues and purples from the neck to the floor. "Tonight," said Laban, "we're playing it cool. We're Egyptians." He wore a white muslin loincloth tied at the hips like a diaper, and a pleated, fringed apron hanging in front. His body from the waist upward was bare except for the nest of hair on his chest. "Clothes make the man," said Laban. Rachel fashioned spectacles of her thumbs and forefingers and peered through them at Beatrice. What exactly did clothes make her stepmother, who wore a form-fitting white sheath that fell from shoulder straps to her ankles and had a square hollowed out to fully expose her large breasts? The veins had been outlined with blue eye shadow by a drunken cartographer and the nipples tinted red by a raspberry picker. She came on strong, head and shoulders back, smiling, happy to be airing her prize pair of poodles, and sat in her place at the table opposite Bernie, who remained bolted to his chair. Leah got up and brought in the leg of lamb on a platter and set the lump of meat in the center of the table, where Rachel eyed it nervously. "You may have noticed," said Laban, seating himself with ceremony, "that Beatrice's tits are bare. The truth is, a nice tit is pleasing to the sight."

"The truth is," said Bernie, lips quivering, "you used to run a first-class three-ring circus. The best aerialists and dancing bears in town. It's very sad that you're reduced to the one and only Little Egypt. Step right up, folks. Watch her shimmy, watch her shake, watch her give you a bellyache. Straight from sensational performances before the crowned heads of Europe and Asia."

"Dance, baby. Dance for the man," said Laban, and Beatrice got up and revolved her arms like sleepy snakes, grinding her shoulders at an itch in the middle of her back. Her breasts did a cocky little ballet of their own.

Bernie snatched the platter of lamb and held it under Beatrice's nose. "Here, Salome. Your reward. Hide it in your treasure chest." Unable to contain herself, Rachel ran upstairs, as Laban called after her, "Baby, where you going?" and Bernie chimed in with "I hope you're satisfied." Rachel found her purse and raced back. She fished for some coins, threw them at Beatrice's sandaled feet and sat down again, flushed with triumph.

"Thank you," said Laban. "Baby, thank the nice lady."

"Thank you," said Beatrice politely.

Laban carved up John the Baptist's head and they began to eat.

"We're ready now for the Bible lesson," said Laban. "What's the good word?"

"The word is, 'Abandon all hope, ye who enter here.' That's the word."

"What's the matter, baby? Throwing in the towel?"

"If I had a towel I'd know where to throw it."

"A towel, please, for Bernie."

Leah brought in a bath towel. Bernie draped it around Beatrice's breasts and tied it at the back of her neck like a bib. Rachel couldn't decide whether Laban or Bernie was being the more idiotic. Once Laban had launched his program of dressing for dinner, finding something to wear had become increasingly difficult. Given his premise—if the shoe or dress fit, one wore it—he had to travel sooner or later to private parts. Breasts, after all, weren't born wrapped in cotton. What of nude statues in front of airports or railway stations? What of French, Italian or Swedish movies and topless bathing suits? When Bernie draped the towel over Beatrice, he flung mud around the Louvre making Beatrice look dirty instead of all of a piece. Laban's folly, perhaps, but all of a piece.

What was Laban's sin anyway? He didn't respect their sensibilities. Only what he felt mattered, and that couldn't be right. Bernie's crime was having a private vision of private parts. The exposure of breast, after all, wasn't by itself either moral or immoral. It was a question of intent, as the judges said, and Rachel's problem was that she didn't, after all these years, know what either Laban or Bernie intended. She didn't even know if Laban intended anything, and if he didn't how could one say he was any more immoral than an idiot? Bernie, thin and serious as a wire, professed to be moral, but was he? It just wasn't enough to be indignant, but Rachel didn't know where to go from there. She was all amuddle, like a Dickens character *in medias res*. She clung to one thought: this was her father and brother and she had to live with them. They were part of what she was and whatever she was to become.

"My lesson for today," said Bernie grimly, "is called 'The Revenge of Jacob's Sons,' and the moral is, God save us from the tricksters."

"Court's in session. You may proceed," said Laban, buttering his bread on both sides.

"A gentile prince, Shechem, laid Dinah, Jacob's daughter, and Jacob's sons were very unhappy about it even though Shechem was crazy about Dinah and wanted to marry her. So the sons cooked up a plot. They said they couldn't give their sister to an uncircumcised dog but if all the males of the prince's city would be circumcised, then the Jewesses could intermarry with them, and everybody'd live happily ever after. Shechem thought this was great, so all the gentile males were circumcised. Three days later Dinah's brothers caught them with their pants down, so to speak, their penises sore, killed them down to the last man and confiscated their wives, children and property. Jacob complained that it would make big trouble for him and he didn't want any trouble. The sons said, 'Should he deal with our sister as with an harlot?'"

Laban tugged at the hair on his chest. "That's some story, baby. God save us from tricksters. Some trick if you can do it."

"You can do it, Laban, I know you can. Have faith."

"Come on, Bernie," said Rachel, "stop fooling around. You make it sound like the Trojan War. Beware of Jews bearing gifts."

"I don't make the Bible, I just read from it."

"Then read it right. Are you trying to say it's a big How Not To book? It sounds like the modern justification for sick, sick literature—that morality lies in the strength of the reaction."

"Try this for size," said Bernie. "Shechem took his uncircumcised penis and with it penetrated a daughter of Israel. He was doing what came naturally. Where's the moral?"

"But he offered to marry her. He wanted to atone for what he did," said Beatrice.

Bernie shook his head. "You're thinking *goyish* again, Mom. Repent and be saved. The handsome prince whisking Dinah into his golden chariot with 'Just Married' hung on the rear. Keep thinking like that and you'll never get to Judaism."

"The way I figure it," said Laban, "is this prince was I mean ugly, with a long, drippy nose, halitosis and B.O. Dinah says, Boys, marrying him is a fate worse than death. I'll die before I marry that piece of *tref*. They figure if they just knock off the prince, they're dead ducks. They're outnumbered. So they put their heads together and come up with a winner. When you're in a fight and you got little fists, hit 'em in the balls."

"Is that what you do in the courtroom?" said Bernie. "If you don't have a case, make one up? Dinah's silent. She never opens her mouth. We don't know what she wants because nobody cares. Her maidenhead is a figurehead."

"They committed mass murder. In God's name, why?" yelled Rachel. It wasn't fair of Bernie to lead them around in circles. Her college Bible course, Geography of the Holy Land and Gospel Texts, didn't do her a bit of good.

"There you said it. In God's name. Not for Harry and Saint George but for God. The Jews were fighting to save their God in the only way they know how, by saving those who believed in him. They inscribed a magical ring around the children of Israel and anyone who crossed the line must die. It was no small thing to survive. Mercy is a luxury that primitive peoples just can't afford. Then history turned the Jews around and any Jew who ventured outside the circle was killed.

"The first commandment was to fight for God's life to the death. The rest came limping after. When you're strong enough you kill the unconvertible. When you're weak enough you remind the strong of the other nine commandments and they hate you for it and kill you off like flies. It was true of the Jews of the Diaspora, and of the early Christians. The final morality emerges when God is strong enough to stand on His own feet without looking over His shoulder, and that time will come when nobody feels strong enough to knock Him down for His own good. When we are weak enough God will be strong enough. In the meantime, let us pray."

"You're a smart boy, baby," said Laban. "I wish I knew what the hell you're talking about. This God. I thought he could knock off the world with a flood or a bolt of lightning by raising His pinkie. He sounds pretty strong to me."

"He was whistling in the dark to keep reminding Himself He *was* God. He always knew His only chance was in not raising a finger to protect Himself. He's got one asset, immortality. He can be beat around the ears, knocked down, disemboweled, but He can't die."

" 'Blessed are the meek: for they shall inherit the earth,' " said Rachel.

"Exactly, and yet not exactly. The ideal for the modern Jew is not the atavistic, nationalistic aberration known as Israel but the early Christian, the Sermon-on-the-Mount Christian. It *must* be; the world for too long hasn't let the Jew be anything else. 'Blessed are they which are persecuted for righteousness' sake: for theirs is the kingdom of heaven. Blessed are ye, when men shall revile you, and persecute you, and say all manner of evil against you falsely.' Every time a Jew gets mad when somebody calls him a lousy coward, he should rejoice instead. 'Blessed are the peacemakers.' When he's condemned for crowding like sheep into Hitler's boxcars and crematoriums instead of gloriously rushing the guards, he should celebrate. 'Verily I say unto thee, Thou shalt by no means come out thence, till thou hast paid the uttermost farthing.' Genesis and Ruth are five hundred years apart and we're a couple of thousand beyond that. Jews have been weak enough long enough to practice what Christ preached, and Christians have the misfortune of having inherited the kingdom of earth. The biggest danger to the Jew is that it's too easy for him to join the restricted country clubs. There won't be enough Christian gentlemen left to make no-Jew agreements."

Laban laughed. "You're some Jew, baby, believe me. Some Jews just can't stand prosperity. What's so bad about being pals with gentiles? Some of my best friends are gentiles. And I could tell you plenty of stories about your meek Jew that would curl your hair."

"I'm sure you could. Jews are only human. That's what I said. It's a historical accident that they've been anything more—which is persecuted. I'm not arguing for more persecution of the Jews or anyone else. I'm just asking Jews not to forget what they've been privileged to learn by it. I'm asking them to celebrate their history of persecution, ritualize it, honor it, not bury it in Christian credit cards."

"Okay, okay. I'll tear up my Diner's Club. How's that?"

"*That* is exactly what I'd expect from you."

Laban raised his hands toward heaven. "You sure are hard to please." He picked up the salt shaker and sprinkled his third slice of lamb. "We Egyptians may not know much about God but we can't believe He doesn't want us to raise a little hell."

Bernie took the salt shaker and flourished it over his shoulder. " 'If the salt have lost his savour, wherewith shall it be salted? It is thenceforth good for nothing, but to be cast out, and to be trodden under foot of men.' "

"There you go again with your riddles. I've got one for you, Baby," he said to Beatrice, "what is it that's red, hangs on the wall and whistles?"

"I don't know."

"A herring."

"But a herring isn't red," said Beatrice, obviously coached.

"So it isn't red."

"But a herring doesn't hang on the wall."

"So it doesn't hang on the wall."

"But a herring doesn't whistle."

"So it doesn't whistle."

Rachel still thought the old joke was funny and laughed, but Bernie grimaced and Leah cleared the dishes from the table. It looked as though Laban would die from laughing. He doubled over as if in pain and laughed so hard that he choked and his face turned gray.

After dinner Rachel and Bernie went for a walk. It was still light with that magical glow of a fading summer evening that makes grass heady with greenness, and bricks of houses as red and blooming as cardinal flowers. Rachel felt like saying, Here's your scared, murderous God, and there's more things, brother, in heaven and earth than you dream of. But she was afraid she'd get Bernie started again and she was sick and tired of his Jewish ecumenics. "What," she said, "do we do about our revolting Jackson Schwartz?"

Bernie was mystified, as he had a right to be, since he didn't care whom his sisters went out with or whom they might marry. For years he hadn't even been able to tell Rachel and Leah apart, simply because he did not try. His only concerns were how to get the better of Laban and how the world would end. Still, he was their older brother, and was very self-conscious about protecting them since he felt Laban wouldn't. "What do we have to do?" he said. "He seems harmless enough."

"Much you know." She tried to hit Bernie where he lived. "He's got the morals of that snake in *An American Tragedy*. Jackson Schwartz would drown his own mother to marry one of Laban's daughters. That's all he's interested in, marrying a Laban's daughter so he can get ahead in the law."

"Really?" Bernie turned an owl face toward her, blinking behind his glasses. He was so naïve when it came to judging people that she had to struggle to remember his high I.Q. It was a question of being interested, and he wasn't. She had to force him. "I had no idea you knew him so well," he said. "Have you talked to Leah?"

"Of course not. That would be the worst thing we could do. Leah *likes* him. He's tall and good-looking and acts like butter wouldn't melt in his mouth. You know Leah. What experience has she had with men? She's ripe for picking by the first opportunist to come along."

"What's so bad if she likes him? One thing's certain: she'd be better off than staying on with Laban. Schwartz strikes me as a safe, dependable fellow. That's all Leah wants, somebody to make a home for. She won't go back east to school with us. I've argued myself hoarse and she won't even consider it."

"Bernie, sometimes I could strangle you. Did you ever hear of the word 'love'? L-o-v-e? I'd die before I'd marry a boy who didn't love me. *Me*, not whose daughter I am. Once he's got Leah tied up and Laban makes him a partner or whatever he's after, he'll treat her like a dog. Can't you see that? It's so clear to me it makes me sick."

"Assuming you're right, what is there to do?" said Bernie. "Contract for his murder? Leah knows what she wants and I'm sure she knows what Schwartz wants. Let her make up her own mind."

"Bernie, believe me. I've never been so positive about anything in my life. He'll make her life a hell on earth. He's a mean, immoral schemer. Would you want your sister to be married to an immoralist?"

"You're making a loose definition of immorality," said Bernie, and she fretted at her error in strategy. Bernie was back playing on his home field. "Immorality implies a conscious selection of inferior choices. From what you've said about Schwartz, he may be conventional, he may accept a static, obsolete moral standard. He may also believe, in fact, that his intentions are strictly honorable. So where's the immorality? He's courting a girl he plans, from what you say, not to seduce but to marry. He treats her with deference. In any army he'd get a good-conduct ribbon."

"Crap," said Rachel. "We're talking about Leah's happiness. How can she be happy with a man who doesn't love her?"

"Granting him the premise of conventionality, I'm not even sure he doesn't love her. His kind of love attaches to labels. He loves who, not what, she is; therefore, he loves."

"I give up," said Rachel. "You don't know what love is. A simple, universal thing like love and you manage to intellectualize it out of existence. I pity your wife if you ever manage to find one."

"I thought we were discussing Jackson Schwartz."

"*I* was discussing him. Forget the whole business, will you? I'll work it out by myself." The truth was, she had gotten excited enough to squeeze Bernie's arm in forgiveness. She had a marvelous idea of how to deal with Jackson Schwartz, really do him in. She'd wait for the right moment; sooner or later it had to come.

When they got back, the others were waiting for them in the living room. Laban, holding the blue-backed document, announced that he had rewritten his will and would like to read it to them if they would be so kind as to listen. As he read, Rachel eyed Beatrice's blue-penciled breasts and thought how true it was that no emotion was so ephemeral as embarrassment. It was merely a trick on the senses and depended on surprise. One yawned at the second lady sawed in half, the second rabbit pulled out of a hat. Even Bernie was regarding the naked bosom as so much bric-a-brac. She considered ripping open her own war chest to test her theory, but she didn't want to get into Bernie's rut of throwing down gauntlets to Laban as a way of life. She preferred to think of her breasts as doves of peace that she'd let fly open only in the face of love.

Watching Laban read the will, Rachel could imagine him, with his craggy face firm and deep-socketed eyes steady, as a fierce, flamboyant leader of a nomadic tribe, laying down the law, fighting the Jews for possession of the Holy Land. Perhaps he was being Pharaoh, letting the Jews go. Only it turned out this time he was letting Bernie and Leah go.

"As you may have heard," Laban said, "I earned my money the hard way. Nobody handed me a bucket of water in the desert. I was my own water boy. So I figured the person who gets my dough has got to earn it the hard way. Bernie was putting up a good fight but Rachel's licked him good. She finally spit that hot potato out of her mouth and kicked it around a bunch of hospital corridors. She didn't tell her old man to get lost, she *got* him lost. You may think it's what I deserve, that one good trick deserves another, but it wasn't good. It was a dirty trick because Rachel didn't play by the rules. She lied just to beat me, not to win the game. In fact, she made up her own game, and that's not cricket. So I say to myself, This Rachel baby deserves nothing but my money. Beatrice gets her third, Miss Trilby twenty thousand, Rachel gets the rest." He stood up, Egyptian apron swinging, went to *A History of the Jewish People* and replaced Bernie's will with Rachel's. She was suddenly struck with the beauty of Laban's legs, long and shapely and still well muscled. He lit a match and set fire to Bernie's will, and they watched it curl into cinders in the fireplace.

Rachel was close to tears. "You deserved it," she said. "The way you treated Mr. Kohler and Mr. Flaker. You humiliated them beyond belief. You have absolutely no respect for anybody's dignity. You stripped them bare, especially poor Mr. Kohler in front of his step-daughter and a bunch of strangers. You left him with less clothes on than your wife."

"No, sir. I was playing the game, and by the rules. I was there to get Mrs. Kohler out of the hospital prison, remember? Charlie and Flaker were there to keep her in. They were my opponents. The chalk stripes were laid down and not once did I hit a foul ball; I didn't even raise chalk. I'll let you worry about Charlie's feelings. My concern was getting his wife loose. That was my job. I didn't point a gun. I didn't raise my fist. All I did was shoot off my mouth because that's what I'm paid to do. My weapon's the law, the only one I had, the only one I used. You, not I, took the law in your own hands. You decided I was to go to the wrong place, Charlie and Margery to the wrong place; you lied to get the job done. You created a farce at other people's expense, and all you had to gain was what it cost other people. I'm sorry, baby, but you really earned my money."

Rachel couldn't take any more. She tore open her blouse. One of the pearl buttons caught and she ripped cloth but didn't care. She unhooked her brassière, threw it on the floor and burst out crying. "There," she said. "Is that playing the game?"

10

Leah went with Beatrice to the neighborhood movie because Beatrice was dying to go and nobody else would. Leah went because she was asked and didn't care whether she went or not. Beatrice was as excited as a little girl. She had seen the movie before and loved it, and she loved to see movies that she liked over again. It wasn't a loss for Leah. She liked the pale gloom, the shadows of people and the sorting out of sounds, smells and touches. The sounds: creaking of worn, anxious seats; slither of leather soles down the aisles; stage-whispering of voices; shrieks of adolescent laughter; popping of lips over gum; forest fires of candy wrappers; scratchings of a nervous leg against the back of a chair like a tree branch at her window; popcorn cracking like knuckles. The smells: gummy sweetness of melted butter, like sick flowers; heavy perfume of Snickers and Hershey's chocolate with almonds; stagnant waters of body and breath odors; ammonias of cologne and face powder; flat, musty layer of too little air. The touches: limp, creamy leather; the harsh saw-toothed edges of a crack in the seat; sea-washed hardness of the gum wads underneath; the doughy roundness of Beatrice's upper arm against hers; a tattoo needle—her own fingernails across her forehead.

William Holden was a sergeant fighting the Germans in Italy in the middle of World War II. Nancy Olsen was a WAC lieutenant who had lost her first lover; Holden was unaware of her tragedy and tried to have an affair. When she wouldn't, he assumed it was because he wasn't a commissioned officer but,

subsequently, he received a battlefield commission for his bravery
and she still wouldn't give in. However, during an air raid she
became frightened and threw herself into his arms. They fell in
love. But Holden had to go back to the front, where, since he was
in love, things were not the same. He became overly cautious
and, as a result, a buddy was killed while he was only wounded.
He was sent back to the hospital and Nancy Olsen; his physical
wounds healed, but he remained psychologically scarred. He felt
he had betrayed his manhood. Nancy appeared to bring him
around and they got married and Holden got a safe desk job, but
meanwhile he was suffering internally from guilt and during the
honeymoon had nightmares. Finally he couldn't stand it and told
Nancy he had to go back to his company to absolve his guilt.
Nancy blinked back her tears, hugged him and let him go. He
wound up missing in action but Nancy refused to believe in his
death. She wandered through cheering crowds in liberated Rome
looking for him. She saw him, on crutches, unshaved, but alive,
on steps going upward. She called out his name. They embraced
to end the picture.

As they left the theater, Beatrice couldn't stop crying. She kept
gulping and blowing her nose. "I can't help it," she said. "It's
such a lovely movie. Wouldn't it have been awful if William
Holden had really gotten killed and Nancy kept wandering
among all those happy people and never found him? I would have
died."

"Death is part of life," said Leah. "Flowers die that flowers
may live. Some day even William Holden has to make room."

"I know that, but for now he never has to die and that's why
the picture makes me so glad. I can cry because he's still alive
forever. Didn't you cry at all? You're so much stronger than I
am. I'm made of peanut butter and jelly; I eat enough of it and
you know how fattening peanut butter is."

"That's true. Peanut butter is fattening."

"Tell me honestly, Leah. I know I can count on you to be
honest. Am I getting too fat? Do I look too terrible?"

Leah obediently looked at the tall woman walking beside her,
at the long graceful legs—her best feature—wide hips, the slightly

thick waist, full breasts, the squared-off shoulders, the bare arms too fleshy underneath, the rosy face with its rawboned nose and too thin lips. "You're not too fat," she said, as she had so many times before.

Beatrice clutched her arm. "I can trust you, I really can. You're the most truthful person I've ever known. I don't want to go home yet. I want to talk awhile. Couldn't we go in here and get some coffee? Please."

They were standing in the orange light of an all-night restaurant, which played with the streaks in Beatrice's hair and turned her blue eyes yellow. "Of course," said Leah and she followed Beatrice into the restaurant, where they found a booth and ordered coffee.

"Here's what I truly want to know," said Beatrice, a lock of orange-blond hair falling across her face. "Are you glad I married your father? Do you think I'm making him happy? Why don't Bernie and Rachel like me? I know they don't, no matter what I say or do. Is it because I married Laban?"

"I don't think about such things. I can't answer you."

"Then you're not glad. You don't like me any more than your brother or sister do. Oh, Leah, why?"

"That's not true. I told you, I don't think about such things."

"But you must. We live together. What else is there to think about?"

"Everything else."

Puzzled and sad, Beatrice stared at her. "I love you, Leah, I honestly do, but you're such a strange girl and you frighten me. You won't laugh or cry at anything. You make me feel like a child for wanting to love you, as though it's not love but fear of being left out in the cold. I won't pretend. I am afraid of being left out, but only because I have so much love to give and I don't want any of it to be wasted."

"Bernie says you like men."

"Is that what he thinks? That I'm promiscuous? I'll bet he's called me some terrible things."

Leah thought for a moment. "He's called you a whore."

"Well, he's wrong, and he's awful for saying such a thing."

Beatrice hiccuped in her excitement and jerked her head so that a bobby pin settled on the Formica table top. "Of course I like men. Men are wonderful. It's unhealthy for a woman not to like men. And I admit I wasn't a virgin when your father married me. He wasn't the first man I ever loved. But I never, never slept with a man I didn't love, and that's the God's truth, may He strike me dead if it isn't." Beatrice raised her arm and dared Heaven. "I love Laban and nobody else. I haven't cheated on him even in my mind. I've never cheated on any man, least of all your father, and I never will, no matter what Bernie thinks." She was crying and Leah handed over her own handkerchief. "He isn't being fair. He isn't giving me a chance. He isn't giving his own father the benefit of the doubt that he knows when he's loved. He's happy with me and I want so much for all of us to be happy together. I've prayed that I could make matters better between us, not worse."

"Bernie doesn't like my doing all the housework and cooking the meals."

"But you wanted to. Didn't you tell Bernie? You father was getting a housekeeper and you said no, you wanted to do the work. Didn't you explain that? Isn't it true?"

"Yes, I told him and yes, it's true."

"Leah, *please*. Be my friend," Beatrice said, and covered Leah's hands with her own.

Leah looked down at the long fingers and narrow, orange-painted nails. Beatrice's palms were hot, dry and brittle, like dead leaves in the sun. "I am your friend," said Leah.

"Then tell me what to do. What am I doing wrong? Will you tell Bernie that I'm not a prostitute, that I love his father more than life itself and would do absolutely anything for him? That I love Bernie and Rachel and you because you're my husband's children, because you're such lovely, intelligent people, because I *must* be loved? Will you tell Rachel?"

"If you want me to."

"I do, I do, but only if you think it will do any good. Help me, I'm begging you. Would it do any good?"

"I don't know," said Leah. Beatrice withdrew her hands.

"Bernie didn't like your showing your breasts."

Beatrice's face tightened into stubbornness. "Your father asked me to dress that way and whatever Laban asks I'll do. I won't deny his slightest wish. He comes first, no matter what."

"Rachel feels Laban got married too soon after Mother's death."

"I did what your father wanted. Believe me, if you only knew, we meant no disrespect to your mother. Is that what you think too?"

"I don't think about things like that. Rachel says you're not careful enough about your hair and clothes. She says you're always dropping objects like bobby pins or earrings."

Beatrice snatched the bobby pin off the table and shoved it in her hair. She felt the earrings at each ear. She sat silently and mooned at her cup of untasted coffee growing cold. "I guess we may as well go home," she said.

Her amusement safely tucked away in her mind, Leah reached out with both hands and sandwiched Beatrice's fingers. It was all Beatrice needed. She swooped down and kissed the back of Leah's hand, leaving behind henna lipstick marks, like fingerprints, for Leah's unblinking eyes.

As she anticipated, Rachel got her crack at Jackson Schwartz; it was as if he were an insect banging against the screen, begging to be swatted. Or, more likely, the drone dancing around the queen even if it killed him. She'd been nice, *very* nice, to him whenever he came to pick Leah up. She made it her business to be around to say, Hello, how *are* you? and give him a nice view of her knees as she crossed her legs while Leah sat quietly by. She let him know which twin had the painted toenails.

And she refused all dates for Saturday nights to be available—which wasn't much of a sacrifice because she preferred a different brand of boy from the locals, different even from those, like herself, back from college in the east. Once home they became pompous and self-conscious as they sucked their silver-trimmed, curve-stemmed pipes. The ones who never went away weren't much better; they felt it their duty to act like all-American truck drivers. Actually, she wanted older men but hadn't met any.

Jackson Schwartz had a friend, it seemed, with the improbable name of Charles Crevecoeur, a roommate from lawschool days. Leah asked Rachel whether she'd like to go out with him; Jackson wanted them to go together to Tangletown, which you could count on Jackson's liking since it was phony. Rachel said she'd love to, without thinking twice. "You know," she said to Leah, "I was beginning to think I'd lost my touch. I haven't gone out on Saturday night in an awfully long time. Do you know Charles Crevecoeur? Is he as gorgeous as Jackson?"

"I've met him once. He's very nice. I'm sure you'll like him. Of course, he's a lawyer."

Rachel shrugged. "I've gotten over *that*. Lawyers do wear pants, and if they're as cute as Jackson they can't be all bad."

"He's quite attractive," said Leah, and Rachel got excited, not for herself, but at the suspicion that Leah might be diverted. Nobody could be as bad as Jackson Schwartz.

Dressing for the evening, she didn't kid around. She wore a brassière that flung her breasts up and out, under a close-fitting black Egyptian cotton sheath that ended two inches above her knees. She finished up with a clutch of thin gold bracelets around one wrist and was ready for Jackson Schwartz and Tangletown. Leah had on a sweet, blue cotton with buttons down the front and a dark blue belt, sandals, and no make-up except for a touch of lipstick. A clear dialectic. An argument as pure as the pairing of professional wrestlers: the whore and the lady. May the best girl win in one fall.

With his first look at her, Jackson revealed she'd pegged her man, had him tied hand and foot in the sun and stretched out to dry. He was a horny one, this one; the only thing that might rule his head was his gonads. A road map was what he was and all you had to do was read him right. You started with the head, by-passed the heart and created havoc in his pants. To tell the truth, sexually he left her absolutely cold. The only kind of sex that gave her a jolt was on the heart-to-heart circuit, and Jackson might just as well have been a mannequin in a better men's store. He was dressed to the teeth, which were even more polished than his shining shoes and cuff links. To keep his balls in an uproar she gave him a hard, blue-eyeshadowed look and a lippy smile. She opened her mouth, patted her upper lip with her tongue like a junior-miss Marilyn Monroe and hoped she wasn't overdoing it.

Charles Crevecoeur was another matter; right off she could tell. He had that disturbing kind of looks that couldn't possibly hide the decency of his character. He was, for all the world to see, a "nice guy"—whatever that had come to mean. For one thing, it meant she had known him all her life, trusted him, liked him, wanted to mother him. He was Spencer Tracy or Van Johnson. It did not mean, necessarily, that one would fall in love with him, which depended on one's needs. He was not Humphrey Bogart, Clark Gable or John Wayne, with whom you'd have to risk the day he'd oil his gun and ride out. Some women couldn't love without that risk. It also meant he wasn't Anthony Perkins or Roddy McDowall, who might, any day, come at you with a carving knife. Crevecoeur's face was an open sandwich that invited you to nibble here and there. Rachel resolved immediately to confide in him about Leah and Jackson, to see if he would help. Of course he was Jackson's friend and Spence or Van couldn't betray a friend in any way, but maybe he'd see he was doing it for Jackson's good as well as Leah's—helping shape up his character a bit. Don't think you're so clever, Charlie, if you turn out to be an axe murderer. I've been wrong before about people and where did it get them in the end?

They went to Tangletown huddled together in Jackson's Volkswagen, and since the back seat of a Volkswagen was no place to conduct a private conversation Rachel did her best to pretend she was out to have one, not letting Jackson or Leah miss a single word. She was playing for high stakes—Leah's future— and she didn't care how many faces, two, three or four, she displayed. "I adore Tangletown. All those offbeat places and funny little people running around. Like Greenwich Village almost, don't you think?"

"I wouldn't know," said Crevecoeur. "I've never been there before, or Greenwich Village, for that matter."

"Marvelous. Did you hear that, Jackie? Charlie's never been to Tangletown before. It'll give us a chance to show him around— the jazz spots, coffee houses, folk-sings, pizza palaces—the works."

"I told you, Creve, it's a lot of fun. You don't know what you've been missing." Jackson laughed. "Every nut in town hangs out there."

"I never dreamed you young lawyers had so much fun," she said to Crevecoeur. "I thought you were serious, hard-working people who didn't have time to fool around. My father says the law is a very jealous mistress and any young lawyer who doesn't give it one hundred percent had better find himself another kewpie doll. That's what my father says and he's a lawyer, you know." That should shake Jackson up a little, make his measly little mind figure he'd better butter up the sister or she might upset the apple cart.

Crevecoeur smiled, which crinkled his face like a benevolent prune. "I'm afraid you're right and that's why I've decided to quit the law."

"You've *what?*" said Jackson from the front seat. "You're kidding."

"Yesterday was my last day. You remember when you saw me at the Lawyers' Club? Mr. Terryhill invited me to dinner to try to talk me out of it. Not because I'm that good a lawyer, of course, but because, as he took pains to point out, he knew my father and owed it to his memory."

"Creve comes from one of the oldest families in the city," said

Jackson. "I still don't believe it. Why would you quit? You've got everything going for you. You ranked our lawschool class, and you said it yourself, Mr. Terryhill is on your team. He was a friend of your father's."

"He wasn't exactly a friend. He knew my father. My father didn't make friends easily—or money either, for that matter."

"What did your daddy do for a living?" said Rachel. She was thrown off course because Crevecoeur had refused to remain a pawn and was sweeping over the heads of other pieces, capturing attention right and left. He wasn't, after all, Spencer Tracy, who wouldn't desert the law until he'd become judge or senator or even President, who wouldn't quit until he was, as Laban would say, on top of the game. Who then? Van Heflin, maybe, examining his conscience and finding it wanting?

"My father was what you might call a free thinker. He worked very hard at any idea he couldn't charge for. This made it necessary for my mother to earn the living, which she did by teaching school."

"Is that what you've decided to be?" said Rachel. "A thinker?"

"For the time being, yes," said Crevecoeur. "On what little I've saved and on my father's inheritance, which *his* father left him: an abandoned farm in the country. Only I'd say it's become a little more abandoned. In fact, it's practically falling down."

"You never know when Creve's kidding," said Jackson.

"It's in the blood. The Crevecoeur men seem to be drawn to that old farm. The family haunted house. My mother had great hopes for me. She said that the Crevecoeurs would finally raise their fuzzy heads in polite society, make watercress sandwiches, walk down winding staircases, bring their daughters out and keep their sons in the office, grow their family tree safely under glass. She even dreamed of restoring the farm, seeding the pastures and stabling riding horses. She doesn't really like teaching small children, which she's doing now on the West Coast."

"You can't be serious," said Jackson. "It's unbelievable. What about your education going down the drain? Wasted. And you ranked the class. It's"—Jackson searched for words—"adolescent and immoral. I'm sorry but I had to say that, and I never thought I'd have to say it to you. Think of what would happen to the world if all the lawyers decided to stop practicing. There'd be anarchy."

Rachel smiled at Crevecoeur. "Your country needs you," she said.

"My country estate needs me," said Crevecoeur. "No one else would have it. Don't be upset," he said to Jackson. "I may go back to the law with my tail between my legs, and you can give me a job."

"Believe me," said Jackson. "If it's ever within my power, the job is yours. You can count on it." He shook his head. "All that may sound romantic right now but don't think it'll be easy when you go back. A lawyer plays with fire when he forgets his sense of responsibility. People have to be able to trust a lawyer all the way."

Rachel said, as sweetly as she could, "Maybe we shouldn't go to Tangletown. Somebody might see us. It's an untrustworthy place if ever I saw one."

"It's all right," said Jackson. "Everybody goes there."

Rachel turned to Crevecoeur. Jackson could wait; she could wrap him up later—around her little finger, when it was free. "I'd like to see your farm. Would you take me there sometime?"

Crevecoeur examined her while she sat at ease under his glance. If he was a confidence man he was a marvelous one. He certainly had hers. If he put a hand inside her dress she would be sure it was to stop the bleeding somewhere and she'd not move a muscle. She wondered if she could fall in love with a Van Heflin who lived on a farm with no visible means of support, whose father had lived off his mother. She thought with a happy grin, This week I'm an heiress, Charlie. Grab me quick before Laban changes his mind.

"It's not really a farm," he said. "It's a shabby, dirty, shaky building surrounded by weeds. No cows, chickens, Lassies, pickup truck, white-painted fences, not even a television set. I thought of running a rental advertisement: 'For the man who has everything, even an executive yo-yo, the farm that has nothing: no bath, electricity, heat, running water, shade or fruit trees, garden, pond, brook, stream, hammock, power mower, root feeder, rake, shovel, Wiss shears, radio-phonograph combination, newspapers, *Time* magazines, Sears-Roebuck catalogs. The man who wants nothing can find it here.' "

"Will you take me?"

"Of course. I'd be delighted."

They crept through the center of Tangletown, a single street that was actually an improvised square, since the buildings were set back some distance from the curbs. People strolled at random across the right of way, like abandoned children. Jackson finally swung around a corner into a dark parking lot, and they got out. Unleashed, Schwartz bounded ahead with his paw on Leah's elbow.

"Shall we join the others?" Rachel said to Crevecoeur.

"If it's the thing to do," said Crevecoeur. He filled up with a deep breath of darkness, something to tide him over until evenings at his farm. "Let's go paint the town."

She huddled against his arm. "I know what you mean. We're figures with white faces, staring out of the crowd, asking, 'How did I get here? What's happening to me?' I hate this place, not for itself, but for how it makes me feel. I hate not being part of a crowd I'm part of. I can't stand feeling superior to what I'm doing and yet that's the purpose here. A community of voyeurs counterspying on each other."

"You've refined my thinking," said Crevecoeur, "but I agree with you. Misery loves company."

"Did anyone ever tell you that you look like Van Heflin?"

"No. Who is Van Heflin?"

"Wonderful," said Rachel. "That's exactly what Van Heflin would say. He's a movie star with a face that does the worrying for him while he remains calm. I love him, so don't be offended. That's why I feel I can trust you with something very personal even though we've just met. I've got a serious problem and don't know who else to turn to in this traditionless age. That's what we are, you know—faithless. Everybody says so. We've lost the old values—God, king, family, social status, money morality. There's only one adoration left—the Movie Star. We still hitch our wagons to a Movie Star. Everybody trusts Van Heflin and that's why I trust you."

Crevecoeur laughed just as they turned the corner into the bright lights and blare of jazz trumpets. She was overjoyed at his amusement. It was like overturning a stone expecting slugs, and finding a Walt Disney creature, aide-de-camp to the princess. When he stopped laughing, she said, "My problem is Jackson Schwartz. How good a friend of his are you?"

"He was my roommate at law school. I haven't seen much of him since. I'm afraid I'm like my father when it comes to friends. I don't make many and don't see them when I do. I actually don't know Jackson very well. In law school he was very serious about studying. He wasn't a natural scholar and he had to work hard. I had the idea he resented me because I fooled around and yet did well, but he tried not to show it. He was very impressed with my family history even after I made it clear we never amounted to much. You remember he made a point of it tonight. I was surprised when he popped up here practicing law and even more so at his persistence in asking me to lunch after I kept refusing. I suppose he liked the idea of going to lunch with the lawschool roommate. By instinct he's the old-school-tie sort."

Rachel eyed Jackson's head bobbing several yards in front like a cobra charmed by the waves of people. "Why did you agree to come tonight?" she asked.

Crevecoeur smiled. "I met your twin and learned there was another at home like her."

"And am I like her? If you had a choice, which would you choose?"

"Do I have a choice?"

"Of course you do." Rachel hesitated but went on. "I think Leah likes you."

Crevecoeur looked ahead toward Leah in her Alice-blue-gown, her hair coiled at her neck, and with a sinking, confused sensation

Rachel fingered her own plunging neckline. Somehow, with her inevitable talent for ignoring road signs, she was in another cul-de-sac. If she could get him, she wanted Crevecoeur for herself, at least for a while, to play out the summer with; and she wanted him to help break up Leah and Jackson. She wanted to save Leah, but she wanted to salvage something for herself. She expected boys to like her because she was lively and fun-loving, and she expected them to love Leah's tranquility and feminine reserve, and yet when it turned out that way, she was shocked into surprise. She knew that in an open fight she could win the Jackson Schwartzes, whom she despised, and she was very much afraid she'd lose the Crevecoeurs, whom she wanted. And to make it much worse, she could never be sure which Leah liked or even if she liked anybody. If it weren't so obvious, Rachel would have wiped off her eye shadow right there on the street—and succeeded only in being more foolish than she already was. She squared her jaw and reminded herself irrelevantly of Margery Schmidt, beautiful with jaw. She was here to do a job in her own way, and if that wasn't Crevecoeur's way it was just too bad.

"What's the problem?" said Crevecoeur.

"Jackson's treating my sister the way you say he treated law school—as a project he has to work at very hard because it doesn't come naturally. I'm sure that he doesn't love her and that he's very serious about her. Leah deserves better than that."

"I'm sure she does. How does she feel about him?"

"I have absolutely no idea. You'd think Leah would confide in me if nobody else, but she's kept mum. I just can't believe she'd fall for a meatball, but Leah's funny—in many ways the most mature person I know and in others the most naïve; the most responsible and the most irresponsible. You know what she's doing? Keeping house for our father and his new wife. She may be ready for a trip to the moon, and God help her if Jackson's to be her pilot."

"What does your mother say?"

"She died last year."

"I'm sorry. What do you suppose she would have done?"

"You're saying I act like Leah's mother. I don't care. I'm Leah's younger sister. I was born five minutes later, so that gives me the right to five minutes of her time. Mother, since you're being so smart, would have loved Jackson Schwartz. He would have brought her flowers and been very courteous. She liked good-looking, conventional, safe men and was always on the lookout for our future husbands."

"Maybe Jackson's exactly what Leah wants."

"I don't care what she wants. She needs love and I mean for her to get it. If she *has* love and rejects it then I'll wash my hands of the whole mess. She can have her suburban home and babies, and Saturday night in Tangletown for kicks. Are you with me or against me? That's what I want to know."

"I'm with you. Down with Jackson Schwartz."

"You mean it? Will you put money where your mouth is?"

"I just quit my job, remember? If it's money you need I can't help you."

"If you're such a smart aleck, why ain't you rich? I don't need money. I need a stout right hand and a true soul."

"I'm your man. What do you want me to do? I could call Jackson out and knock him down."

"That comes later. For now I want you to play up to Leah while I handle Jackson." There. Her plan was out and it sounded stupid. In her mind it had been brilliant. She had jolted Charlie, and from the way he looked at her she suddenly realized that he was a stranger and she knew nothing about him except her own fantasies. What, after all, did she really know about Van Heflin? Did he growl at the extras on the set, complain about his position on the marquee, cry over spilt milk, hesitate when he was lost, never try again when he couldn't at first succeed? What she kept forgetting was that even with the author's name on the back you couldn't tell a book by its cover unless you knew the author.

"It sounds tricky," said Crevecoeur. "What if you didn't gain a brother-in-law but lost your sister? And it might work in reverse. You could drive them together."

"They *are* together. Look." Jackson was swinging Leah's arm like a pendulum. "And Leah is used to tricks. We live in a house of cards. You should meet my father if you want to see what people can have up their sleeves. In fact, you have to meet Laban. He'd like you."

"What about you? What about our trip to the farm and other great plans in the offing?"

Rachel stopped and faced Crevecoeur. "Listen, you, get this straight. I like you. If we see each other more I'll like you more. That's a promise. I want to see you again, but that's entirely up to you. Leah and I were launched five minutes apart but that doesn't mean we're in the same orbit. You'll find that out soon enough if you haven't already. You pay your respects and you take your chances. For all you know, all you'll get from Leah is a fish stare, and we may bore each other to death the second time around. Right now I despise Jackson more than I like you. Is that perfectly clear?"

"It's clear. Okay. I'm your boy."

"I'm sorry about just one thing," she said, scuttling for cover. "That there isn't another one at home like you. Let me show you the sights."

She pointed out a cleaning establishment that had a single light burning over a long counter, which Crevecoeur agreed was picturesque. Next was an importing company with twisted metal figures playing the aftermaths of war in the window. They listened to the blare of jazz emerging from a loudspeaker hung above a neon sign that flashed a trumpet off and on. They examined a blood-red oriental rug figured with orderly spiders. They passed a black-painted coffee house and bumped into Jackson and Leah backtracking. "How about pizza?" said Jackson. "There's a place here that's got the greatest pizza in the world and the guy who makes it is a show all by himself."

"That sounds grand, Jackie," said Rachel, leaning forward, inviting his eye. "I'm starved and I adore pizza."

"Right across the street here," said Jackson, taking charge and moving in front of the traffic with the authority of a policeman.

"Here we go," Rachel said grimly to Crevecoeur. "Make yourself felt."

They sat down at an outside table before a man who was

throwing a floppy round of pizza in the air, and Rachel jumped up. "How exciting. Can we go in and watch him, Jackie?"

"Sure. It doesn't cost any more."

"You go on," said Leah. "I'll watch from here."

Jackson looked from her to Crevecoeur, who gave no signs of moving. "Creve?"

"I'll keep Leah company," said Crevecoeur. "You two go."

Jackson flushed. "I didn't mean to leave you sitting by yourself," he said to Leah.

"Let's go, Jackie. Leah won't melt. We'll be right back," said Rachel, pulling him along by the arm, resting it uncomfortably against her breast. The pizza chef gave them a broad smile and extra performance. He banged out a Congo rhythm on a lump of dough, pounding it flat. He sailed it at the ceiling and had to lunge to catch it. He danced it toward the oven and back to his worktable. He sprinkled bits of Parmesan cheese, pepperoni and mushrooms with a frenzied wrist, and charged the oven. "Isn't he sensational?" said Rachel. "Nobody's ever taken me here before. How did you ever discover it?"

"It's new," said Jackson, "but the word gets around. While we're here we may as well order. I think two slices apiece would be enough, don't you?"

"Oh, Jackie, you should have asked Leah if she wanted any. I don't think she likes pizza. Imagine someone not liking this heavenly stuff. Just smell." She took a deep, eye-closed sniff. To save her life she couldn't remember what attitude Leah took toward pizza. "Maybe they have something else. Do you have lox and bagels?" she asked the chef.

He wrinkled his nose. "No, lady, just pizza. The lox and bagels is next door."

"Then it's settled. We'll order our pizza here and go next door and get lox and bagel for Leah. She'd love that and it shows how thoughtful you are."

Jackson hesitated. "Maybe I ought to ask her."

"Don't be silly. Surprise her. She'll appreciate it so much more. Leah loves surprises."

Jackson ordered three sausage slices, three pepperoni and four cups of coffee, and they went for the lox and bagel. Leah and Crevecoeur were talking quietly and didn't even notice them. Great campaigns were won by attention to small details. It couldn't hurt for Jackson to think Leah a crank. Crevecoeur could work on Leah. And it gave Rachel a few more moments to pal around; it takes time to carve up a block of wood. The lox man was beefy and businesslike. He smeared cream cheese on a bagel, slapped on the lox, wrapped it in wax paper and held out his hand for the money. For Jackson's benefit Rachel raised her eyebrows toward the ceiling, where no pizza played. He paid for the sandwich and they went back to the table.

"This is for you, Leah," Jackson said, and handed her the sandwich.

Leah unwrapped the wax paper and examined the lox and bagel. "Thank you," she said.

"That's the queerest-looking pizza I've ever seen," said Crevecoeur.

"It's lox and bagel," said Jackson, managing to be uncomfortable. "Leah doesn't like pizza."

Leah folded her hands and said nothing, and while they waited for the pizza Rachel spent some time meshing Jackson with Tangletown. It was created for him and would disappear with him. The girls with loose-swinging hair, sweat shirts and blue jeans, and their bearded, paint-smeared friends were conjured by him, pumped with air and tied to life by a string attached to his wrist. And his would be the prick that would pop them into nothingness when he found a newer, more improbable place—he and the other handsome, well-dressed people who owned the place by default; no one else would mistake façades for faces and be willing to pay for the mistake. Yet they weren't as stupid as they seemed, because they remained outside for the most part, fearing a trap. Occasionally a restless one entered a door and discovered that the front wall was a Hollywood set, and that he was in an alley among garbage cans.

The pizza and coffee arrived and they started eating. Jackson nudged her elbow (hers, not Leah's—a good sign. Think, Jackie, how much more comfortable life is with old-shoe Rachel).

"Look over there," he said. A young Negro was standing at the next table exhibiting a portfolio of charcoal sketches to two men.

"Please, Cal. He's very good. Let him sketch you. For me. I want him to."

"I'd rather not. It makes me uncomfortable to pose."

"Please, Cal. I'll never forgive you if you don't."

"All right, all right! Don't make a scene."

"Fairies," whispered Jackson. "They're all over the place."

"Really, Jackie? Are you sure? How can you tell?"

"I saw plenty of them in the army. They give me the creeps. How can people get that way? It just doesn't make any sense."

"Leah," said Rachel. "Jackson says fairies don't make sense."

"Hey," said Jackson. "Not so loud. They'll hear you."

"When we were little, Leah and I had a whole collection of fairies. Our favorite game was to tie each other up and then decide which fairy would kiss us and set us free."

Leah munched her lox and bagel. She looked up and met Rachel's eyes. "That was a long time ago."

"But what if I got some clothesline and tied you up and put a gag in your mouth and locked you in Laban's survival shelter? Who would rescue you?"

"Jackson would rescue me," said Leah.

"You can count on me," said Jackson. He laughed. "I'm a knight in shining armor."

"At the very least," said Crevecoeur. Rachel noticed that he hadn't touched the pizza but was merely sipping coffee, and she thought contritely, He's the one who doesn't like pizza and nobody thought of asking him.

Jackson had started on his third piece when they had a visitor, a creature in a wheel chair, with a misshapen jaw, rolling white eyes and withered arms and leg. He said something in a tongue-less jabberwocky voice and held out a tin measuring-cup. Rachel felt dizzy with the shame of her repugnance, and a giggle bubbled into her nose where, mercifully, it was smothered by membranes. Jackson took command. He waved his arm. "No. Move on."

The man's vocal chords, unanchored, splashed around.

"I said beat it," said Jackson, shaking his head violently. The man dropped his cup and it clattered on the bricks. He wheeled after it; a waiter caught up with him, picked up his cup and moved him toward the street.

"That guy's always around. Every time I've been here. They better do something about him before they lose their business. I don't care how good their pizza is."

"Maybe he's part of the atmosphere," said Crevecoeur. "He didn't put on much of a show, but he was worth a dime, wasn't he?"

"That's where you're wrong," said Jackson. "You can't encourage him. You ever hear of that guy downtown who rolls around on a platform? He got robbed one night and guess what he had under the mattress at home? Fifteen thousand dollars. Fifteen thousand!"

"Jackson," said Crevecoeur, and his eyes didn't look quite right, so Rachel kicked him under the table to shut him up. "Jackson," Crevecoeur began again but in a milder way and Rachel, worried, had to let him go. "You put me in mind of that day in law school. Remember the torts class, the rearing horse and the miscarriage?"

Jackson turned the color of the pepperoni that was disappearing into his mouth. Rachel stood up. "I feel like dancing. Why don't we go some place else?"

"Yeah," said Jackson. "I'll get the check."

"Our torts professor taught by the Socratic method," said Crevecoeur. "The case involved the question of whether a pregnant woman frightened by a rearing horse and suffering a miscarriage could collect from the rider, even though she wasn't touched. Jackson thought this was going too far. 'Why,' he said, 'what if a cretonne'—c-r-e-t-o-n-n-e—'was walking down the street and frightened a pregnant lady? Could she collect from *him?*' The class thought it was very funny."

"I meant cretin and everybody knew it."

"It wasn't at all funny," said Rachel, patting Jackson's hand. "I think Charlie's got a warped sense of humor."

"I can still visualize that bolt of cretonne walking down the street. Very unnerving."

"Okay. You've had your laugh," said Jackson, staring at Crevecoeur. "Forget it."

"Schwartz," said Crevecoeur, "when I want to I'll forget it without any help from you. And while we're at it, it was you, not me, who never had a girl at law school. You've got a short memory."

Anxious, Rachel nevertheless savored the image of Jackson's perfect nose being bent. Maybe some blood on his white shirt. She wasn't bloodthirsty, but honestly, they used to apply leeches to people in better shape than he was in. "I swear," she said. "I never saw full-grown men acting like such babies. Charlie, what would your mother say?"

Crevecoeur had already begun to relent and she gave him the necessary excuse. He held out his hand. "I apologize," he said. "I didn't mean to offend."

Jackson took it big. He smiled like a plantation owner. After all, the apology was from Crevecoeur, old family in the city. "That's all right. Forget it, buddy."

The place Jackson picked for dancing was called The Combo. It had the biggest sign on the street, a huge golden trumpet bordered with lights that chased each other in a perpetual relay. Inside were small, round wooden tables surrounded by straight-backed wooden chairs, and there was a small dancing area in front of a bandstand. A four-piece group—trumpet, saxophone, piano and bass fiddle—was rendering a marshmallow version of "Smoke Gets in Your Eyes." The Combo was half-filled, with Jackson Schwartz people. She didn't spot any blue denim shirts with rolled-up sleeves.

Seated at one of the tables, they were so close together that Rachel's knees struck legs wherever she turned. She dug in at Jackson on the left and was gratified to see him sitting stiffly at attention. She examined his face, smiling to hide her distaste. She couldn't believe that she had once considered him handsome. If he wanted to remain attractive, he had to remain static, or run for cover to a magazine or billboard. If he were asked to appear on Johnny Carson's show, or the old Jack Paar's, he'd have to work twice as hard as, say, Crevecoeur to prove he wasn't trivial. His face was as naked as Beatrice's breasts in her Egyptian costume, and just as meaningless after the first impact. The most durable movie stars always had some bite to their faces: Humphrey Bogart, Clark Gable, John Wayne, Bette Davis, Joan Crawford, Katharine Hepburn. The pretty-all-over people rose and fell like the length of dresses.

After a whiskey sour Rachel knew what was wrong with The Combo, why only the "right" people went there. The band modeled its music on the Lawrence Welk–Mitch Miller syndrome, which meant it played what was old and borrowed and nothing new or too blue. It was the half of marriage that old people preferred to remember, the uncomplicated, comfortable part, devoid of tensions, passions and revolt. The couples on the floor clung to each other's bellies for dear life through "Star Dust," "A Pretty Girl Is Like a Melody," "Harvest Moon," "It Had To Be You" and on "April in Paris" Rachel decided to join them. It was time to shoot Jackson down with a little well-aimed sex. "Would you care to dance?" she asked him. "I just adore this song."

"Sure," said Jackson. "Do you mind, Leah?" Leah merely looked at him.

As soon as they were up, Rachel set the pace. She laid her cheek against Jackson's shoulder and let him have the full benefit of her soft, round belly against his groin, which responded manfully. All hero from the neck down, he was a sensationally smooth dancer. He hummed the melody and she joined in with glee, their legs sticking to each other like Con-Tact paper. When she figured she'd brought him to a boil, she said, "Jackie, don't think me nosy, but I have to know. Is it serious between Leah and you?"

"What do you mean?"

"You know what I mean, but I'll spell it out. Is there a chance for me? I dig you, Jackie."

Jackson laughed. He had a whinny that by itself would have

been enough for her to put him out to pasture. If Leah had any
idea what this was costing she'd appreciate her sister's true worth.
"You Laban girls are something," said Jackson. "You come right
out with what you're thinking."

If he had the slightest notion of what she was thinking he
couldn't be the man she thought he was, and then she'd have to
change her way of thinking and he still wouldn't know. Still, it
annoyed her, as it always had, to be lumped with Leah, like so
many pounds of the same meat. "You find Leah and me alike?"
she said. "Can't you tell us apart?" She crowded him with her
belly.

"Sure I can tell you apart. You've got more hell in you."

"Level with me. Don't you like a little hell? I love Leah dearly,
but honestly, Jackie, don't you find her a little *square?*"

"She's a very fine girl."

"Naturally, and when you're in the soup she's the one to ride
the river with. Right now we're on dry land and I want to know
if Leah's got you wrapped up in her pretty pink ribbon."

"Wait a minute. I like Leah very much and I think she likes me
but that's as far as it's gone. There's no understanding between us
if that's what you're getting at. I take out who I please."

"That's the boy. How about taking me out?"

"Sure. Why not?"

"How about Wednesday night?" That was his next regular
dinner with Leah. "Or does Leah have it sewed up?"

"Where do you get that idea? Wednesday night. It's a date.
We'll go to dinner."

Rachel wrinkled her nose. "I've got a better plan. Let's come
back here and have a ball. I mean, let's have ourselves a time. Pick
me up at nine."

"It's a deal." Jackson couldn't help himself. He looked over at
the table, frowning. Leah and Crevecoeur had their heads together
and were talking a blue streak.

Rachel stopped dead. "Let's sit," she said. "After all, I'm with
Charlie tonight and he deserves a *little* attention."

As they sat down, Crevecoeur made a point of jerking back
from Leah; he was certainly laying it on thick. Jackson had

barely got settled when Leah said, "Jackson, I'd like to dance," and he jumped up like a puppet driven by any stagehand. Rachel watched them move to the dance floor before she zeroed in on Crevecoeur.

"Well, Charlie boy, how's it going?"

"No complaints. And you?"

"Jackie and I have a date for next Wednesday night. What do you have?" She was horrified at the edge sharpening her voice.

Crevecoeur said, "I wish you'd consider what you're doing. From where I sit, Leah's not likely to get carried away. You should trust her to make the right decision about Schwartz."

"You and Jackie are birds of a feather. Are you sure *you're* not twins? Maybe your mommy put Jackie in a basket and left him on a doorstep when he was a baby. He agrees with you that Leah is a very fine girl. Don't you think I know Leah better than somebody who's talked to her for all of five minutes? Spare me the analysis and just tell me how you made out."

"I'm invited to dinner at your house. On Wednesday night."

Rachel sat back stunned. Leah, holding her tongue, watching Rachel sweep Jackson off his big, fat feet, instead of trying to prop him up was going to let him fall and then sit on top of him. Rachel searched for salvage. So Jackson would see Crevecoeur on Wednesday, but the invitation, she could imply, had come from her and not from Leah. The main problem was Leah, whose counter could only mean that she was fighting fire with fire—that Jackson meant enough to fight for.

Beyond all that, which was bad enough, she was angry with Crevecoeur for doing what she'd asked him to do. If he was at all taken with Rachel, and she insisted he was, he would never have gone ahead and tangled himself up with Leah. What she was doing with Jackson Schwartz, LL.B., didn't count and he knew it. She made a decision: She didn't need his help. "I can take care of Jackson by myself. I'm sorry I involved you and I want you to forget everything I said or asked of you."

"It's not that easy. Why don't we let nature take its course and see what happens?"

Rachel stared. "What do you mean?"

Crevecoeur thought a moment. "I don't know. If I did I'd certainly tell you."

Unable to look at him she jerked her head around toward the dance floor and noted clinically what she already knew, that she was a much better dancer than Leah. As she watched, a couple came through the front door. It was her brother Bernie, eyeglasses glinting, unruly hair combed, dressed in a blue suit, with a proud, watchful hand on Mrs. Margery Schmidt's elbow.

Jackson took Charles Crevecoeur home first. "I owe my mother a letter before I move to the farm tomorrow. My last official act as a civilian," said Crevecoeur. "I hope you don't mind, Rachel."

"It'd take just a few minutes to run the girls back and then I can drive you home," Jackson said stubbornly.

Leah took a hand. "I think you should take him home first," she said, and Jackson offered no further resistance.

They drove westward on the expressway and Leah watched the stretches of deserted road sweep up to engulf her as they moved, reviving her sense of the loneliness of manmade objects. Leaves and grass didn't need conversation, but highways did. The end of the world was a city empty of voices. For the first time everybody, even Rachel, was silenced by the fear of being abandoned in a place without bird calls. They passed a park on the right and Leah was renewed by the sight of trees. "You turn off at the next exit," said Crevecoeur, and Jackson slowed down.

Crevecoeur's apartment was in a modern building with little

iron porches. It rose in ribs of steel like an Erector set, and Leah credited Crevecoeur, as he said good night, with having the sense to trade in his mess of geranium pots. As they continued home Rachel, curled on the back seat, closed her eyes. When they arrived she ran ahead, saying, "I'm dead. See you later, Jackie." She opened the front door of the house and disappeared inside.

"Well," said Jackson, playing with the wheel, "I guess I'd better get going. It's pretty late."

"Not yet," Leah said. "I want to talk to you. Let's sit on the side porch for a while. Tomorrow's Sunday."

"I don't know, Leah."

"I do. For a few minutes."

They went in and she sat in the middle of the glider so that he had to sit next to her. She swung the glider into motion with her foot. It creaked back and forth and swayed under their weight. A breeze brought delicate odors from the peony beds.

"What do you want to talk about?" said Jackson.

Leah placed her forearm and hand, palm down, on his leg, and felt him grow rigid. Her role—harsh, implacable, unsexed—suited her. She was the Apache princess hungering for the white man's golden hair and blue eyes, deaf to the babble of his foreign tongue. Her body, an instrument, had no use for pride. Pride was too public a show of feeling to be unlocked from the hidden places of her mind. She would bind Jackson to a stake and light a fire under him. She would inform the chief, her father, that if Jackson burned, so would she. She cared nothing for pain; she was beyond pain. Grave under a cliff of brown face fissured with warrior scars, Laban would nod and she would untie Jackson and lead him to a private place.

Leah flung her arms around Jackson's neck and kissed him on the mouth, finding his teeth. She hung on while his arms remained at attention by his sides. About pride: it involved lacy garments and going-away dresses, but once it simply meant sexual desire. If he remained loggerheaded, she'd give him back to the Indians. Those sticks of inertia, his arms, came up around her, and his lips sucked as if he'd realized that he, a thirsting man, was being offered melting snow. Her hand, bold as a woman who had nothing to lose, clung to his hip socket. She loved to slide down cliffs with only strength of covert purpose to hold on to. His body lifted and with a murmur she lay back and let his primed pump take over. She was proud of her handtooled body, of the knobs and hollows and swellings that triggered even *his* imagination. His lips closed her eyelids, smacked at her breasts, nibbled her belly. He moved under her dress and she spurred her rider. He poked peremptorily and at random, a baby with a wooden stick, and then, when it seemed a thrust might strike home, she felt him retracting like a mounted artillery piece. He lunged again and collapsed with a groan.

He lay breathing on top of her and she hid him with her arms. He buried his wet face in the curve of her neck and she increased the pressure of her arms. "Good show, Jackson," she said. "You can try again."

He lay motionless and then got off with care. He stood up and fussed with his zipper. She remained in her vulnerable spread-eagled position and he looked away. "I'm sorry, Leah. I don't know what came over me for a minute but thank God I couldn't go through with it. I've just too much respect for you. What if your father had seen us? We took an awful chance."

Leah sat up. The breeze was cool on her legs. "Forget Laban. He believes in live and let live."

"Anybody could have walked in. There are other people living in this house. It would have been an awful mess."

"That's my worry. You just worry about me. Or is it Rachel who's on your mind?"

"What do you mean?" he said. He hesitated. "I thought you didn't like to talk about people."

"That doesn't mean I won't," she said. "Don't change the subject. Rachel's trying to make a fool out of you. Do you want to make it easy for her?"

He turned to face her. "Leah, no matter what it costs, I believe in being honest, especially with you. I'm taking Rachel out on Wednesday night."

"You *are* a fool." She was pleased with him. He was her private lump of dough and all she had to do was put him in the oven and bake him. "You don't know Rachel any better than you know Laban. I don't care about any of that. Come here by me and I'll tell you what I wanted to talk about."

He sat down, taking pains not to come into contact with her. "I feel lousy," he said. "I ought to go."

"Just one simple question," she said. "How would you like to marry me? You see? I'm no cat-and-mouser. I'm like you. I have no secrets."

He jumped up but she wasn't distracted by the move. She had him pinned and could win the match any time she wanted to. It was his own fault for trying to wrestle with the big girls. "Talk about Rachel making a fool of me," said Jackson. "I hope you're enjoying yourself."

"I am," said Leah. "Come on, what's your answer? Don't be afraid. Rush in. Don't be afraid."

"You've got no right to talk to me like this. What have I done to deserve it? If you're sore about what happened I've told you I'm sorry. Anyway, thank God, nothing happened."

"If I were angry it would be because nothing did happen. As a matter of fact, you've got me worried. Tell me, Jackson, do you have a normal sex life? You're not a little queer or anything?"

"I act decent and try to show you proper respect and you think I'm a pervert. Leah, you shouldn't go on like this. It isn't right."

"Are you a virgin? I am."

"I've had my share of women," said Jackson. "You made me say it. You can't say I wanted to."

"I'm proud of you," said Leah. "You certainly are the frank one. Now then. We've settled your sex life, so I feel much better about marrying you."

"Will you please wait a minute, Leah? Marriage is a serious business. You have to be mature about it. You can't decide on the spur of the moment. You have to find out first whether you're really in love or just carried away. Are you that positive you're in love with me?"

"Don't be silly," she said. "Of course I'm not in love with you. I wouldn't dream of marrying you if I were. Love and marriage don't mix. Everybody knows that. People in love marry the worst possible mates. We're very mature, you and I, because we're going to marry in cold blood." Leah pointed her finger at him and shot him down. "Laban wants us to get married."

He sat down again. "Mr. Laban said that? In so many words?"

"In seven words. He said, 'I want you to marry Jackson Schwartz.' He said more. He said I needed a steady, hard-working, sober provider and he thinks you're the best one around. That's what he said, and, Jackson, he's ready to do a lot for his son-in-law."

She waited and listened to Jackson think.

"I admire your father very much, I've already told you that. But I wouldn't be marrying him, Leah. I guess I'm old-fashioned, but I believe that two people shouldn't get married unless they love each other."

"Old-fashioned? Arranged marriages have a thousand-year head start on love. Don't let Laban hear you go on like this or he'll begin to think you're a radical."

"I don't know what to say to you. You're making me afraid to admit I think I'm in love with you. I'll be honest. It's pretty hard to take, your saying you don't love me."

"I'll tell you what to say. Just say yes. Play it smart. Marry me before Laban changes his mind about you."

"I feel like I'm in a dream world. I can't believe any of this is true. If I took you seriously I bet you'd laugh at me."

"I don't laugh at anybody. Say yes, and I'll marry you. It's a promise and I never break a promise. Think of what you're getting. A smart, pretty, willing, rich girl, and a virgin to boot. I can cook, sew and keep house. Make up your mind because you don't get a second chance. A deal like this comes along once in a lifetime."

"I need to be sure I'm in love with you. I'm sorry but that's the way I am. That's the only thing that counts."

"All right," she said. "I tell you what. You're afraid you've landed the wrong Laban girl. Don't bother to deny it. You want a Laban girl. That's your secret. Go out with Rachel and think it over. You've got until next Saturday night. If it's yes, we'll get married. If it's no, I never want to see you again, and I'd better warn you, that goes for Laban too."

"You don't have much respect for my integrity," he said. "I can't marry you unless I love you. That's all that matters even if you don't love me. What happens to my career doesn't matter."

"It does to me. I want a man who's going places. Laban says you'll be a partner if you put that ring on my finger. Otherwise you get the axe. It's up to you."

Jackson shook his head. "All right. I'll go home and think about it. At least it'll give me a chance to digest the situation and decide if I'm really in love with you and whether, in time, you'll learn to love me. It's got nothing to do with Mr. Laban's plans for me."

"Saturday night, then. I'll wait to hear from you." Where, her mind giggled, had he been sleeping for the past century? He was the last shirt stuffed with cardboard armor. He was her man. She could buy him with her body alone and be home free. With the sword of her fingernail against his cheek she dubbed him Sir Jackson and put her hand on his lap. She felt him spring into life before he jerked away and stood up to go.

By Wednesday, to save her life Rachel couldn't devise a plan of attack against Jackson Schwartz or even remember exactly why one was necessary. Watching Leah go about the house armored in self-possession that protected her like a boned corset, Rachel regarded herself as a Salvation Army worker beating the drum

against deaf ears. She longed to start over again with Crevecoeur
not as an accomplice but as a playmate. In a few hours Jackson
would come for her in his German-made tumbrel, and she felt
like screaming, No, I'm innocent. My only crime is foolishness. A
poltergeist entered my soul, made me run onto the field and
interfere with the game. Look, I'm waving my little flag of truce.

She watched Crevecoeur and Beatrice trailing after Laban on a
tour of Laban's one-man show, and she begged Charlie to notice
how sweet she was tonight, how demurely dressed in her but-
toned-up white blouse with the Peter Pan collar and blue pleated
skirt. Her sandals were thick-soled and heavy-strapped, suitable
for a quick getaway from Schwartz if she needed one. She wore
no make-up at all, not even lipstick. The mantel was covered
with Laban's signs, but she moved one over and faced the mirror,
her eyes darkly ominous. See here, Mr. Jackson Schwartz, she
whispered, I'm a no-nonsense girl. In fact, if you really want to
know, I don't like boys. You may as well know the whole truth,
so help me God. I'm frigid and terribly sadistic. Also, I'm a lady
cop well trained in judo and karate, and I could very easily break
your neck. She dropped her eyes because she couldn't bear the
thought of Jackson. She regarded his handsomeness as a superior
brand of evil, like chocolate cake to a dieter.

All she had to do was pick up the phone and tell Jackson the
date was off. She couldn't, because Crevecoeur would think she
didn't have the power of positive thinking—even when she was
no longer positive. As it was, she was an idiot but at least a
heroic idiot. Though fighting in a mock war, she was willing to
be struck down for the sake of her sister, whether or not it did
Leah any good. Even if she left the coast clear for Leah to find
Crevecoeur, it would be a far better thing than she had ever done
before.

The house was littered with Laban's signs. They were everywhere, lined up along the walls in the living room, propped up on
the mantelpieces and around the dining room. The table settings
had little ones. "Every man," said Laban, "when he's ready, when
he's absolutely sure, should have his exhibition. I've worked two

years and I'm ready." Bernie had escaped, hurrying off to meet Margery Schmidt. He was seeing her every night, staying out till all hours, and Laban complained that Beatrice's religious instruction was suffering. Bernie, beefed up with sexual juices, laughed in his face and said he was gathering new source material.

Crevecoeur had gone native on his farm. He'd started a beard, which promised to be reddish, and wore a blue work shirt and khakis, and heavy boots strapped to his calves. Laban succumbed right away to his Van Heflin magic and Crevecoeur took Laban and his signs in stride. Their immediate rapport exasperated Rachel. It had been barely possible that Van Heflin would take a firm-jawed look at Laban and his signs, lock understanding glances with Rachel, and inform Laban pleasantly but firmly that if he expected his daughters to grow up straight, with no crooked and bizarre schemes on their minds, such as seducing each other's lovers, he'd have to pull up some weeds. No young girl would rather have a turnip for a father, as Sam Johnson might have said, so beware lest they cry turnip at your funeral.

Laban threw an arm around Crevecoeur's shoulders. "Baby, the next time you see one of nature's noblemen on a boatswain's chair up in the sky, you'll experience pride in the human race. Here's an early one, plain Egyptian, upper case." The sign, in black letters on a white background, read:

THERE'S NOT A MAN THAT LIVES
WHO HATH NOT KNOWN
HIS GODLIKE HOURS

"Not as easy as it looks. For example, the E is three fourths as wide as the A and yet they seem to be the same width. Measure it if you like. It's because the E has three horizontal strokes—the same kind of problem a fat lady faces with horizontally striped dresses. She's got to have those stripes running up and down. This one is Roman, a little fancier but still basic. The strokes alternate between thick and thin and we're introduced to serifs, those squiggles at the end. The letters are more square than the Egyptian." The sign read:

SIX HOURS IN SLEEP, IN LAW'S GRAVE STUDY SIX,
FOUR SPEND IN PRAYER, THE REST ON NATURE FIX

"Here's another before we go in to dinner. One of my favorites." Laban tapped the sign and it made a metallic sound. "Sheet aluminum, transferred from a paper layout. The layout's perforated with a tracing wheel, placed on the metal and pounced with charcoal powder. The printing's Old English." It read:

We Are No Other Than a Moving Row
Of Magic Shadow Shapes That Come and Go

"Mr. Laban, that's a beautiful piece of work," said Crevecoeur.

"Thank you, baby. It takes an impression to make an impression. Signs can be beautiful. I drive along a highway, see a billboard painted by a master and thank God we didn't leave roadsides to the trees. Nature's got its place, mind you, but I've got no use for people traveling seventy miles an hour complaining about billboards. Nature's free and easy and you've got to enjoy it slow to enjoy it at all. The phonies can't tell a daisy from a sweet scabious, else they wouldn't throw out babies with bath water. Who tells them to read 'Three Miles to Joe's Place, Five Yards to Joe's Place, You Just Passed Joe's Place'? They should be looking at the letters. Are they modern Gaspipe, lightface Gothic, Broadway, what? Are they crisp and clean, or sloppy? When they look around in an art museum are they trying to read? Hell, no. If they're so worried about beauty let them look for it. Don't blame signs, blame how they're made and how they're looked at."

Crevecoeur smiled. "I never thought of it that way," he said.

"That's the whole trouble. Let's go have a drink. Rachel baby, you got yourself a good boy."

Rachel felt temper rising to her face. "He's not my boy. Leah invited him."

"Is that a fact?" Laban grinned from one to the other. "How can I tell the players without a program? You should have let me know and I would have gotten up a batch."

Rachel let her tongue run away with her. "Charlie's an irresponsible, shiftless renegade lawyer, Laban. Don't get too high on him. He's two-timing your jealous mistress. He's quit the law and gone to live on a skid-row farm."

"I love beards," said Beatrice. "Laban, that's what you ought to do. You'd look lovely in a beard."

Laban shook his head. "They'll carry me out feet first, with my head resting on *Corpus Juris*. Hell, I'm not criticizing you, baby," he said to Crevecoeur. "You've got to follow your nose. You go where it smells nice, right?"

Leah came in from the kitchen and said dinner was ready any time they wanted to sit down. "We'll have a drink and then we'll eat," said Laban, rattling a pitcher and dropping cherries in cocktail glasses. "A whiskey sour?" he asked Crevecoeur.

"Fine, yes, sir."

"Leah, you've got a good boy here. He likes my signs."

"I just wish I knew how to make them as well," said Crevecoeur.

"Good enough. You want to paint signs? No sooner said than done. You'll be my apprentice, baby. I've been looking for somebody to take over the sign-painting business. What's the good of it if you've got nobody to leave it to? You live on a farm? Perfect place. I'll bring my gear out and we'll go right to work."

"If you're serious, Mr. Laban, I'd like to, though I'm not good with my hands."

"Sure I'm serious. I'm always serious. What Laban promises Laban does. A handshake is all you need from Laban." They shook hands. "Baby, I've got signs in the blood like alphabet soup. I'll make you the best sign painter in the world. They'll hang one of your signs outside the Louvre. I'll be honest with you. I'm good but not that good. It's a young man's game and I started too late. You've got to make your move early when you're barely able to lift the brush, like in tennis. You're still young enough to take a real shot at it. But you'll have to work hard. Not spare yourself."

"I'll work like a mule," said Crevecoeur.

"Did you ever see a jackass paint a sign?" said Laban. "No sir, you'll work like Michelangelo, that's how you'll work."

Rachel could choke Laban, and she wouldn't relax her grip even at the signs of aging, the gray hair and skin that he couldn't paint away. There was a law, not passed by any legislature or indexed in any library, which she had learned could not be violated with impunity. The law was: Do not permit any person to meet Laban whom you wish to preserve for yourself. It was a simple rule of thumb you'd think would be easy to apply, and yet only after the victim was thrashing about in Laban's net did she remember it. Laban was an octopus, each of whose legs was painted with a lure. He was the Good Humor man. If you wanted a double dip of moonbeam in a cone of star dust, just wait for his bell to clang. She had very little time left. They would be at dinner and then Jackson would come and the situation could harden and she might bang on Crevecoeur with her puny fists forever without making a mark. And then there was Laban straddling Crevecoeur, pushing signs in his face, and if Crevecoeur could ever be tempted to look up, which was unlikely, Laban would press his head down with a length of modern Gaspipe. It would never occur to Laban that Crevecoeur might have been invited for some purpose other than to get involved in Laban enterprises; that he was, possibly, more interested in one of his daughters than in Laban's fireworks, waxworks, waterworks, clockworks, the works.

When they went into dinner, they found a card propped against each water glass. Rachel's read, in phony Chinese:

WE RESERVE THE RIGHT
TO SERVE WHOM WE PLEASE

The two other nearest her read, in the same Chinese:

WHAT IS FOOD TO ONE MAN MAY BE FIERCE POISON TO OTHERS

and:

TELL ME WHAT YOU EAT AND I WILL TELL YOU WHAT YOU ARE

Rachel could tell Laban what she was eating all right—bitter pills—and even what she was—parricidal. Crevecoeur had given her one look, to show she existed. When they sat down he placed himself next to Leah, leaving Rachel and Beatrice on the other side of the table and Laban at the head. Rachel felt as if she were in an overloaded lifeboat, and she would be the first thrown overboard. She felt so waifish that she began to long for nine o'clock although it would bring nobody less fiercely poisonous than Jackson Schwartz.

At eight forty-five she was upstairs in front of her mirror, still trying to work out a plan. She had to escape from Crevecoeur and Leah before she forgot who her friends were. About all Crevecoeur had required of her through dinner was the butter and salt. He'd spent his time attending to Laban's sign language and murmuring to Leah, making it clear that he was riding a hobbyhorse built for three, marked Crevecoeur, Leah and Laban, sí; Rachel, no. Okay, she'd asked for it, but he didn't have to rub it in. She'd misjudged him. He was turning out to be Van Heflin in one of those other roles—Van insisting on not being typed, letting the public know he could be as miscreant as Dan Duryea.

She gathered her loose-flowing hair tight against the sides of her head and clipped it together in back with a barrette. She looked alarmingly like Leah, and as she undid the barrette and let her hair flow into its usual sweep, slanted across a temple, she had a great idea. Something to get through the evening with. She would will herself into Leah's frame of mind. She would ask herself, What would Leah do or say? She'd give Jackson two Leahs for the price of one and see what that would do to his monogamous mind. It could preserve her sanity because, being herself, she'd blow her top if he tried to finger her. She was proud to be thinking straight again. She had another idea and put her pocketsized date book and a pencil in her purse.

Rachel sized up her uncluttered face with its dark brown-on-hazel eyes, decided that in a pinch she would always stare Jackson down, checked her watch and hurried below to make sure he didn't get inside. She passed by the dinner table without getting a single glance, which made her madder than ever. You'd think she'd covered herself with instant vanishing cream. Crevecoeur, you'd better keep your hands and knees freshly oiled, because someday you're going to need them to come crawling. She was careful not to make any noise as she went out the front door to wait for Jackson on the porch. When he arrived she ran down to meet him before he could even get out of the car. "Like hi, Jackie boy," she said as she bounced into the front seat before she remembered she was the other one and added weakly, "Hello, Jackson."

"Hi," he said. "You ready to go?"

She looked at the house with the lights glinting from the dining room, she listened to the motor running, she examined Jackson poised at the wheel—and she could think of nothing but Alice in Wonderland. Of course she wasn't ready really, she would never be really ready, but any fool could plainly see she was merely ready, and only a fool could ask. Leah, Leah, she thought desperately, and said, "Yes, I am, Jackson."

"You know," he said as they moved away. "If I didn't know it for a fact I'd never believe in a million years that you and Leah are twins. You're not at all alike."

A fine beginning. "How's this?" She grabbed her hair and pulled it tight.

"I don't mean your looks. You look pretty much alike all right.

I mean the way you act and talk. Entirely different. Take my word for it."

Rachel sighed. "How different?"

"A lot. Did you ever stop to realize how much personality affects the way a person looks? I never thought about it before I met you two."

She twitched in her seat. If he started bombarding her with what he called insights, she couldn't last. She'd stick fingers in her mouth and cross her eyes; she'd make Jerry Lewis faces; she'd start bawling, borrow his handkerchief, and twirl it and snap it at him. What would Leah do? Nothing. A beautiful insight. She'd do nothing. She interlaced her fingers and imagined she was a football.

"Leah's a wonderful girl but you never know what to expect. She's quiet and all of a sudden she can do the craziest thing. Like one night at the Lawyers' Club she gets down on her knees and starts feeling the carpet right in front of other people. It was really creepy." He hesitated. "To tell you the truth, she scares me a little bit. Do you know what I mean?"

"Not exactly," said Rachel, excited with a brand new plan. "You mean she has psychiatric problems?"

"Oh, no, I didn't mean anything like that." It was clear he meant exactly that. His careful mind was adding up the cost. Twenty-five dollars an hour four times a week is a hundred times fifty-two weeks is fifty-two hundred a year. Just what was Leah up to? There had to be more to it than stroking a rug. Rachel couldn't imagine what Leah might do. She wasn't supposed to do anything that wasn't sweet and nice. Ask anybody. Ask Laban or Beatrice. Ask the mailman or milkman. Leah cooked and sewed and was made of sugar and spice. Rachel was the nut. Ask anybody. Honestly, it was getting terrible. As Laban said, you couldn't tell the players without a score card and it was about time she stopped trusting to memory. Just as she made up her mind to tell Jackson that Leah had just a little psychological problem, nothing serious, mind you, just a little problem with her father, a wee mite jealous, maybe, of Beatrice, and the doctor, Dr.

Wanderscheid, was doing wonders, saying only the other day that he hoped to bring her around in much less time than anticipated, probably less than five years even—just as she made up her mind, Jackson put his hot hand on her knee. "I feel a lot more comfortable with you," he said. "You make a guy feel at home."

She stared at his hand and hadn't the faintest idea what to do about it. She was having enough trouble keeping her various projects in mind without being distracted by sex and the single girl. To begin with he had a lot of nerve treating her like an old shoe. Leah was the old shoe. Rachel was high heels and low-cut dresses; at least that was the way he should remember her. But she was supposed to be acting like Leah, remember? And that made Rachel Mother Hubbard. But he said he was scared of Leah. Then what was he doing with his hand on her knee? Obviously he had no idea she was being Leah and was playing fast and loose with comfortable old Rachel. He squeezed and she hated him too much to let him go on. She appealed to his legal mind. "Hey, Jackie boy," she said, throwing Leah to the wolf, "that's private property. Look at the sign. No trespassing." Plain English, lower case. "If you need to strengthen your fingers, get a handball."

Jackson laughed and withdrew his hand. "You're a picnic," he said. "We'll have a ball."

"That's what I said—you need a handball."

By the time they got to the Combo, Rachel decided that she'd overestimated Jackson. She'd credited him with devotion to the main chance above and beyond the call of emotion, and he was displaying far too many human responses. A craftier person would be hedging, feeling out the lay of the land mentally more than physically, and holding on to the wren in the hand until he caught the cardinal in the bush. "You know," he said, "I never meant to take Leah out in the first place. It was a misunderstanding. I saw you at the courthouse that day—remember?—and I went for you right away. I asked Mr. Laban if it was all right to take you out and he must have thought I meant Leah. You see, I didn't know your name and just asked about his daughter and he told me, 'Sure. You can call Leah any time.' "

With difficulty Rachel recalled her irritation at Laban's switch. It seemed so trivial—a part of a different lifetime—now that she knew Jackson. She'd supposed it was merely a Laban gag but now she wasn't so sure. He wouldn't have let it rock along so far on its own energy.

"You haven't quarreled with Leah, have you?" she said. "I thought you and she had a thing going. Don't you think it'd look funny to drop her like a hot potato and take up with her sister?"

Jackson turned red. He pulled the white handerchief from his breast pocket and wiped his face. "I wanted to ask you out before but you didn't seem interested, so I just let matters take their course. I guess I let it go a little too far, but I want you to know I'm not sneaking around behind Leah's back. She knows about us."

"What does she know?"

"That we're out together tonight."

"And did she tell you she invited Crevecoeur to dinner? That he's there right now?"

Jackson stared. "Are you sure?"

"Of course I am." One of his irritating qualities was a skepticism of basic communication and his swallowing whole of the frivolous. He was the sort of man who'd watch a drowning girl waving her arms and crying for help and say, Stop trying to make a fool of me. If, on the other hand, the swimmer was Laban dressed in a gay-nineties suit mugging for all he was worth, Jackson would jump in.

"Boy," said Jackson, "she's sure been taking me for a ride. I had an idea all along. Any girl who'd pull the things she did."

"Like for instance, Jackie," said Rachel, leaning toward him, smiling, hoping she had him set up for a few indiscretions.

"I'd rather not say," said Jackson. "But you can take my word for it. Your sister can be pretty rough when she wants to be. She doesn't care who she hurts."

"You can tell me. I'll understand. I'll be mad at you if you don't tell me." She put a hand on his arm to show she was on his side.

"Well, you'll know soon enough anyway, I guess. She came right out and popped the question. Can you believe it? She asked me to marry her just like that, and all the time she's fooling around with Crevecoeur. What do you think of that?"

"It's a gasser, Jackie," she said. She thought it was horrible, and getting very late in the game. Leah didn't kid around and Jackson, whether he knew it or not, had Leah in the palm of his sweaty hand. Rachel's brain got busy again. If Leah went to market and bought a slab of beef that turned out rotten, she wouldn't complain or take it back. Leah was buying Jackson's brand of beef and wouldn't be diverted by the Pure Food and Drug Act. That left Jackson. Rachel went over her arsenal and came up with only one weapon: herself. She was back to sex. What if—nauseating thought—she let Jackson sleep with her? Would he be able, in all good conscience, to marry Leah anyway? She'd answered her own question. Jackson had no good conscience. He'd go right ahead with Leah, turning red when he saw Rachel. What a safety valve this boy had. A little blood to the surface was his public defender. She was wearing herself out on exercises and getting too tired to pick herself up off the floor.

She, Rachel the First, Queen of Questions, could marry Jackson. The proposition reared up like one of Laban's signs. She could marry Jackson for love of her sister. She could be Joan of Arc, Sydney Carton, Jesus Christ. She could not. She wouldn't marry Jackson Schwartz because she couldn't survive the wedding night. She'd die laughing. She pulled out her memo book and pencil and wrote, *Jackson, you're a desecration. A pox on your pubic hairs.*

"What are you writing?"

"A few notes on this place. It's our place and I love it and want to remember what it looks like." *Since Jackson Schwartz eats dirt the trick is to keep a goodly supply on hand.*

"You don't have to. We can come here as often as you like. What do you say to a dance?"

"In a minute. Let me finish." *1. Jackson lays Rachel.*

2. Rachel tells Leah. 3. Leah marries Jackson. She scratched
that out. *1. Jackson lays Rachel. 2. Rachel tells Laban. 3. Leah
marries Jackson.* She scratched. *1. Rachel leads Jackson on.
2. Jackson tries to lay Rachel. 3. Rachel punches Jackson in
the nose. 4. Jackson (a) is too humiliated ever to show his
swollen face in the Laban household again (b) punches Rachel
back and decides the Laban blood's too much for him (c) marries
Leah.* She stared at the words and decided they'd have to do.

"Okay," she said, slipping the pad in her purse. "Let's dance,
Jackie."

The combo was playing an Irving Berlin medley and Jackson,
making the most of it, welded her to him and drifted along with
the other true-love couples. The floor was crowded and impossible to really dance on. She let her head drop against his shoulder
like a dumb animal in pain at the Bryl Creaminess of him and
remembered Robert Young in an old movie revived on television.
Robert was being tortured to reveal secret government information. Being all-American, Robert forced his mind away from
suffering into happy memories of wife and family, shade trees
and white fences. This carried him through until the F.B.I.
rescue. She jammed her reception of Jackson with rag dolls, her
first Schwinn racer, playing jacks, house or fairies with Leah,
walking to kindergarten hand in hand with Leah, and later
trading menstrual secrets. She sniffed for memory smells of her
mother and buried her five-year-old tearful face in Mama's neck.
She went to the zoo with Laban and hiccuped from laughing at
his imitation of prairie dogs blinking from their burrows. It was
no use. Robert had more will power than she because Jackson
was suffocating her.

She pushed him away. "Not so tight, Jackie," she said. "Save a
little for later."

He relaxed and she looked down for breathing space. He
blushed and looked away and she wanted her memo book. She
had turned this Jackson Schwartz on, but the problem was how
to turn him off. By the time the set was over she'd established the
ground rules and was able to survive. She would close, work him
up to a pitch and move back. It was almost satisfying as kicking

him in the stomach, which possiblity would be added to the list as 3(a).

As the evening went along Jackson started looking at his watch, and she knew why. He wanted to get her parked where she was nobody's business but his own, but he couldn't gather the nerve to prod her to leave. Finally she was too bored even to tease. "Jackie," she said, "let's leave. I could dance all night with you but let's go some place we can be alone."

"Swell," said Jackson. "Whatever you'd like to do is A-okay with me." He thought a moment. "How about a drive into the country?"

"Why waste gas, Jackie? There's no place like home. We'll sit outside in the car and let the rest of the world go by." No deserted roadside for Rachel, Jackie boy. She didn't know how fast he was with his dukes and it was better to be safe than sorry. Even household pets have been known to turn on their mistresses.

He didn't fool around on the way. No sideswipes with his arm, no hands on the knee. He was a boy in a hurry to score. Meanwhile, she tested the door handle to make sure of a fast getaway. She chattered, "We're an awful lot alike, you and I. We've both learned the ropes and found out that life isn't all a greasy grind. We both like fun and dancing. We're young and know how good it is to be young. And above all, we're not ashamed of our God-given bodies. Oh, Jackie, it's great to be alive and pretty. Don't you think I'm pretty?"

"You're as cute as a bug in a rug, Rachel, and that's the truth."

"You're sweet, Jackie, and pretty too. Did anyone ever tell you how much you looked like Tony Curtis? If you had darker hair you'd be his spitting image."

"Do you really think so? I never thought about it."

"Do I ever. Oh, Jackie, Jackie, Jackie," she said, remembering in the nick of time how often they repeated names in the soap operas. "You're a living doll."

Jackson laughed. "Anything you say. I ought to quit while I'm ahead."

You can say that again, she thought.

When they parked in front of the house, Rachel noticed that the lights were on in the living room. Jackson moved swiftly. He turned off the motor and lights, and reached for her. She flung her head back on the seat and waited for the onslaught, wondering how in the world he expected to get anything done in the front seat of a Volkswagen—it was like having money in the bank. He came down hard with his lips on hers and cupped a cherry-picking hand on her breast. He squeezed as if her breast were the handball she'd recommended. She curled an arm around his neck as her contribution and this led him downward. He snorted and pawed, and she closed her hand in a fist, swung with all her might and caught him flush on the end of the nose. He sat stunned, and she noticed with interest the blood trickling toward his mouth. She didn't wait for afterthoughts. "That'll learn you, you bounder." She jerked the door open and ran toward the house. At the door she added a fillip: she reached inside the neck of her dress with both hands, ripping for all she was worth. The second tear of the month. She burst inside, cloth flapping, and stood poised in the hallway before the raised eyes of Crevecoeur, Leah, Laban and Beatrice. "I've been on a scavenger hunt," she said, trying her best to look raped. "When you lie down with dogs you get up with fleas." And she ran upstairs before they could say a word.

Leah watched Rachel come and go. From outside came the sound of Jackson's Volkswagen starting up and moving off. She moved a rag dipped in ammonia across her mind and washed it clean of sight and sound. The pungent odor of the ammonia dilated her nostrils and she concentrated on it until it existed as the only reality. It spread outward and bleached the roomful of people into nonbeing. Rachel and Jackson were of no concern to her and never would be. Tomcats were gray at night and returned home for the warm bed and bowl of milk, while a tiger, burning bright, might drape himself like a fur piece around her neck and lick her to death. She'd put a dish of milk in the corner, clean Jackson's whiskers and reap her reward with his purring body. She dumped his moral sense in the alleys he traveled. His love she assigned to anyone who was willing to treat him like a dog.

"Don't you think I should see what's wrong?" Beatrice asked Laban.

"Can't hurt, baby. Go ahead," said Laban, and Beatrice went upstairs.

Crevecoeur said, "I'm in the way. I'd better go."

Laban shook his head. "Sit tight. We've got plans to make. I'm anxious to get you painting. You're getting older by the minute. How about tomorrow afternoon? I've got nothing on that can't wait and I can use some of that country air. I'll bring the equipment and put you to work."

"I'm sorry but tomorrow is out." Crevecoeur hesitated. "I'm sitting in at three o'clock at John Smith's Restaurant next to the university."

"What you mean, sitting in? Negro sitting in?"

"That's right, sir. A Negro friend and I."

"That's the ticket. Why didn't I think of it? We'll make some terrific signs like 'They're good enough to fight with, they're good enough to eat with' and 'Black is a color, not a disease.' We'll be a great team. Tell you what. My next job will be 'Laban and Crevecoeur, Color-blind Master Painters.' I'll put it on wood and we'll nail it to your front door. We'll put that farm of yours on the map. Let's see. The rest of the week is out. How about Saturday morning?"

"Fine with me, Mr. Laban. My friend will appreciate the sign. He's a painter, too."

"Good. We'll start an art colony." Laban smiled and stood up. "I better check upstairs on the womenfolk. See you Saturday."

Leah, left with Crevecoeur, eyed one of Laban's signs, which read EVERY MAN'S WORK IS ALWAYS A PORTRAIT OF HIMSELF. She felt uncomfortable with Crevecoeur. Something about him invaded her privacy. She rose and moved away from him, her back turned to his probe.

"Would you like to go on the sit-in with me tomorrow? Would your father object?" said Crevecoeur. "I want to see you again, and asking you to The Combo seems silly. Correct me if I'm wrong. There'll just be Ronnie Birch and me. You may remember my saying hello to him in Tangletown. He was doing the charcoal sketches."

"I remember," said Leah, pressing her hands to her face and finding it hot. "Why should you think I'd want to get involved? You're confusing me with Rachel."

"I can't say. It's just an impression I have. If I'm wrong, forget I mentioned it."

"I thought you were trying to escape from things."

"I hope I'm not so much running away as exploring. I may be kidding myself. How about you? Wouldn't you like to explore a little?"

Mixed in Leah's mind was a terror of steel and brick crowding out earth, the pull of Crevecoeur's regard and the tension of getting involved with emotions she had no use for. "I guess I'll go," she said.

"Good enough. I'll come by at two-thirty."

She retreated in alarm from her spasm toward public exposure. "I'll ask my brother Bernie to go along. I'm sure he'd want to."

"Fine. I'd like to meet your brother." She turned to face him as he stood up. "I'd better go," he said. "Thanks for inviting me." He held out his hand and she engaged cool flesh. "My regards to Rachel. I hope she's okay," he said. She withdrew her hand and went with him to the door.

"Would you want me to ask her too?" she said, restored to control.

He paused. "If you like."

Upstairs Rachel stopped crying and felt better, although she found it hard to believe she'd crawled into Beatrice's arms and all but called her Mama. Whatever the justification, Rachel was a liar and a cheat and had to suffer for it. She'd flopped into bed shaking all over, staring hot-eyed at the ceiling, giggling at the memory of Jackson's nose, and Beatrice merely had to come in, sit at the side of the bed and hold out her arms for Rachel to fall apart. She'd burrowed into the cushiony breast and cried her eyes out while Beatrice said, "There, there, baby. It's all right," rocking her back and forth. In a way it was another betrayal. There was no end to Rachel's perfidy. All Mother had to do was die and Rachel, eyes screwed shut and lips puckered, nuzzled the nearest red-painted nipple and baked in the cozy oven of blue-eyeshadowed breasts. She could imagine Bernie's reaction. He'd pull out a Boy Scout knife and stab at the drapes if they so much as rustled. She didn't care. The more she despised herself the less she cared. A fist, the one launched at Jackson's nose, was lodged in her frontal lobe, and it pressed against her forehead. She had provoked a sneak attack from an overexposed person in order to annihilate him and claim self-defense. She was no better than an undercover policewoman who paraded the streets at night in order to flip male egos over her shoulder. An admirable woman, a credit to her race, but who would invite her on hay rides?

She lifted her head. "I'm sorry, Beatrice. I'm being silly. Nothing happened. Really."

"Do you want to talk about it? Talking helps, you know."

"It's nothing. I'm just tired."

Laban stood in the doorway and Rachel pulled away. Beatrice's arms clung and for a moment there was a timid tug of war before Rachel fell back on the bed. She brushed angrily at her eyes and fiddled with the torn cloth at her breast. Now there'd be the devil to pay. She was Laban's basketball and he would bounce her up and down or lob her toward the ceiling. This was Laban's kind of game and he'd play her for all she was worth, which was two cents marked down in a bargain basement because she'd sprung a slow leak. He moved to the bed and rested a hand on Beatrice's shoulder. His face was tired and gray-looking and she thought with a surge of alarm, Dear God, no. I want the ribbing, nothing else. If you go soft on me I'll run away from home. I'll join a nunnery. I might even confess I'm a wicked girl.

"Baby," Laban said to Beatrice, "would you mind leaving us alone? I'd like to talk to Rachel for a minute."

Beatrice kissed Rachel on her moist cheek and left her rubbing at the lipstick marks. Laban sat on the bed and curled his fingers around Rachel's hand. It was too much. Damn him, anyway. She burst out crying all over again and he sat as sober as somebody else's father, waiting her out. She stuffed her fingers in her mouth but kept sobbing anyway. Finally she subsided.

"Did he try to rape you, baby?"

She coughed and then, beautifully, in the midst of her turmoil, tumblers clicked, a bolt slid back and the door swung open on its iron hinges. Laban had unbuckled his gun belt, unpinned his badge, saddled a horse and had it fresh and ready in the back. She paused breathless, in a mountain pass on the road to freedom. She had only to say, Yes, he did. He's a beast who doesn't care who he hurts. What kind of a man would take out twin sisters at the same time? He's morally corrupt. He's grasping and ambitious and all he wants from us is your blessing. Please, Laban, fire him. Get rid of him. Beat him up and show him you're still boss. All she had to do was lie and cheat a little longer.

She said, "No, Laban. I encouraged him because I wanted to hit him in the nose."

"And did you?" The Laban smile, a network of wrinkles forming connections and eyes squeezing shut, began and aborted.

"Yes. I made his nose bleed. Just before I came in I tore my dress to make it look good." The fist in her mind uncurled and decent fingers patted the inside of her skull. She felt light-headed. She'd discovered that her father, of all people, was a confessor.

"Let me tell you about Schwartz," said Laban. "He's a horse's ass but a competent lawyer. He works hard and he'll work harder. He does whatever I tell him because he doesn't know any better. He doesn't know that if he wasn't such an ass-licker he'd make it with me even without marrying my daughter. But that's what he's going to do, marry Leah, because that's what I want."

Rachel sat up and in her excitement forgot to be penitent. "Why? If you know him for what he is how could you do that to Leah? She's your own flesh and blood. It must count for something. He doesn't love her. In fact, he'd rather marry me. I'm sure of it. He doesn't even like Leah. She scares him."

"Sure she scares him. She scares me. You know why? Your sister's a twenty-four karat radical and, baby, that's scary. She's a yogi in a corner inviting chews on her own fat. She's got her tit in a wringer. Whatever she's asked, whoever asks her, she's liable to do, God knows why. She's a gal who refuses to value the difference between yes and no, and unless she's awfully lucky she's going to be eaten up alive. Either that or she'll explode and chew up everything in sight. I don't want to be around to see it. Meanwhile, I've got to do what I can."

"What's that got to do with Jackson Schwartz? If what you say is true and she's somebody's dish, why throw her to a dog? Frankly, Laban, I'm amazed. I didn't think you worried that much about us."

"I don't worry about you. You can take care of yourself. I'm not a crutch and you're not a cripple. Leah's another matter. Something's eating her alive. You see someone who chooses to drown and you throw her a lifeline. Schwartz may be her lifeline."

"How? He's awful."

"Because he's a square. He lives by the book. She's too screwed-up for a complicated person. She might get through with a striped-tie guy like him to tell her what to do. She needs to be told what's on the next page because she's thrown away the book. She's not like other women. The ordinary women make the conventions. They decide on what spoon to use. They make us class-conscious and sex-conscious. Men make up the game and women the rules and God help the woman who makes up the game. The only hope for her is to field a grounder like Schwartz. He sees a sign, 'Don't step on the grass,' and maybe the grass has a chance to grow."

She was grateful to Laban. She was proud of him for caring about Leah. She wouldn't trade him for all the daddies in the world who took their kids to circuses and ball games, who helped them with their homework and went to P.T.A. meetings, who wore floppy hats and barbecued on Sundays. But he was terribly wrong about Leah and was making a fatal mistake, killing Leah with his definition of kindness. She felt wise, like a benevolent, bent and twisted old lady with arthritic joints and sad, watery eyes, lying in her bed with its massive headboard, explaining to a wide-eyed war orphan about life. Laban, trying to decipher a woman's heart, was fabricating English words out of a foreign language. "Laban," she said in a faint wisp of a voice, "don't sell Leah short. She's my twin, after all, and I know her. She's not different from other women. We live by our hearts. We'd do anything for the man we love, anything they ask us. We don't care if they're gangsters or African missionaries as long as they love us. Don't tell me Leah loves Jackson."

Laban shook his head. "She doesn't love anybody, but that's beside the point. One of her parts got lost. She marries Schwartz. Look, baby, she wants to. I'm not forcing her, just helping her get what she wants."

Rachel's heart sank. It was hopeless, much more so than when she thought Laban didn't care one way or the other. For the first time she saw where Bernie got his moral fixes. They were there all the time, buried under Laban's false noses and baggy pants. Only a moralist could be naïve enough to believe he could save a woman from herself. Not sparing herself she made one last try. "What about Charles Crevecoeur?"

Laban grinned, happy to be diverted. "I'm going to teach him sign painting and he's going to learn me Negroes. He's not for Leah. He'd make her explode in a thousand pieces. What she needs is a tight, neat package wrapped in cardboard, marked 'Open for Inspection.' With Crevecoeur, baby, it'd be touch and go all the way."

In the midst of her concern for Leah, Rachel felt a friendly feather of anticipation tickle her throat and she coughed. Through no fault of her own, she'd live to fight another day. And there was always the slim chance that Jackson Schwartz had had enough even for him.

Ronnie Birch, in a T-shirt and khakis, was slim and round-shouldered. Leah thought he was a beautiful color. She wanted to smudge her palm against his cheek. She was glad she'd agreed to come, and was calm about Crevecoeur, steady-eyed over his beard and boots. She wouldn't have needed Bernie and regretted inviting him. He looked silly in his neat blue suit and regimental tie, on his best behavior as if he were the one on trial. "I'm very glad to meet you, Ronnie," he said, the sunlight glinting on his glasses and making him look like an animated cartoon. He extended his arm. "I confess I've never done anything like this before but I'm anxious to help in any way I can. The world's past the point where anybody can sit on his hands."

Ronnie looked at the hand and thrust his own in his pockets. He barely nodded his head and Bernie, his lips squirming over each other, withdrew his arm. "Don't mind Ronnie," said Crevecoeur. "He didn't really want to come."

"Then why did he?" said Bernie.

"Because I asked him to," said Crevecoeur. "This is my show. I promised he'd just be a supernumerary. Ronnie's a painter. He doesn't go in for group activities."

"Who does?" said Bernie, fidgeting with his collar. "I don't exactly regard this as a picnic myself, you know, but I felt it was something worth doing. If anybody feels I'll just be in the way, tell me and I'll go home."

"You're welcome," said Crevecoeur. "Ronnie didn't mean anything personal. Let's go in."

Crevecoeur pushed open the door and they sat down at the

nearest table. It had a black enameled surface; the chairs were plastic with metal legs. Conscious of the air space between herself and Ronnie, sitting to her right, Leah looked past him around the restaurant. A man was seated behind a cash register next to the door. She could see only two customers, two men in overalls, crouched over beers at a table on the other side. As she watched, the men drained their glasses and walked out. "There's a wait-ress," said Bernie in a hushed voice, "in a green uniform sitting in that rear booth staring at us without moving a muscle. I don't think she's about to wait on us."

"Let it ride," said Crevecoeur. "They'll have to do something."

"What do you paint, Ronnie?" said Leah.

"Pictures."

"Of people or things?"

"Both."

"Are you good?"

He sat hunched in his shoulders, refusing to give an inch. "I like to think so."

"Have you sold anything?"

"No."

"Ronnie's staying at the farm with me for awhile," said Creve-coeur. "We've got an artists' colony going. Your father's going to teach me sign painting."

Against Ronnie's reticence, Crevecoeur was a babbler and Leah found herself sharing Ronnie's silences. The man behind the cash register stood up and came over to them. He was dressed in dark, unpressed trousers, a long-sleeved sport shirt and a tie dirtied at the knot. He had a long, thin nose hammered flat, small eyes and a short, square body.

"I'm Mr. Smith. You want something?" he said. He had an accent.

"We'd like to see a menu, please," said Crevecoeur.

"The kitchen's closed." He looked at his watch. "The kitchen closes from two-thirty to five o'clock."

"Then we'll have beers."

Mr. Smith looked at Leah. "You, girlie, you got identification you're over twenty-one?"

Leah raised her eyebrows at Crevecoeur and he shrugged. "I'm twenty," she said, "but I'll have coffee."

Mr. Smith wagged a finger. "No good. I can't serve beer to a party with minors. It's against the law. Who knows who drinks?"

"We'll all have coffee," said Crevecoeur.

"The kitchen's closed."

Crevecoeur smiled. "We're not going any place. We may as well wait until the kitchen opens. Five o'clock, you said."

Mr. Smith watched as three men in work clothes came in, glanced around, and almost without breaking stride, turned and walked out. "You see that? You see? Three regular customers. Every day they come in like clockwork. Do me a favor will you? Go some place else and sit."

"We'll have beers except for the lady," said Crevecoeur. "We'll drink our beers and then we'll leave. That way we'll be out in fifteen minutes."

Mr. Smith leaned over and rested hairy-backed hands on the table. "Look. You look like nice, educated people. Give me a break. I'll be honest with you. Who's Smith? My name is Rabinowitz. Samuel Rabinowitz. Understand? I plead with you. Start up with somebody else."

"We're here to help you, Mr. Rabinowitz," said Crevecoeur. "You're close to the university and when the word gets around you're a person of good will you'll get all the college trade. You'll get in on the ground floor."

Mr. Smith-Rabinowitz jerked back. "Listen, smartie, don't tell me from good will. What good will? You kids would keep me in business maybe a month, no more. Without my lunch and supper trade I'm dead. Look. Colored people eating at my place, you think I care for myself? Their money's as good as anybody else's, no?

"Yes, Mr. Rabinowitz," said Crevecoeur.

"Okay. Listen, I'm a Jew. You think I don't know what prejudice is? I know, believe. Start with another place. Then when things open up a little bit, I'll let this colored gentleman have a meal absolutely free from charge. He brings his girl friend—no charge. I got respect for the colored people. They got rights like everybody else. Don't run me out of business. Please. Start with the others."

"Mr. Rabinowitz," said Crevecoeur. "You may not remember me but I've been here before. You know the way you have Negroes wait at the cash register while you fix them a sandwich to go? That's not fair, to take their money and not give them a place to sit down."

"I lose my business. Look. I'll be honest with you. I'm a refugee. Give a refugee a break, can't you? After what I've been through in my life, don't I need a break? You think my life is peaches and cream? You want to know how many hours I'm on my feet every day, with my wife in the kitchen working like a dog? You want to see her hands? As red as an Indian. We got a little place here. You think we're millionaires?"

A man reading a newspaper came in and sat at a table. After a moment he saw them, folded his newspaper under his arm and walked out. "You see the look he gave?" said Smith-Rabinowitz. "You're killing me."

"If you'd taken our order, we'd be finished and gone," said Crevecoeur.

"Sure. That's all I need for them to see food and drink on the table and I'm up for auction." He backed off a foot. "You want I should call the police?"

"You forget we have a public accommodations law, Mr. Rabinowitz. *You're* violating the law, not us. I don't think you'd want the police in on this but if you want to call them, go ahead. Come on, how about some hamburgers? We're getting hungry."

Smith-Rabinowitz wrung his hands. "An educated boy like you. A college boy acting like a bandit, picking on an old man who knows plenty from persecution. What am I, a Ku Klux Klan? I'm a Jew. You know what they say. A colored man turned inside out is what they say. Plenty of places they don't serve me in my lifetime."

Bernie had been twitching in his seat. "Mr. Rabinowitz," he said, "why do you call yourself Mr. Smith?"

"Why, he asks. You think I got Jewish clientele? I got Polacks, Bulgarians and Rumanians, that's what I got. My restaurant feeds *momsers* is why. I make a living by the skin of my teeth. If they know I'm Rabinowitz they go to Corboni's a half block away, which is where you should go. You think I'm a bad man not to serve you? I'm twice as bad. I don't serve Sam Rabinowitz even."

"Mr. Rabinowitz, you're a liar," said Bernie, and Crevecoeur shook his head but Bernie ignored him. "It doesn't matter if you have a Rabinowitz or a John Smith restaurant. This is America. People go where they like to eat unless they're Negroes and I can't imagine a restaurant being boycotted because its owner is Jewish. I think you're ashamed of being a Jew. I think you're greedy and immoral and that's why you won't serve Mr. Birch here, who is an American citizen with inalienable rights."

Smith-Rabinowitz looked searchingly at Bernie. "You're Jewish, hah?" he said, and Bernie's lips tightened. "I beg you," said Smith-Rabinowitz. "Don't ruin my business. Go to Corboni. Let him suffer a little bit for Mussolini."

Ronnie laughed and Smith-Rabinowitz eagerly joined in.

"We'll have our hamburgers now," said Crevecoeur.

Smith-Rabinowitz concentrated on Bernie. "You want to act like a Nazi and murder an old man who came from a concentration camp? Is this why I came to America, to find Nazis?"

"Sure," said Bernie. "Roll up your sleeve and let me see your arm."

Smith-Rabinowitz glared. "Bandit," he said. "Sit till you drop." He went back to the cash register but he couldn't stay still. He ran to the rear, pushed through swinging doors and emerged with three giggling, aproned young Negro women, who trailed him to the booth. "You see these three ladies? They work for me in the kitchen. I make them a living. Girls, you like your jobs? I treat you right? Go ahead, say what you want. This is a free country." They laughed and tossed their heads. One made eyes at Ronnie and they laughed even harder. "You wreck my business and you throw these fine girls out from work. What does that accomplish for the colored race? What kind sense is that? Okay, girls." As they moved away, their whispers and giggles floated to the booth.

"Mr. Rabinowitz," said Bernie, "I'm pleased that you produced those women from your kitchen because it highlights the problems of race relations. They prepare food, wash dishes, handle everything and yet they remain invisible. It's as though they're shadowpunching a time clock. It's old-fashioned slavery, Mr. Rabinowitz, gone underground, and it won't change until black man serves white and white man serves black and nobody even notices the difference. The world isn't black and white. I've got nothing against you personally, just the color scheme of your restaurant."

"It's exactly like I bought it," said Smith-Rabinowitz. "You think I'm a millionaire? Who can afford to redecorate?"

Ronnie laughed. "You've got a sense of humor, Mr. Rabinowitz," he said. As he spoke, Smith-Rabinowitz's little eyes widened toward the entrance. A policeman was coming in, dressed in his summer uniform, badge over his heart, a thick black belt strapping a gun holster to his side. Her pulses thudding, Leah saw that it was Laban.

"Goddamnit," said Bernie.

"What might be the trouble, baby?" said Laban to Smith-Rabinowitz.

Smith-Rabinowitz shrugged his shoulders and raised his eyebrows. "No trouble, Officer."

"A bit of peace disturbance maybe? I got a tip there's a donnybrook in here."

Smith-Rabinowitz wet his lips. He hesitated. He shook his head. "No trouble in here, Officer. I'm just taking these people's order. Four hamburgers, three beers, one coffee, right?"

"Right, Mr. Rabinowitz," said Crevecoeur.

"Anything for you, Officer?" said Smith-Rabinowitz.

Laban looked stern. "Might that be in the way of a bribe, baby? I'll have you know it's an honest cop I am, a law enforcement officer with no ifs, buts or maybes."

"I'll be out in a few minutes with the order," said Smith-Rabinowitz, and he hurried toward the kitchen, pulling out his handkerchief on the run.

Laban grinned at Crevecoeur. "I told you I had a free afternoon. It's a little bit of hell raising I'm after."

"Mr. Laban, this is Ronnie Birch. Ronnie, this is Leah's and

Bernie's father." Ronnie smiled and shook hands. He seemed in very good humor.

"To be sure and it's a pleasure," said Laban. "You're a fine broth of a lad."

Bernie slammed his fist on the table. "You're going too damned far as usual. Who asked you to stick your two cents in? It would serve you right if they arrested you for impersonating an officer, and an Irish one at that. Talk about prejudices. Isn't anything sacred to you? Life isn't one big playground. You're so busy laughing at your own gags you haven't time to notice nobody else is amused. Keep rolling that barrel of fun until you knock everybody flat and completely humiliate your family, and then maybe, just maybe, you'll be satisfied. Didn't it occur to you this might be serious business? If you have to play dirty, do it in your own grubby sandpile."

"Who's your crepe-hanging friend?" said Laban to Crevecoeur. "Tell him to button his lip or I'll run him in. But in a manner of speaking, he's right. I wouldn't want to be spoiling your fun as long as I've had a bit of my own. Nobody likes to have a policeman at a party. My, did you see that poor man run to the kitchen, now? Well, I'll be saying good-bye to you, Crevecoeur, till I visit you at the farm. And good-bye to you, miss."

"Good-bye, officer," said Leah.

Laban leaned over to shake hands once again with Ronnie. He walked away with a wave of his arm.

"You shouldn't quarrel with success," said Crevecoeur. "Here comes our food."

"Great," said Bernie. "Is that what you've learned from history, that the end justifies the means?"

Crevecoeur looked steadily at Bernie. "Don't be so edgy, friend," he said.

Smith-Rabinowitz arrived with a full tray, which he set down on an adjoining table. "What happened with the officer?"

"He left, Mr. Rabinowitz," said Crevecoeur. "He said it was a joy to behold such happy, peace-loving people and he was sorry he couldn't wait to say good-bye." Smith-Rabinowitz dumbly delivered the sandwiches. "Three beers and a cup of coffee and we're all set," said Crevecoeur. As Smith-Rabinowitz started away, a woman entered the restaurant. Smith-Rabinowitz paused, shook his head and kept going. Leah recognized Mrs. Margery Schmidt even without Bernie's "Margery, what's going on here?"

Blond, blue-saucer-eyed, stubborn-jawed, dressed in a tight, pale blue dress and blue spike-heeled shoes, Margery Schmidt drove toward them with fast, choppy steps. She stood, hands on hips, and stared at Ronnie. She shook her head and turned slowly to Bernie, eyes translucent. "You dirty fink," she said. "You bloody Communist. If my ex-husband were here he'd have you horsewhipped." She spun around and clicked out. Bernie, sweating, half rose and then settled back.

"That's a tiger," said Crevecoeur. "At least you can't say she pussyfoots around. Bernie, our business is well in hand here if you'd like to go after her."

"I didn't know I needed your permission," said Bernie. "I'd be obliged if you didn't use that condescending tone."

"I wasn't aware I was being condescending. I'm sorry if you got that impression."

Bernie looked from Crevecoeur to Ronnie, who was grinning at his hamburger. "You people seem to get a kick out of seeing a couple of Jews chew each other up, don't you?"

"You're reaching, Bernie," said Crevecoeur. "If you keep putting a chip on your shoulder, someone's bound to knock it off. Nobody but you seems to be worrying about Jewishness around here. Why don't you let it alone?"

"I know you phony Anglo-Saxon liberals from way back," said Bernie.

"I'm French," said Crevecoeur.

"As you said before, this is your show, isn't it? Ronnie's along as Exhibit A and I can join in as long as I know my place. You've got the Jew figured as the real Uncle Tom of history, haven't you? We've got a history of Jerry Lewises and Danny Kayes. We're experts at pratfalls and nimble footwork. If we play ball, help entertain the troops and finance the demonstrations, maybe later do the dirty work with dishes, okay. Otherwise, there's always the flaming cross to fall back on. After all, no matter what an ecumenical council says, every true Christian knows in his heart we killed Christ. I don't think it was an accident that Mr. Smith was Mr. Rabinowitz. I think you knew it all along. I think it was amusing for you to show up a Jew as a Bircher turned inside out. Well, this Jew won't stand for it."

Smith-Rabinowitz brought the beers and coffee. "Okay, anything else? You got everything you came for?"

"We're fine," said Crevecoeur. "How much is the bill?"

Smith-Rabinowitz whipped out a pad and started figuring. In the middle he looked up and breathed heavily. "Ah, forget it. It's on the house. I'll mark it down for good will. Mr. Rabinowitz shows there's no hard feelings."

"We'd rather pay," said Bernie. "How much?"

Smith-Rabinowitz moved away, shaking his hand across his chest, and went back to his seat behind the register.

"Bernie," said Crevecoeur, "if you want to set up a morality play, do it on somebody else's time."

Bernie spoke to his hamburger, as if he were sitting alone at the table and hadn't even listened to Crevecoeur. "We see the worst part of ourselves," he said, "by looking only for that part. Not all of us changed our names to Smith. Not all of us became the one Jew to belong to the Christian club, to keep it honest. It's hard to resist trying to belong. It's hard to be proud of a heritage that's a suitcase left in the lost and found, so battered and mud-caked and pasted over with peculiar-looking labels that we're ashamed to claim it even though it's loaded with value. In a grim way, the Negro is lucky. He sticks out like a sore thumb, so he can't be tempted to live a lie."

Leah looked at Ronnie. "My brother likes to talk," she said.

"I can see that," said Ronnie. "It doesn't bother me. It's like rain on the roof."

Bernie had shot his wad. He didn't react to Ronnie's comment. "I was supposed to take her to the art museum this afternoon," he said heavily. "I forgot all about it. I can't understand how she knew I was here." He turned to Leah. "Did you tell her?"

"No. I guess it was Rachel. I asked her if she wanted to come along."

"Rachel. It's just like her to make trouble for me." He made a face. "To hell with Margery."

"She's a beautiful girl," said Crevecoeur.

"She's an idiot."

They finished eating and filed out past Smith-Rabinowitz, who—evidently to speed them on their way—didn't look up. Crevecoeur said, "Thank you for the service, Mr. Rabinowitz," but he merely grunted. His brief honeymoon with civil rights was over and it didn't promise to be a particularly happy marriage. On the walk to the car, Crevecoeur said to Leah, "Would you like to visit the farm on Sunday? I'd like to show you around." He hesitated. "Unless you'd rather come with your father on Saturday."

Leah thought a moment. "Sunday would be fine," she said.

"I'll pick you up," said Crevecoeur.

"That won't be necessary. Laban has two cars. I can borrow one."

"Good. Come out any time you feel like."

"All right."

She felt Bernie's hand tugging at her elbow. "What do you want to do that for?" he whispered in her ear. "He's a phony."

Leah shrugged him off and didn't bother to answer.

Bernie explained why he allowed Rachel to take the lower bunk while he took the upper. They were in the survival shelter. "Conventionally," he said, "the lower bunk is considered preferable due to the convenience of getting in and out. Convenience, however, is the curse of our time. We press buttons, flip switches, and don't even notice our toes and fingers falling away. Soon we'll be nothing but bloated heads blinking our eyes to turn our machines off and on. Hardship, even contrived, is the *sine qua non* of the human spirit."

Rachel swung her legs upward and rested her bare feet against the springs; nursing her fist, that was still bruised from Jackson's face, she bounced Bernie about. "You pant turning book pages. Every muscle you have swings like an old woman's underarm. You're the world's weakest man and belong in a side show."

Bernie reached over the side and knocked her legs down. One of her knees, unprotected by her shorts, struck the concrete basement wall. "You bastard, Bernie, look what you've done. You don't have to be so rough. Jackson Schwartz has more respect for a woman than you do."

"I've got a right to kill you if I want to. Why did you tell Margery I was at John Smith's Restaurant?"

Rachel grinned while she dabbed her knee with a handkerchief. Dots of blood had formed. "Your love was worried. She was in a real sweat. I think her exact words were, 'Where the hell is he? He was supposed to pick me up forty-five minutes ago.'"

"She didn't say 'hell.' She never says 'hell.' She never says dirty words because ladies don't use profanity. 'Fink' and 'Communist' is as far as she goes."

"So she didn't say 'hell.' 'Where the heck is he?' is what she said. So I told her. Who dreamed you kept secrets from Margery? I thought you and she shared nothing but the naked truth."

"Have your fun. Your pal Crevecoeur asked Leah out to the farm. Did you know that?"

Rachel didn't know. So that was the way it was going to be. Crevecoeur hadn't let out a peep about his plans—hadn't called even. She was the one who was supposed to go to the farm. He was zeroing in on Leah then, doing Rachel a big fat favor. It was getting very tempting to write accommodating Charlie off, to just tell him to go to hell if he ever gave her the chance—which it looked like he wouldn't. No, sir. She was never one to lose a match by default. When she had him where she wanted him, she'd decide if she wanted to keep her prize package or donate it to her favorite charity, which was fast not becoming Leah. She might even slam the door on his fingers; there was more than one way to skin a tomcat.

Bernie crawled out of the upper bunk and examined her knee. "God," he said. "When is this bloodshed ever going to end?" He pulled out drawers from the desk, dumping them on the floor, until he found a bottle of iodine. Gently he swabbed her knee and she forgave him. She had the heart of a Hemingway whore. All it took was a little tenderness. "You know what that fool father of yours did at the restaurant? He impersonated a police officer. I seriously think we ought to have him put away. He's a menace to society."

Rachel took back every bit of her forgiveness. "That isn't funny in the least," she said. Bernie should know without being told that overnight Laban had become sweet and adorable, and she would die to defend him. She considered Bernie thoughtfully. "If you despise Laban so much, why are you imitating him?"

"What is that supposed to mean?"

"Why are you going to law school?"

"I'm a spy in the enemy's camp. When I've discovered the

weak spots I sneak back to my own lines and organize the attack."

"That's just what you've become: a sneak."

"Be careful," said Bernie. "Remember, you've got another knee."

"You've become a puppy tugging at Laban's trouser leg. Keep it up and you'll never amount to anything."

"That's Laban's daughter. Why do I have to amount to anything?"

"Because," said Rachel grimly, "you're Laban's son."

Bernie surveyed the room. "All right. Let's take your cue. I'm Laban's son. He thinks I'm a weakling because I carouse with low characters. His crowned head is uneasy. I have to prove I am really a Prince Hal. So be it. What would the king do under the same or similar circumstances? He'd have a party. So we celebrate my reduction to Labanism. We prove that man can endure only if he risks grandly the failure to survive. You willing to join the Grand New Party of the Grand New Person?"

"You're the one who should be put away," said Rachel. "What are you up to?"

"The book on Labanism is that life is a big Tinker Toy, right? Okay, let's tinker. Let's debase Laban's coin and see how much it takes to get a nickel's worth." He rushed around the room, dragging out paper cups, bottles of bourbon, cans of fruit, chocolate bars. He turned on the transistor radio and tuned it to jazz music. She watched, fascinated and immobilized by his burst of energy, knowing she should do something, if it were only to leave him with no audience, but instead she sat motionless on the bunk. Even more than her curiosity to see how far he would go, her feeling that she couldn't desert him kept her there. If she left he might transform the room into a padded cell. Bernie poured bourbon into two cups and handed her one. She committed herself and took it. She began to get excited. She was never a person to stay sober at a drunken party and she did love parties.

Bernie touched cups. "To the Grand New Person of the Grand New Party." They drank, and as the whiskey curled her lips and heated her chest, she decided it was possible that Laban had conned her. Leopards didn't change their spots and Laban had big, round, painted ones that went with fright wigs and unicycles. She might be getting so starved for love that she looked for it in a hyena's mouth. She tried to visualize Laban's face as the sympathetic papa's, and couldn't. She looked for the burning match stuck between her toes before she remembered Laban wasn't there.

"To Labanism. The show must go on," Bernie said, and they drank.

"To Laban, the patron saint of the Grand New Party," said Rachel, and they drank, and she was dizzy.

"To brave men everywhere who stand on soft soap boxes in squares. To helpless men whom God won't help. To the second team that has to pay to play. To the dirt-eaters who nibble away the shore." Bernie opened a can of peaches and fished out sticky slices with his fingers. She gobbled with him. He went to the closet and unloaded cans on the desk. He opened all of them with admirable no-nonsense briskness. Obviously, someday he'd be up for chairman of the board. She'd bide her time and then, when she could demand something really big, she'd threaten to tell about how he'd joined a sit-in demonstration in his youth, and make him pay through the nose. If he balked she'd remind him of Jackson Schwartz and what she could do to noses.

"To Jackson Schwartz," she said, "and how to succeed in business without really trying." They drank.

"Guess who I saw sneaking into a church?" said Bernie. "While I teach her Judaism at night she confesses to the priest by day."

"I've read Graham Greene. Think up your own slander."

"The truth, sister, is a defense to slander."

Bernie picked up two buckets of water and carried them out. She heard him emptying them into the basement drain. He came back swinging the empty buckets and banging them together. He took out the remaining water bucket and she admired his devotion to duty. No waste of energy was too great for the cause. He was a dedicated Grand New Party member. He staggered off with two buckets of sand and she heard the garage door open. He came back with two empty cardboard boxes and filled them with ballpoint pens, transistor-radio batteries, envelopes, stamps, first-aid kit, toothpaste tubes, toothbrushes, soap, safety razors, packs of blades. She helped him. Laban must be taught a lesson. Everyone should have a survival shelter, or no one. It wasn't democratic. None of her best friends had shelters, so why should Laban?

Bernie carried out a box, came back and picked up another. She gathered an armful of World Encyclopedia volumes and followed him. He'd created a dump in the driveway and she gravely unloaded the books on the pile. The late afternoon sunlight struck her face and left her nauseated. They hurried back to the dim safety of the shelter. "The Grand New Party," said Bernie dreamily, "will be the nothing-doing party. Our insignia will be a lily of the field."

He pulled a mattress off a bunk and slung it across his back. She collected a pillow and blankets and stumbled after him to the dump. "For a nothing-doer you're awfully busy."

"Merely mopping up. You can't make an omelet without breaking eggs. We'll have a secret word, something you hear every day around the factory. The word is 'waste.' The category is dispossession and the word is waste. Waste and want not. The greatest freedom is wantonness. The greatest evils are work and thrift."

When they had finished carrying out the encyclopedias their rubbish heap filled the driveway. "What happens when nothing's left?"

"What happens? We'll have reached the state of Labanism. We play games. We swing from blackened trees. When the evil serpent raises its head we stomp on it."

They ran back and forth with cartons of cigarettes, newspapers, chairs, the Holy Bible, a four-volume set of Shakespeare, thermos jug, Coleman lamp, bedpan, tool box. She helped Bernie drag a ladder.

"Leah would never join the party," said Rachel. "Would you leave her behind?"

"Leah? Who's Leah? The party *is* my sister. Leah's hand-brushed front steps. She's the P.T.A. and the R.S.V.P. Let her sink or swim in alphabet soup." He examined the remains of the shelter. "We're finished in here," he said. "Let's go." They went to the junk pile and she watched while Bernie held his cigarette lighter against a layer of newspapers.

Flames sprang up and licked book bindings. Rachel turned sober. Her head pounded. "Put it out, Bernie." She started forward but he held her arm. The fire gained momentum and she tried to twist away, but he wrestled her to the ground. They sat on the concrete.

"You should have the courage of your convictions," said Bernie.

"This is crazy, Bernie. Don't be a fool. Let me go."

Immobilized, she heard the screen door slam and Beatrice, bouncing out of a housecoat, curlers riding her head like metal snakes, rushed toward them down the back steps. Rachel wanted to curl up with Beatrice's yellow-streaked hair and die. She stared at the flames; her eyes burned with the smoke, and she thought how fitting it would be to add the rest of her flesh. It would serve Bernie right and prove that suicide was the final solution of the Grand New Party. Since she was no heroine and had no intention of dying for any cause whatsoever, she wrestled free of Bernie and dove for Beatrice, seeking shelter once again in the round of her breasts. She had her own yellow streak to match Beatrice's; she kept proving that by getting swallowed up by whatever opened its mouth. "Beatrice," she said, deserting him, "Bernie's gone mad."

Beatrice wrapped her arms around Rachel, who peeked around at Bernie still sitting on the ground. "What are you doing, Bernie?" said Beatrice. "This is terrible. Your father's home. He's liable to see you any minute. Please, put out the fire."

"No, Mama," said Bernie. "I'm saving the world. See those red-rimmed eyes and dripping fangs? Hear them snapping at their own tails? Only the fire stands between us and doomsday, while Laban fiddles with props."

"Let's get the hose," Rachel said, and ran under the porch. She turned on the water, dragged out the hose and sprayed the fire, making sure she sprayed Bernie on the way. The flames hissed and sent up reptilian twists of smoke. Something smelled to high heaven. In a few moments the pile was a soggy, smouldering mess.

They stared at the charred chairs, gutted bedding, Hitlerized books, at the blackened bottles and flashlights cradled in ashes like baked potatoes, and Beatrice said in a hushed voice, "I don't know what your father will say. I pray to the Lord he isn't upset."

"I pray to God he is," snapped Bernie, water streaming from his hair, his shirt glued against his body. "Who is Laban not to be upset? He should be here. He should hit me in the face. Like this." Bernie's palm smacked his wet cheek. "I've earned my punishment and mean to have it. This is no laughing matter."

"Stop it, Bernie, please," said Beatrice. "Don't talk so crazy. You mustn't try to hurt your father. If you only knew. He's got enough to worry about."

"That, Mama, is the misconception of the century. Where did Laban find you, in the nunnery where you'd been deposited on the doorstep at birth? Laban's baby, you're a big girl now. Hurt Laban? How? Just tell me. He's got four inches of armor plate for skin. I'll make you a bet. When he sees this, he'll call a wrecker and have him pull the whole house down. Nobody tops Laban."

Laban stood at the porch landing looking down at them. The sun struck at an angle that made his eyeballs look like the blind smooth cups of a Greek statue and accentuated his tufted eyebrows. With his rugged, lined, gray, unsmiling face, his business suit seemed like a defilement, as if giggling schoolchildren had draped a museum piece. Seeing his features in repose, Rachel thought how heroic he'd look captured in a frame on a wall. Unless the painter knew him and was true to his knowledge. Then he'd be—what? Moved by his silence, despising Bernie for having made her his accomplice, she struggled to fashion a valid glimpse of Laban hung on a wall. He would be smiling. His eyes would be leaking imps that tumbled through the air. If an imp was in danger of falling on its head, his hand would reach out to steady it. If another, more daring than the others, darted into a blazing furnace, what then? If it was his own child and the only way to save it was to spring from the canvas into the fire after it, what then? She couldn't picture Laban facing a last laugh.

"I want to thank you, baby," said Laban to Bernie, "for cleaning out the basement room. I've been meaning to do it for some time." His voice was tired and Rachel's throat closed. He wasn't rolling with the punch. He was fighting on his toes but his responses were sluggish.

"You're welcome," said Bernie. He took off his glasses and wiped them against his pants. "I knew I'd be doing you a favor."

Laban lifted his head and extended his arms. "I declare the state of emergency officially over. I declare the survival of mankind secure. I propose a period of celebration. The survival shelter is hereby converted into a game room with the first game to be held tomorrow night, Saturday. Every year hereafter tomorrow will be a national holiday to be called Survival Night. And to make it worth your attendance I'll have an important announcement and free gifts for everyone."

"You see?" said Bernie to Beatrice. "He's got *six* inches of armor plate." But Beatrice was already up the stairs, taking Laban's arm and leading him back into the house. Bernie kicked a bucket. "Thanks, sis, for running out. You're a real trooper."

"I told you to quit, didn't I? You don't know when to quit. Forget about Laban for a change and live your own life, can't you?"

"Don't worry about me. Worry about yourself. You're not doing so hot."

"Is this what you call hot? Trying to set the world on fire? Hey, everybody, look at Bernie. The man who killed Lincoln, Kennedy, Mahatma Gandhi and Jesus Christ. Look at him, everybody."

Bernie's face was tight. He pulled his shirt away from his chest and flapped it in the sun. "For a little-girl traitor you've got a big mouth," he said.

"You want to know what's the matter with you? You ain't got no body control. You still need a nursemaid to take you to the potty, to keep you from drinking cleaning fluid or playing with matches." He turned and went into the garage and slammed the door behind him. "And what's more," she shouted, "you have no sense of humor." The field hers, she surveyed the wreckage in misery. She felt like the little girl orphaned by an Indian raid, wandering aimlessly until the cavalry rescued her. Only there would be no cavalry.

The large, round wooden table supported by claw legs was covered with a green felt pad and lighted by a naked bulb hanging from the ceiling and swaying just above their heads. The rest of what used to be the survival shelter was in shadows that shifted as the bulb stirred. A breeze from an open window blew across Leah's brow, which was mantled like the others' with a green eye shade furnished, along with arm bands, by Laban. The six of them were sitting on wooden chairs with cane seats. Laban had provided four new decks of cards, poker chips, a bottle of bourbon, ice in a bucket, a pitcher of water and glasses. He had also set the rules: The ante was a quarter with a fifty-cent limit, and he was the banker.

Leah fingered the edge of a chip and settled down. She and Laban and Beatrice had played a great deal of poker during the winter. She had read Laban's books on poker. She had no intention of losing and would be merciless, especially toward Jackson Schwartz, who had to declare himself tonight. He had actually averted his eyes as he came in. He was there at Laban's invitation, not hers. All she required was that he say yes or no, nothing more; it didn't matter which. She examined his fair face under the eye shade. His nose was red and swollen. He looked like a farm boy stung by a bee, who'd come to town for the weekend and been lured into a professional game.

They were playing dealer's choice and Laban, choosing seven-card stud, dealt with exaggerated clumsiness. He took a deep gulp of whiskey, which Leah discounted. He could hold his liquor, and he drank only before he bet, to create the impression that he was getting careless. He was the only one she really had to worry about. The rest of them were mechanical toys programmed to lose. She couldn't help winning, in any event, because she had an ace in the hole. The game was the only thing on her mind.

Leah exposed her straight and Bernie turned in fury to Rachel. "If you hadn't stayed I'd have gotten my third queen. You go riding right along no matter who gets hurt."

"What are you talking about? I had you beat. Why didn't you get out? Don't be a poor loser."

"She's right, baby. If you can't stand the heat stay out of the kitchen. You people play like there's no tomorrow. Maybe you didn't hear the rules. No checks, no I.O.U.s, no lending. I started you each out with twenty-five bucks and that's all you're going to get. The moral is, Money doesn't grow on trees. The well does run dry. You'd better start knowing it."

"Old Ben Franklin. Big Daddy Warbucks," said Bernie. "How much is the banker allowed to lose? When does your well run dry?"

"Baby, I'm the Bank of America, insured to ten thousand dollars. The bank doesn't run dry. I'm a lamb waiting for you city wolves to eat me up alive."

"Laban," said Bernie, "meaning no disrespect, you're full of crap."

"That puts me in mind of a client story," said Laban. "This ninety-three-year-old millionaire lady. Nobody but one nephew took any interest in her for years. He kept her in his home with a battery of nurses. So she decided to draw a will in his favor. I went to the house and there was the old lady lying in bed on a bedpan. For years she just lay there on her bedpan. She was skin and bones with two cataracts staring under a green eye shade like ours. I yelled in her ear, 'How you making out?' She yelled back, 'Fine, mister. I want to leave my money to Billie. Billie's a fine boy and I want him to get my money.' I had her sign the will before two of the nurses and as I left, there they were, changing bedpans."

"All of which means what?" said Bernie.

"All of which means that money talks louder than diarrhea. If you think I'm full of crap, why do you take so much of it?"

"Is that what you think?" said Bernie. "What a miserable soul you've got. Take your goddamn money and shove it. Dangle your carrots somewhere else."

"That's the spirit," said Laban. "I'll look around. Maybe I can find a nice ditch for you to dig." He turned to Jackson, who was shuffling and reshuffling the cards. "How you doing, baby? You like being with the Labans on a Saturday night?"

Jackson ducked his head but there was no place to hide. "Yes, sir," he said.

"You hear that?" said Laban. "That's what I like about this boy. He respects his elders. Jackson baby, I like your style."

"Yes, sir."

"And that's why, since my money's going begging, I'm going to proposition you. I've noticed you making cow eyes at my little daughter Leah. Don't think I haven't. You thought the old man was asleep at the switch, slobbering over his gums, but he's been following your train of thought right along. Yes, sir. I've watched Leah, in her shy, modest way eying you back. You're both fine, sturdy people and you'll breed hefty kids to carry on the Laban line. I want you to know here and now you've got Laban's blessing and when you've got that you don't go away empty-handed. What I mean to say, Jackson baby, is that Laban's with you all the way. I consider you like one of my own flesh and blood."

"You have my sympathies, Jackson," said Bernie.

"Laban," said Rachel, "there's a limit and it's fifty cents, remember?"

"All right, the gallery's heard from. Let's hear what the principals have to say. Jackson Schwartz, do you want to take this pretty little woman for your lawful wedded wife? Before you answer, here's my deal. First, you get to call me Laban like the rest of the family. No more sirs. Second, I've got this contract here." He reached under his chair and produced a thin leather case, which he unzipped. He extracted some documents. "It's already signed by Warder, Silvermintz and me. A partnership agreement, baby, that needs one more signature—yours. Marry Leah and you get ten percent starting now, which means at least twenty grand a year. If you don't marry her you get five thousand dollars and a boot out of the firm. On your wedding day your percentage jumps to fifteen percent. If Leah dies, if you get divorced, or Leah so wishes at any time in writing, you're finished and you get the five Gs and the boot. Now hear this, baby. When old man Laban dies you get a twenty-five-percent slice of the pot roast. All you've got to do is marry my little girl, keep her alive and happy, and you're on the gravy train. What do you say?"

Leah watched Jackson's hands shuffling the cards. He kept dividing them into two equal piles, bending them back with strong, broad thumbs and riffling them over and over as though his hands had been mechanized into a permanent single function. His eyelids blinked rapidly at her but she wasn't taking any secret messages.

"Am I to understand, Mr. Laban, that you're offering me a partnership in the firm?"

"I told you, baby. You've got style. No nonsense about you. First things first and no beating around the bush. I'm offering you a partnership and along with it, as a kind of tickler you might say, you get my beautiful little girl. Marry Leah and you don't get a measly twenty cows or fifty sheep or a handful of beads. You get a partnership, savvy? Lots of wampum."

"What are you waiting for, Jackson?" said Bernie. "The moon in June? April in Paris? The great white father has spoken. He's treating you like a son."

Jackson riffled the cards and set them down in a neat pile.

Laban reached over and cut. "Your deal," he said, and Jackson, quoting from memory, said, "Seven-card stud." He dealt the cards but nobody picked them up.

"Come on, baby," said Laban. "Get off the pot."

Jackson looked at Leah and blushed red. "Sir, I was going to ask Leah to marry me tonight even before you raised the question. If it's all right with her, I'll be honored to marry her. I'd consider myself the luckiest man on earth."

"Leah, what do you think of that? He'd marry you if you didn't have a penny. A straight-shooter. This is what I'd call a happy meeting of the minds."

"Sure," said Bernie. "Happy families are all alike. Hey, Schwartz, come on. Now's your chance. Don't let him take you with his disappearing ink. Tell him what he can do with his contract."

"I'll be your wife. I accept your offer," said Leah. She was lying in the bottom of a boat in the middle of a lake, staring up at an unclouded sky. If she didn't move she could lie there forever. She examined the blond hairs on the back of Jackson's hand.

"Good. It's settled," said Laban. He shoved the contract under Jackson's nose and offered him a pen. "Sign, baby, all four copies. Life is a bowl of cherries. You really know how to pick them." Jackson took the pen, dropped it on the table, picked it up and signed, and Laban inserted three copies in his case, zipped it and lowered it to the floor. Jackson folded one copy, making sure the edges were even, and put it in the inside breast pocket of his coat, which was hanging on the chair. His forehead was beaded with perspiration. "Let's play poker," said Laban.

"Just a minute," said Bernie. "I think Schwartz should know the facts of life. Schwartz, don't let his Western clothes fool you. This is an Oriental potentate who's got the power of life and death over souls. You're selling yourself short. The least you should get is your weight in rubies and emeralds. After all, Leah's no ordinary girl. She's a mystic princess, a valuable medium of exchange. Think, Schwartz. Don't let your heart rule your head."

"Jackson baby," said Laban. "We understand each other? Any time she wants she can blow the whistle."

Jackson wiped his face. "Yes, sir. Leah can terminate the agreement any time she wants to. I understand that."

"That's the ticket," said Laban. "*Quid pro quo.* Nobody gets something for nothing."

Bernie turned on Leah. "Just like that?" he said. "Enough's enough. Leah, are you in love with *this?*"

"I'll answer that," said Laban. "Your question's out of order. We're talking marriage. Property rights. We lawyers say, Never go courting when you're drunk on wine or love."

"You lawyers." Bernie pointed a finger at Beatrice. "Is that how you married her?"

Laban reached out and patted Beatrice's hand. "Beatrice baby? She's a luxury. I can afford a little love."

"The rules are different for the king, is that it? He can marry for love but nobody else."

"That's right, baby."

"And Mother? What noble instinct made you lower yourself to her?"

Laban winked at Bernie and shook his head. "If you want to know the truth, I made an honest woman of her. You were on the way."

Saliva coated Bernie's lips and he spit words. "Go to hell."

"It's nothing to be ashamed of. Your mama was a wonderful woman. What do you say we play the game?"

Bernie picked up his cards and threw them across the room. He stood up and said, "If I'm a bastard you're a son of a bitch."

"Now is that a way to talk about your grandmother?"

Bernie turned and walked out and Laban watched him go. "A nervous boy," he said, and got up to pick up the cards.

Beatrice leaned toward Leah and kissed her on the cheek. "I think it's wonderful. I hope you'll be very happy," she said.

Rachel couldn't believe that Jackson and Leah could go on playing as if nothing had happened. Jackson took Laban at his word and acted like a member of the family. He rolled up his shirt sleeves, loosened his tie, filled his glass with bourbon and was having himself a victory celebration. She eyed his swollen nose with satisfaction. That, at least, was something to remember her by. She wasn't his enemy any more. It wasn't worth it; it would be like hating a scarecrow because his rags flapped in the breeze. To know Jackson was simply to ignore him. As far as she was concerned, brother-in-law-to-be or not, he'd ceased to exist. With Leah she could only stand helplessly by. What Laban had said must be true. Leah had no use for love. Maybe she saw herself being business manager of a rich man's home life while he swam in warm waters off his yacht. Maybe she was being Bette Davis in one of those devotions to family; the image of the starched white collar, black silk dress and prim lips, sharp nose and huge, floating eyes, was unnerving. She might be secretly fashioning leg and arm shackles, getting ready to beat the family into submission with leaded sticks. After this, who knew what Leah was capable of? All Jackson had to do was step out of line and Leah could lower the boom. It was a cruel contract, and Rachel worried about her father. Was he becoming a sick comedian? He wasn't having that much fun. His face sagged and his skin was gray with fatigue.

And what demands would Leah make in the privacy of the bedroom? Rachel, working herself into a state, looked for telltale lines of sadism around Leah's mouth and saw only the reflection of her own lips. Things had come to a pretty pass when she could suspect her twin of meanness. After all, Jackson had asked for whatever he would get, and it was an old story for merchant princes of the twentieth century to find their manhood being nibbled away at home while they ordered people around at work. She washed her hands of the whole business. Everybody else seemed well satisfied except Bernie, and he'd already abandoned the ship. Beatrice was murmuring about wedding announcements and Laban was setting the date. It was all over but the shouting.

"We'll have the wedding in three weeks," said Laban. "Bernie and Rachel will be going back to school soon and I wouldn't want anybody to miss out. You got folks?"

Jackson lowered his eyes. "My family lives in New York. I don't think they can get away." They don't speak the English, thought Rachel excitedly. They live in a cold-water flat in

Spanish Harlem. His father's an escaped murderer and his mother walks the streets. Whatever they were, she despised Jackson all over again.

"You crazy? Sure they can get away. Why can't they? Their son's getting married, baby. If they need plane fare, I'll send it to them. What's the problem? What's your papa's line of work? I'll call his boss."

She watched Jackson mulling it around in his mind. He could say his father had an important deal on the fire. His mother was dying of cancer. His sister was a congenital idiot and his parents couldn't leave her alone for a minute. "I guess they can come," said Jackson.

"Sure they can," said Laban. He gave Jackson a straight, hard look. Maybe, Rachel prayed, a miracle could happen. It still wasn't too late for Laban to pull the rug out from under. They could all have a big laugh. "What did you say your father did?" said Laban.

Jackson cleared his throat. "He works in a bakery. He's a baker." He continued rapidly. "My brother works in the post office."

"Okay, so what's the sweat? Send them a telegram. They come to the wedding. In fact, they come a week early on me, all expenses paid. Tell them they've struck it rich, right?"

"All right, sir."

"Laban."

"I mean Laban."

"Good boy. One of the family," Laban said, and punched him on the arm. "We'll show them a wedding that'll knock their eyes out. You'll have a night to brag about to your grandchildren."

Rachel had an old theory about Laban. Hands off the children, she fancied him muttering. You're only their father so don't mother them. Now he was killing Leah with kindness. He reminded her of a television play in which a rich father kept getting his son off the hook. Finally, the son committed a robbery for kicks and, escaping, murdered a watchman. The father tried to get him to Mexico and when the police caught them, all he could say was, "He's my son. What else could I do?" Laban, don't you know you were right before? There's no such thing as a bad marriage, only bad spouses.

"Sir— I mean Laban," said Jackson, "three weeks is awful short notice. We'll have to look around for an apartment. I just live in a room. And we'll have to make wedding arrangements."

"Forget it, baby. It's all arranged. I've already talked to my good friend, Rabbi Sam Isaacson. Everything's set. As far as living quarters go, what's wrong with this place? There's plenty of room. One big happy family, that's us. I'll tell you what. You move into Leah's room and Rachel can sleep in the guest room until she goes back to school."

"What am I, a stray alley cat?" said Rachel. The idea of Jackson smearing her childhood objects with his meaty thumbs was revolting. He'd hang his pin-striped suits in her closet, look out her window at her tree.

"All right, baby," said Laban. "We'll fix up the Schwartzes in the guest room. It'll do fine."

It was no victory. Rachel made up her mind. Whatever happened she would not sleep in the same house as Jackson, not for one minute. She could ignore him all right, but only if she didn't have to see him. She felt like a baby bird that had fallen out of its nest and was looking for bread crumbs in snow, and when she found some a starling would come along with his ball-point beak and eat them up. She had the feeling, the unhappiest one yet, that Laban, pushing the wedding along and her out of the house, was fully aware that the whole setup was strictly for the birds. She looked him over. He really didn't look like himself. He didn't have the old bounce. Twins ran in families. Maybe he had a double he'd never told them about who'd taken his place, and he was lying bound and gagged in a basement somewhere, praying for rescue. Things like that happened to people with money. "Laban," she said, "what did you always use to call Leah and me when we were little?"

Laban smiled. "The two-timers. What made you think of that?"

Rachel shook her head. He'd passed the test. He was Laban all right, and she had no more excuses for him.

At noon on Sunday Laban wore a white linen dressing gown, a silken, fringed prayer shawl around his shoulders, a black skull-cap on his head and Provincetown sandals on his feet. Leah, engaged to be married, had nevertheless gotten up at dawn, while the house was dark, and had prepared boiled chicken, matzo balls in soup, brisket, gefüllte fish, potato pancakes, carrot pudding. She'd bought braided white bread and a box of matzos the day before. Beatrice had hidden bits of Tip Top bread around the house and Laban, in robe, shawl and skullcap, carrying a soup-spoon in one hand and chicken feathers in the other, traveled around to unleaven the house. Beatrice went before him with a lighted candle to suggest the hiding places. When all the pieces of bread had been discovered, Laban put them in his spoon, wrapped and tied the spoon in a rag. He dropped the package into the fireplace and set it on fire, and they went in to dinner.

"With a Jew like you for a father, who needs synagogues?" said Bernie.

"Take it easy, baby," said Laban. "I've got that old-time religion. A man's got to start somewhere."

"How about in the mind, or is that too obvious? Ceremony without faith is a refinement of barbarism only you could think of."

Laban went to the front door and threw it open and called, "He that's hungry come and eat. He that's needy come and join our Pesach." He returned to the table and poured a glass of wine at an empty place. "For Elijah," he said. "If ever a squabbling pack of Jews needed the old boy, it's us. Leah, bring out the *chomets*." She rose and waited to be told what they were. "The unleavened bread, baby." She brought in the bread and handed it to Bernie. "Here you are. According to the custom all *chomets* must be sold to a non-Jew before Pesach. A penny'll do it. When Pesach's over you can sell it back to me for a profit."

Bernie ignored the offering. "In the first place, it doesn't happen to be Pesach," he said. "In the second place, it's one thing to be irreligious; it's something else to be profane. You get a hodgepodge of ingredients out of a book and make a half-baked devil's food cake out of them. You won't let anything alone. You smear mud even on the temple walls."

"We're here to learn," said Laban, filling the wine glasses. "Better late than never. Listen to my story. I sat in the synagogue when I was a boy and listened to the babel. I went to the Hebrew teacher until I was thirteen and memorized sounds. I gave a speech and became a Jew, they told me, so I sat with the men, *tallis*ed and *t'fillin*ed, and mouthed more sounds. I became rich so I moved up to the Reform temple and listened to reviews of best sellers. I became an expert on *Marjorie Morningstar* and *Goodbye, Columbus*. When the rabbi said to stand, I stood; when he said to sit, I sat. I sneaked guilty looks at the prayer book. I had coffee and cake. I became richer so I moved up to the Ethical Society and listened to ways to pour new wine in old bottles. I was kicked out for sneaking guilty looks at the Bible. I'm telling you, baby, I'm as anxious to be a Jew as you are, but it isn't easy."

"It isn't easy for you to read handwriting on the wall so I'll spell it out for you. There are babies in your dishwater. There's duty, conscience, good will, commitment, love. Ever hear of them?"

Laban studied Bernie. He adjusted his prayer shawl on his shoulders. "Bernie baby," he said, "since you're a one man Salvation Army you should learn to travel on your stomach. Pass the chicken."

Leah chewed at a matzo ball. It tasted like the inside of an undercooked biscuit. The boiled chicken was like wrapping paper. She swallowed, a spy devouring cooking secrets, and checked her watch, having decided to make a basket lunch and drive to Crevecoeur's farm in midafternoon.

After dinner, Laban assembled them in the living room. He'd made a new will, which he held in his hand. On the mantelpiece over the fireplace he had placed two polished brass candlesticks that held slender white candles. He lit them and drew the curtains. In the dimness, in prayer shawl and skullcap, he was the rabbi of an ancient sect, laying down the law to his disciples. "As you know, Bernie is the philosopher in the family. However I've developed a few ideas of my own that will explain my new will. I'm weary of hearing about the failings of the American. Sure he's killed off Indians, cattle-boated and lynched Negroes, but like Bernie's pointed out, genocide is an old story. The American's kept plugging. He believes that if God didn't create natural laws, man has to invent them. He keeps trying his damnedest to remember that all two-legged animals are men even though historical precedents are against him."

"Laban has spoken," said Bernie. "How about circus animals, Ringmaster?"

"And that's why I've decided to leave my money to Leah. She's going to get married and have children. She's going to preserve our way of life. She's proving that she can be more than a toady in her father's house, by bringing new Americans into the world. Blessed be the fruit of Leah's womb."

"Laban, you treat your slaves nice," said Bernie. "See what he thinks of you, Leah?"

Leah saw chunks of bills bound with fat rubberbands lining the walls and ceiling, muffling the creaks and groans of the old house. The money meant nothing to her. It was paper with ugly faces on it. Whatever tricks Laban played with it were of no concern to her.

Laban bent over and clutched at his stomach. His face twisted and he let out a grunt. Beatrice jumped up and hurried to him.

She kneeled at his chair and wrapped him in her arms. "I'll get the pills," she said and hurried out. Laban rocked back and forth, the tassels of his shawl swaying.

"What's wrong now?" said Bernie. "Is this one of your jokes?"

Beatrice returned with a pill box and a glass of water. Eyes closed, Laban swallowed the pill and kept rocking. In a moment he sat back, breathing heavily, and Beatrice wiped his face with her handkerchief. Laban opened his eyes and smiled.

Bernie stood over him. "You all right?" he said. He sounded angry.

"Sure, baby," said Laban. "You want to arm wrestle?"

Bernie shrugged. "If you're so damned rich, why aren't you healthy?" he said.

"You know better than that," said Laban. "How can you tell an American businessman without his ulcer?"

"Laban," said Rachel, "all I can say is, it would be a dirty trick if anything happened to you before I get another crack at your money."

"Don't worry. The germ isn't made that can get to Laban. Remember, I've got a bulletproof car."

Leah prepared ham-and-cheese sandwiches and a jar of potato salad, and put them into a wicker basket with two bottles of burgundy. She left the house at four o'clock and drove to Crevecoeur's farm. Even after consulting his map she might have missed the turn-off onto the dirt road if Charles hadn't been sitting in the dust waiting for her. His beard was filling out, and in his old clothes, his face rust-colored with sun, he looked like a beggar.

He settled in the seat beside her. "I didn't tell you when I was coming," she said. "How long have you been waiting?"

"Not too long. I didn't want you to go right by. People do. You'd better drive slowly. The road's rutted."

"I would have found my way."

"I'm sure you would, but sitting in the sun's become my major pastime."

They rocked along. Trees crowded thickly on either side and

embowered the road with leafy overhanging branches that scratched at the roof of the car. The filtered light transformed the baked earth into what seemed to be a soft, tan gelatin and she felt capsulated and at the same time freed from cyclone fences and television aerials. She was the last woman on earth with the last man, and she remembered with detachment her initial uneasiness with Crevecoeur.

She hardly needed him to show her the way. They forded a shallow stream and the water gurgled against the wheels. The trees closed in until the branches seemed impenetrable, but she drove on without hesitation and the leaves parted before her face, whispering at the windshield. The road ended about fifty feet from a slanted, weather-beaten frame farmhouse with peaked windows and a pointed roof. She stopped the car and sat still. Crevecoeur smiled. "It's a dump but it's home."

She shook her head. "I like it."

The ground around the house was overgrown with weeds and wild flowers in random profusion. A cluster of orange milkweed caught her eye and she reached down and picked a bouquet while Crevecoeur waited at the door with the wicker basket.

Inside, the house was dark and damp and smelled of mildew. The front room was furnished with an easy chair that sagged on broken springs, packed bales of hay in the corners and a pot-bellied stove with its door open. The walls were bare. "It's not Windsor Castle, is it?" said Crevecoeur.

She set the basket on a bale of hay and said, "I want to see it all."

He led her into the kitchen. It had a gray metal sink with a rusty-handled pump, an old wooden icebox and a knobbed chest of drawers that went higher than her head. Somebody must have worked on the wood with linseed oil, for it glowed darkly. She opened the icebox without waiting for permission and saw a melting block of ice, a carton of milk, a slab of cheese and a wilted head of lettuce. "One minute," she said, and went back to get her wicker basket. She put the food and wine in the icebox. "What's next?" He led her to a small back room, where there was a rake, a shovel and an axe, and a small hand mill on a wooden table. Next to the table was a bag of corn, and she dipped her hand into the kernels. "May I?"

"If you like. It's hard work. Here's a paper bag."

She put the corn into the mill and turned the handle until an inch of grain had flowed into the bag.

"Would you like to see the barn?"

"All right," she said, and they left the house by a back door that complained of rusty hinges. After a few yards they were in a meadow. She took off her sandals and sank her toes into the turf. She ran ahead of him toward the barn until she stepped on a pile of cow dung, which brought her up short. By the time Crevecoeur got to her she was sitting down scraping her foot against the grass.

"I should have warned you," he said. "Buffalo chips."

She swiped a few more times at the grass and stood up. The barn had a dirt floor and was cluttered with cans, a roll of sign paper, a palette and other materials she recognized. "Your father's been very kind. Come look at my handiwork," he said. Reluctantly she went to the easel and stared at a collection of black dashes, curves and wriggles on white paper. "I'll never make much of a sign painter, I'm afraid."

Fighting to keep her mind clear, she turned away. "Is there a loft?"

"Yes. I sleep there on hot nights." She climbed the ladder after him, hugging the round rungs with the soft balls of her feet. His bed was two bales of hay pushed together. Two more bales huddled in another corner. Part of the floor was broken through and they had to step around the hole. Crevecoeur stood gazing out an opening at the rear of the loft. "You can see for miles from here," he said. "If you're interested in seeing for miles."

Below, some distance away, she saw two toy cows flicking their tails, in a meadow that merged into the hazy grayness of further meadows beyond. She hugged the scene, cows and all, to her breast. "Could we go visit them?"

"They'll be flattered," said Crevecoeur. "They don't get many visitors." She felt his eyes on her but turned to the ladder without looking at him. She climbed down and he followed her and they started across the field. The sun was warm on her skin and a breeze tugged at her blouse. Her clothes clogged her pores and she envied the animals their nakedness.

"Cattle are nice people," said Crevecoeur. "They come from the best stock. The Hindus worshiped them and made it a crime to kill them. Do you think it's a crime?"

"I eat beef," she replied calmly. "We had it when you came to dinner." She wished he wouldn't talk. In the country she had a right to expect silence.

When they reached the cows she reached up to pat one on the head. He had a diamond-shaped spot between his eyes and a spongy, flesh-colored boil of a nose. He rolled a round eye at her. "This bull is Trigger," said Crevecoeur. "I'm glad you don't hold anything against him."

"Why should I?"

"It was his factory that manufactured the manure."

She looked at her flaked toes. "It's his meadow, not mine."

"It's my meadow. If you want it, I'll give it to you," he said.

"Thank you. Have you any other animals?"

"These aren't mine. They're my neighbor's, a working farmer. All I've got is two of everything in my head waiting for the Flood." She stroked the dip at Trigger's haunch; it was hot and taut as a drum in the sun. When she didn't answer, he went on. "I haven't any livestock because I wouldn't know what to do with them. I'm on a desert island trying to find out what a man does with nothing to do."

"I suppose he starts talking to himself," said Leah. "I'm ready to go back if you are."

"All right," he said. They walked toward the house. "I warned you," he said. "It's not much of a farm."

When they reached the house a faded black automobile was parked in front of the house. "Ronnie's back," said Crevecoeur. "He's been sketching at the river front for some Biblical painting he has in mind."

Inside the house, Ronnie was sitting on the floor propped against a bale of hay, munching one of her sandwiches. A bottle of wine was standing open beside him. He was dressed in a paint-spattered work shirt with the sleeves rolled to his biceps, and his blue-grained work pants were cut off raggedly at the knees. The calves of his legs were smoothly turned and she vibrated to the rhythm of his sprawled limbs.

"Ronnie, you remember Leah," said Crevecoeur.

"Hello," he said, without getting up. He tilted the wine bottle at his lips. "That's Leah's wine and sandwich. You might say thanks," said Crevecoeur.

"That's all right," said Leah quickly.

"Thank you," said Ronnie, staring at the floor.

"How'd the sketches go?" asked Crevecoeur.

"Okay."

Leah felt aroused. She had the sense that Ronnie and she belonged there, that Crevecoeur was the outsider. She felt compelled to fill in Ronnie's silences. "What are you working on? Charles says it's a Biblical scene."

He chewed on the sandwich and Crevecoeur said, "Gideon and his soldiers. You know, where some of them lap water from their hands like dogs and others get down on their knees to drink. I've been meaning to ask you, Ronnie. How are you going to make the two groups look different?"

"You know better than that," said Ronnie.

"Do I? I guess I do." Crevecoeur turned to Leah. "Ronnie hates to talk about his stuff."

"I don't blame him," said Leah. "Could I see something you've done?"

Ronnie shrugged. "If you like," he said without moving. "There's a finished one upstairs."

"I'll take you," said Crevecoeur. As they went up, he said, "Ronnie has a good heart but it's hard for him to show it. He's really a nice guy."

"He doesn't require any explanation."

"He'll be happy to hear it. He's afraid to let people know how much he wants to be liked. He's like a rich man, always suspicious of the basis for people's friendship."

"Is he suspicious of you?"

"You sound as though you already know the answer. I guess he is. But it isn't all one-sided. He didn't have to come."

"Why did he?"

"To paint, for one thing. This is a nice place to paint. For another, maybe he needs to learn to live with me as much as I do with him."

"He didn't want to go to the sit-in. Why did you make him?"

"I didn't make him. I suppose he realized a Negro can't be a loner. If he buries himself in art he can still be dug up by one white man's calling him 'nigger.' "

"That's your opinion."

"That's right. I'm getting the impression you don't approve of me. Why did you come out here?"

"To see the farm," she said.

They passed through a room containing two cots and a bureau and went into Ronnie's studio. On an easel in the center was a large, elongated stretch of canvas with perhaps forty children standing in three rows. From the heads of those in the last row grew the stems of huge, round, red flowers. The children were dressed in bright shades of red, orange, blue and green. They had pearly-gray-colored faces; each had sunken black eyes, puffy elliptical cheeks, sensuous lips and a heavy-nostriled nose. Their faces, sharply delineated, were too old for their bodies.

"You notice the color of their skin?" asked Crevecoeur. "Always the same whoever he paints."

"They're very sad," she said.

"They're beyond sadness. To be sad they'd have to have known some joy. They were born not to live but to die, like mosquitoes or flies."

"Ronnie didn't tell you that," she said.

"That's true. Ronnie doesn't discuss his paintings."

When they came downstairs Ronnie was standing at the open door looking out. He didn't turn when they entered. "I liked the painting," she said to his back.

He turned. "Are you through upstairs?" he asked.

She was unwilling to let him go. "I saw you drawing charcoal sketches at Tangletown," she said. "Would you do one of me?"

He wouldn't look at her. "They're ten dollars apiece," he said.

"I'll pay."

"I'll get my sketch pad," he said, and went upstairs.

Crevecoeur picked up the half-empty bottle of wine. "Shall I get the sandwiches?"

"I'd rather wait until he finishes."

"All right. We'll wait." Crevecoeur extended the bottle. "You want any of this?"

Conscious of the imprint of Ronnie's lips, she accepted the bottle and took a swallow. She handed it back and Crevecoeur drank. He watched her silently. She had finally run him out of words. Ronnie returned with a sketch pad and a stick of charcoal. "It'd be better outside," he said.

"Then we'll go outside." She opened her purse and found a ten-dollar bill. "Here's your money."

He took it and shoved it in his pocket and they went outside. "Shall I sit on the ground?" she said. "I wouldn't mind."

"No, just stand there," he said. He drew quickly, huddled on the ground against the side of the house, darting quick glances at her face. Every time he looked up she challenged his eyes, but he might have been examining a fence post. He worked swiftly; in a few minutes he ripped off the sheet and handed it to her, then turned and went into the house.

Crevecoeur stood at her side, and together they looked at the sketch. It had bold, economical strokes. "He's caught you," said Crevecoeur. "Big dark eyes and strong eyebrows."

Shadows were lengthening across the ground and it would soon be dark. Leah felt a swell of peace rising within her as she looked at the sketch. She let out her breath and it was as though she'd been holding it for an hour. She felt hungry. "Let's take the food and wine to the barn and look out over the fields."

He came back with the wicker basket and they went to the barn. She followed him up the ladder. They sat on the bales of hay, and when he started to reach inside the basket she said, "No, not yet. Let's just lie here for a while." She sprawled forward on her stomach and let the breeze play with her hair. He sat beside her.

"You ever hear of *Letters from an American Farmer?*" he said.

"No. Should I?"

"It was written by a namesake of mine who lived around the Revolutionary period. He made a catalogue of our cruelties and innocences. I wanted to reach out and touch his sky and earth, but I can't, because of the cruel part. It hasn't worked for me. I think it might for you."

Leah turned over on her back, facing him. "You talk too much," she said. She pulled out his shirt and slid her hand inside, fingers spread over his heart. She felt it beating. She inserted her other hand, locked her arms around his waist and pulled him forward. His beard tickled her chin. He was nothing if not innocent. She twisted on her side and rammed her body against him, pinned his leg with hers, drove her lips across his mouth. Her fingernails roweled his side. Tame animals could make love if they were shown how. His body lay before her like a peaceful town bedded down for the night, and she was the marauder galloping through. Leah vaulted on top of him, knees straddling the straw, and hung over him like a veterinarian dealing with a stallion. She bent down and blotted out his face. Making quick work of him, she fell back on her bale of hay to catch the breeze. It was lovely.

Crevecoeur lay still where she'd left him. She hoped that by unfettering the rest of him she'd bridled his tongue.

"It may surprise you to know that most male animals indulge in courtship," he began. "Take your friend Trigger. He hangs around a cow for two days before she's in heat. And then, when the time comes, he licks, smells, paws and horns the ground, throws dirt over his back, rubs his head and neck on the ground. The buck rabbit goes around chasing the doe, who runs until she wants him to catch her. They weave around the whole country-side. They stop and pretend to feed, and as soon as the buck makes a rush, the doe is off again. Even when she's ready, he walks away with his tail in the air. He wants it in the worst way, but it has to be the right way."

Leah lay with her eyes closed. His words were a swarm of insects that buzzed about her head but never alighted. She was sleepy and it was a strain to move her lips. Nevertheless, since it no longer mattered, she made conversation. "I'm sorry if I rushed you," she said. "I don't believe in making a man wait. I don't believe in teasing."

"Aren't you the honorable one?" He shook his head. "I'm sorry. I didn't have to let you twist my arm. I'm acting like a spoiled brat who has to play the game his way or not at all. It's not your fault if I have a juvenile notion of how tides move and plants grow. God knows what I expected. Maybe stars on the nipples. Teach me to love dirt, Leah. I'm willing to learn."

She smiled into the fading light. Once he'd made her uneasy, tempted her to curl up in his manhood, but never again. She'd tasted his flesh, swallowed it whole, and discovered he was good for nothing but fertilizer. "I'm sorry, no," she said. "I don't have time. I'm getting married in three weeks to Jackson Schwartz. Will you come to the wedding?"

He sat up. His feet thumped on the floor and his hand closed hard about her arm. She expected to be hurt and waited patiently, but he let her go. "No offense intended," he said, "but I had to do that. I had to make sure once again that you're real. I've been alone too much. If you're going to marry Jackson Schwartz, what have you been doing, shadowboxing for the main event? Getting a little premarital experience? Excuse me—I'm being vain. You don't need any lessons."

"You're the first man who's ever had me," she said.

"Come on now, Leah. You're the girl who shoots from the hip. Why did you make love? You owe me an explanation, if not for myself, at least for the sake of what we haven't meant to each other."

"I did because I did."

"I won't settle for that. You had a reason and I want to know what it was."

"Because I liked your body."

"You hated my body. You couldn't wait to get rid of it. Is that it? You hate men and that's why you're marrying Jackson Schwartz? What about love? Did you think you might be marrying the wrong man? I'm throwing you a lifeline. Why don't you take it? Love seals cracks in the spirit."

"I don't love you. I never pretended I did."

"Very commendable. Very honest. Leah, you're a fraud. You've got an idea of yourself that makes me glad it's hidden behind a steel door with double padlocks. I don't want to understand you. It might make me a little sick."

In the dusk birds had begun calling to each other, and she listened to their trills and chatter. She picked out a piece of straw and held it to her cheek like a flower. "I'd better go now," she said.

"You're right," he said. "Somebody might get the right idea." He looked down at her body sprawled on the hay, her skirt hiked to her waist. She let him look. "I hope you and Jackson Schwartz will be very happy," he said.

"Thank you," she said and sat up.

He looked away. With his beard and his sober profile, he looked like an Orthodox rabbi at a funeral. "I mean it," he said.

It was hot. The cool summer had finally turned mean and Rachel perspired while she dressed. She cursed Laban as she slipped her short-sleeved dress over her head. He'd heard of air conditioning because his bulletproof car had it, and Beatrice's Chevy had it—and besides, ignorance was no defense, especially for a lawyer. He hadn't air-conditioned the house because he said that a man's home was his castle and who ever heard of air-conditioning a castle? He would live like a king and sweat like a king. So they sweated, and she chewed Laban out. When I want to be an ice cube, he said, I'll turn the house into a refrigerator. Her skin felt sticky enough to trap flies instead of men.

Life owed her something after Jackson Schwartz. Just thinking of him made her double her fist and jab at the mirror. Hot or not, she was determined to look good enough to eat. A delicious morsel in a cool dress that was beginning to spot under the arms.

They were going to visit Crevecoeur. In the car she said to Laban, "A rich man like you letting his daughter sweat like a pig. You should be ashamed of yourself. You should wrap me in cellophane and keep me safe from seepage."

"Read the signs on plastic bags," said Laban. " 'Keep away from children.' " He turned on the air conditioning, and the fan swept cold air along her bare legs.

She jumped. "I forgot," she said. "I'm in good hands with my sugar daddy."

"That's right. You're my little girl. I tell you what. Why don't we just keep moving? Shake the dust of this town. Change our names and start a new life. Mr. and Mrs. Pharaoh. Like Bernie says, the king can do no wrong. Would you like that?"

"Gee, Laban, I don't know. This is so sudden. I don't know what to say. I like you and all that but I've never thought of teaming up with an older man. I guess not. My daughter would be my half sister. What would the neighbors say?"

"I forgot about the neighbors. I guess it's not such a good idea," he said, and his tone disturbed her. Was he getting sensitive about his age? He was the eternal youth; he should know that. Besides he was only fifty and people lived easily now until eighty and ninety. Look at Churchill and his whiskey and cigars. She hated the idea of worrying about what she said to him, and realized what a luxury it was to have a father to whom she could say anything. She preferred it even to an air-conditioned house.

He brightened up after a moment and she relaxed. He was just playing the rebuffed father-suitor. "Now that we've got Leah settled, what about you? Too bad we're not Mormons. Then you could both marry Jackson Schwartz. He wouldn't mind that a bit."

"I guess he wouldn't," said Rachel. "Even if one of his wives can beat him up."

"You did a nice job, baby. It did me good to see Schwartz's nose."

Rachel couldn't help saying, "Yet you think that Leah, a partnership in your firm and every slimy ambition his heartless heart is set on are coming to him."

"Don't whip dead horses in midstream. You'll have to take my word that Leah could do worse. Schwartz is an all-American Jewish boy who can be bought, so I bought him. He'll give Leah her money's worth. More marriages are made in smoke-filled rooms than in heaven. Not everybody wants the same thing." He grinned. "You can hustle for your own mate. Not that I don't stand ready to stick a finger in the pie. How about Crevecoeur? It's not too late to carve out another partnership."

"If you make me one of your games I'll hit you in the nose."

"I believe it. I don't know if I could. Crevecoeur keeps his cards close to his chest." Laban looked pained. "Give me credit for knowing hearts aren't my long suit."

"You and your meeting of the minds," she said.

"Minds, yes; hearts, no. Hearts don't fool around. They're too busy pumping blood. Whoever said love is a game is crazy in the head. I don't mess with love. You can get killed doing that."

Clutching for her infancy, she said, "Would it kill you to show a little affection for your children? You're our papa."

He looked at her quickly and she wished she could withdraw her words.

"That's what I called my father," he said. "Papa." She became anxious. He hardly ever mentioned his parents. "It's too bad they died before you were born," he said. "Papa was a landowner and cattle buyer in the old country and got out during a pogrom. In America he wound up selling junk in the alleys off a wagon pulled by an old spotted horse, King Solomon. It was so sway-backed its belly scraped the ground. Papa kept him in the garage. I spent hours looking at that horse. I even loved the smell. We

were the only family on the block with a horse. Papa couldn't
feed us, so my mother worked in a factory as a seamstress. He
was a religious man and wore a *yamulke* and prayed all the time
he wasn't out peddling. One day Solomon flipped over and died
in one of the alleys and Papa gave up trying to earn a living. He
sat in a corner and rocked all day over his Bible. Mama got us
through. I worked after school. Newspapers, then in a clothing
store. Mama never let me quit school. She had the Jewish
mother's fanaticism about her son being a professional man, and
she was willing to starve to make me one. Papa didn't express
himself one way or another. He left decisions up to God and
Mama. A landowner without land, he sat in his corner and
prayed. Mama was old-fashioned enough to believe his soul was
valuable household property and she never complained. She
would point at him and say, That's what you should be, a learned
man. She preserved his dignity through fifteen years of non-
support and let the rich ladies worry about general indignities. I
never went hungry. I had patches in my pants but no holes. My
parents' lives were forfeit. They could keep body and soul
together only by one being the body and the other the soul."

Laban shook his head. "I'm disturbing you, ain't I? People are
amused by a clown only as long as he doesn't mean a word he
says. There's nothing more painful than when he tries to get
serious."

"Of course you're disturbing me. What does all that mean?
Why do you have to treat us like kids at a circus? Why do you
ward us off with parodies?" Rachel was close to tears. She'd
imagined Laban springing full-blown into manhood. He'd never
given her any history or tradition in which to place him. His
image was a series of current events. He had no right to have
once been a little boy who cried for his mama during the night,
who stared round-eyed at his papa's mangy horse, who wore
patches on his knees.

"I don't parody, baby. It may seem that way because we live in
a 'pro' world. I'm acting in good faith. I just don't happen to
believe life should be subdivided and stuck into little locked
prefabs, with one key for each man. What should I be doing—

building a body beautiful and preparing for the Olympics, or fasting on a board of nails? Christ knew the score. He performed magical tricks and told riddles. He moved around and kept himself busy. He didn't sit in a corner mumbling to himself."

"Your father did."

"He couldn't help it. Like I said, his life was forfeit."

Rachel's mind swam with iridescent fishes. They darted about and flicked their tails in her face. Where in a hodgepodge of hypnotism and green eye shades were Laban's apologies and best wishes? She was depressed and wished she'd never gotten him started. As long as she could consider him a crazy mixed-up adult she could be indulgent, but his attempt to give his runaway rocket a control system made him seem as pathetic as yogurt eaters or flagpole sitters or goldfish swallowers. "Without experts we'd be back living in caves," she said. "You want a world of bunglers."

"Baby, I'm a pro. I've got a key to the law building. But I want to see it unlocked and the law books checked out for thirty days by doctors and carpenters. And I demand the same privilege with their hypodermics and doweling jigs. The locked doors are mirages made of hot desert air. Look. Man invented the wheel. He put it on a wagon, filled the wagon with popular mechanics and went out to rescue damsels in distress over their dishpan hands. He didn't live, breathe, eat wheels for the rest of his life."

It was silly to feel sorry for him or to give him an inch. He was a professional arguer. His actions spoke louder than his words. She thought of Beatrice in her bosomless dress. "I suppose," she said, "dressing up like an Egyptian is your way of not eating wheels."

"That's what they wore," he said.

All she could think of were Laban's fishes, and she felt herself being sucked in. They were having such a good time swimming around, and she felt miserable standing on the shore, a lifeguard drowning them with dirty looks, afraid to go in because they were strange creatures with goggle eyes, and hardly worth saving besides. Laban was jumping from a diving board in a one-piece black-and-white-striped bathing suit, scissoring his legs as he dropped feet first.

"Take our friend, Crevecoeur," said Laban. "Here's a boy who locks himself out of his own room. He's not lazy. He's got a fine legal mind. I told him he could come to work for me in a minute and he looked at me like I was offering him a handful of snakes. 'Law is good for a lawyer,' I said, and you know what he answered? 'It's a matter of degree.' "

"He's young," she said recklessly. "He can afford to be foolish."

Laban smiled. "You've got it backwards. Gaffers can afford to be foolish because only they have the time. The young people should be out making the world safe for the gaffers."

She had enough. The reference to Crevecoeur reminded her that she had her own fish to fry. She looked out the window as they turned off the main highway onto a gutted dirt road muddied by rain. She realized with annoyance that she was overdressed. She should have been warned by Laban's old clothes and his pants tucked into laced leather boots. He could have warned her, but it was too good a joke to see her clicking off in high heels to high tea on the landscaped terrace of a country estate. She was in for a hard time. Every activity had its uniform and it wasn't easy to be a good sport in the wrong one.

The car had to ford several shallow streams between dips in the road and Laban charged them to get across. Her bones felt like dice in a cup, and not being forfeit—not just yet—she attended to the business of keeping her body and soul together. They drove to within fifty feet of a weather-beaten, decayed farmhouse that looked like salvage from a world war. She stared at the intervening mud and at her white pumps. "Am I supposed to walk through that?"

"Take off your shoes. Live a little."

"Why don't you carry me? Make believe you're Sir Walter Raleigh."

"You see any coupons on my back? You're not crippled. My daughter's got to learn to stand on her own two feet."

"Boy," she said. "Pity the poor, standing pregnant women if you rode the buses."

"Get pregnant and try me. Beat Leah to it and I might even leave you my money. I've got a special place in my heart for mothers." He got out, opened the rear door and pulled out a wicker basket of fried chicken and potato salad—courtesy of Leah—and a bottle of whiskey, and slopped toward the door. He stopped and looked back at her. "I'll tell Crevecoeur to carry you," he said.

"No you don't," she said and quickly removed her shoes. She stepped into the mud and made a face as it oozed through her toes. She took a hop and sank in to her ankles. By the time she looked up, the door had opened and Crevecoeur, bearded, sunburned and naked to the waist, was watching her. She made it inside, perspiration rolling down her armpits, and dared him to laugh, but he seemed displeased at the sight of her. She became conscious of the fact that she hadn't been invited. Looking for a place to sit down, she chose a grubby easy chair in the corner. The seat was sprung and she thudded down as though it had been pulled out from under her. She stood up. There was a bale of hay against the wall and she sat on that. She examined her feet. They were coated with caramel-colored muck and she'd made tracks coming in, but she didn't care. The place was filthy and swarming with insects. She said good-bye to her dress.

"I've got some dig stuff in the car. I'll be right back," said Laban.

"I'll help you," said Crevecoeur.

"No, I can manage. Stay put."

Crevecoeur, with his back to her, looked out the door. Thanks for the warm welcome, buster, she thought. "I was in the neighborhood and thought I'd drop in," she said, scraping her feet against the hay. If he wouldn't give her a rag she wouldn't ask for one. She decided that she hated him. Any ex-roommate of Jackson's was no friend of hers. Besides, he was a filthy bum.

He turned and said, "This is hardly a place for a lady." She looked down at her dress and gritted her teeth. Who did he think he was, El Aurens?

"Listen, Charlie," she said. "You once invited me, remember?"

He refused to bend. He remained poor but proud. She tried to fit him into the proper pigeonhole and all she could think of was *Gone with the Wind*, Clark Gable putting Vivien Leigh in her place, and that would never do. What had happened to the Van Heflin she used to know and love? "I warned you it was a dump," he said.

"Why don't you think of me as a missionary? We've brought chicken and potato salad, true, but we're really bringing you the Word."

"Thanks for the food. What's the word?"

"The word," she said, "is 'courtesy.' I'd like something to wipe my feet with."

"Sorry. I'm so used to dirt I didn't notice." He went into the next room and came back with some newspaper. She scrubbed at her skin. Actually, the mud felt good, like salve, and she wriggled her toes. She didn't really care about it and was willing to forgive and forget if he'd stop putting her off with manners.

Laban returned with a pick, two shovels and a bucket. "I'm off to inspect the dig," he said, and disappeared.

"Have I offended you in some way?" she asked.

"Of course not. Why do you ask?"

"You're handling me with kid gloves and I hate to be treated like the brittle type. Loosen up, Charlie. I knew you when."

"When what?"

"When you were loose. Smile, Charlie. To know me is to love me."

"I'm sure of that," he said. "The word for the Laban family is love."

His tone was so savage that she looked at him in alarm. "What do you have against the Laban family?"

He sat down beside her. "I'm sorry. I had no right to say that and I don't know why I did. Let's start over."

"If I'd known you disliked me I wouldn't have come. My skin isn't as thick as you think."

He touched her hand. "You have very nice skin. Soft and

fragile. Skin anyone would love to touch. It's no excuse, but I've had a tough week."

She felt better. She was never one to limp on a healed leg; one nice word and she was ready to wag her tail. "What's wrong?" she said. "Is there anything I can do to help?"

He finally smiled and she gazed happily at his prune of a face restored to benevolence. "I'll be all right," he said. "I need a change of scenery and your father's providing that."

"What's he up to?"

"We've got the ruins of an old concrete house in back. Parts of the walls are left standing. Mr. Laban thinks there's something interesting underneath."

"He would. What does he think he'll find—buried treasure? Laban was a very urban little boy. All he had a chance to explore were garbage dumps."

"He says there are some underground slave cells in this area. It's a scientific venture."

"Naturally. Science is a man's way of acting like a boy. I suppose you're going to help him."

"Ronnie and I both. Your father's enthusiasm is infectious."

"You remember my brother Bernie?" Crevecoeur nodded. "He'd call it a disease," said Rachel. "Who's Ronnie?"

"Ronnie Birch. He lives here with me. He's a painter."

"I've heard about your sign painting."

"No. He's a real painter. An artist painter."

"Is that so? Will I get to meet him?"

"I don't see why not."

Laban came back with another load of tools, which he dumped on the floor. There was another pick and shovel, a ball of string, several bricklayer's trowels, whisk brooms and two small hand-shovels. "That's everything from the car," he said. "The dig looks fine."

"I hear you're looking for a direct route to India," said Rachel.

"You know," said Laban, "there just might be an Indian burial mound out there. I figure we'll start our right-angle trenches today. We make them three feet wide and four feet deep, according to the book. Of course we'll leave balks."

"Of course," said Rachel. "He's crazy," she said to Crevecoeur. "Don't let him gull you. He doesn't know archeology from a hole in the ground."

"Wait and see. You'll laugh from the other side of your mouth," said Laban. "Where's Ronnie? Let's have a drink and get to work."

"He's upstairs. I'll get him," said Crevecoeur.

Laban took off his sport shirt. "This house needs air conditioning," he said. "Maybe I'll buy the boys a ton-and-a-half." He laughed. "Like sending refrigerators to the Congo."

"Charity begins at home, Laban."

"Baby, my money's booby-trapped. Reach for it and it'll blow up in your face."

Rachel sighed. "You and your money. Don't you know your children are your jewels?"

"When they start speaking my language, I'll consider them precious. Meanwhile, money talks."

Rachel's eyes wandered around the room. "Look at Crevecoeur," she said. "He seems to be doing all right. The sun rises and sets for him without any help from the U. S. Treasury. How much does it take?"

"I'm with you, baby. Like Lincoln said, God must love poor people because he made so many of them. Me, I'll have to rock along the best I can and try to sneak through the eye of that needle."

Crevecoeur came in with a Negro. Rachel was aware of knotting up as though a strange animal had bounded into the room. She couldn't help herself, though he was slight and round-shouldered and had a puppet-like face with a wide mouth and cupped nostrils. He looked as harmless as "Cuddles" Sakall and yet her breath came faster and her body was triggered into wariness. She resisted jumping up and sticking her hand out to show what a democrat she was. "Pleased to meet you, Ronnie," she said, without waiting to be introduced. She tried so hard not to be the Southern lady that her face snarled like the backlash of a fishing line.

"Hello," he said, not looking at her. She felt like a threatened turtle and pulled in her neck. Had he seen through her already? His face seemed vaguely familiar. Had she met him before and didn't remember? She thought of the Negroes at Laban's trial. They were all too old, or so she'd believed at the time. She had a good heart, really she did. Was this how a good heart behaved?

Ronnie had turned to Laban. "I see you brought the gear, Mr. Laban. You're a man of your word."

"You better believe it, baby. I'm taking over this territory, see, and nobody quits the organization except feet first. Play ball and you'll be on easy street. Got the messsage?"

"You're the boss, Mr. Laban," said Ronnie.

"You hear what he said?" said Laban to Crevecoeur.

"You're the boss, Mr. Laban," said Crevecoeur.

"Okay. You're good boys and you'll wind up driving Cadillacs. I'll take good care of you, just so you stay in line. You got any beefs, you come to Laban. You need anything—bread, dames—you come to Laban. Let's have a drink on it and get to work."

"I'll get the glasses," said Crevecoeur.

"Forget the glasses," said Laban. "From here on in we're blood brothers." He removed the seal from the whiskey bottle, pulled the cork and took a swallow. He passed it to Crevecoeur, who drank and passed it to Ronnie, who drank and thrust it at Rachel. She held it like a hot potato in her hand and they watched her. "Where does an alien go to register?" she said.

"Drink, baby, and you'll be water boy," said Laban.

She touched the bottle to her lips and returned it to Laban. "Fine," said Laban. "Ronnie, I've got a commission for you. Five hundred bucks for Rachel's picture. How do you like them apples? That's a lot of lettuce."

Ronnie looked at his feet. "It's a lot of lettuce, Mr. Laban."

The bottle came around to Rachel again and this time she took a swallow. The warm whiskey almost made her gag. "What if I don't want my picture painted?" she said.

"You'll be immortal, baby," said Laban.

"What if I don't want to be immortal?" She had visions of Ronnie's banked eyes examining her like a customs inspector; at the same time she would be at the farm as much as she liked. In any event she knew she couldn't refuse and admit she was afraid to look Ronnie in the eye. "All right," she said. "If Ronnie's willing, I am."

"I can be bought, Mr. Laban," said Ronnie.

"It's a deal. Ronnie, you and I'll take the first shift. We'll leave Crevecoeur to entertain the doll. Then he'll come out and spell us. Rachel baby, don't forget the water. It's hot out there."

"You're the boss, Mr. Laban," said Rachel. They collected the tools and went out the door.

Crevecoeur smiled and sat down beside her. "Your father's quite a fellow," he said.

She was angry. "You're patronizing him. Both of you," she said.

"Why do you say that? *He's* the patron. He's paying Ronnie five hundred dollars for your picture."

"You know what I mean. Humoring his projects. It makes you feel ten feet tall."

"We like your father, and believe me, Ronnie doesn't like many people. Mr. Laban's good for Ronnie."

"You see?" she lashed out. "That proves it. What a crummy thing to say. Laban isn't a bag of tricks for the amusement of the underprivileged. He's a human being."

"Who said he wasn't?" said Crevecoeur. "I have a lot of respect for him. He's an unusual man." He hesitated. "Or don't you think so?"

He caught her retreating from her own remark and she was covered with confusion. "Of course I do," she said, and added inanely, "but he's my father." She began to feel like Margaret O'Brien as a little orphan, enormous eyes in a dewdrop face, brought to the home of her crusty maiden aunt, Edna Mae Oliver, and waiting in a darkened parlor for Edna to appear and say, 'Just as I expected. I knew my sister who ran off with a drunken sailor would produce a scrawny half-starved brat. Don't just sit there. Stand up and let me take a good look at you.' Edna would turn out to have a heart of gold, but meanwhile Margaret must cower among china cups on fragile tables she mustn't touch, praying for the chunky, dimply self-confidence of Shirley Temple, who would have tap-danced on the parquet floor the minute she arrived, compelling Edna to break out the fudge squares and milk and the unwilling smile.

"Ronnie disturbs you," said Crevecoeur. His voice was reasonably gentle, and she thought with amazement, He doesn't hate me. He's on my side, or at least he's willing to lead me by the hand. She relinquished her maturity and was willing to remain Margaret O'Brien.

"I guess he does," she said. "The way he treated Laban made me upset. It doesn't make me look very good, does it?"

"Don't worry about it. Ronnie's trying to be an artist rather than a Negro. It's not easy."

"Wouldn't it make more sense for him to try to be both? To try to be what he is?"

"He doesn't see it that way. Take your father—he's a lawyer, not a white lawyer. The white is taken for granted."

"My father has labels too. He's a Jewish lawyer."

"And I was a Protestant lawyer. It's not the same thing. It's an artificial coupling, and the Negro's is real. Why else would Ronnie's attitude have bothered you?"

She sought refuge in honesty. "I must be a very small person. At school I bum around with the few Negro girls in the dorm and break my arm patting myself on the back. I rant and rave about how monstrous the Southerners are. All the time I wear a sign around my neck: Get down on your hands and knees, little Negress; I let you share my tennis racket but not my humanity. I'm a nasty fraud."

"You're too hard on yourself. Ronnie has the right to be amused at your father and you've the right to be annoyed at his amusement. It's not your fault if history makes it wrong."

She thanked him with her eyes. Their glances met and held, even as she was aware she was even using honesty to be dishonest. She wanted to impress him in any way she could. "How about you?" she said. "How did you overcome history?"

"What makes you think I have? Because Ronnie's living out here? It's not much better than your dormitory. We both try too hard. That's what I meant about your father. He's not on the make. Ronnie gets more than a kick out of him—he really likes him."

She took a deep breath. "Thank you for being so nice to me. I envy Ronnie. If anybody can make a go of it, you can."

"Sure," he said and waved his arm at the room. "You call this making a go of it?"

"Of course I do," she said, her confidence restored on firmer ground. "It took a lot of courage to throw up the law because you didn't believe in it and try something else. He who fights and runs away lives to fight another day."

"Now you're the one that's being nice," said Crevecoeur. "Another way of looking at it is that I'm holed up with blankets over my head, punch-drunk, jabbing at shadows."

"Is that the way you look at it?" she said. "I don't believe it." She was happy at being the confidante of his self-doubts. A strong man made love by a confession of his weaknesses, and nobody, not even Crevecoeur himself, would ever convince her he wasn't strong.

"I'm not sure what I believe. I came out here to find out, and so far it hasn't done me much good. I've even developed a nostalgia for the law. All the things I despised—the make-believe seriousness; the exposure of people at their most selfish, irrational, vindictive moments; the mock war of words—have a perverse fascination for me. Did you know your father offered me a job?"

"Yes, he told me."

"I was tempted. Sitting here doing nothing makes me feel like a prisoner of war in solitary. Everything gets blurred and even working on a rock pile seems like too good a chance to miss."

"Or painting signs or working on a dig?" she said. She put her hand on his. Things were going well. She felt tender.

"I suppose. I guess I've learned something. I'm not cut out for living off the land."

"You can always go back to law if you really feel you want to. I still say it takes courage to find out what you really want to do and do it."

"The courage of a spoiled brat."

"You're being too hard on yourself," she said. "I'm quoting you. How did you feel when you first came out here? You must have had plenty of good reasons."

"Oh, I did. All sorts of fantasies. In the heart of every lawyer lies the wreck of a frustrated poet. I think Clarence Darrow said that. He neglected to warn me that trying to live like a poet wrecks a lawyer. I saw this article about some Americans who went to Tahiti to live. There was a cover picture of one of them lying on a white beach in swimming trunks holding a Tahitian girl. He turned out to be the owner of an import-export business. Others owned resort hotels, laundries, and one was starting a bank. They all said they were escaping the conformity of American life. The businessman—the American missionary, and welcomed too—trying to escape from materialism by bringing it with him. All right, I figured. So I ran in a circle to America's backside to make those Tahitian Americans honest. I do without in the land that despises its plenty. Mine was a very grand and new idea. Revolting *to* poverty—how brilliant. I would go stand on my mountain not because it was there but because I could look down on the busy ants. So where am I? Helping your father dig holes in the ground."

Rachel squeezed his docile hand. She was warm inside as well as out. Let him live on a farm or fly to the moon. He'd forgotten the most important thing, the love of a good woman, and he made her feel good. She wondered if those ragged men with placards hanging from their shoulders had women to go home to? Scientific tests had proved that women were fifty percent more effective than beds of nails. "I think you're wonderful," she said. "You refuse to settle for a mess of pottage."

"Is that enough?"

She leaned forward and held up her face to him, a few inches away. He looked at her offering for a moment of silence and then put his hands on her shoulders. He dipped forward and she closed her eyes as he kissed her on the mouth. His beard tickled her chin. His lips and hands dropped away and she opened her eyes. "There's more," she said. "There's me." To make it sound less demanding, she added, "And there's Ronnie."

He sat back, and she regretted her spasm of delicacy. "Ronnie," he said. "Another of my myths. A case of mistaken identity. You ever hear of Crevecoeur the writer?"

"*Letters from an American Farmer*," she said promptly. "I've heard of it in American Lit but I never read it. Is he your ancestor? I meant to ask."

"No. I wish he were. He had some genes I could use. He tells this story about being invited to a neighboring plantation. Along the way he sees this swarm of vultures around a tree. He fires his gun at them and as they fly away he sees a Negro suspended in a cage, left to die. The birds have pecked out his eyes and laid bare his cheekbones but he's still alive, and he begs Crevecoeur for water. Crevecoeur says if he had another ball for his gun he would have shot him. He finds a container of sorts, fills it with water and puts it to the Negro's lips. The Negro thanks him and begs for poison. Crevecoeur asks him how long he's been there and the Negro says, 'Two days and me no die; the birds, the birds; aaah me.' Crevecoeur goes on to the planter's house and learns that the slave is being punished for having killed the overseer of the plantation. They tell him the laws of self-preservation made such executions necessary."

Rachel buried her face in her hands. "Charlie, that's an awful story."

"After that every Negro I saw on the street was in a cage begging to die. I wanted to rush up and offer him water. So I offered Ronnie a place to paint and I wind up envying him. He has a purpose. He's an artist. And I'm still looking. What does one do? Merge corporations? Play golf? Take off a shoe and pound it at the United Nations? Drink beer before the television set? Chant 'We Shall Overcome'? Turn tan in a motel swimming pool?"

"Laban plays games," said Rachel. "In a way you remind me of him."

Crevecoeur shook his head. "I don't see how. That may work for him but I don't play very well." He stood up. "Forgive me for bending your ear. You've been patient."

"I loved every minute of it."

"Okay," he said. "I at least know enough to quit while I'm ahead. We'd better get out to the dig. I promised your father."

"I'm ready," she said, jumping up. "Where's the water pail?"

It didn't take long to ruin her dress, but Rachel wouldn't have given up her job as bucket girl for anything. She filled the bucket with the loose dirt and rocks they threw from the trenches and carried it over to a pile she'd made to one side. Her shoulders ached and her fingers were blistered, sweat and dirt made streaks all over her, but she felt wonderful and had to give Laban, the old goat, his due. If the project made any sense it would have been ridiculous. As it was, they'd worked themselves into a state of euphoria and had entered into a secret pact that no one would complain or ask why. The men were caked with dirt and almost indistinguishable from each other; she thought that an easy solution to racial problems would be for everyone to wear masks and gloves. Ronnie seemed as gay as a bird and she felt no tension at all with him. Even Crevecoeur's cage story didn't dampen her spirits. She had great hopes for the human race.

Two men would work while one rested. Two trenches were almost finished; Laban was beginning to conk out but he wouldn't admit it. Esthetically Rachel considered the holes quite fine, with their even, vertical walls. Good enough to be graves if nothing turned up—and nothing had, not a fragment of pottery, an old coin, an arrowhead. There was nothing but a foundation under the walls. Gone were visions of a treasure trove. She looked at her spattered dress and laughed aloud. The dig made her feel like a little girl.

Ronnie heaved himself out of one trench and they went over to the other and watched Crevecoeur scraping with a hand shovel. He looked up. "Enough?" he said.

"That little hunk right there," said Laban.

Crevecoeur scraped. "Enough?"

"Fine. Next time we'll start on the other two outside trenches, then move out from the inside. We've got a first-class dig, so get this, see?"—he was head of the mob again—"You're good boys. You do what you're told. I ain't a fink. Tonight you live it up.

Hot food and baths at the big boss's house. That's Laban for you. All heart."

"It's a wonderful idea," said Rachel. She could have hugged Laban.

Crevecoeur looked at her and hesitated. "I appreciate it, Mr. Laban, but I'm sorry. I can't make it."

"Can't make it—you crazy? You want me to send the word out on you? Sure you can make it."

"I really can't, Mr. Laban. I would if I could."

With one sweep Crevecoeur had flattened her house of cards. She was no longer happy, and she glowered at Laban for wrecking her dress, matting her hair with dirt and cracking her fingernails. She looked at Crevecoeur's filthy beard and thought she'd never seen anybody so repulsive in her life. One shove and he'd be where he belonged, in a hole with the other rats. She could cover him with dirt if he liked being dirty. When he tried to climb out she'd hit him with the shovel. Did he have another girl in mind? Somebody who disliked taking baths as much as he did? What did she know about him? Why on earth did she expect anything from him? She was a big girl now and remembered that if she lay down with dogs she got up with fleas. She scratched her shoulder blade and pretended it was Crevecoeur's eyes.

Laban turned to Ronnie. "How about you, baby? You going to thumb your nose at the old man? You think he's had it too?"

Ronnie looked at Crevecoeur. "I don't know, Mr. Laban."

"What's to know? The organization's still behind me, see? Don't look at Crevecoeur. A pin's stuck in his name. Look here, you guy. I'll put bubbles in your bath."

"Go ahead, Ronnie," said Crevecoeur. "I'd go if I could. Don't worry about me."

"Who's worried about you?" said Ronnie quickly. "I'll be glad to go, Mr. Laban."

"That's more like it. You had me worried. Two defections in one day and I'm dead. I'm in Siberia." He took Crevecoeur's arm. "Come on, baby. To show you there's no hard feelings we'll unload the tools and look at your plain Egyptians."

As they went toward the barn she lagged behind, testing the way with her bare feet, and Crevecoeur dropped back to join her. She concentrated her attention on the terrain. "I want you to know," he said, "how much our talk meant to me."

"Glad to oblige, Charlie. Whenever you need a shoulder to cry on, call on me." It came out nastier than she intended. After all, he had a privilege against self-incrimination and she hadn't warned him anything he said would be used against him.

"I'll do that. I hope you'll visit the farm often. Whenever you like you'll be welcome—but I don't have to tell you that."

"Oh, I'll be here. Ronnie's painting my picture, remember? But I appreciate your offer anyway. The same goes for me. Our house is always open to you."

He said slowly, "I'm sorry about tonight."

"Don't apologize to me. Laban invited you."

They walked on in silence and she realized she was being silly. Back to her old trick of exaggerating. Crevecoeur liked her and wanted to see more of her; she should be grateful for crumbs. What she really wanted was to see how he acted with Leah—a childish wagging of a doctored tooth. She put her hand on his forearm. "It's been a wonderful day," she said.

On the trip home, with Ronnie in the back seat, Laban said to Rachel, "Schwartz and I are catching a plane tonight. We're going to the West Coast on a deposition. When we get back, he's moving into the guest room."

"Before the wedding?"

"Sure. He's around all the time anyway. Why should he keep traveling back and forth? It cuts down his office productivity."

"Since when have you become an efficiency expert?" she said bitterly. The thought of seeing Jackson in his pajamas nauseated her. "Can't you wait until the wedding? Then Bernie and I'll clear out. We'll be going back to school."

"He's going to be your brother-in-law, baby. You'll have to learn to live with him."

"That's what you think," she said and made up her mind: "Either he goes or I go."

Laban smiled. "Think it over. We won't be back for three days. It's only for a couple of weeks. You won't desert your sister. She's the only one you've got."

"I'm warning you, Laban. I won't be here when you get back."

"We'll see. I'm calling your hand."

"Go ahead. Play around. Shuffle our lives like a deck of cards. What do you care if you make me miserable?"

"Come on, it's not that bad. You're my chip off the old block. You're not going to let a fourflusher like Schwartz bluff you out. Use your imagination."

In a way he was right. She could really do a job on Schwartz. Tie knots in his bed sheets. Steal his underwear. Put a snake in his bed. Salt his coffee. The possibilities were endless. She shook her head; she was through playing it Laban's way. It was time she remembered she was a woman, and there was such a thing as a strategic withdrawal. Her problem was more than Jackson. She couldn't bear to hang around watching them prepare for the wedding, and she'd thought of a wonderful place to go. She turned around, to be nice to Ronnie.

The dishes, cups and saucers were white china, the crystal winked with refractions of light, the tablecloth was an expanse of snow and Leah couldn't take her eyes off Ronnie's hands, moving like brown-black birds on the table, glowing against the opaqueness of Jackson's blond hair and pale linen suit.

"Bernie, baby," said Laban, dressed in a going-away business suit, "you should visit the farm, shake those cobwebs out of your mind. Give you a fresh slant on life. Ask Rachel."

"Bernie would make a perfect farm boy," said Rachel.

Bernie wriggled his shoulders. "Think of how much forward motion it took to allow Crevecoeur the luxury of sitting the world out. Trees had to be cut, shipped, milled, shipped, distributed, sold, fastened with nails on a foundation that had to be dug. Food was grown, baked, canned, packaged, shipped and marketed. All that to let Crevecoeur spin his wheels."

"And for you to beat your gums," said Laban. "Don't forget that. What's so bad about going around in circles, baby? It gets you off the turnpike."

"To some people every bum's a hero because he's too lazy to shave. They think he's great every time he thumbs his nose at a Cadillac. Jesus dies on the cross, so creeps go around sticking their tongues out at gendarmes. Take Ronnie here. He's a painter. He's got his mission; coupled with Crevecoeur he joins the misfits. They both become nitrate on the back of a windowpane. Society's image is forced back on itself and it becomes uneasy, starts whining and bares its teeth."

"What have you got against Crevecoeur? What did he ever do to you?" said Rachel.

"Nothing. It's what he's doing to Ronnie. Tell me, Ronnie, for whose benefit did he prod you into the sit-in, his or yours?"

"Will you stop meddling," said Rachel, "in something that's none of your business?"

"Let him talk," said Laban. "It's his hobby. Everybody's entitled to a hobby."

"You should know. What's the matter, run out of costumes? How about it, Ronnie? Ever think about what Crevecoeur's doing to your public image?"

"I've got no public image," said Ronnie. He looked at Beatrice. "Would you please pass the butter, Mrs. Laban?" he said. She quickly handed him the dish.

"Of course you do. You're the Negro artist. That's your image."

Ronnie buttered a slice of bread. He sawed at the beef on his plate. "Butt out," he said.

Laban laughed. "You hear that, baby? Butt out."

Bernie bit his lower lip. "So that's the way it's going to be," he said. "I forgot. Rudeness is one of the prerogatives of the artist."

"That's enough," said Laban. "Ronnie's a guest in this house and don't you forget it. Save your cleverness for the family. Better yet, why don't you clean out your mind and start over? You're starting to fester. Be like the fox and his fleas. He puts a piece of moss in his mouth and backs into a pond until the fleas collect on the moss. Then he lets the moss go. No more fleas. No more bees in his bonnet. No more bats in his belfry."

"You'd love that. For me to be as much of an animal as you. I prefer being human, thank you. I'm proud of the fact that human beings, with nubs for teeth, skin for fur, flippers for wings, lungs for gills, have conquered the earth. You want parables? I'll give you one. Hans In Luck starts out with a lump of gold, trades it for a horse, the horse for a cow, the cow for a pig, the pig for a goose, the goose for a stone. Loaded down by the stone, he stoops to drink from a well and lets the stone fall in. He watches it disappear and jumps for joy. He cries that he's the luckiest man in the world for getting rid of his burden. You know what the stone is? Human intelligence. You know who Hans is? People like you."

While they waited for Laban to answer, Leah looked at Ronnie's hands. She wanted to crawl inside him and be safe until the blast of conversation was over. When the silence lengthened she turned to Laban. He seemed distant, as if Bernie's barrage had finally struck him deaf and dumb. He looked shrunken in his collar. Beatrice was standing over him but he waved her off. "Bernie," he said. "I'm going to Rabbi Isaacson's retreat next week end. I'd like you to go with me. Just you and me, father and son."

Bernie stared. "What have you got up your sleeve?"

"Nothing. A change of pace would be good for both of us."

"Forget it," said Bernie, looking down at his plate. "I'm perfectly happy the way I am. If you wanted to take me on a fishing expedition, you should have thought of it a long time ago."

"Bernie," said Rachel, "Laban's trying to be nice to you."

Laban took a deep breath and worked up a grin. "No, he's right. I can't pull the wool over his eyes. We've taken a vow of silence, just like the Catholics. It would have been a neat trick, shutting him up for a whole weekend."

"Why don't you tell the rabbi about your Passover service? He ought to get a big kick out of that. Be sure to take some candles with firecrackers in them."

"Why didn't I think of that?" said Laban. He looked at his watch. "Time to go, Schwartz. Call a cab, will you?"

Jackson, still as a graven image, jumped up and went to the phone. Leah realized he hadn't said a word throughout dinner, and wondered why his silence seemed so noisy.

"I can't get used to Laban's out-of-town trips," said Beatrice, settling in her chair. "The house seems empty without him." She smiled at Ronnie. "It's nice to have an overnight guest. Laban says you're painting Rachel's picture. I can't wait to see it. It must be wonderful to be able to paint. I have absolutely no talent."

"You've got female talents," said Bernie.

"Oh, you," said Beatrice. "Ronnie, maybe when you've finished with Rachel you can do me if it's all right with Laban."

"It's okay with me," said Ronnie.

Bernie eyed him. "Say, Ronnie," he said, "tell me. When Negroes get their slice of the pie, what are they going to do with it?"

"Don't you start again, Bernie," said Rachel.

"What am I starting? I'm asking a civil rights question. I'm interested in what Ronnie has to say. If he doesn't want to he can always notify me to butt out."

Ronnie didn't answer. "All right," said Bernie. "Then I'll tell you. You'll worry about filling up your leisure time, about your loss of individuality, whether you're really a success, whether the braces are helping the kid's teeth, whether the air-conditioner gives the baby colds, whether the nanny is loving enough, whether your friends invite you to only their big parties. You'll have two cars, an electric stove, refrigerator, can opener, toothbrush, shoe polisher, and you'll pile gadgets to the ceiling that you'll never take out of the crates. You worry me, Ronnie. Don't you want more than what we've got? Don't you have a message for me?"

"*I* have," said Rachel. "Drop dead. Ronnie's going to do just what he's doing now. Paint."

"That's true. I forgot about that. He'll sit out at the farm and paint. He'll let everybody else stew in their own TV-dinner juice."

Ronnie locked glances with Bernie and Bernie fidgeted with a spoon. "That's right," Ronnie said.

"We're not all as lucky as you," said Bernie. "What are the rest of us to do who aren't artists?"

"I wouldn't know."

"I do," said Rachel. "We start taking some of those gadgets out of the crates."

"Sidney Poitier's a doll," said Beatrice out of the blue, looking wildly from Ronnie to Bernie. "Did you see *Lilies of the Field?* Wasn't he wonderful in that? He won an Academy Award."

Rachel lay in the dark listening to Leah's even breathing. Very soon they would no longer share even the same room. Rachel fretted that it could well be the last of their joint properties to go, rather than the first. Between them—she blamed herself as much as Leah—they had constructed a narrow corridor down which they walked, suitcases in hand, in opposite directions. If either of them tried to look back now, she risked turning into salt and vinegar and everything not nice.

She blamed Jackson Schwartz, not because it was finally his fault, but because it was easier to pick on an outsider. The thought of him made her twist on the bed and bury her face in the pillow, and she felt better. She understood why primitive tribes killed strangers; it let them live with their hatefulness. It was comforting to displace so much of her emotional pool into such a shallow vessel. She saw his soul as a shriveled-up pea busily preserving itself in successive layers of pod. Just fashioning his image made her feel homeless, made her reach instinctively for her wallet to make sure she had her passport and wouldn't be shunted from border to border.

"Leah," she whispered. There was no answer or even a break in the rhythm of Leah's breathing, but Rachel refused to quit. "Leah, I know you're not asleep."

"What do you want?"

"I want to talk. God knows when we'll have another chance. I hardly see you anymore."

"You still like to exaggerate. We see each other every day."

"Not really. I want to help with the wedding. Is there anything I can do?"

"Certainly. You can spell Beatrice and me with the invitations. There's going to be over a thousand people."

"A thousand people! You're letting Laban get away with that? Who does he think he is, Cecil B. DeMille?"

"I wouldn't know. It's his affair and he can invite whomever he likes."

"Okay," said Rachel. "It's your funeral." It slipped out before she realized how it would sound. She would never convince Leah that she hadn't intended to be nasty. Her chances for rapport were fading fast. "I'd love to help with the invitations," she said. "I'll tell you what. Let's make a game out of it. We'll each draw thirteen letters out of a hat and keep count of the letter each name starts with. The one with the most common letter wins. Okay?"

"If it makes you happy."

"It'll be fun. You'll see. We've got to have a prize. What do you want to bet?"

"Whatever you like."

Since Leah put it that way, she'd like to have the wedding called off if she won. Rachel thought a moment. "Mother's gold wedding band. That should make it interesting."

"Since I'm the first to marry it should be mine anyway," said Leah. "But it's not that important. We'll bet the ring."

"No, you're right," said Rachel quickly. "I wasn't thinking.

You're entitled to it. We'll bet Muffin." Muffin was a stuffed aardvark they'd squabbled over as children.

"I have no use for it," said Leah. "It's yours."

"No," said Rachel stubbornly. "We'll bet Muffin."

"All right."

Rachel floundered in the face of Leah's detachment. As a child Leah had played hard, and Rachel refused to believe she'd turned into a complete spoilsport. Somewhere an imp must be waiting to be reborn. "Do you remember how we used to pin a mood chart to the wall? Every day we'd each make a dot to show how happy or sad we were. Mine would go up and down like the Himalayas while you stayed at sea level. Remember when we saw *Pinocchio?* I cried for a week when his ears turned donkey. I thought my line would never go up again."

"But it did."

"You said you'd be my nurse when we were big because I was always skinning my knees. You promised you would."

"A child will promise anything."

"I believed you. No matter what kind of life I imagined for myself, you were always in it."

"As your nurse?"

"Not always. We would climb mountains together, marry twin brothers, live in a duplex and advertise Doublemint gum— just so we were together."

"And now there's Jackson Schwartz. Is that what you're trying to tell me?"

"I realize we have to grow up sometime. I just hate to see us drifting apart the way we are."

"I'm not going anywhere. You're the one who went away."

"We begged you to come east to school with us—Bernie and I both. We went down on our hands and knees. I wish to God you'd come."

"Because of Jackson Schwartz?"

"Because of what staying at home has done to you. All right, because of him. I have nothing against him really. He's just not right for you."

"I think so."

"For the life of me I can't imagine why. What do you see in him?"

"What I'm looking for."

"What are you looking for? Tell me and maybe I'll shut up."

"I don't mind your chatter. Bernie and you like to talk."

"Don't treat me like this, Leah. Don't shut me out. Help me to understand. Do you love him?"

"He's very good-looking."

"Sure," said Rachel. "You'll look great walking into restaurants." She passed beyond restraint. "I'll tell you what else he is. He's insensitive. I don't think he'd hang children up by their thumbs but he wouldn't cut them down either. He has no sense of humor. All he'll laugh at are pratfalls. He won't ever drink too much and he'll watch his weight. He'll tell you where he goes at night. He won't ever quit his job but he'll go crazy if he's ten minutes late for work."

"Jackson said you didn't like him," said Leah. "He said it's because you made a play for him and he wouldn't play."

"He had the nerve to say that? He's a lying sneak. He tried to seduce me right in front of the house, knowing you were inside. Where do you think he got his swollen nose?"

"I prefer to believe Jackson's version. I know how much you like to make up stories."

"I give up," said Rachel. Her eyes were hot and dry. She was ready to cry. "You and Jackson will make a perfect pair. Two hearts that beat as one. I hope you'll be very happy together. All gondolas and Italian tenors in the moonlight."

"Thank you. That sounds very romantic. Good night."

Rachel lay on her back and stared upward into darkness. She'd made a real mess of things and gotten what she deserved. Maybe romanticism was her trouble and she was trying to live by childish rules in the grown-up world. Maybe she should throw away her heart and apply to IBM for a new one. Submit like Leah to an o-82 computer and let a punch card serve up her mate. Anyway, what did she really know about hearts that wasn't the tired language of songwriters? The heart was a muscle that pumped blood. She should settle for that. But her mind wouldn't let her. She saw her heart as a castle surrounded by ramparts, with archers at the crannies and a moat crossed by a drawbridge. It was impossible for anyone but a fairy-tale prince to get inside; who would ever try? Somebody. She had to believe in more than Jackson Schwartz.

She couldn't sleep. She still had to come to grips with the fact that Jackson was moving into the house. Soon the bedsprings would creak down the hall and Rachel would writhe on her conventual bed, feeling ravished by proxy. In the morning she'd be awakened by the swish of a toothbrush across those enameled teeth. The firing of his urine at the toilet bowl would riddle holes in her inner ears. It was intolerable, she'd told Laban, and he wouldn't listen to her. This time she'd show him that one of her idle threats could be put into action, that some people still believed there was honor in deserting a lost cause.

It was obviously the only thing to do. At the age of twenty, some five or six thousand years from the beginning of the world according to the Jewish calendar, she had to run away from home. She would put a few simple possessions (including Mother's wedding band, since all bets were off) in a duffel bag and hop a freight to Shangri-La, Oz, Wonderland or wherever grown-up children ran off to. She knew where she was going. She'd known all along. Home was where her heart might be unlocked with ease, and her heart was not here. She would drive Ronnie out in the morning and just stay. She saw herself running through the muddy fields, her hair blowing freely across her face, and she stumbled—not, as she first thought, over Laban's dig, but over Crevecoeur's foot. Why should she expect him to let her stay and complicate his life in the middle of his trying to disentangle it? Because she had to know if he would, was why. She'd make herself useful. She'd clean the place up. God, how the dust would fly. People would come from miles around to eat off the floor.

Then there was Ronnie. Think of the history they could make. She could see the lead article in *Ladies' Home Journal:* "The Aryan, the Jewess and the Negro." They would introduce a brand-new concept into social studies: the Eternal Ethnic Triangle. It would be an immediate sensation, topping the Beatles and even Lawrence Welk. They would authorize buttons, T-shirts, caps. They would dispense slide smears of compounded blood. They would franchise a parlor game, complete with three toy figures, a spinner to determine the number of spaces a player could move, and an elaborate cardboard track with plenty of returns to Go and extra-space advances. Their names would become as familiar as those of Mickey Mantle, Anne Frank and Sammy Davis. If Rachel landed on the square marked *Pogrom*, she would return to Go, but if Crevecoeur did, he'd go forward ten. If Ronnie hit Mississippi, it was back to Go; for Crevecoeur, forward ten; for Rachel, stay put. If they landed on Civil Rights Bill, back to Go for Crevecoeur; ten forward, Ronnie; stay put, Rachel. Junior League, We Reserve the Right, Cossacks, Hitler, Senator McCarthy, John Birch Society, Would You Want Rachel To Marry Ronnie? Lox and Bagels, Pigs' Knuckles, Hominy Grits, Auto-da-fé, Underground Railroad, Harlem, Black Muslim, Irgun, U.A.R., N.A.A.C.P., K.K.K., D.A.R., Nazi, A.D.A., The Pope. She couldn't lie still any longer. She had to talk to somebody. Late as it was, it was as good a time as any to break the news to Ronnie of the imminent invasion of his and Crevecoeur's privacy. If one of the natives was friendly, she might survive.

As she prepared to sneak out of bed, Leah got up and went to the bathroom. Rachel subsided in a sweat of impatience. She wouldn't want Leah to get the wrong idea. It might make Jackson look good. People found it easy to make two wrongs an inalienable right. She speculated. Leah might have been more affected by their conversation than she let on. It wasn't like her not to fall asleep as soon as her head hit the pillow. She couldn't be that blind to Jackson's defects. Rachel began to work up to another try at Leah but couldn't think of a new argument. How could one argue with a slide rule?

She listened for sounds from the bathroom but heard nothing. Leah was taking a long time. She decided not to wait any longer and went to the bathroom to prod her sister along. The door was open and the room was unlighted. She felt a little scared. Was Leah sitting in the dark? Maybe in concentrating on Jackson she'd forgotten Leah might be chewing internally on a private brand of misery. She switched on the light. Leah wasn't there. Rachel turned off the light, and as she stood in the darkness, a suspicion pricked her skin, dissolved and reformed in a mushroom-shaped cloud. She went downstairs to make sure Leah wasn't having a glass of milk. She checked the side porch before she slowly walked back up. She peeked into their bedroom to see if Leah was back in bed, and then, fighting herself every inch of the way, she moved down the hall to the closed door of the guest room. She knocked lightly and whispered, "Ronnie? You awake?"

She heard a hissing sound, a human sound of breath going the wrong way. "Ronnie, it's Rachel. I want to talk to you for a minute. It's very important."

The door opened and Ronnie, clear-eyed, making no pretense of having been asleep, stuck his head out. "What do you want?" he said.

"Could you come downstairs? There's something I've got to tell you. Please."

Ronnie blinked his eyes slowly, like shades being pulled down by a person in no hurry. "All right. I'll meet you downstairs," he said, and closed the door.

She returned to her bedroom and sat on the edge of the bed. In a few moments Leah walked in without saying a word. Rachel felt her throat closing and for a few seconds she stopped breathing. She fought back a cough, got up and walked downstairs. All she could think of was Pinocchio's ears growing longer, hairier, more pointed, and she moaned, No. She turned on a lamp and waited for Ronnie. He came into the living room dressed in rumpled striped pajamas that were much too large for him, and she thought, They're probably Crevecoeur's. To her horror she started giggling and Ronnie watched her grimly. "What's so funny?" he said. "What do you want?"

"Nothing's funny," she said. "I don't know what's wrong with me." She stopped laughing and moved into something even worse—hiccups.

"Well?"

"I'm in a terrible spot," she said, forcing words past her runaway glottis. "I can't stay in this house any more."

"Why tell me? What am I supposed to do about it?"

"You can help me. You really can."

He stared at her with low-fused, sullen eyes. "I don't know what you're talking about. Why can't you stay here?"

"I have reasons."

He made a gesture of impatience, like a man pushing aside papers on his desk. "It's none of my business what you do or why. We got nothing to say to each other."

She swallowed several times but it didn't do any good. She still had her hiccups. "Yes, we do," she said. "I want to live at the farm—just until my sister gets married. Then I'll go back to school and get out of your hair. Do you think it would be all right?"

"What you asking me for? It's not my farm. I told you, I don't care what you do."

"I couldn't if it was hateful to you. I don't want to mess anybody up. Can't we be friends, Ronnie?"

"Just like that," he said. He shrugged. "You're talking to the wrong guy. It doesn't matter what I want. I just got squatter's rights. Why don't you ask Crevecoeur?"

"I will but only if you don't mind. I just couldn't."

"It doesn't matter to me one way or the other."

"I'd be coming out a lot anyway for the painting," she said.

"Is that all you wanted?"

She hesitated and hiccuped. "I guess so," she said.

He turned and started to walk out, stopped and came back. "You want to get rid of your hiccups?" he said. He made it sound like a threat and she nodded quickly. "Get some water," he said. "Bend over until you can drink from the far rim of the glass. Good night."

"Good night and thank you, Ronnie," she said. She watched him go and then the tears sprang to her eyes. Crying, coughing, hiccuping she ran into the kitchen for water. She'd drive Laban's bulletproof car to the farm in the morning and make him come out to get it back. She'd be damned if she'd disappear without a ripple and let him off scot free. It was all his fault anyway. Everything was. As she bent over and the blood rushed to her face she prayed that Crevecoeur wouldn't humiliate her, would welcome her with open arms. If he didn't, she'd have to pack up her troubles and crawl back home with her head forevermore between her legs. No matter what, she couldn't finesse the wedding. Whatever Leah thought or did, she was still her sister.

Laban didn't come after the car for three days. In the meantime the sun was shining and Rachel made hay. She'd had fifty dollars. She bought an aluminum-framed cot and installed it in an upstairs room next to Crevecoeur's and Ronnie's bedroom. She bought the largest washtub she could find, which could do for both washing clothes and taking baths. She bought a mop, broom and dust pan. They already had buckets from Laban's dig. With the last of her money she got a cheap barbecue grill, a bag of charcoal briquettes, two bottles of California burgundy, three large T-bone steaks, two heads of lettuce, tomatoes, a box of salt and a bottle of oil-and-vinegar dressing.

Crevecoeur let her stay, but only after he tried to talk her out of it—for her own good, he said, as if he were a truant officer, inspecting her blue jeans, white blouse and red tennis shoes. She should realize it wasn't any picnic out there.

"I'm a big girl now. I know what I'm doing. Just tell me if you want me."

"Of course I want you. That's not the question."

"It is, as far as I'm concerned. Don't worry, I won't compromise you," she said and pulled her suitcase out of the car. He took it from her but made no move toward the house. "Ronnie says it's fine with him," she said.

"I said it was up to you and that's all I said," Ronnie stated and disappeared inside, leaving her to battle it out alone.

"I've got to know what it's all about," said Crevecoeur.

"Don't disappoint me, Charlie. I had you figured as the chivalrous type, who wouldn't ask questions of a lady in distress."

"I don't see any dragons chasing you. It'll more likely be your father with a horsewhip."

"Very nobly said. Is Laban worrying you? You should know him better than that. Much he cares."

"I think he cares a lot. I care a lot. I wouldn't want you to do anything you'll be sorry for."

"Listen, Charlie," she said. She couldn't take much more. "I'm not going to beg you but I'm desperate, I really am. I feel like your man in the cage getting his eyes pecked out." She swore that if she started crying again she'd rip out her tear glands and feed them to the pigeons.

He took her arm. "Let's go inside," he said, and she allowed herself to be led like a blind child. He put her bag down and they sat on a bale of hay. When he put his arm around her she leaned against him. "Now tell me what's wrong," he said.

"Jackson Schwartz is moving in for good," she said. "I can't live in the same house with him. I warned Laban I'd move out but he did it anyway. I can't go back." She lifted her head and looked at him. "It'll only be until the wedding. Then I'll go back to school."

He smiled. "It doesn't sound so terrible."

"It doesn't? Could you live with Jackson Schwartz?"

"I did for three years."

"Could you now?"

"I guess not." He looked around the room. "That cuts both ways. I can't imagine Schwartz living with me. But then I can't imagine you either, and here you are."

"And here I stay," she said fiercely, permitting no backsliding. Aware she was weakening her position but unable to help herself, she added, "There's more but I can't tell you. You'll have to take my word for it."

"Have you ever really looked at this place?" asked Crevecoeur. "You'll go nuts. It's filthy dirty but that isn't the half of it. It's got no insides. No bathroom, no electricity, no television set or radio, garbage disposal, dishwasher, vacuum cleaner or fan. Water comes from a pump that breaks your arm. Cockroaches, water bugs, mosquitoes, chiggers and rats. You still want to stay here?"

If he was trying to frighten her, he'd succeeded. She didn't know what she'd do if she saw a rat. "Women rode in the covered wagons, didn't they?" she said. "You can't scare me off."

"All right," he said, and smiled. "I'll get you a stick to keep by your bed. Just remember. I don't know what you're trying to prove but you don't have to prove anything to me. When you've had enough, say so."

"I'm not trying to prove anything," she said, and as if to peg the lie she tilted her face toward him. His hand came up and cupped her cheek as he looked at her.

"Sealed with a kiss," he said, and bent toward her lips. Beggars couldn't be choosers. She responded with all her moated, ramparted heart.

She set up the grill on a flat stretch of ground in front of the house. While she watched with pride the flame roared up and she felt like a princess caught in a spell, terrified that it might be broken. It wasn't true that the princess was better off being awakened. She remembered a magazine cartoon. The princess was sitting up in bed in the morning staring at a huge, grinning toad next to her, and the caption read: "You lied." All the fairy tales lied. Her prince was disheveled, bearded and wrinkle-faced. Frogs were blond, blue-eyed and handsome, in Brooks Brothers suits.

After a few minutes the fire died down, flickered and went

out. The briquettes weren't even singed. Too late she remembered there was some sort of fire-starting fluid. She tried again,
with the same result. Things were getting desperate. She had to
prove her value to the team. It was easier for women going across
the prairies; they had buffalo chips. Crevecoeur must have something for starting fires in the iron stove. In the house she found a
pile of loose straw and sticks in a corner. When she returned to
the grill with her arms full Crevecoeur was standing there, and
she dropped the load at his feet.

"Surprise," she said. "We're having steaks and wine for
dinner."

Crevecoeur looked at the grill. "Damn it, I wish you hadn't,"
he said and her heart plummeted from its high of the morning.

"Why not? I thought we'd celebrate my declaration of inde-
pendence. What's so bad about that? I got plenty of food for all
of us if you're worried about Ronnie."

"We can't afford steaks. I thought I'd made it clear we weren't
running a country club."

She refused to take him seriously and sidled up to him. "I
wanted to show my gratitude," she said in a small voice. "Don't
be angry with me."

"I don't want you buying anything like this grill for me again.
I'm no Jackson Schwartz."

"It won't happen again. I promise. Besides, I don't have any
more money. I'm completely at your mercy. Charlie," she said,
"it's such a little grill."

"Okay, just so it's understood. No more."

She nodded. "Will you help me start the fire?" she said. "I'm
having all sorts of trouble."

The floors were hopeless but she tried anyway. She pumped
water until her arm ached, and splashed the floor, but it was
so caked with dirt that she merely made new designs with the
mop. When she swept, the dust flew in her mouth and she
coughed it back on the floor where she let it rest in peace.
Although there was no furniture she tried to rearrange the living
room anyway. She pushed one bale of hay into a corner and

placed the broken-down chair near the stove. Her biggest problem was where to take her washtub baths. The fields were too flat to provide any cover. She could put the tub in the kitchen and carry the dirty water out in buckets, but while the weather was nice, the thought of soaping in the sun was too marvelous to give up. Crevecoeur worked it out; he built a small, roofless lean-to against the back wall by the kitchen door and hung an army blanket across the door space.

Her aluminum cot with its foam-rubber mattress was heavenly. After she got used to the snoring from the other room she slept like a baby log. Crevecoeur gave her food money and one day they had hamburgers broiled on the grill, the next, wieners. She saw no rats but heard scamperings at night; she was covered with mosquito bites, and she didn't care. Before they went to bed, they sat in the living room and read by kerosene lamps. Crevecoeur had given her *Letters from an American Farmer*. In the mornings she sat upstairs in an armless wooden chair while Ronnie painted her portrait and she became fond of him.

At first it seemed impossible to break through. Ronnie gave her no more of himself than if he were painting a still life; she struggled to find an opening. On the second morning, simply—it seemed—by her sitting there hour after hour, his face muscles relaxed, his eyes responded to hers and he began a tuneless whistle. They began to talk and she discovered the importance of her truth that hearts could be unlocked only with ease. He had been very poor all his life. His father was a janitor in an apartment house and his mother did housecleaning by the day. He was used to doing without central heating, hot water, or plumbing. His agony during childhood was due to his resistance to the school gangs. He refused to belong and kept getting beaten up. He hated physical violence. His break was getting a scholarship to art school. After that he figured the world owed him nothing. "You know," he said. "Your brother might be right. Negroes won't be any better than whites when they make it. If you live for *things* your spirit goes dead. You find some idea to live for, and you shouldn't give it up to be a junk collector."

"Bernie's a fool," said Rachel. "He doesn't know what he wants and he tries to mix everybody up. He's jealous of anybody who's not as miserable as he is."

"Negroes are like everybody else. They want as much as the next guy and when they get that, they'll want more. It's funny. They say religion is the opiate of the masses but what's money to the fat cats? I want no part of it. I don't care about justice. Freedom is all I need and I got that. Freedom to be left alone."

"You can't mean that, Ronnie," said Rachel. "Maybe for yourself but not for everybody. Maybe an artist can do without. Or a saint. Most of us can't. Why shouldn't the rest of us start out with an equal chance at what the world has to offer? Why should one person have to suffer more than another because he's born with more pigment—or maybe, someday, with less? You don't know how comfortable justice is when you've got it. It lets you accept what you can't do for the only acceptable reason—because no one else can do it either. Without justice, what kind of freedom can you have? The freedom to fight or the freedom to hide, like a wild animal. Your idea of freedom scares me to death."

"The freedom to paint is all I want. I'm not fighting and I'm not hiding."

"Aren't you? Aren't you letting other people carry your fight?" She was afraid she'd gone too far but he stood unperturbed, with his brush in the air.

"Let them. It gives them something to live for. They want to make the world safe for democracy. Okay. They're doing themselves a favor, not me. When they've made the world safe they got to look around for something to do. Me, I already got something."

"But what if everybody felt as you do? People would still starve in the land of plenty. Nothing would get done."

"Why not? We got all these machines. If they got no bread let 'em eat paint. Science can do anything these days."

"Well, if that's the way you're going to argue—" she said, and was very pleased to see him smile.

. . .

She lay on her back in the cot, looking through the open window at the stars, waving away mosquitoes, listening to the steady large-toothed buzz of Ronnie's snoring—playing the game all by herself of being the last to go to sleep. She was the mother who didn't eat until her children were fed, the captain who left the ship after everybody else was in the lifeboat. She had settled herself on her right side, head cradled in her arm, when the snoring stopped. Instantly she was wide awake wondering what was bothering Ronnie. After several minutes, the snoring still hadn't started again. When she heard no sounds of movement, she lost out to her imagination in spite of herself. She had blocked out all memories of the last night at home with Leah and Ronnie but now, with her body tied to the rails, that miserable train of thought bore down. Maybe she'd been naïve and Ronnie had an entirely wrong idea about her overtures. Maybe he wasn't her friend at all but thought that all Laban girls were gray at night. Maybe he meant to fix her good and send her home with her tail dragging between her legs. She knew she was being absurd, he was lying in the dark with an upset stomach or something, but her primordial fears of blackness were not to be suppressed. She trembled all over. She was crazy. Ronnie was her friend and wouldn't hurt her for the world.

The door of her room opened and reality caught up with her fantasy. She was too frightened to tell the difference. The sounds of crickets and birds became that of vultures waiting to tear at her white flesh. She longed to fly home and huddle in her own bed, Jackson Schwartz or no. She reached for the stick by her bed. A blurred, dark shape moved toward her. She couldn't believe it was happening. It was so stupid she could have cried from frustration. With Crevecoeur lying in the other room, Ronnie must know it could wind up only in a horrible mess. In the middle of her anguish she turned giddy. Maybe, walking in his sleep, he was looking for God. He would kneel at her side and bow his head. When he did, she'd crack him with the stick and teach him she was no church. There was no more time to speculate. He sat on the side of the cot and bent over her. She kept her eyes closed, pretending to be asleep or, even better, a corpse. He'd have respect for the dead, wouldn't he? His lips closed on hers and as she thrashed to get away, she realized with horror that he wore a beard. She rolled away and fell off the bed with a thump.

"Ssh," said Crevecoeur. "You'll wake up Ronnie."

"Are you nuts?" She groaned. What kind of a Van Heflin had he turned out to be anyway? All this time he must have been thinking, like one of the boys in the back room, She came out here to live with me, didn't she? Okay (leer, wink), we know what that means. She felt miserable.

He stood at the window. "I'm sorry," he said. "It was an unforgivable thing to do, but I had to find out."

"Find out? That's a laugh. Why didn't you ask me? I'd tell you. What do you want to know? If I put out whenever a man in heat walks at midnight into my bedroom? If I'm one of those foolish, simple-minded girls who still believe sex and love are baked in the same cake? Don't worry, Charlie. I'm very easy to seduce. Just say you love me and the walls come tumbling down. You don't even have to mean it. I'll believe it anyway. It's rape I'm not particularly fond of."

"I'm sorry. Good night," he said and started toward the door.

She glared at his retreating, indistinct shape, bitter at her lack of character in assuming he was Ronnie, and all she could think of was yelling, for Ronnie and the rest of the world to hear, "Crevecoeur, you snore." Worse, to make her feel even more corrupt, as soon as he was gone, she wanted him back, wanted him, no matter what he wanted from her.

When Laban came, early in the morning, he didn't arrive empty-handed. He brought her a brand-new jeep station wagon. "It's got four-wheel drive, baby. You'll never be a stick-in-the-mud. Here's a Mobil credit card to boot. Now can I get my Cadillac out of hock?"

He was dressed in a business suit, so obviously he hadn't come to spend the day. She was disappointed. She didn't know any more where she stood at the farm and Laban looked good to her. He may have sensed something because he said, "Listen, baby, everything all right?"

She wasn't prepared to fall apart and tell him everything with the boys getting ready to get up any minute. She couldn't trust his sense of humor; he was liable to tell her she'd made her bed and she could lie in it. "Aren't you sore?" she said. "Aren't you going to play the outraged father? Aren't you even worried about my reputation?"

He grinned. "Baby, this is junior year abroad. You're a big girl now. If you want to play with the big boys why should I spoil your fun? And I know about your right hook."

She was right. It was useless to confide in him. She had to stand on her own feet and slug it out. She handed him the keys to the Cadillac. "Look," he said, "I've got to get downtown, so tell the boys I'm sorry I missed them." He hesitated, then reached out and squeezed her arm. "Tell you what. If you're not doing anything tonight, how about coming in and helping me celebrate the Days of Awe."

"The what?"

"Sure. The time between Rosh Hashanah and Yom Kippur. One day for the price of ten. A little early this year but what the hell? I've got a lot of years to make up. Get a package-deal Jewish education out of your old man."

If he had any idea how tempted she was. She could drive in right now, stay the evening and forget to leave. She'd never have to face Crevecoeur again. Even the thought of Jackson parading around didn't seem intolerable. One of Laban's evenings might jumble her memory track.

"I'm sorry, Laban," she said. "I can't, but thanks anyway. I've got some unfinished business here. And thanks loads for the car. It's very sweet of you." She reached up and kissed him on the cheek and he eyed her.

"Look, baby," he said. "You know where to reach me."

She struggled past the lump in her throat that arose whenever he talked to her like that. "I know. Give my love to everybody and tell them I'll see them very soon."

"I'll do that. Tell Crevecoeur I'll be back tomorrow afternoon to work on the dig. My boys still with me?"

"Sure," she said. "They'll be waiting for you." She watched him get into his car and drive off. He waved, and feeling lonely, she waved back.

Laban had resurrected his white linen dressing gown, fringed prayer shawl and skullcap. They were sitting at the dining room table waiting while Leah drew the curtains and lit white candles in a seven-branched candelabrum. As she struck the match Bernie, fidgeting, said, "Schwartz, have you learned the score? You're marrying the assistant to a stage magician. He'll never let her quit the theater. Make up your mind to that."

"I don't know what you mean," said Jackson. He sat stiffly, a new arrival at a boarding house. Leah went about her duties. She placed a prayer book, a pitcher of water, a dime-store tin horn, a leather riding crop and a platter of bread and honey on the table. The rooster was making a racket in his box in the kitchen.

"Baby," said Laban to Bernie, "you sound like a politician who's been out of power too long. You think if you point a finger at me you can shoot me down. Why don't you be the loyal opposition for a while? You might grow to like it."

"I mean, Schwartz," said Bernie, "your wife-to-be is a slave and her marriage vows won't be worth the paper they're printed on unless you do something about it."

"Bernie," said Beatrice, as Leah sat down with the rest of them, "why must you talk like that?"

"Ah, yes," said Bernie. "Another slave heard from."

"Bernie my son," said Laban, "I get the idea you're having a lousy summer. Why you sticking around? You need a vacation before school starts. How about a Caribbean cruise, all expenses paid? Would you like that?"

Bernie ducked in a rapid series of nods. "You'd love that. With Rachel and me both out of your hair, you'd have a real ball fiddling with your puppets. You can't even wait until we go back to school. I've got news for you, Laban." His lips quivered. "You'll have to force me out the way you did Rachel. I want you to admit you hate my guts."

Laban shook his head. "You do carry on, boy. Why would I do a fool thing like that?"

"Because you're a fool."

Laban looked at Bernie, who dropped his eyes. "Honor your father once a year, baby. That's a commandment."

"You don't honor a father without honor. That's a rule of reason."

Laban looked gray and dispirited, and Leah felt a string of rage tying her brain into knots. Staring coldly at the candle flames she succeeded in shaking herself free. "The rule of reason," said Laban. "I learned a long time ago that a lawyer who defends himself has a fool for a client. I wouldn't want to prove your case." He heaved his shoulders, smiled, winked at Leah and turned to Jackson. "Tell me, baby, how often you go to temple?"

Jackson shifted his weight. "I always go on the High Holy Days," he said. "Every year."

"That's what I wanted to hear. I'd hate to think of my daughter being married to a boy who didn't go to temple two times a year. It'd be a shame for the neighbors. Well, you're lucky. We're here for preseason training. You're going to be ready for that rabbi's first pitch."

"What you might call a Laban exercise in sacreligion," said Bernie, unable to look anybody in the eye, unable to sit still.

"Did you know," said Laban to Jackson, "my son reads the

Old Testament backwards, just the way it was written?"

"Did you know my father gets everything in the Bible backwards?"

"I've got to give the devil his due," said Laban. "You're sharp as a tack today.'" He picked up the tin horn and blew on it. It sounded like New Year's Eve. "To let God know we're here," he said. "May all of you be inscribed and sealed for a good year. *L'shanah tovah.* Leah, pass the hors d'oeuvres. Start the year sweet and it'll stay sweet."

Leah offered the plate of bread and honey. Everybody accepted but Bernie. "Won't you take some, Bernie? Honey is good for you," said Beatrice.

"Congratulations. You've made it. You sound just like a Jewish mama. No, thank you," said Bernie.

Laban picked up the prayer book. He glanced at Bernie. "I don't want any interruptions. I mean it."

Bernie glared back. "You'll just have to take your chances," he said.

"And so will you." Laban read aloud: " 'How many are to pass away, and how many are to come into existence; who are to live and who are to die; who are to accomplish the full number of their days, and who are not to accomplish them; who are to perish by water and who by fire; who by the sword and who by hunger; who by earthquake and who by plagues; who shall have repose and who shall be troubled; who shall be tranquil and who shall be disturbed; who shall be prosperous and who shall be afflicted; who shall become poor and who shall become rich; who shall be cast down and who shall be exalted?

" 'How weak is man. He comes from the dust and returns to the dust; must toil for his sustenance; passes away like withered grass, a vanishing shadow, a fleeting dream.

" 'But Thou, O God, art eternal; Thou art King everlasting.' "

Beatrice was crying. Her sobs filled the room. Leah watched her with distaste. What a child she was. Laban patted Beatrice on the shoulder and she clutched at his arm. When she subsided, Bernie said, "Can I talk now? But Thou, O Laban, art eternal; Thou art King everlasting."

"Blasphemy, Bernie," said Laban.

"Look who's talking. What do you think your whole performance is?" asked Bernie, nostrils distending, a young warrior watching the old chief wither, ready to leap in for the kill. "You make a mockery of ritual and expect us to clap our hands and shout Hallelujah. I don't buy it."

Laban looked as if he was in real pain. Beatrice said, "Are you all right? You want your pills?"

He waved her off. "You've got it wrong. I'm not playing God."

"You've been playing God all your life. You collect people and place them on a checkerboard and move them around for your amusement. When they're not funny any more you sweep them off and find new ones."

Leah couldn't restrain herself. She had lost all her sense of detachment. Her cool, dark places glowed with hot coals. Her eyeballs smarted. Bernie had got Laban to fight his way, and Laban was standing with his arms down, helpless. He couldn't afford to be serious with Bernie. She picked up the pitcher and flung water in Bernie's face. "You've got a dirty mouth," she said, and went to the kitchen to refill the pitcher.

When she returned, Bernie had his glasses off and was wiping his eyes. "You crud. You coolie," he said. Her diversion had worked.

Laban was back in the groove. "We're ready for the water now," he said, grinning, and took the pitcher. "We'll remind ourselves of Abraham and Isaac. Satan bet God that Abraham would chicken out before offering his only son. Satan turned himself into a deep stream to block Abraham's way to the sacrifice grounds. But God dried up the stream. In memory we still go to the stream to prove that for Him we're willing even to go to the devil." He crumbled some bread in his hand and dropped the crumbs into the water. "For you, Satan. We cast our bread on the waters. Get thee behind us."

Bernie wiped his glasses and put them on. "Keep it up," he said. "A thousand and one nights of Jewish fairy tales. If somebody squawks, send your hatchet woman after them."

"Good idea. Leah, we're ready for the rooster."

She went into the kitchen and picked up the crate, and with the rooster thrashing around, she carried it into the dining room and set it down at Laban's feet. He unfastened the wire catch and pulled the bird out by its feet. It flailed its wings. While it gabbled in terror, its comb arched, he whirled it around his head. "This is instead of me. This is in expiation for me. This bird shall grace the poor table of my daughter, Rachel, and may we enter a long and healthy life." Breathing hard, he lowered the rooster into the box and fastened the lid.

"Go, Laban, go," said Bernie. "Unload your guilt and parade around as pure as Crisco. Help us to remember the Jew is a caricature, an animated cartoon in a black alpaca suit with long nose and beard, galloping after a runaway fowl, shouting, 'God is everywhere.' "

"That's the ticket, baby. God is everywhere, even inside that strait jacket you wear." He reached for the riding crop and extended it to Bernie. "Here's your spot. A small part but loaded with dynamite. Knock 'em dead in the aisles. Play it any way you like." Laban got up and stretched face down on the floor.

Bernie stared at the riding crop. "What are you talking about?" he said.

"*Malkus*, baby. Time for *malkus*. You flog me for my sins. Beat the devil out of your old man."

Bernie flung away the crop. "Don't be a bigger fool than you already are."

"Beatrice, you know what to do. Thirty-nine times."

She picked up the crop, and treating it like a wand, repeatedly touched Laban on the shoulder. Laban counted, and Bernie appealed to Leah and Jackson. "He's hopeless. God damn it."

When the exercise was over, Laban got to his feet. He pulled a crumpled bill from his pocket. "This is a hundred dollars. They used to use a goat. A red sash was tied to his horns and he was led to a cliff over a ravine. They cut the sash in two and tied one part to the cliff, then pushed the goat over the cliff. I've got no goat. Only money." He held the bill to a candle flame and dropped the burning paper into a bowl. They watched it curl into ashes.

"That does it," said Laban. "I'm going to bed. Bad boys go to bed without their supper, right, Bernie? Good night." He walked out, his prayer shawl floating like wings behind him.

"Wait. I'm coming with you," said Beatrice. And she left Bernie, Jackson and Leah sitting in the dim candlelight, like guests who had overstayed a party.

"Well, Schwartz," said Bernie, "how do you like your new father-in-law?"

"It was very interesting," Jackson said, with a cautious glance at Leah.

"How about it, Leah the Baptist? Was it interesting?"

She started to pick up the rooster crate and Jackson hurried over. "I'll do it, Leah. Where do you want it?"

"Laban's room, of course," said Bernie. "Birds of a feather flock together."

"In the kitchen," she said, and turned grimly to Bernie. "You wanted somebody to admit he hates you? All right. I admit it: I hate you. Are you satisfied?"

Laban sat at the edge of the bed and pressed the heels of his hands hard against his stomach. His eyes closed around the pain and he began to call out, "Beatrice, the pills," before he remembered she wasn't there. He was at Rabbi Isaacson's retreat. Bent forward, he made the bathroom and found his pills. He'd have to remember to keep them with him. The pain retreated and he ran cold water over his face, which had the look of moist, gray putty. Bernie would say it was the price of applying too much stage make-up—the body could take just so much abuse. Laban tried to smile when he thought of Bernie—it was what the rabbi would have suggested—but it was too much effort.

When he arrived at the chapel the others were already there. Besides the rabbi there were perhaps two dozen, dressed in slacks and T-shirts, most of whom he recognized but no longer felt he knew at the retreat. The rabbi was of medium height, sturdy, with a long face and soft brown eyes; as if to start him out without illusions, God had given him a short, thick blob of a nose. He too was in sport clothes.

Rabbi Isaacson said: "God is everywhere. In the stone, the stream, the grass and the living heart. He embraces the universe although the universe cannot embrace him. The eternal question 'O God, where can I find Thee?' is answered by 'And where can I not find Thee?' 'Alas,' it is said, 'the world is full of lights and mysteries, and man shuts them from himself with one small hand over his eyes.' We must sanctify our desires, not suppress them. We must live each day, not as if it were our last, but as if it were our best. 'Defraud not thyself of a good day; and let not a portion of a good desire pass thee by.' The enjoyment of life is no sin when our first enjoyment is of God. A rabbi asked one of his rich, pious followers, 'What do you eat?' The man replied, 'I eat very modestly, just bread and water.' 'Starting tomorrow,' said the rabbi, 'you eat steak and drink champagne. If you live on bread and water, what will you give to the poor—stones?'

"For the sake of God and those you love, you must enjoy life even in sorrow. It is said of a man that his only daughter died as a child. He was heartbroken and took to his bed. Nothing could rouse him. He had a dream. He was in heaven watching a parade of child-angels. Every angel but one, his own little girl, carried a lighted candle. He ran to her, embraced her and said, 'Why is yours the only unlit candle?' 'They keep lighting it,' she said, 'but your tears keep putting it out.'

"It is said that God does not entirely heal those who have broken hearts. He only eases their suffering lest it torment and deject them. For dejection is not good and not pleasing to God. A broken heart prepares man for the service of God, but dejection corrodes service. We must distinguish between the two as

carefully as between joy and wantonness; they are so easily confused and yet are as far removed from one another as the ends of
the earth.

"The psalmist says, 'O taste and see that the Lord is good.' You
should taste everything and see that the Lord is good. Our physical pleasures are derived from the heavenly source of delight.
While we enjoy, we must think back to the spiritual fountain of
all bounties and blessings. In this way, eating, drinking, sex and
other appetites only serve to make us realize the Lord is good.
The Baal Shem says, 'If the vision of a beautiful woman comes
suddenly to a man's eyes, or if he perceives any other fair and
lovely thing, he should unhestitatingly ask himself: Whence
comes this beauty except from the divine force which permeates
the world? Consequently, the origin of this beauty is divine, and
why should I be attracted by the part? Better for me to be drawn
after the All, the Source of every partial beauty. If a man taste
something good and sweet, let the taster conceive that it is from
the heavenly sweetness that the sweet quality is derived. Such
perception of beauty, then, is an experience of the Eternal,
blessed be He. . . . Further, if he hears some amusing story and
he derives pleasure from it, let him bethink himself that this is an
emanation from the realm of love.' It is said in Proverbs, 'The
righteous eateth to the satisfying of his soul: but the belly of the
wicked shall want.'

"I speak, not of pantheism, but of the immanence of God.
Rabbi Baruch said, 'What a good and bright world this is if we
do not lose our hearts to it, but what a dark world if we do.' I
speak, too, not of self-mortification, but of the immanence of
God. A man who wore nothing but a sack and fasted from one
sabbath to the next came to the *maggid* of Koznitz. The *maggid*
said, 'Do you think the Evil Urge is staying away from you? It is
tricking you into that sack. He who pretends to fast but secretly
eats every day is spiritually better off than you, for he is only
deceiving others while you are deceiving yourself.' "

Before the evening session, Laban walked to the lake. He had
no desire to talk to the others even if it were allowed; he was

content to sit on the bank and stare at the water. His pain had
subsided into a dull ache. He threw a pebble and listened to the
soft splash. "Stones for you," he said. "Steak for me."

In the evening, the rabbi said: "Every man high of spirit can be
a high priest. Every spot on earth can be the Holy of Holies. We
need ask of God only that He make His face shine upon us. We
are asking Him for His greatest gift and the only one He has to
give. It is said that a great sinner lived in Lublin. Whenever the
sinner wanted to talk to the rabbi, the rabbi always consented and
talked with him as if he were a close friend and a man of integrity. Many of the holy men were annoyed and asked, 'Is it
possible that our rabbi—who has only to look once into a man's
face to know his life from first to last, to know the very origin of
his soul—does not see that this is a sinner? And if he does see it,
can he possibly consider him worthy to speak to and associate
with?' The rabbi answered them: 'I know all about him as well as
you. But you know how I love gaiety and hate depression. And
this man is so great a sinner. Others repent the moment they have
sinned, are sorry for a moment and then return to their folly. But
he knows no regrets and no doldrums, and lives in his happiness
as in a tower. And it is the radiance of his happiness that over-
whelms my heart.' The *dav'ner* who mouths ashes instead of
fire—of what value is his prayer? The sinner's fervor may lead
him to God at the very moment the *dav'ner's* death-in-life is
leading him away. Once the Baal Shem stopped on the threshold
of a house of prayer and refused to go in. 'I can't,' he said. 'It is
crowded with teachings and prayers from wall to wall and from
floor to ceiling. How could there be room for me?' When he saw
those around him staring at him, he said, 'The words from the
lips of those whose teaching and praying does not come from
hearts lifted to heaven cannot rise, but fill the house from wall to
wall and from floor to ceiling. If a man has fulfilled all the commandments, he is admitted to the Garden of Eden, even though
he has not experienced delight. But since he has felt no delight
on earth, he feels none there either. He says, "And they make all
that to-do about Paradise," and he is thrown out.' "

Laban went to bed early but couldn't sleep. He dozed off

several times but awoke each time in bed sheets wet with perspiration. Once he had to take a pill.

On the final day, Rabbi Isaacson said: "A mechanical and lifeless performance of a religious ordinance is valueless. A man is nowhere if he thinks he'd done his duty to God when he had recited a whole round of religious laws. The inspiration of true service is its own end, which is God. Out of enthusiasm springs spiritual progress. We are eternal penitents cheerfully making progress every day, never merely repeating today a religious routine of yesterday. Mere freedom from active sin is not enough, if sin is concealed in the heart. Only uninterrupted communion with God will ennoble your thoughts and cause the roots of sin to die. There is no short cut, there is no alternate, but the route to God only seems to be devious and filled with obstacles and temptations. The obstacles and temptations are illusory and God is real. We are told of the king who built a great palace. By means of magic he created illusory corridors and mazes preventing access to himself. Actually one could approach him directly. With much gold heaped in the entrance halls the people were content to take their fill of treasure and go no further. No one thought of pushing forward against the imaginary walls.

"We have a choice. The gold gatherers, like all people trapped in fantasy, will see nothing but the fantasy, while those who push on will be able to see God in the stone, in the stream, in the grass and in the living heart. Some will have picked up the gold and others the world. Some will shape dead hearts and wear chains around their necks, and others will join living hearts in an eternal chain. Only the living heart can enjoy even gold.

" 'Let the heavens rejoice, and let the earth be glad; let the sea roar, and the fulness thereof. Let the field be joyful, and all that is therein: then shall all the trees of the wood rejoice. Let the floods clap their hands: let the hills be joyful together before the Lord. The wilderness and the solitary place shall be glad for them; and the desert shall rejoice, and blossom as the rose. It shall blossom abundantly, and rejoice even with joy and singing: the glory of

Lebanon shall be given unto it, the excellency of Carmel and Sharon; they shall see the glory of the Lord, and the excellency of our God.'

"We have found, you and I, that we yearn for faith. Our belief in nothing circles to a belief in everything. We sell our souls even to the devil to believe, and in the believing get them back. The fire of reason, drenched with skepticism, is fed with eternal fire. As the last man on earth dies without having answered his question, Why? he may yet thank God for having lived.

"May the Lord bless thee and keep thee. May the Lord make His face to shine upon thee and be gracious unto thee. May God lift up His countenance to thee and give thee peace. Amen."

Laban stopped to say good-bye to the rabbi. "How's it going?" said the rabbi.

"If you want the truth, baby, not all my way, but then you're not Barry Fitzgerald. You're some rabbi. You still marrying off my daughter?"

The rabbi laughed. "That's like asking me if I'll attend my own funeral. I wouldn't miss it for the world." He leaned forward and placed his hand on Laban's shoulder. "Take care of yourself," he said.

"Sure, baby. You keep pitching and I'll keep catching and God'll keep watching."

"What better does He have to do?" said the rabbi.

It turned out that Jackson's family—his parents and brother
Arnie—were Orthodox Jews; since Leah had prepared a baked
ham, there was nothing for them to eat when they came for
dinner. In any event they wouldn't have eaten from the plates.
Mrs. Schwartz insisted they should go ahead and eat already, she
wasn't hungry, with a big lunch from a Jewish restaurant. Laban
proposed that they all go out to the Jewish restaurant—what, he
should eat while others starved?—but Mrs. Schwartz wouldn't
hear of it. "Ssh," she said. "Go ahead, eat. Come, Abe, Arnie.
We'll wait in the living room." Leah was impressed. The woman
took the play right away from Laban.

During the hurried dinner, Laban said to Jackson, "Dirty pool,
baby. Why didn't you tell us they were Orthodox? You think I
like to pull wings off flies?"

Head lowered, Jackson said, "I guess I forgot," and added
inanely, "My parents keep kosher."

"That's telling him, Schwartz," said Bernie. "I can understand.
A man leaves his father and mother and cleaves unto Laban.
Render unto Laban the things that are Laban's."

"Just once, baby," said Laban to Bernie, "I wish you'd put
money where your mouth is."

"Just once," said Bernie swiftly, "I wish you'd put God where
your money is."

They finished dinner in fifteen minutes. Leah cleared the dishes
and stacked them in the dishwasher, then went into the living
room and sat down quietly with the others. Mrs. Schwartz, a
round, very short woman, wore a black silk dress and imitation

pearls at her neck. She had a broad, flat face and thick, gray hair, and she sat stiffly and deeply on her chair so that her feet hung like suspended weights several inches above the floor. She had little pebbles for eyes, which bore down on Jackson, and he looked in every direction but hers. The father was the source of Jackson's looks. He was a tall, lean man with a strong nose, shy faded-blue eyes and light, carefully brushed hair that showed no signs of gray. His hands were big, with long, interlaced fingers. Jackson's brother, Arnie, was a fleshier, less handsome version of Jackson. He had the father's blue eyes and blond hair but his face had too much of the mother's broadness.

"Mr. Schwartz, baby," said Laban, "with your hair you could pass for a Swede." Mr. Schwartz shrugged and examined his hands.

"He comes from a crazy family," said Mrs. Schwartz. "*Goyishe kopfs.* Don't ask me why." She pronounced her *w*'s as *v*'s. Jackson got up and went to the window.

"Jackson, baby," said Laban, "come back and join the party."

Jackson turned and sat down. He was perspiring and wiped his face with a handkerchief.

"Jackson tells me you're a baker, Mr. Schwartz," said Laban.

Mr. Schwartz nodded.

"Bagels and *challah?*"

"Bagels, *challah,* rye bread, wedding cakes, cookies. Anything you want," said Mr. Schwartz in a deep voice. Like his wife he spoke with an accent.

"That's great, baby. You know what everybody's favorite smell is? Fresh bread. There's a scientist who manufactures smells and he complains the one smell he can't put in a bottle is fresh bread. It's like God meant for us to leave it alone. To hell with prefab pies. I'm with you."

"My husband had his own shop," said Mrs. Schwartz.

"Mom, please," said Jackson.

"What's the matter?" she said. "For two years he had a shop. You think he always slaved for somebody else?"

"The American Dream," said Bernie. "That crazy mixed-up American Dream."

"Shut up, baby," said Laban. "I mean shut up."

Bernie blinked behind his glasses.

"Mr. Schwartz, how long does it take to learn to make bagels? I mean, really, the way you do," said Laban.

Mrs. Schwartz laughed. "Like Abe? A hundred years maybe."

"A man wants to learn, he learns," said Mr. Schwartz. "You don't have to be a college boy." Jackson blew his nose in his handkerchief.

"I envy you, Mr. Schwartz. You can make a bagel and I can't," said Laban.

"How long, Mr. Laban, would it take my father to be a lawyer like you?" said the brother, Arnie. He hunched forward with an angry-looking jaw.

Laban studied him. "I meant no disrespect to your father," he said. "I admire skill. I hear you work in the post office."

"That's right. I work in the post office. I sort mail. You know how long it took me to learn? Two months, because I'm lazy. All lazy bums go to work for the U. S. Government."

"Baby, I've got nothing against the U. S. Government."

"Laban, the man of good will," said Bernie. "A kind word for everybody."

"My name is Arnie, not baby," said Arnie.

"He calls everybody baby," said Bernie. "It's simple. Everybody calls him Laban and he calls them baby. It's not bad once you get the hang of it."

"So, Mrs. Schwartz," said Laban, "what do you think of your son's choice of a wife?"

Mrs. Schwartz rolled her head. "A face like an angel. How could a fine boy like my Jackie pick anything but an angel? Marriages are made in heaven, *Gott zu danken.*"

"That reminds me of a story they tell about King Solomon's daughter," said Bernie. "Stop me if you've heard this one. Solomon had a beautiful daughter, the fairest girl in all Israel. Dove's eyes, lips like a thread of scarlet, pomegranate temples, and breasts like young roes feeding among the lilies. A real doll, something like Leah here. Solomon asked the stars who was possibly good enough to marry his daughter, and the stars said his future son-in-law would be the poorest man in the country. So he built a tower by the sea and locked his daughter in, under the guard of seventy old men. There was no conceivable way to get in. Solomon said, 'Let's see God work this one out.'

"One night a ragged, bone-weary young traveler wandered by. He was fainting with hunger and cold. Looking for a place to sleep he saw the skeleton of an ox, crept inside and fell asleep. An eagle swooped down and lifted up the carcass and flew it to the top of the tower where he dropped it on the roof. The next morning when the princess went walking on the roof, there he was. She got him bathed and dressed up and saw he was the best-looking boy in Israel. Without even asking Solomon, they got married. They wrote out the marriage certificate in the boy's blood since they had no ink. When the guards found out they went to tell the king, expecting him to have their scalps, but he was very happy and said, 'Blessed is the Lord who giveth a wife to man and establisheth him in his house.' Or, as you pointed out, Mrs. Schwartz, 'Marriages are made in heaven.' "

She had been following Bernie's story closely. When he finished she said, "My Jackie's a fine boy and he never went around in rags. My son's a lawyer. He could marry a hundred girls in a minute."

"Mom," said Jackson, wiping his face.

"She's right to be proud of you, Jackson baby," said Laban. "It isn't easy for a poor boy to make it. I know, Mrs. Schwartz. I was a poor boy myself. Many's the time I fell asleep over my law books I was so tired, but you know what pulled me through? The same thing as Jackson: my mother. There's nothing like a mother's love. Nobody can deny that."

There was a silence, Arnie said in a savage voice, "We all pulled him through. What's to be proud of?" Mrs. Schwartz unglued her eyes from Jackson and stared at her other son. Her dark little eyes flashed a warning.

"Arnie," said Mr. Schwartz. "Enough. Be a *mensch*."

"Look at him," said Arnie. "Sitting there like a lump of clay, like he doesn't know what's going on. Mister," he said to Laban, "I worked so he could go to college and law school. Our parents wouldn't take a penny from me so it could be saved up for him. Do you think we get a thank you? He doesn't even send a post card. Look at him sweat. Do you think he ever sweated for us? Like you said, mister," he said, glaring at Bernie, "he's a bum."

"You're some baby, Arnie baby," said Laban. "I'll tell you what. I'll buy the post office and make you chairman of the board."

"Don't do me any favors. Save them for him. He needs them."

Jackson was a puddle. He kept working at his face with a handkerchief that couldn't hold any more moisture. Leah noted clinically that he was suffering.

"Mrs. Schwartz, now that we've had a nice chat," said Laban, "and gotten better acquainted, let's talk a little about the wedding. My friend, Rabbi Isaacson, has agreed to officiate. He isn't, I'm afraid, exactly Orthodox but he isn't exactly Conservative or Reform either."

"He's an Isaacson," said Bernie. "Pure Isaacson."

"He suggests that since your son is Reform, we should have something like a Reform ceremony. But we can throw in a canopy and breaking the wine glass—a few things like that. What do you say?"

Mrs. Schwartz sighed. "What can you do? It's the modern generation. Why make a fuss?" She turned to Mr. Schwartz who kept his head down. "*Nu?* What you got to say for yourself?" He shook his head and said nothing. She swung suddenly toward Leah. "Your sister," she said. "She'll be at the wedding?"

"Of course, Mrs. Schwartz," said Leah. "She's sorry she couldn't come in today but she's staying in the country. She wanted me to apologize for her and to say she's looking forward to making your acquaintance."

"She looks like you, hah?" said Mrs. Schwartz.

"Very much so, Mrs. Schwartz. She's my identical twin."

Mrs. Schwartz's face expanded into a wide-mouthed smile. "Jackie," she said, "how can you tell them apart?"

By challenging her imagination, Rachel had predicted the kind of wedding Laban would cook up for Leah. It was a mixture of smörgåsbord, ragoût and pig's knuckles, with a topping of chopped liver and Nova Scotia salmon. Laban wore a top hat, gray spats and a cutaway, with a soft gray vest and pearl buttons; he looked like Jack Benny playing John Jacob Astor. The ceremony was being conducted in the ballroom of the biggest hotel in town, under a fringed, curtained canopy supported by four poles—a four-poster without the bed. The ceiling was festooned with multicolored formations of crepe paper. On the back wall facing the guests were giant pictures of Jackson and Leah, each at least eight feet by six. Blown up, Leah's serenity looked menacing, like the simple soldier who, when ordered, would press the doomsday button. Jackson was bloated, a man on the way to the bathroom when the picture was snapped.

The guests, seated on wooden folding chairs, overflowed the hall. There must have been two thousand of them, and their chatter and laughter were deafening. Looking at the front row, at flesh overflowing collars and holes in mouths where cigars belonged and would soon return, Rachel felt she could very well be at a national political convention, with the rabbi there to deliver the invocation. Wearing a light blue faille dress, she stood with Jackson's mother behind Leah in her sacrificial white. Bernie and Jackson's father supported Jackson, who she was forced to admit, was breath-taking in his pale blue jacket that matched his eyes. Like Jackson, Mr. Schwartz wore a skullcap, which made her squirm when she looked at Laban's top hat. Not that she'd become a temple Jewess in one surge of indignation, but it would be nice, once, at a ceremonial time of life to let the ceremony speak for itself.

Her eye picked up familiar faces at random. Neighbors, the Negro boy at Laban's parking lot, Margery Schmidt, Mr. Flaker from the hospital. Laban must have invited everyone he ever knew and, like a precinct captain, anybody who could be bought for Laban's ten-dollar bill and the promise of free food and whiskey. Intimidated, she waited for favorite-son banners to bob up, but as the rabbi raised his arm for quiet, the crowd relapsed into the exaggerated silence of displaced persons who weren't certain of their rights—she imagined them fumbling in their pockets to make sure of their invitations. But there was Laban, big as life, standing before them in his cutaway. He would let them know the time to cheer and begin their demonstrations.

The blessed rabbi refused to be one of Laban's props. He was decently dressed in a black suit and skullcap, and made it perfectly clear from whom he took his orders. "God," he said, "supremely blessed, supreme in might and glory, guide and bless this groom and bride." She thanked Heaven for his clear, resonant voice. She'd expected a gobble or cackle to come out—a record slowed down or speeded up. She still didn't quite believe that Laban had delivered a straight man of the cloth. Laban was docile but who could be sure a firecracker wouldn't go off under the rabbi's feet?

"Standing here in the presence of God, the Guardian of the home, ready to enter into the bond of wedlock, answer in the fear of God, and in the hearing of this assembly. Do you, Jackson Schwartz, of your own free will and consent, take Leah Laban to be your wife, and do you promise to love, honor and cherish her throughout life? If so, answer yes."

"I do," said Jackson, and Rachel thought with satisfaction that he'd seen too much television and muffed his line.

"Do you, Leah Laban, of your own free will and consent, take Jackson Schwartz to be your husband, and do you promise to love, honor and cherish him throughout life? If so, answer yes."

Now, Leah, prayed Rachel, now's your chance. At least throw the question open to the convention floor.

"Yes," said Leah.

"Unto Thee, God and Father," said the rabbi, "we lift our souls in praise. Thou, Source of all life and of all joy, sanctify the covenant which this groom and bride are consummating in Thy name. Be with them at this hour of their gladness, bless their covenant, and seal their bond of wedlock with love everlasting. Amen."

The rabbi picked up a crystal cup of wine from a small table behind him. "Praised be Thou, O Lord, our God, King of the universe, Who has created the fruit of the vine." He handed the cup to Jackson, who brought it to his lips. "No, Jackson," said the rabbi, "first your bride."

Jackson's hand shook and the wine spilled over the edge and dripped on the floor. "I'm sorry," he said, and he held it out toward Leah. She took it, sipped and handed it back. Jackson took a deep gulp.

"As together you now drink from this cup, so may you, under God's guidance, draw contentment, comfort and felicity from the cup of life, its bitterness sweetened, and all things hallowed by true companionship and love." He stopped. Jackson stood with the glass in his hand. "The cup," said the rabbi. "Break the cup." Jackson bent down and placed the cup on the floor. He stamped on it with his heel and Rachel heard a buzz from the mob. This was what they'd come to see; this was a Jewish wedding. Rachel's eyes clouded with tears. The rabbi had a chubby round nose for God. His tone and manner kept the faith. It wasn't his fault if he was casting words before swine.

"The rings," said the rabbi. Bernie handed one gold band to Jackson and Rachel unwound her moist fingers from the other and gave it to Leah. She failed to catch Leah's eyes.

"Jackson Schwartz, place the ring upon the finger of your bride as token of wedlock. Repeat the words which I now say: Be thou consecrated unto me."

"Be thou consecrated unto me."

"With this ring as my wife."

"With this ring as my wife."

"According to the faith of Israel."

"According to the faith of Israel."

"Leah Laban, place the ring upon your groom's finger as token of wedlock and repeat these words: Be thou consecrated unto me."

"Be thou consecrated unto me." Her voice had the flatness of a menu recitation; Rachel couldn't believe the rabbi didn't know what was going on. Shouldn't he at least ask if anybody knew? With blurred vision, she saw the dim outlines of Jackson and Leah as a pair of hungers eating each other up, drifting with bare cupboards on the matrimonial sea.

"With this ring as my husband."

"With this ring as my husband."

"According to the faith of Israel."

"According to the faith of Israel."

"As by these rings you symbolize your marriage bond, may their meaning sink into your hearts and bind your lives together by devotion and faithfulness to one another. Praised be Thou, O Lord, our God, Who sanctifiest Thy children by the holy covenant of marriage.

"Now that you have spoken the words and performed the rites which unite your lives, I do hereby, in conformity with the faith of Israel and the law of this state, declare your marriage to be valid and binding; and I pronounce you, Jackson Schwartz, and you, Leah Laban, to be husband and wife before God and man.

"May the Lord bless thee and keep thee.

"May the Lord let His countenance shine upon thee and be gracious unto thee.

"May the Lord lift up His countenance upon thee and give thee peace. Amen."

It was finished. Leah was over and done with. Jackson put his arms around her and kissed her noisily on the mouth. The tears streamed down Rachel's cheeks. A roar swept up from the hall, as if "The Star-Spangled Banner" had been played and the game was about to begin. Laban pulled a surprise and hundreds of colored balloons floated toward the ceiling. Jackson, face flushed, on the prowl, stood over Rachel, groomed for her kiss. She darted past him and pecked like a timid bird at the rabbi's cheek. "You laid them in the aisles, Rabbi," she said. He smiled and started to speak, but she turned and ran into the hall to find Ronnie. The rabbi had saved her sanity. As long as there was one righteous man, nobody could damage the old words. Jewishness was hereditary, like royal blood, and even abdication couldn't unlink the identification bracelet. Leah and Jackson were Jews in hiding but the rabbi had smoked them out, if only for a moment, and Rachel saw that it was good. She was radiant. She was a daughter of Israel and the Jewish God was love, not wrath. Pride in heritage, all but lost, rattled around like a pea in her chest. Even if she married a Buddhist, she'd remain a Jew because she'd marry in the spirit of faith, of truth and of the fear of God. Nobody was going to rip pages from her book of life, even if to the ironic or savage eye they read like "God Bless Our Home," in modern Gaspipe.

She stood at bay before a seething mass that was regrouping itself in pockets of conversation. Dozens of hotel men were removing chairs while others wheeled in long tables jammed with food and whiskey, which they lined up along the side walls. A group of musicians materialized in front of the hall, as did music stands and chairs. In the wink of Laban's eye, the room was transformed into a dance floor and banquet hall. As the music started she saw Ronnie and pushed toward him. He was moving toward the front and kept melting away but she caught him by the elbow. "Ronnie, I've been looking all over for you."

"Be right back," he said. He looked different and it wasn't only the dark blue suit and polished black shoes. He seemed like a tuning fork that had been touched off and was vibrating to an alien pitch. She watched him go up to Leah, lean forward and kiss her on the mouth. Jackson's face turned red. Leah said something to Ronnie; he answered and then came back to Rachel.

"What did you do that for?" she said. "What's gotten into you?"

"I did it because I felt like it," he said. He looked at her. "Stop taking me for granted."

"What's that supposed to mean? What did she say to you?"

"Well, she said, 'You kiss real good.'"

"Ronnie, please."

"She said she was glad I could make it to the wedding and I said, 'Thank you. I hope you'll be happy.' What's bugging you? Ain't I allowed to kiss the bride?"

She accused him with angry eyes. "You're pulling race on me," she said. "You know that wasn't what I meant."

"No? What did you mean?"

She refused to consider what she meant. "Let's drop it. Dance with me."

"No. What did you mean?"

She shook her head dumbly, and he said, "I got it. That night at your house." She couldn't look at him. "Okay," he said. "Listen good. Nothing happened—and I mean nothing. She was there all right but you think I'm a fool? I've got my own life to lead and Leah wasn't doing me any favors."

Rachel felt her heart lift and she was ashamed of her joy. She raised her eyes to his. "Thank you, Ronnie. It's a nasty thing to say, but thank you. Will you forgive me?"

Ronnie said slowly, "You sure do live a complicated life. Take it easy. I'm just a country boy."

"Will you dance with me?" she said.

"Sure," he said, but couldn't resist setting her down hard. "I better set you straight on that too. We're not all great dancers."

"I'll take my chances," she said. He held her loosely. "Ronnie," she said. "Why wouldn't Crevecoeur come to the wedding?"

"Your guess is as good as mine."

"I think I know. It's Leah, isn't it?"

He shook his head. "There you go again," he said, and she knew she was right.

"What happened, Ronnie?"

"I don't know and that's the truth. Forget it." He grinned. "You're his girl."

"If I am, he's got some funny ways of showing it, and I'm running out of time. In a little while I'm supposed to be going back to school. I'll probably never see him again."

"If you want to see him, you'll see him. He's not going any-place. Cut it out, will you? Talk to him, not to me. What you and him do is none of my business."

"Don't you think friends should help each other? I'd listen to you if you were in trouble."

"Like I told you before, some people like to do social work and some don't. I don't. I thought you wanted to dance."

They stumbled silently around the floor, bumping into other couples. He was right; he was a bad dancer. "Hey now," he said. "Look at your daddy." She turned her head and Laban twirled by in his top hat with—she looked again to be sure—Margery Schmidt. "I remember that lady," said Ronnie.

"She's no lady," said Rachel.

"She's some looker. I think I'll ask her to dance."

"What's turned you on? You're acting crazy tonight. What are you trying to prove?" She was so exasperated with him that she stopped in the middle of the floor. "All right. If you're deter-mined to be a comedian I'll be your straight man—I've had plenty of experience. Just remember, I won't catch you until you stop bouncing."

"A friend in need is a friend indeed," said Ronnie.

"Come on," she said, and pulled him to the side where they watched Laban and Mrs. Schmidt hopping around the floor. When the music stopped they went over.

Laban was fanning Mrs. Schmidt with his top hat. "This is one red hot mama," he said. "If I put her in a package I'd sell a million." Mrs. Schmidt faked a smile.

"Laban, you know Ronnie," said Rachel. "Mrs. Schmidt, this is Ronnie Birch."

Ronnie put out his hand. "Pleased to meet you, Mrs. Schmidt."

She looked at the hand and said, "How do you do?"

"Would you care to dance?" said Ronnie.

"Not right now, thank you," said Mrs. Schmidt.

"Go ahead, baby," said Laban. "Don't mind me."

"I'd rather not," said Mrs. Schmidt. "I'm tired."

Ronnie grinned. "News travels fast. You must of heard what a lousy dancer I am."

Laban shrugged. "That's the way the ball bounces," he said and Rachel whispered, "I told you you'd get bounced."

Beatrice appeared out of the crowd and murmured into Laban's ear. He nodded. "Ronnie wants to dance with you, baby. Go ahead."

She looked anxiously into Laban's face and turned to Ronnie. "Thank you for asking me," she recited.

They started off and Laban laughed in Mrs. Schmidt's face. "You're good as new, Margie. Excuse me, ladies. Got to say hello to the Governor."

Left with a tight-lipped Mrs. Schmidt, Rachel watched Ronnie and Beatrice through the woman's clear blue eyes. Anger collected like ice water in a pail and she wanted to dash it against Margery's face. "You mustn't mind Ronnie, Mrs. Schmidt," she said. "He's uppity. He doesn't seem to appreciate what we've done for him. If it weren't for people like us he might be jumping around Africa with a spear in his hand."

Mrs. Schmidt's shoulders engaged in a delicate shiver. "I noticed you dancing with him," she said. "Everyone to her own taste."

"I'll let you in on a secret. It doesn't pay to rile Ronnie. He looks scrawny but he's a tiger when he gets mad. God knows what he might do. It pays to be nice to one of them. You know, if something crazy happens and they take over the country. Speaking of being nice, your mother must be terribly grateful to you for getting her out of the booby hatch."

Mrs. Schmidt looked away. "She's dead," she said.

Rachel felt sick. "I'm terribly sorry to hear that. Was it sudden?"

"Very," said Mrs. Schmidt. She met Rachel's eyes. "Yes, she did, if it's any of your business."

"You were going to take her away from Charlie. Didn't it help?"

"She wouldn't go," said Mrs. Schmidt shortly. "Excuse me." She walked off.

Nobody wants to talk to me, thought Rachel. I'm as old and gray as I feel. No wonder she was having her troubles with

Crevecoeur. Farm life aged a woman prematurely, what with chores and all—everybody knew that. Since his attempted rape, he'd treated her with kid gloves, had been the perfect gentleman; she didn't know how much longer she could stand being treated as a house guest. What if she'd welcomed him with open arms that night? At times she wished she had. At least it would have been a resolution. She felt like a trapeze performer swinging from one day to the next, depending on each day in turn to decide her future; Crevecoeur was her safety net. She waved a spangled arm over him. She wasn't above bribery. That was part of the game, at least the way Laban played it. She would go to Laban and say, Look, Laban, you may as well know I'm in a bad way about Crevecoeur and believe in happily-ever-after miseries, and it's obvious we need a few laughs. So get up an entertainment for the troops. Squirt a little Kickapoo joy juice into his prune face.

At the liquor table she ordered a scotch on ice and found Bernie getting two martinis. "Big brother," she said. "Watch over me. I need to talk to you."

"Hurry up," he said. "I'm busy. I'm spending the night getting Margery away from the old goat."

"I thought you'd had it with her."

"Not quite. There's more to her than meets the eye."

"I'll bet there is. Give me the party line on your new brother-in-law."

"He's neat. May be the first Jewish President. Leah will have a ranch house, maid, car, two and a half children, and subscribe to *House Beautiful* and *The Wall Street Journal*. He's the answer to a Jewish mother's prayer—*his* mother's."

"He doesn't have a grain of love in him."

Bernie smiled. "Stop riding him. You should be happy we're getting a go-getter in the family. It's nice to think that when Laban's gone we'll have another Laban to carry on. Think of the wear and tear it'll save us. Imagine how miserable it would be to become one of those families who goes from shirt sleeves to shirt sleeves in two generations. As long as Jackson squats in the corner counting money, he's my boy."

Rachel gulped her drink. "You're no better than Tommy

Manville and Lance Reventlow. You and your Margery Schmidt. You spend your life listening to the tunes of a piper you don't have to pay."

Bernie sipped at one of his martinis. "We've had our talk. Good-bye."

"Not yet. Don't you feel the slightest bit worried about Leah?"

"Why should I? She's been very careful to make the bed she's going to lie in. She'd probably kill anybody who tried to muss the sheets. She's a girl who prizes property. Nobody gets a bigger charge out of pillows, rugs, furniture, pots and pans. Watch her rock and roll with Jackson's punches. They're made for each other—ask Jackson's mother. They'll never have an argument. They're two sensible people who will map their lives to the grave: vacations on time, meals on time, life insurance, cemetery lots. Excellent people with whom I intend to have as little to do as possible."

"You've lost a sister but picked up a good business manager, is that it? Your family means nothing to you."

Bernie finished his martini and asked for another. "You always say I don't know how to enjoy myself. Let me go enjoy myself."

"No. Tell me about Margery Schmidt. She's a bigot."

"She's beautiful and I like the way she makes hate."

"What do you talk about afterwards?"

"Who talks? Can I go now?"

She drew a deep breath. The air mixed with scotch made her dizzy. "Give me your idea of Crevecoeur and I'll let you go."

"He's a bum, a good-for-nothing bum, and I think you're making a fool of yourself. He's laughing at you. He's a rich man's Saint Francis, a poor man's Thoreau."

"I'm thinking I might marry him."

Bernie shrugged and looked irritated as his martinis dripped on his hands. "Take a sauna; it'll do the same thing. You don't marry bums, you send them to the Salvation Army. Hell, I don't care. Do what you like. I'm going."

"Go," she said. "Go, you delivery boy of conclusions." She felt sad. How could her brother be so intelligent and yet so unwise? He was enigmatic only to himself. He played with millions of ideas but didn't believe in any of them, and that made him the heavy-handed person he was. That was why Laban frustrated him so: Laban had some ideas he wouldn't play with; Laban, the showman, had a private life.

As she watched Bernie move off holding the martinis above his head, she caught sight of Leah in her wedding gown dancing with Ronnie. Her eyes were closed and her face glowing. She looked like a bride. Rachel felt weak in the knees, and to justify her giddiness got another scotch on the rocks. She drained it in quick gulps, standing next to a fat-bellied man who looked like Eugene Pallette and was talking in Pallette's gravelly voice to several men grouped around him. He turned and smiled at her. "Hello, Miss Laban," he said. "Your daddy throws a very nice wedding."

"You know it, baby," said Rachel.

He laughed. "Would you honor an old man with a dance?"

"No, thanks," she said. "I don't dance with strangers. You have to draw the line somewhere." She moved away, looking for Laban to tell her who the man was. She couldn't find him, but discovered Ronnie standing alone against a wall. She ran to him. "What's the matter?" she said. "You look like a private eye watching the silver and crystal. I expect my dates to circulate, be popular. See that big fat man over there at the bar? Do you know who he is?"

"That big fat man is the Governor," said Ronnie. "He runs the state."

Rachel was delighted. "He tried to pick me up. Imagine," she said, and darted off to Jackson Schwartz, who was sitting with Leah on folding chairs, sipping champagne and swiveling in all directions, making sure he was getting his money's worth. Leah was looking less like a bride and more like a housewife, ready to pull out a bundle of socks for darning. Rachel tugged at Jackson. "Come on," she said. "I haven't had a crack at you all night."

Jackson turned his head toward Leah and she nodded. "Feeling pretty cocky?" Rachel said as he swung her around. She put her head on his shoulder. His body felt as bland as ever and she marveled at his inability to arouse her even when she was drunk.

"I feel great," said Jackson.

"Life is just a bowl of cherries. Like Laban said, all you have to do is pick the right one."

"Rachel," said Jackson. "Seriously, I want us to be friends. I'm your brother-in-law now. We may not have seen eye to eye in the past but I want bygones to be bygones. I'm going to devote my life to making Leah happy."

"Ducky," said Rachel. "You've got a heart of gold, pure gold." She jammed against him, trying to get him excited, because, God damn him, he was such an ass, and there he was, probing for all he was worth, and she couldn't stand his guts. The hell with him. She was off again, leaving him flat before the music stopped, running back to Ronnie. "You're my last friend on earth, Ronnie, and you're stuck with me," she said. "Why are you so much more man than Jackson Schwartz?"

"You're drunk," he said.

"Ronnie," said Rachel, head hurting, ready to cry, "talk to me about Crevecoeur."

"Don't start that again."

"I know you," said Rachel. "You think you're opaque but I see through you. You're soft as mush. You need friends as much as I do but you won't admit it. You're afraid to be hurt and that makes you a coward. Well, get it through your skull you can't fool me."

"You don't know what you're talking about," said Ronnie. "Like I said, you're drunk." She had no chance to answer because he suddenly added, "Come on," went past her and ran toward the center of the hall. She swung around and saw a swelling knot of people crowding each other in the impudent way of people watching something they knew they shouldn't. They looked like a group of children around a fight, and she rushed forward in a mixture of dread and exhilaration.

She pushed through fiercely, surprised how buttery the massed forms were, made the inner circle and found, of course, Laban. He was lying on his back on the floor, his face as still as if he were holding his breath on a bet, and another man, plump and round with short arms, held his head against Laban's chest. She recognized him. It was Dr. Wanderscheid.

She whispered to Ronnie, who was beside her gripping her elbow, "Laban's kooky, you know. And that Dr. Wanderscheid's another screwball. Everybody knows what Laban'll do for a laugh."

Dr. Wanderscheid lifted his head. "He's gone," he said, his voice as conspiratorial as Rachel's, so much so that she laughed aloud and made people stare. She heard a sob and saw Beatrice a few feet away, big breasts heaving, eyes wide, and thought, The last person to know. Always the last person to know.

Somebody—could it be Ronnie?—hit her on the top of the head and her knees buckled. She leaned against him to keep from falling and realized that she'd been struck with the improbable fact of her father's mortality.

Beatrice dropped beside Laban on the floor, her dress sliding up her thighs, and cradled Laban's head in her lap. Her mind flying apart in every direction, all Rachel could think was, Laban, this isn't funny. This isn't funny at all. Get up and do it right.

Leah stood with Jackson at the back of the crowd. As soon as people noticed her they whispered and nudged each other. Their deference to tragedy created a corridor for her to pass through but she refused to budge, and soon their curiosity plugged the gap. Weeds of hair shrouded the tunnel through a mountain of skulls and hip-sockets, and the hole of light at the other end led, as she suspected, to death. She was buried alive, in her wedding dress, by an avalanche of human flesh. She was cold. The watery blood stopped flowing in her veins and turned her heart to ice. She stood on a frozen spring in a sunless age, bits of coal planted in her eyeballs; an arrowhead became her nose, a steel comb her teeth.

"My God, my God," said Jackson. "What a terrible thing to happen. I still can't believe it." He tried to ease her forward with a gentle pressure on her elbow. "We've got to join the family, Leah," he said. "Somebody's got to take charge. It's awful, I know, but we can't leave him lying there."

She was stuck to the frozen floor, her feet reorganized into molecular blocks without human properties. He tugged. "Please, Leah, we can't just stand here. It doesn't look right."

She turned and carved words into the wooden planes of his face. "We've got to hurry," she said, "or we'll miss the train."

He stared at her. "Leah, please listen. I know it's a shock, but you've got to face facts. Your father has just passed away. We can't possibly think about going away now. Look, there's Bernie and Rachel and Beatrice. Let's talk it over with them and see what's to be done."

"You talk. Give me my ticket."

His face traveled through its various shades of red and wound up glistening with iridescent globules. He was sweating a rainbow of blood. She saw him as a carcass suspended on a hook above a sawdust floor. She meant what she said; he could stay behind if he wanted to.

"You know I wouldn't do that," he said. "I want to do whatever's best for you. If you really think we should go ahead as planned and take the train, that's what we'll do." He struggled with his collar and gulped for air. "Do you mind if we stop for a second at the house? I forgot something."

She was a dark room pierced by a ray of light projected on a screen. The first slide was a survival shelter. Click. The second was a foreign language painted in old Gothic. Click. The third was a prayer shawl swaying back and forth beneath a green eye shade. "I do mind," she said. "We're going straight to the station. Come, if you're coming." As she clanked on armor-encased legs toward the rear of the hall, she became aware of hot needles piercing her refrigerated back. The pain couldn't be denied, and turning to face her tormentor, she met her magnified face hanging on the front wall. It moved toward her in a swollen wave of tears and drowned in her neck, and Rachel said, "Leah. Honey. Poor Daddy."

Leah pried loose from Rachel's coupled arms and stepped back. "Let's go, Jackson," she said. "We'll miss our train." She pushed her heavy feet toward the door.

Rachel ran in front of her, eyes burning wetly—gasoline on the surface of a lake. "Don't do it, Leah. It's tough on all of us. You can't go. Laban's dead. He's dead."

Leah's arm, encased in chain mail, elbow locked, moved in a metallic arc that ended hard against Rachel's cheek. The blow made white marks that turned red before Rachel's hand came up to cover them. "Get out of the way," said Leah. Rachel sobbed and ran away. "Hurry up," Leah said to Jackson. "We've wasted too much time already."

Only after the fact did the fact become real. It wasn't Laban's death that affected Rachel, but the realization that Laban was no longer alive. Huddled against the door of the station wagon as Ronnie drove her home, she tried to imagine where his vitality had gone. It couldn't simply disappear. In apothecary shops all over the country his energy was being conserved in corked bottles. Laban's Magic Elixir: one sip and cripples danced; a cupful and God cupped you in the palm of his hand and stroked your ruffled feathers.

Her face throbbed from Leah's blow. The rest of her body was numb. She tried to think of a poem to do Leah justice: A cheek for a nose/Is a rose is a rose. She could never forgive Leah for running out on Laban when he needed her. If they'd all stuck together and massaged his heart, Laban would have smiled. They could have worked miracles. Instead Laban would wear a long face throughout eternity.

She was grateful to Ronnie. He seemed sad, as if he had lost something of value. He made no effort to cheer her up with talk of this or that. He left her with the dignity of silence and gave her confidence in her grief. She hated to see Laban go, and nobody would ever talk her out of it. When they stopped in front of the house, Ronnie came around and opened the door for her, and this obsolete act of courtesy moved her to tears. "Take the car to the farm, Ronnie," she said. "I won't be needing it for a while." She ran past him, crying, hearing Laban's voice saying, Thanks for the tears, baby, but no thanks. Play the game.

Inside, she looked for Bernie and Beatrice upstairs and down, but they hadn't come back yet. Sitting in the living room and waiting, she composed her face in melancholy, but images of loincloths and skullcaps and poker chips kept interfering. Laban's face kept dissolving into upper-case aphorisms: THERE WAS A GREAT CRY IN EGYPT: FOR THERE WAS NOT A HOUSE WHERE THERE WAS NOT ONE DEAD. CALL NO MAN HAPPY TILL YOU KNOW THE NATURE OF HIS DEATH. SPARE ME THE WHISPERING, CROWDED ROOM, THE FRIENDS WHO COME AND GAPE AND GO. She wound up with THE GODS VISIT THE SINS OF THE FATHERS UPON THE CHILDREN. What sins had he left them with? He hated to break appointments: Leah had kept her date with the honeymoon train. He loved to dance: They'd all danced at his death. He gave God a hard time: So did Bernie. And she herself? It wasn't whether you won or lost, but if you played the game.

She eyed the bookshelves. There it was, *A History of the Jewish People,* cuddling against *The Decline and Fall of the Roman Empire.* The lion's share to Leah—and now that meant Jackson Schwartz. "Dirty pool, Laban. Let us not to the marriage of false minds admit treasure troves."

Go ahead, baby. Here, I'll give you a helping hand, and he shoved her with fingers at her back. She glared. "Cut it out. Just play dead like you're supposed to. Stop trying to make a dishonest woman out of me. Haven't you done enough?"

God helps them who help themselves, baby. Where there's a will there's a way. All can be lost, even the unconquerable will. Didn't I teach you anything?

"Listen, Laban," she said, "you taught me plenty."

Come on, baby, add up the score. Don't strike out on me now. Leah's doing the Watusi on my grave. Jackson married her for my money. There's no honor among thieves. Get with it.

"All right already," she said. "I'll do it." She ran to the window. Nobody was in sight. She went to the bookshelf and pulled out the will. She held it, a dead cat, by two fingers, put it back in *A History of the Jewish People* and the book back on the shelf. She heard a car pull up and grabbed the book again and took out the will. She looked for a hiding place. The chair cushion —she unzipped the cover and slid the will in on the bottom side and rezipped the cover. They were fumbling at the door when she ran upstairs and fell on her old bed like an escaped convict who hadn't slept for days.

Leah lay in the lower bunk of the compartment and listened to Jackson tossing above her. He hadn't made any effort to touch her, as if waiting for a sign. She hadn't given him any. The compartment was cool and she lay nude under a light blanket, encased in a block of black ice. Her eyes probed the darkness of lids that might never bother to open again. She saw Laban as a Roman warrior with skirt, breastplate and arching helmet, exposing hairy legs, pushing meatballs and spaghetti through his face guard, and without warning, her body got so hot she began to perspire. She found herself in a swelter of sensation and dug a hand into her goin. "Jackson," she said.

"Yes, dear. What is it?" he said.

"I want you."

"I'll be right there." He climbed down and got in beside her. She threw herself at him, pinning his lips and legs with hers. His hand found her breast and squeezed. She unbuttoned his pajama tops. He pulled away and stood up to take off his clothes. He was breathing hard.

"Hurry up," she said. "Will you hurry?"

"Don't you think I should put something on?" he said.

"No, no, it's all right. Hurry."

He fell on top of her. "I'll try to be gentle," he said. "It may hurt a little."

"Yes. Be gentle," she said and tore at his flesh.

He finished almost at once, and lay with all his weight on her like a stranded whale. Suffocating, she said nothing and waited for him to make the next move. He got up and stood by the side of the bunk. "Why didn't you tell me?" he said. "It wouldn't have mattered to me. You at least could have told me."

She searched for an epitaph her father might have appreciated. "Gentlewomen don't tell," she said, and turned on her side to go to sleep.

He wasn't through; he climbed back into bed. "It doesn't matter," he said. "Really it doesn't. In a way I'm glad."

She pulled him toward her and nibbled at his lips. "Thank you, Jackson," she said.

Rachel sat on top of the will and wondered how Bernie and Beatrice could miss the scarlet letter on her forehead. She was relieved she hadn't burned it. She could put it back any time and no one would be the wiser. She could organize a treasure hunt and furnish clues like, If you stand instead of sit, You will have less chance of finding it. She wondered about herself. While Beatrice sat with a swollen face and eyes swimming in tears, she felt gay. And yet, Laban, she informed him, I've lost my best friend. You can understand that even if I can't.

"He knew all summer he was going to die and didn't tell us," said Rachel. "But you knew."

"Yes," said Beatrice, wiping her eyes and blowing her nose. "Cancer is such an ugly word. He made me promise not to tell anybody, especially the children. He couldn't stand being treated like a dying man."

"The hero," said Bernie. "He could never give anybody a chance. Keep it light and gay. He deserved everything I said to him. I don't regret a word."

"God forbid you should, Bernie," said Rachel. "He'd hate that. He'd want to keep a clear picture of your loving-kindnesses."

"Bernie," whispered Beatrice, "can't you find any sorrow in your heart? He loved you very much. He told me so."

"I bet he did. I bet he came right out and said, I love that Bernie baby. Knock it off—you're safe now. Stop pretending to be the patsy. He's dead, remember? The masquerade's over and you can take the mask off. You made it, sweetie. You're a rich, young, pretty widow. You outlasted the old Jew."

Beatrice shook her head. "Your father said you have a good heart and didn't mean what you said. Why must you say such things?"

"The truth hurts, baby. You don't mind my calling you baby? I can't let the word go begging."

"Speaking of beggars," said Rachel, waving her red flag of guilt for all to see, "what about you and me? According to the will we're penniless orphans, or don't you care as long as you've got your gift of gab?"

"That's right. The will," Bernie said to Beatrice. "What were you saying about love?"

"He loved you all," said Beatrice.

"Sure. Some joke. I'll tell you what. I'll live on love while I finish law school. And Rachel can offer love for sale. It's what makes the world go around. Clue Rachel. How does she catch a rich old Wasp who likes to sting young Jewesses?"

"He thought of you," said Beatrice. She reached into the pocket of her housecoat and took out a pair of checks, which she handed them. "He said if anything ever happened I was to give you each five thousand dollars out of the joint checking account right away."

Bernie folded the check and placed it in his wallet. "Five thousand bucks from a millionaire philanthropist to his son. Okay. I deserved it."

"He loved both of you very much."

"Will you cut it out?" said Bernie. "You can't be that much of an idiot. Try hard. Pretend for a minute you don't have to pretend. See how easy it gets."

"Let her alone," said Rachel. "Stop picking on her. She hasn't done anything but be nice to you. If she didn't want to she didn't have to give us the checks."

Bernie rubbed his eyes. "Okay," he said. "Beatrice, I wish you all the luck in the world. Have fun on the Riviera. You're my favorite stepmother." Beatrice cried into her handkerchief.

"When's the funeral?" said Bernie, his mouth working into a spasm. "We've got to get back to school."

"The day after tomorrow," said Rachel. "I talked to Rabbi Isaacson." She braced herself. "But you'll have to go back without me. I've decided to quit for a while."

"What kind of foolish statement is that? Don't you go haywire on me. Of course you're going back. What's around here for you?"

"I'm going to stay on at Crevecoeur's farm."

Bernie twitched. "Look, Rachel, listen to me. A week or two, okay. Crazy but okay. Foolish but not fatal. This would be fatal. You'll turn into a coffee-house girl who talks about Life."

She decided he was trying to be nice and patted his hand. "I'll be okay. I'll probably go back, but not for a while."

"I'd love to have you stay here with me," said Beatrice. "It would mean so much to me."

"I'll come visit. I promise," said Rachel.

"Is this your house now?" asked Bernie. "I thought you only get one third."

Beatrice looked at him, wide-eyed. "I don't really know. I haven't thought about it."

Bernie shrugged. "It's yours as far as I'm concerned—as if that'll do you any good." He turned to Rachel. "What about Leah? You contact her about the funeral?"

"No, I didn't and I don't intend to," said Rachel. "She knows she should be here. I may never speak to her again."

"Don't say that," said Beatrice. "Please. Families should stick together. Think how terrible she must have felt with Laban dying at her wedding. The poor thing must be out of her mind."

Bernie stood up. "Beatrice, you're too much for me—I mean, you're in a class by yourself. I'll send her the telegram, I'll go to the funeral and then I'm getting the hell out of here. With a little luck and if I don't look back I might even survive."

Rachel got up and put a hand on Bernie's shoulder. "Bernie," she said, "he's dead. You've got nobody to argue with. Don't you feel anything?"

"Yes," he said. "Free."

Leah lay behind the drawn wine-colored curtains of the hotel room, her sheer white silk nightgown bunched around her neck like an ancient Spanish nobleman's ruff, and listened to the muffled sounds of Jackson in the bathroom. After each sexual episode he took a shower and scrubbed every inch of his skin. The streets of the city were too far below for even the ordinary traffic noises of midmorning to reach her, but she strained to catch the sound of an occasional horn. She fingered the gold band on her finger.

Jackson came back, glanced at her quickly and averted his eyes, and fumbled for cigarettes at the bureau. With his gray checked dressing gown belted at the middle, he was a boy dressed up in a father's clothes. He picked up the telegram and quickly put it down when he saw her watching him. "The funeral's tomorrow," he said.

She straightened her legs and folded her arms across her middle. She was lying in an unpainted pine box waiting for the lid to slam her shut. He had only to order her body shipped to Laban's funeral and she would go. While they shoveled dirt on the coffin she would stand with blank eyes and await further orders. He puffed on his cigarette. "I hate to keep bringing it up," he said finally, "but what will people think of us for not being there? It will look terrible. They'll say we have no respect for your father." He hesitated. "It'll seem especially bad when they find out he left you the residue of his estate."

"If you order me to go, I'll go," she said.

"Why would I do that? You know I wouldn't. I'll always respect your wishes. If you don't feel you're up to going to the funeral, that's the end of it."

She didn't know what to do with him. What she wanted was that he *not* respect her wishes; that was all she asked. She wanted to be a machine into which he fed relevant data; she would respond when he pushed the red button. But the only buttons he pushed were the nipples on her breasts. "Jackson," she said, "I'll never interfere with your position in the law firm. No matter what you do I'll never write a letter asking that you be fired."

His hand trembled as he raised the cigarette to his lips. "Why did you bring that up? I wish you wouldn't. I want only to make you happy. I'll never mention the funeral again."

"All right," she said. He was over Laban's pork barrel and he would sprawl there, waiting with an anxious smile for kicks in the rear end. She had intended to be the wife baking bread from crumbs, clothes from rags, standing at the switchyards in early morning to buy vegetables. She had expected to be in his sight and out of his mind. Instead, she was yoked to a sober man determined to keep his good fortune intact by humoring her. She was left with a life-size puppet she took to bed.

She stretched out her hand and he extended his. She ran a finger along the blond hairs of his arm. When they got home, it would be better. There would be socks to darn, meals to prepare, washing and dusting and sweeping. And there would be Beatrice, sufficiently demanding in her helplessness. In time, when Jackson saw he could get away with anything, he might command it. He was too good-looking, too blue-eyed and light-haired, too broad-shouldered and narrow-waisted. He must be observing the waiting period until he could decently find a willowy Scandinavian playmate who understood him; then he would find the courage to snap his fingers at Leah for the morning-after Alka Seltzer. He would forget to beg her pardon and she would, once again, be free behind bars.

She dressed for breakfast with care: her hair caught in a bun, the simple black dress and pumps, the strand of imitation pearls around her neck—his kind of lady. He would, of course, buy her real pearls as soon as he could afford it. He wore his Cambridge gray suit, striped tie and button-down, French-cuff shirt.

When they stepped out of the elevator directly in front of the desk, Leah heard a groaning from the sitting room on the left. The desk clerk was talking on the telephone. A tall, silver-haired man with a pretty woman and two little girls moved past them toward the restaurant on the right. "Do you hear that noise?" she said.

Jackson listened. "It's probably a television program," he said.

"Don't you think we'd better go see?"

"Do you think we should?"

"Yes."

She walked quickly into the deserted room and he trailed behind. The groans came from the rear, where she could see the cables of an elevator car exposed in an open shaft. She went over and looked down. A young man in overalls was lying at the bottom of the shaft, twisted on his back. "Help me, lady. My leg's broken," he said and moaned.

She turned to Jackson and found him lingering in the front of the room. "There's a man down here with a broken leg."

He came forward slowly and stared down. "Are you hurt?" he asked.

"Mister, you must be kidding. Get me out of here. I'm dying."

"We'll go tell the clerk," he said.

Leah got down on her knees and bent over the shaft. "We'll help you," she said. "It'll just be a few minutes." She jerked her head at Jackson. "What are you waiting for?"

"Aren't you coming?"

"I'll wait here. Will you please go?"

He rushed off and she said to the man, "I wish there was something I could do. Does it help to talk?"

He smiled between clenched teeth. "Sure. Let's you and me do the Frug, what do you say? Would it get your hubby sore?"

"No. He likes me to get plenty of exercise."

"I bet he does. He keeps you hopping, huh?"

"All the time." She felt possessed. She stared down the rectangular hole at the man bent like a discarded toy and she started to cry.

"Jesus, lady. What you doing that for? It's only a broken leg. I'll be okay." She couldn't stop. A backload of tears streamed down her cheeks and she swayed blindly at the edge of the shaft. Hands grabbed her shoulders and pulled her up.

"Leah, for God's sake, are you all right? You almost fell," said Jackson. "What's the matter?" She shook her head in anger and jerked away.

Jackson leaned over the shaft. "Hey, fella, they're on the way. We've sent for the fire department and an ambulance."

"Thanks, buddy. The dame okay?"

"Of course she is." He looked at Leah. "You all right?"

She wiped her face. Her tear ducts sealed shut at the sight of Jackson's face. She nodded and dropped back to her knees at the elevator. "Mister, I'm back."

"Jesus, lady, you had me scared. I know I ain't pretty but I didn't think I had a face that made women cry."

"You have a nice face," she said.

"What do you know? Lady, if I had any guts I'd climb up the cable for that."

"Leah," said Jackson, "I think we'd better go. We can't do him any more good."

"You go. Get a table."

"Leah, please. Let's not get involved. This may boil down to a law suit and we'd get all tangled up as witnesses. We've done enough for him."

"You go." She paused and said, "That's an order."

His face reddened. He walked away without a word. She called down, "You still there?"

"No, ma'am. I just got out through a secret panel. Listen, lady. I don't want to get you in dutch with your old man."

"Don't worry about him. You married?"

"Don't bet on it. I'm footloose and fancy free."

"As soon as you're well, we're going dancing. That's a promise."

"Sure we are. What's your name, lady? Who am I going out with?"

"Margery Schmidt. My husband's name is Jackson Schmidt," she said without hesitation. "He's the only one in the phone book."

The man let out a groan. After a moment, he said in a choked voice. "Excuse me, Margery. I got a hair in my throat."

She heard movement behind her and looked around; the firemen were coming in. "Don't forget," she said. "Jackson Schmidt, the only one in the phone book. Good-bye."

"Good-bye, Margie, and thanks."

In the restaurant Leah saw her husband at a table and pushed past the maître d'hôtel. Jackson examined his napkin while she was being seated. The dining room gleamed with crystal chandeliers and huge Negroes in silken robes, African kings with curved swords strapped to their waists and turbans wound around their heads. She examined Jackson in his gray suit, cuff links glinting in the flame of a nearby brandy dessert. He said slowly, "Did you give them your name?"

"Yes, indeed."

"Did you have to? You mark my words. We're right smack in the middle of a personal injury or workmen's compensation case."

"I've decided to go home the day after tomorrow," she said.

"The day after the funeral? But that's the very worst time. Be reasonable. If you don't want to leave tomorrow let's at least stay out the week. Everybody'll think we're terrible."

"The day after tomorrow," she said, "and that's an order."

He said in a low voice, "Do you have to keep talking to me like that?"

"Somebody has to take charge," she said and turned to a Negro sultan. "We're ready to order now," she said.

As they examined the engraved menus Jackson said, "Maybe

it's not such a bad idea at that. We've got to get the will pro-
bated. Do you happen to know who the executor is?"

"I get two thirds of everything."

"I know, Leah."

She gazed at him wide-eyed until he was forced to meet her
stare. "It must be frightening," she said, "to be married to such a
rich woman. Aren't you frightened?"

He looked away again. "I wish you wouldn't talk like that," he
said.

Through the rear window of the limousine, Rachel could see the
interminable line of cars, headlights glowing dully in the sunlight,
bulling through traffic. Laban was undoubtedly pleased at the
turnout although he would never know which of his people were
only fair-weather fans. It was a perfect day, clear and warm, for
Laban's last game of the season. She sat between Beatrice and
Bernie and wondered how Leah could live with the knowledge
that she'd played hookey. Never had she felt more twinless. It
made no sense at all for Leah not to grant Laban his last rites. If
it were Bernie she could understand—a final thumbing of a well-
thumbed nose—but Bernie sat as quietly as a doped mouse. Leah
had spent her life making Laban comfortable and she should be
there to help put him to his final rest. Rachel thought of the will
nestling in its cushion, and she clung to the vision of Jackson's
face when he discovered it was missing. It was the only pleasure
she had left from the theft and it wasn't enough. She had made
up her mind to produce the will as soon as possible, but her body

still hesitated to execute the order. Laban, she thought, you've got two swell daughters. One ignores your funeral and the other picks pennies off your eyes.

Worn but composed, Beatrice was the perfect widow in her black dress, pearl-white skin and puffy eyes. Bernie huddled within himself at the other window. Rachel was determined to play it Laban's way. She couldn't believe he wanted to go out draped in a black-bordered flag. If he could have managed it he'd have painted signs along the route: FIVE HUNDRED YARDS TO LA-BAN'S; FOUR HUNDRED YARDS TO LABAN'S; ONLY TWO HUNDRED MORE YARDS TO LABAN'S. At a hundred yards he'd have five girls in short, red, flaring skirts waving pompoms and chanting, You're about to arrive at Laban's Retreat—fun and free gifts for all! Poor Laban, she whispered. They've poured all that black coffee into you and sobered you up.

The casket, with lowering straps attached, was waiting at the grave. Rabbi Isaacson nodded and smiled at them. Rachel smiled back; here was a man who knew how to pay his last respects. The park was filled to overflowing. Wherever she looked people stood massed. The grave was the center circle of an arena. Still people kept coming.

And Rabbi Isaacson in a clear voice that quieted the shuffling feet and made them still as the grave, said: "We know, O God, that Thy ways are sure, that not without wise purpose dost Thou afflict Thy children. In Thine abundant goodness Thou didst give us this loved one in whose rejoicing life we have rejoiced."

There was a sharp, amused cough and Rachel glared at Bernie. With his head thrown back, he let out a whoop, oblivious to stares. Rachel, her heart pounding, said, "Shut up." He hadn't folded. He intended to have the last laugh on Laban, and it wasn't fair.

Rabbi Isaacson said: "Thy richest blessings we shared with him in overflowing measure. His love, answering to ours, his gay companionship with us, his tenderness, responding to ours, filled our days with beauty and gladness. We praise Thee for Thy boundless goodness unto us." Bernie giggled.

Rabbi Isaacson said: "Now his earthly end has come. We give him back unto Thee in faith and submission. We do not murmur against Thee."

"Go on. Murmur," said Bernie.

"Though our pain be deep we trust in Thee and praise Thee for Thy goodness unto us. We thank Thee for all these years of life and joy and love with him. We cherish that love, that joy, though he be gone; and reverently we shall hallow his memory in love, in joy undying."

Bernie dropped to his knees in the piled earth and laughed into the grave. The rabbi watched him and waited. Bernie stood up with spots of dirt like elbow patches at his knees, and the rabbi said: "It is said that when his son died, Rabbi Levi Yitzchak danced as he followed the coffin on its bier. Some of his followers expressed their astonishment. 'A pure soul,' said Rabbi Yitzchak, 'was given to me. A pure soul I render back.' "

Bernie, lips twitching, confronted the rabbi. Beatrice was crying. Rachel heard sobs from the audience.

"Quiet Thou, O Father, our vain yearnings after him. Make our true love a constant inspiration to lives of service and gladness that his memory may live through us and endure among men. May all of us come to Thee strong and rejoicing, for with Thee is the fountain of all life. In Thy light we shall see light.

"All flesh is grass and the goodliness thereof as the flower of the field. The grass withereth, the flower fadeth. The body dies and is laid in the earth. Dust returneth to dust but the spirit returneth unto God Who gave it. God gave and God took away. Praised be the name of God.

"May God spread the tabernacle of His peace over William Laban. We lift up our hearts unto Him Who is the source of all light and all joy. He wounds and He heals. He causes death and He gives life. May the Father of peace send peace to all who mourn. Amen."

"Take *me* away," Bernie said, and he jumped into the grave. A sound, speech without words, moved through the crowd. Through blurred eyes Rachel saw Crevecoeur and Ronnie materialize at the graveside, lean down and pull Bernie out. It happened so quickly that all Rachel could feel was gratitude toward Crevecoeur and Ronnie for coming to her father's funeral. She ran forward and buried her face in Crevecoeur's chest and he held her while she sobbed.

On the way back to the house Bernie sat at one window, hands over his eyes, and Rachel sat at the other, with Beatrice in between. Rachel had decided to keep as far away from Bernie as possible; watching him, she felt sorry for him. He was suffering —whether over Laban or his own foolishness didn't matter. She was a push-over for repenters. Beatrice must have felt the same way, for she reached out and patted Bernie's knee. "I know you loved your father," she said. "It would make him so happy, Bernie."

His shoulders shook and he uttered muffled noises behind his hands. He dropped his arms and revealed himself. He was occupied with another spasm of laughter. He pulled out a handkerchief and wiped his eyes. "Jesus, Beatrice, you're a peach," he said. He sobered and with a swift gesture slid his hand between her legs. "The king is dead, Mom. Long live the king."

Beatrice closed her eyes. She made no move to protect herself but seemed to dissolve in a collapse of will. Rachel, after a wild look at the driver, grabbed Bernie's arm. "Are you absolutely mad? Do you want to be put away?"

Bernie withdrew his arm and wiggled his fingers. "When the fat cat's gone, the mice live on," he said. "You know how long I've been stuck in my hole?"

"Bernie the rat," said Rachel. "And just a minute ago I was feeling sorry for you. I thought that for once in your life you had an honest emotion. Just keep it up. Fight with a ghost. It's all you deserve."

Bernie ran his hand along Beatrice's cheek. She kept her eyes shut. "Did you ever realize how pretty Beatrice is? Laban had real taste. I could do a lot worse than with his leavings."

"What happened? Did Margery Schmidt kick you out?"

"That's right. She wrote a letter to the Pope, carbon copy to the United Arab Republic, claiming she has my signed confession that the Jews killed Christ. The problem is, Margery just doesn't understand me. Beatrice understands me. Beatrice likes Jewish men. She knows that Jews are too humane to crucify apostates. They laugh them to death. Bea, Mom baby, how about you and me going steady?"

"You know what's going to happen to you?" said Rachel. "It's inevitable. Fewer and fewer people are going to listen to you. You'll move from place to place wearing out new acquaintances faster and faster. Finally you'll wind up standing on an orange crate in the middle of a square. You'll wear a wooden cross on your back and drive nails through your hands and nobody will pay the slightest attention. You'll get gray at the temples and take chorus girls to night clubs. They'll steal your money and break your cane over your head. You'll write your memoirs in a shabby, filthy room with newspapers stuffed in broken windows in the dead of winter. And when you die nobody will discover your body for ten days. After the city buries you they'll hang the pages of your manuscript on a nail in an outhouse."

"That's a pretty picture," said Bernie. "I'll paint you one. You're going to meet a dirty, diseased, bearded stranger rooting with a pointed stick in your garbage can. You'll invite him into your modest, decent apartment and give him a bowl of hot Campbell's chicken soup with noodles. He'll take a bath and shave and turn out to be tall, handsome and gentle. He'll sleep between your clean white sheets. You'll work in a laundry to keep him in creature comforts until he gets back on his feet. You'll kiss him and make him well and he'll confess he's really Reginald Courtney, the billionaire plankton king, and he loves you because you're the first woman to love him for himself. You'll sail into a honeymoon sunset on his America's Cup yacht. You'll have five children—three pretty girls and two handsome boys—a Siamese cat, an Irish setter and a Shetland pony. You'll sit at the grand piano in your living room and strike an occasional key while you look through the bay window at the gardener sprinkling powdered pecan shells over the iris beds and clipping the contoured hedges. You'll read in the society section about a certain plankton billionaire and an Italian actress doing uncertain things on the Riviera. You'll read about Reginald being lost at sea during a cocktail party, and you'll become Rachel Courtney, the plankton queen. Your children grow up. One girl will have a junior year abroad and never come back. One girl will marry an insurance man from the West Coast and send you pictures of your grandchildren by registered mail. The other girl will go into show business and take an overdose of Nembutal. One boy will marry a Negro princess and move to a medical hospital in Nigeria; the other will be homosexual and move to Tangletown. You'll move from place to place wearing out new acquaintances and dyeing your hair orange. You'll pose standing on a bank vault in the middle of Trafalgar Square. Your hair will fall out in patches and you'll take chorus boys to night clubs. You'll write your memoirs in a Scottish castle on newspapers piled to the ceiling with hundred dollar bills slipped between each page. You won't leave the castle for ten years and when you die it will be another ten years before they discover your body, when the first group of paying tourists comes through. Your memoirs are published posthumously by a vanity press. You leave your money to the state and your birthday becomes a national holiday. The Rachel Laban Courtney Day. You'll be remembered one day a year."

"At least I'll be remembered," said Rachel. "Who'll remember you?"

"Please," said Beatrice, clenching her hands. "Please don't quarrel. I can't bear it any more."

"Gee, Beatrice," said Bernie, "there's *your* future yet to consider," but Rachel turned her back and refused to listen.

The desk was down to its natural grain, a light oak with dark knots, and Leah was sanding it with a ball of soft steel wool. Soon she would rub it with linseed oil. The desk, one of the objects that had survived the fire because it was too heavy to move, stood its ground in the poker room. The round table with its claw feet and green covering was undisturbed, and even Laban's eye shade hung by its elastic band on one of the wicker chairs. She sat at the table, put the eye shade on her head and shuffled the cards. She dealt herself a hand of seven-card stud, made a pair of eights and satisfied herself that she would have folded on the fourth card if it had been a real game. She picked up the collection of signs gathered from Laban's workshop and went upstairs to her room where she tacked them side by side on the wall.

THERE'S NOT A MAN THAT LIVES
WHO HATH NOT KNOWN
HIS GODLIKE HOURS

MAKE ME A CHILD AGAIN JUST FOR TONIGHT

When in Doubt Win the Trick

A CHILD SAID WHAT IS GRASS?

She put up fifteen of them in all. Tomorrow she would put up more.

The telephone rang and she answered it at the same time as Beatrice. It was Jackson and she waited until Beatrice hung up. "I'm with Mr. Hoy Sing," he said. "He wants to go to the Squirrel Club." He seemed to be pleading with her, but she didn't know what he wanted.

"Who's Mr. Hoy Sing?" she said.

"He's our biggest client and an old friend of your father's. I thought you might have heard of him from Mr. Laban. Hoy Sing Adult Toys? He invented the Toy Man. Leah, he'd like very much to meet you."

"I don't like the Squirrel Club," she said. "Do you insist that I go?"

"It's very important, Leah. Mr. Sing made a special point of it. Please come."

"Is that an order?"

"You know it isn't."

"All right," she said. "If he'll bring me a Toy Man."

"Be reasonable. They're very expensive. I can't go up to Mr. Sing just like that and ask him for one."

"Why not?" she said. "You said he was an old friend of Laban's. What are old friends for? That's the deal."

Jackson surrendered. "All right," he said. "I'll ask him even though I'll make a fool of myself. I hope we don't offend him too much."

She gave him another chance. "If you insist I'll go anyway."

He paused. "I can't. I'll never force you to do anything. I respect you too much for that."

"Then go ahead and ask him. Now."

"All right. Hold on a second."

In a few moments he was back on the line. "It's okay," he said. "Mr Sing says he's flattered that you're interested in his Toy Man. He'll bring his personal one. Wait till you see it, Leah. It's really something. We'll pick you up in an hour. Does that give you enough time?"

"I'll be ready," she said. She hung up and went into Beatrice's bedroom.

Beatrice was standing in front of her bureau mirror brushing her hair, which had finally lost its orange streaks. She was wearing one of her housecoats, her usual costume since Laban's death. She almost never left the house; it was as if she was waiting for Laban to tell her what to do. "Look," she said to Leah. "I'm pure blond again. It gives me a funny feeling to be blond again and not have Laban know."

"Jackson and I are going out to dinner," said Leah. "With a Mr. Hoy Sing. Do you know him?"

"Oh, yes. He's very nice."

"Would you like to come along? We're going to the Squirrel Club."

"You're sweet, Leah, but I couldn't," said Beatrice, continuing the strokes on her hair. It fell in a silken sweep around her shoulders. She looked young and pretty. "I know it seems silly but I can't. Not yet. But I'm glad you're going. You deserve to have a lot of fun."

"I haven't prepared dinner. What will you eat?"

"I'm not helpless, dear. I'll scramble eggs. I'll be fine."

"Do you know how to scramble eggs?"

"Of course. Stop pampering me. Anybody can make eggs."

"Don't let them cook too long. Take them off while they're moist."

Beatrice sighed. "You're a darling, but it's time I did things by myself. I'm going to be a marvelous cook—I've made a resolution. Someday I'll invite you to dinner and you'll be amazed."

"I'm sure I will, but meanwhile let me make something clear. I want you to stay on with us. Laban would like that."

Beatrice gave Leah a hug. "We can't go on like this. We really can't. It doesn't look right. I'm sure it makes Jackson very uncomfortable."

"You're wrong. It excites him. He stays awake nights thinking about it."

"Don't say that, Leah."

"It's true."

In her room Leah put on a black dress with a high oval neck. She wore no jewelry except a round gold watch that hung between her breasts by a gold chain. It would suit Jackson's idea of class in a classless society, and it amused her to dress for him. Her presentation would be something he remembered from eastern lawschool days. She'd be a D.A.R. girl standing on her grandmother's dignity, a vision of vested interest. She would alternate between low mumbles and loud, hard tones that made people look around, and Jackson would blush with pride. He existed by what he imagined he and she should be.

When she was ready she went downstairs to the living room and sat, hands folded in her lap, facing the front hallway, to give Mr. Hoy Sing the full impact of a wife who spent her days waiting for her husband. They came in, Mr. Sing carrying a tuxedo-clad dummy the size of a small boy. Jackson held what resembled a typewriter case. Mr. Sing was a slender, olive-skinned, middle-aged Eurasian, overdressed in a silk suit and hand-painted tie, who said with an exaggerated roll of eye, "I knew your dad well. A wonderful guy. His death was a loss to us all." His voice was hoarse around the edges. He deposited the Toy Man in a chair and Leah found herself caught in a fierce hug. She let her body flow into the squeeze before he released her. "Your daddy saved my business. No fooling. I was going under when he bailed me out, and it wasn't only money. He gave me the big idea. He said to me, 'There's plenty of toys for kids. What about the grownups?' That's what got me started on the Toy Man. Now I've got more money than Bayer has aspirins. I'd give that Laban guy the shirt off my back." Mr. Sing flung open his coat. "You want my shirt? I'll give it to you."

She shook her head. Jackson stood by, a regular fellow with his anxious set grin. "That won't be necessary, Mr. Sing. I just want the Toy Man. Show me how it works."

"You never saw one? You're missing the greatest show on earth." He opened the case and uncovered a machine that, in fact, looked like a typewriter. "This is the remote control console. Look. The lower keys type words. The upper ones handle motions. What do you want him to say and do? Just name it."

"You go ahead, Mr. Sing. Anything will do."

"Okay. Nothing tricky to start." Mr. Sing typed. "See this red button? That's the activator. Watch." He pressed the red button. The Toy Man stood up and said, "How do you do, Mrs. Schwartz? Let's you and me make music together." He had a thin, reedy, perfectly clear voice.

"He's marvelous, Mr. Sing," said Leah.

"Try him," said Mr. Sing. "Go ahead. If you want him to move, hit one of the motion buttons."

Leah selected GO AROUND IN A CIRCLE. She typed a message and pushed the red button. The Toy Man walked in a circle, avoiding a chair on the way, and recited, "I can't give you anything but love, baby." He completed the circle and stood still.

"See that?" said Mr. Sing. "How he went around the chair? All that's built in."

"You're a genius, Mr. Sing," said Leah.

"I'd be nothing without your daddy and don't think I'll ever forget it," said Mr. Sing. "You need anything, ask Mr. Sing." His hands cupped her shoulders. "This guy Schwartz, if he lets you down, runs after the Squirrels—anything—just let Sing know and I'll fix his clock. Got that, Jackson?"

Jackson imitated a laugh. "You don't have to worry about me, Mr. Sing."

Comfortable under Mr. Sing's hands, Leah looked into his eyes and didn't doubt his sincerity. He was a robber baron who would die for his family while he mowed down strangers in the course of trade. Every friend was a member of his family. "All I want," she said, "is your Toy Man."

"Leah," said Jackson, "I told you this is Mr. Sing's personal one. We'll buy another one."

"No, you won't," said Mr. Sing. "You'll never get one like this. It's yours, honey, with my blessing."

"Thank you, Mr. Sing," Leah said, and kissed him on the mouth. He winked and squeezed her shoulders. "His name," she said, "is Laban."

Mr. Sing laughed. "He'd get a kick out of that. You're a chip off the old block. Let's go tangle with the Squirrels."

"In a minute," said Leah. "I have to put Laban to bed." She

picked up the dummy, which was very light. "Jackson, would you carry the console upstairs for me? We'll be right back, Mr. Sing."

In the bedroom Jackson said, "Leah, Mr. Sing is very attached to this particular Toy Man."

"He's also very attached to me," said Leah. She placed Laban in her bed under the covers so that only his head showed.

"In the morning he may have second thoughts about it," said Jackson. "If he does would you mind giving it back if I get you another one right away?"

"You'd better not try."

Leah sat between the two men in the front seat of Laban's Cadillac, which Jackson had taken to driving. Mr. Sing promptly put his hand on her knee. Jackson couldn't help seeing the hand, with its little finger rubbing along her inner thigh. She didn't know her husband's business practices; perhaps he passed her name along to Chinese clients in Turkish baths. The best lay in town, Mr. Sing. My wife's a classy number, Mr. Sing, and my customers are always right.

When Mr. Sing's hand followed his little finger, she looked at him and he grinned. This was only the beginning of course. There would be more at the Squirrel Club; he would ogle the propped-up breasts, the flaring bushy tails, the masks—those squirrel heads on beautiful, bared bodies: an irresistible coupling of disguise and perversion—and tackle her under the table. She sat still under his fingers because he was a friend of her father's, he'd given her an expensive gift, and he was a man.

At the Squirrel Club, Jackson grew animated. He was in his element in the overflow crowd of bare shoulders and evening gowns, in the shower of diamonds and furs. His nostrils were quick on the scent of French perfume and his hands were busy back-slapping, hand-shaking, sleeve-touching the men they passed. Fingers touched and made a connection. Give an arm and there was an immediate short circuit. Eyes went up in smoke. Introduced by a breezy, "The wife," Leah followed Jackson through the daisy chain and Mr. Sing was content to press on from behind, body and breath hot on her trail. Mr. Sing knew what he wanted and he was out to get it all in one piece.

There were no tables to be had. Jackson Schwartz, attorney—as he'd proudly announced—for the Squirrel Club, floundered in front of his client Mr. Hoy Sing. The most he could do was get drinks and plates of little meatballs and hot potato salad and chicken slices; they stood with hands filled and wondered what to do. Finally Leah sat on the carpeted top step of a staircase, balanced the paper plate on her lap and started eating. Mr. Sing dropped down beside her, and with a worried look around, Jackson did the same on a step further down. People went past in a steady stream of curious glances; Jackson, squaring his shoulders, attacked his meatballs with a flourish as if to say, Aren't we swingers? His making-do had lasted hardly a minute when a man in a dinner jacket came over and said to Leah, "I'm sorry, ma'am, but you can't sit on the stairs."

She went on eating. "This is my husband, Jackson Schwartz," she said. "He tells me what to do. I take my orders from him."

This struck Mr. Sing as funny, for he let out a burst of laughter that brought Jackson to his feet. "Where do you expect us to go?" he said, his voice shaking. "Find us a table and we'll go there."

"I'm sorry, sir. There are no empty tables at the moment. You'll have to leave the stairs." He was very polite.

Jackson said, "We're not leaving until you find us a table."

"I have my orders, sir. You're not allowed to sit on the stairs. It violates the fire code."

Mr. Sing said, "Tell him who you are, Jackson. Tell him you'll have his badge."

"I'm Jackson Schwartz, attorney for the Squirrel Club," said Jackson.

"I'm sorry, sir. I have my orders."

Leah waited, poised over her food. She was prepared to sit there until two men came out and carried her away or until Jackson typed a command on her console. Jackson's plate lay unheeded on the stairs, vulnerable to the spikes of feminine heels.

"All right," said Jackson. "What's your name?"

"My name, sir, is Peterson."

"Okay, Peterson. Don't think I'll forget this." Leah stood up with her plate and glass.

"That's telling him, Jackson," said Mr. Sing. "Peterson," he shouted, as they moved into the mainstream on the second level, "he'll have your badge for this." Jackson left his plate on the step and Leah turned and watched Mr. Peterson pick it up; there, in the glittering palace of entertainment, where everything was promised and nothing delivered, she hung over the roundness of her last meatball and the hardness of an iron railing that pressed against her. They wandered through the crowd between tables, Mr. Sing happily bumping hips at her side, and she eyed the rich, brown gravy stains on her paper plate.

Rachel filled both hands with kernels from the sack of corn the neighboring farmer had given them. She stuffed them into the grinder, blew on her fingers and wound the crank. It seemed just as impossible as ever that she would fill the paper bag beneath the spout, but she went on cranking. When her arm ached she stopped and swept the wooden floorboards, watching the dust settle back stubbornly, like a resident population after an invasion.

She went into the front room and sat on the floor, propped against a bale of straw, holding out her hands toward the smoking potbellied stove. It was the first cold day of fall and she felt she'd never be warm again; she shivered in two sweaters, blue jeans and two pairs of woolen socks. Her miserable, smarting eyes pierced the smoke, bidding Laban's ghost to rise like a genie. Here I am, Laban, she said, working my freezing fingers to the bone, living in a broken-down farmhouse with bales of hay for chairs and broken windowpanes through which the wind whistles dirty tunes, so what have you got to say? Don't tell me. I know. It's a charming rustic atmosphere far from the machine-tooled life, where one can paint signs and dig digs. Only I don't dig.

Laban's millions were piling up in banks like the cow heaps in the fields while she pumped water, washed in a cast-iron kitchen sink, scooped dirt from her ears, listened to the obscene remarks of rats and made no plans. She wasn't even telling herself that she was biding her time any more. Her emotions, rubbed raw, lay on the surface of her skin, a row of Laban's signs for anybody to read, and Crevecoeur treated her with impenetrable kindness as if she were a waif with a SAVE THIS CHILD placard around her neck. The days confronted her like panes of glass. When she looked at one she saw another and through that another, with nothing in between. She set her jaw and tried to imagine a future. She would travel first class around the world, drink cocktails at the captain's table, have shipboard romances, change the guard at palaces, deliver Hyde Park orations, give parties on the Left Bank and the Riviera, reorganize Schweitzer's colony into a Laban Hilton, float in blue-green waters off Tel Aviv or Acapulco, ride a donkey cart in the Azores. Crevecoeur would go to medical school and when he graduated she'd become his office assistant. They'd treat only the poor and be paid in homemade jellies. They'd go to dinner with his old shaggy-dog of a professor in a small restaurant dripping with candle-waxed wine bottles. In the middle of dinner the professor would look at her, and then his eyes would meet Crevecoeur's. They'd smile and nod.

She couldn't stay at the farm much longer. Neither could Crevecoeur or Ronnie; they'd get spinal meningitis and die. One morning Crevecoeur would dress in a dark suit and go out to sell vacuum cleaners or World Book encyclopedias or insurance.

He'd work in a box factory or be a scrivener in a law firm run by IBM machines. He'd become a professional sign painter.

They could fix up the farm with her stolen money. They would put in central heating and plumbing and oak-paneled walls, get riding horses, put up a caretaker's cottage and a spiked iron fence. They'd give an annual ball for the county welfare fund.

Crevecoeur came in with a load of wood and dumped it in the corner. He stood with his hands stretched toward the stove. They'd become like an old married couple, speechless from a lifetime of having talked each other out—except that their silences were unbearable because they'd talked nothing out. Rachel couldn't stay in the same room with him; she escaped outside and stood on the bare, brown earth. Having to do something with herself, she strayed to the back and started across the field to the barn. She looked for the woodchuck's head bobbing from his hole, but he wasn't in sight. He had enough sense to come in out of the cold.

She went past the barn to Laban's dig and examined the trenches. Two were completed and a third was half-dug. There was a lot yet to be done, and she decided that while she waited for her ship to come in, she'd dig clams. She dragged a shovel from the barn and jumped into the unfinished trench. In a few minutes her hands were blistered and bruised, but she persisted and managed to loosen a little dirt. Perspiration clouded her vision and when she wiped her eyes she left streaks on her face. She had nothing to complain about. A little physical therapy and she'd level out from her tail spin and have a coming-out party. She'd buy a mink coat and diamond necklace, and boys would kiss her dirty toenails. All she had to do was get in there and dig. She filled half a shovel and tossed the dirt over the side of the trench before she noticed Ronnie. He shook his shoes clear and watched her.

"What you doing?" he said.

"What does it look like?" she said and worried the earth with a burst of energy.

"It's cold out here. Why don't you come in and get warm?"

"That's a laugh, it really is. If you haven't noticed it's not so hot inside either. I like it here just fine. I'm a cold tomato."

"If you wanted to finish the dig, you should have said something. We'll help you. You can go back on the bucket."

"This is a Laban project. Go fry your own fish. Stick to your paints. Don't you have anything better to do than bother a working girl? Go away."

"I thought you said we were friends."

She shook her head. "Too late, buddy. I gave you your chance. I don't have a friend in the world and that includes you. I've just got this hole, so go away."

He shrugged and walked toward the house. She leaned on the shovel and poked at the earth. If she was patient and didn't ask too much of her body, she'd finish the dig someday. She'd do the outside trenches to the four walls and hollow out the inside. First the farmers would hear about it and stand around gaping. Then the city folk would begin to ride out. A Good Humor truck would peddle ice cream. There'd be caps and buttons and pennants. Get your souvenir of the Laban Dig, folks. Jars of Laban Dirt cheap while they last.

Crevecoeur, wearing an old checked mackinaw jacket, approached her from the house. She got busy, and pushed hard on the shovel and hummed to show what a fun-loving creature she was. By the time he reached her she had another load ready and was pitching it over the side. Her arms quivered and she had trouble handling the shovel but she kept humming.

He reached out his hand. "That's enough," he said. "You've done enough for one day."

"You and Ronnie," she said. "Both Eagle Scouts. One day you drag Bernie out of a hole and now me. I'm happy where I am, Charlie, thank you."

"Then I'll join you," he said and jumped down beside her.

They stood looking at each other nose to nose. "Would you mind stepping back?" she said. "I don't have room to work."

"I don't want you to work. Ronnie and I will finish the dig. I don't think your father would want you to kill yourself doing it."

"Is that so? The greatest living authority on Laban. If you're so smart why ain't you rich? I can die as hard as Laban. He kept digging and so will I."

"He died the way he lived. What's your excuse?"

She glared at him, trembling with cold and fatigue and an immense desire to lie down and turn ice-blue. She was tired of her fluffy white flesh. "I don't need to justify myself to you. I don't owe you anything. We're strangers passing the time of day, that's all."

Crevecoeur put his hands on her shoulders and she sagged under the weight. "You don't owe me anything," he said, "but we're not exactly strangers if I'm in love with you."

There it was, the magic formula, the key to a woman's heart, the words that were to lift her from the trench and float her into the featherbed. She closed her eyes and felt buried by a thousand copies of *True Confessions*. The forests were raped, the bison and Indian slaughtered, the water polluted, the flowers aerosol-bombed, and Nelson Eddy and Jeanette MacDonald had played in too many movies. "You make it sound like a curse," she said. "Is that the way you feel?"

"No. Is that the way you feel?"

She opened her eyes and looked at him. She felt like a time bomb that busily ticked away at its business and discovered at the zero hour it wasn't going off. His features were bits of stone and straw improvised into a face by a brutally careless child. Then the pieces came together, the silence moved and shifted, and she felt a burst of joy. "I go for you too, Charlie," she said. "Love me any way you like."

He put his arms around her. She closed her eyes and he kissed her. "I'm glad you love me," she said. "I'd hate to marry a man who didn't."

He disengaged himself, climbed from the trench and held out his hand. "Let's go back," he said. "It's cold." She let herself be pulled up and he took off his mackinaw and put it around her shoulders.

As they walked toward the house she hugged his arm and said, "We'll be the nicest couple we know and that's a promise."

"Rachel," said Crevecoeur, "I love you very much, and I'm

grateful you have some feeling for me. But of course I couldn't let you marry me. I'm sorry."

She dropped his arm and stopped short. He turned to face her. "You're sorry? Thanks a lot. What do you think I am, anyway? What are you trying to do to me?" She lost control of her voice. "What do you want? To sleep with me? Sneak back into my bedroom? Make a score? All right."

He shook his head. "I'm sorry about that night. It won't happen again."

"Tell me what you want. To chop me up in pieces? Why don't you get the axe out of the barn? You want to love me like a sister? I've got references. Check with Bernie."

"Stop it, Rachel. I had no right to tell you how I felt. It was self-indulgence."

"Is that what it was? Indulge yourself some more. Why of course can't you marry me? You see—I'm not proud. Wipe up your dirty floor with me."

He looked away, his mouth hidden by his beard. "You said it yourself. I keep a dirty floor. Bums don't marry."

Her eyes opened until they felt like flying saucers, and in her relief she couldn't help giggling like the schoolgirl she no longer was. She felt two thousand years older than he. He was an American hero, the last of the saddle-bum innocents. He'd stay to die for her but if he lived he'd ride away. He didn't know it but she'd hobbled his horse for good. Nobody was going to not marry her for her own good. Nobody roamed the prairie on a nice Jewish girl's time. She demanded love, not protection. If she had to, she'd make him sit in a corner and think about it while she worked like a slave. "No dice, Charlie," she said. "You're one bum who *is* going to marry. There's only one way for you to get off the hook: if you don't love me."

"I love you."

"That's it, then. You're stuck with me."

"That's not it. I won't be another Jackson Schwartz." He tried to smile, a quick, anxious affair that made him look like Adlai Stevenson with a beard. "I'm not as noble as you. I'm too proud a poor boy to marry a rich girl."

"You love me, Charlie, remember? Jackson doesn't know the meaning of the word. You love my thirty-five-inch chest and my dark passionate eyes, right? You love *me*."

"When you handed me my week's allowance would I say, I love you, or, thank you?"

He succeeded in upsetting her. He'd reminded her of the will. "What if I didn't have any money?" she said. "What if I wore a hair shirt and lived with you in a cave?"

"I couldn't let you do that."

"What if I'm a fraud, a liar and a thief and you're my only hope? Would you make an honest woman of me? Would that violate your code?"

"I just don't want to drag you down. From where I'm standing I don't see any future for us. A woman needs a man who has at least a vague idea of where he's going."

She couldn't take any more. She felt she was losing ground. "What if I were made of stone?" she said. She started crying and ran into the house.

Ronnie was sitting in front of the stove; at bay, she glared at him and ran for the stairs. Crevecoeur caught up and held her and she sobbed against his chest. "Let's sit by the fire," he said. "Come on. Don't cry. We'll work things out."

They sat on the floor next to Ronnie. "I'll leave," he said.

She wiped her eyes with the back of her hand and drew a deep breath. "Stay, Ronnie. This is confession time. The more witnesses the better. I'm a thief."

"What did you take—some dirt from the dig?" said Ronnie.

"No. I stole Laban's will. The one that left me out. What does that make me? You want to hear something funny, Ronnie? Crevecoeur won't marry me because I'm rich. Isn't that a gasser?"

"Why did you do it, Rachel?" said Crevecoeur.

"Why? he asks. Why, to have all the nice things in life. Mink coats and diamonds. To buy myself a handsome husband like you. Why does anybody steal?"

"I don't care about anybody. I care about you."

"All right. I did it because I thought it would make Jackson unhappy. I don't know why I did it. I did it because I'm a rotten person. I meant to put it back."

"Do you still have it? You didn't tear it up or anything?"

"It's in one of the seat covers in Laban's living room. I never want to see it again."

Crevecoeur smiled. "That's a relief. You're not so much of a crook. We'll go in tomorrow and produce it. No harm done."

"No harm done? Don't you hate me?"

"No, I love you." He looked at Ronnie. "We've decided to get married. Rachel wants me to make an honest woman of her."

"Congratulations," said Ronnie. "I'll dance at your wedding." He stood up. "I mean it. Congratulations. I tell you what— Rachel's portrait is my wedding present." He went upstairs before she could thank him.

She leaned against Crevecoeur. He laughed. "You know," he said, "I'll bet your father's getting a kick out of this."

"You know it," said Rachel. "Let's find out. Here. Put your hands flat on the floor and we'll touch little fingers."

Crevecoeur did as she asked and they waited patiently for a sign. The wood in the stove made a noise. "You see?" said Rachel. "There he is."

"Mr. Laban," said Crevecoeur, "glad to have you with us. We're spending our honeymoon finishing the dig, so rest easy."

"Laban," said Rachel standing up, "don't take any wooden nickels." She turned to Crevecoeur. "Did I forget anything?"

"Yes," said Crevecoeur. "You forgot to invite him to the wedding."

30

During the evening Leah got tired of playing poker with Laban. She decided to go out, and she knew exactly where she wanted to go. "Do you realize," she said to Laban, "that in all these years I've never seen your office?"

She typed, and Laban said, "Baby, that's nobody's fault but your own. It's always been ready and waiting."

"Do you still have your keys?"

"No. Jackson has them now, remember?"

"I'll get them from him and we'll go together," she said. "You don't mind? Maybe you'd like to play more poker."

"You know the old warhorse better than that. It'll be nice to put my feet on the desk again and swear at Miss Trilby."

"But she won't be there. She quit when you died, remember? I could call her and say you're back on the job."

"Hell, no. It'd scare the daylights out of her. She hates to go out at night. Just you and me, baby, all the way."

Leah snapped the cover shut on the console. Carrying Laban and the box, she went upstairs and found Jackson sitting in the living room, his glasses on and papers in a pile beside him on the floor. When he saw her he took off his glasses and put them in his pocket. "Hello," he said. "I'm just finishing up."

She propped Laban in a chair and sat on the floor beside the console. "I want my keys, baby," said Laban. "I've got work to do. My vacation's over. And I want to show Leah the office."

"The office? Now?" said Jackson. "Leah, it's awfully late, really. Why don't you wait until morning and drive down with me? I'll show you around. The office is mine now, you know."

"Knock it off, Schwartz. You get my office over my dead body. The keys. Now."

"Leah, please. Make sense."

"I'll ask you one more time, Schwartz," said Laban. "If you don't give me the keys you're through. Finished."

Jackson stared at her, then reached into his trouser pocket and handed her his key case.

Leah took the keys. "Now you're playing it smart, baby," said Laban. "Just remember where your bread's buttered." She shut the console and picked it up, tucked Laban under her arm and started for the door.

"Wait a minute, Leah," said Jackson. "Let me go with you. I'll drive you down." She shook her head. "Let me at least get your coat. It's chilly." As he ran toward the closet she opened the door with her free hand. She didn't bother to look back as she put Laban beside her on the front seat of the car and the console on the floorboard at his feet.

It was a pleasant ride. The streets were quiet and dark and neither Laban nor she felt like saying anything. It was enough to be running an errand together, just the two of them. When she got downtown she made herself ask a policeman where the Olympic Building was; he directed them to a tall building two blocks away, which they found without trouble. She parked in front of a No Parking sign and carried Laban and the console inside the lobby. A middle-aged round-faced man in work clothes was sitting in front of an open elevator reading a newspaper. She begged Laban's forgiveness and forced words into her mouth. "Mr. Laban's office," she said.

He looked at Laban. "Say, that's one of them Toy Men." He smiled, showing ragged teeth.

"Mr. Laban's office, please," she said.

"Ma'am, there ain't no more Laban's office. He passed away."

"His firm's still here, isn't it?" she said angrily.

"Yes'm. That's on the twelfth floor."

She stepped into the elevator and the man rode her up, eying Laban. "Those Toy Men are sure something," he said. She said nothing. The elevator stopped and he opened the door; "Around the corner," he said.

She walked down the hall and unlocked the door to Laban's offices. When she turned on the lights she found herself in a large room with several desks at the rear; on top of the desks were telephones and green-hooded typewriters. After two wrong guesses she found Laban's private office. Her picture was in a gold frame on the desk, and she laid it face down. She sat Laban in the brown leather swivel chair, put his feet on the desk and drew up a chair facing him.

"I like your office, Laban," she said. "It's peaceful."

"Sure, baby. This is where I keep the vintage Laban. You knew it all along, didn't you? That character at home was just to throw people off, so they'd follow the wrong trail."

"I know, Laban," she whispered. "I played the game too. We fooled everybody."

"It was fun for a while," said Laban. "The only trouble was it got tiresome. Fun gets to be hard work."

"I know, Laban. Why don't we get serious while we have the chance? Let our hair down?"

"For you, baby, I'd do anything," said Laban, and Leah unpinned her barrettes and bobby pins and let her hair fall free to her shoulders. "It feels wonderful to say exactly what one feels," she said.

"You're the only child I ever really loved," said Laban, "but I don't have to tell you."

"Yes, you do. I want to hear it," said Leah. "Words mean something if they come from the heart. Words become shining new."

"I'm sorry about Schwartz. We made a mistake there."

"It's not your fault, Laban. But you shouldn't have died so soon. I wasn't ready."

"I'm sorry, baby, but I was tired. All those damned games I played. It wears a man out. I couldn't stop, you know. Bernie and Rachel would have swarmed all over me."

"They killed you. They kept hammering at you. They wanted to crack you open like a coconut and suck out your insides."

"They couldn't leave a body be."

"They're no better than Jackson. They tried to make you what they wanted you to be, and he tries to be what he thinks I want. They're all invaders of privacy."

Laban stood up and walked around the desk. She pulled out the chair for him when he got back and put his feet on the desk.

"I'm worn out, baby," he said. "I'm not the man I used to be. I'd like to rest now."

He closed his eyes. Leah watched him without moving for several minutes. She typed a message, then got up and turned off all the lights in the suite and went back to her chair. She sat in the darkness with Laban, not seeing him but able to feel his presence. She carried the console to the window, placed it on the inside ledge, and opened the window. A blast of cold wind ruffled her hair as she climbed out and sat on the stone ledge. Reaching back, she picked up the console and placed it on the ledge beside her. She looked down at the scattering of lights in the street, then across at the lights from other buildings. Just before she pushed out to engage the darkness, she pressed the red button of the console. As she swept downward toward the fireflies, like a hawk upon chickens, the Toy Man, sitting in Laban's chair with his feet on the desk, said, "Miss Trilby, take a letter. To Hoy Sing, of Hoy Sing Adult Toys. Dear Mr. Sing baby. In response to your letter of the fourth instant, please be advised that I will be unable to attend the coming shareholder's meeting of the corporation due to the fact that I am taking my daughter Leah on a trip around the world. With best wishes, William Laban."

According to Laban's diagrams, it was a picture-book dig. The preliminary trenches had been laid out with plumb lines at right angles to the walls. The balks of soil left standing had been examined and three Mason jars and one tin spoon carefully removed and tagged. The boys were clearing out the last of the balks and would soon have a tidy square hole bounded by the walls. They had started digging again after Leah's funeral as if their lives depended on it, while Rachel filled her bucket and dumped dirt.

A lump of vagrant clay had levitated from the bucket and seemed permanently lodged in her throat. How awful Leah must have felt, how much alone. Rachel couldn't forgive herself for having walked out on her. How little, after all, she'd known her twin. The horror of it overwhelmed sadness.

Why did somebody commit suicide? Look at Laban, knowing he was through: his last act was to dance at Leah's wedding. How could her sister's life be so miserable as to make her want to end it? She'd always been the sturdy one. Leah's was the brick house while her own was straw. Yet the first storm to come along had toppled Leah, while she herself stood with a bucket of dirt in her hands. The moral of "The Three Little Pigs" was phony; if you build with straw you ride the wind instead of meeting it head-on. She shook her head stubbornly. She refused to drift. She had an anchor, Crevecoeur. Live and let die and let others live and let die. If she was reduced to a desert island it didn't matter because

Crevecoeur would be shipwrecked with her.

Charlie and Ronnie threw out their shovels and climbed up. "That's it," said Crevecoeur.

"We've got ourselves a first-class dig," said Ronnie.

Crevecouer picked up a pole that was sharpened at one end and had a sign nailed to the other, and jammed it into the dirt at an inside corner of the walls. The sign was in Roman, upper case, and read LABAN'S DIG. "I'm best at Roman," said Crevecoeur. "Laban might have preferred Gothic or Old English."

"It's perfect," said Rachel. "Let's go in and have a drink on it."

As they moved across the field, a figure in a topcoat came around the side of the house. It was Rabbi Isaacson, and she ran forward to greet him. "How thoughtful of you to visit us, Rabbi," she said. "We've just finished Laban's Dig."

"He told me about it," said the rabbi. "He mentioned it several times. I'd like to see it if I may."

"Come on." The boys stood by. "Do you know Charlie and Ronnie? This is Rabbi Isaacson." They shook hands and all went back to the dig.

"It's a fine job," said the rabbi, looking into the hole and at the sign. "Laban's Dig. A good piece of work."

"Look what we found," said Rachel. She showed him the Mason jars and the spoon.

The rabbi smiled. "Congratulations," he said.

"Would you like to come in with us and celebrate over a glass of wine?" said Rachel.

"Fine. First I have something to ask of you."

Rachel gave him a quick look. "All right. Charlie, you and Ronnie go ahead. We'll be there in a minute." She stared at the dig as they walked off. "I guess you think I'm not behaving very well," she said. "Fooling around like this."

The rabbi smiled. "You forget I knew your father. There are many ways to light candles."

"Thank you, Rabbi." She kicked at the earth. "How could she do it? How?"

"One can only guess. Perhaps she saw a forest instead of trees. When a tree fell she thought it was the whole forest."

"I failed her. I knew something was wrong. I'm her twin and I failed her."

"Her vision failed her. You couldn't have helped that."

"If only she'd given somebody a chance. I'd do anything for her and it's too late."

"It's not too late," said the rabbi. "More than one soul can abide within a person. You can make room for your sister."

She knew what he meant; she also knew that she wouldn't if she stopped to think about it. "Rabbi," she said, "I like you. May I?"

He smiled.

"Something else. A big favor. I'm getting married very soon. Would you perform the ceremony?"

"Of course."

"He's not Jewish, Rabbi," said Rachel bravely. "I'm marrying Charles Crevecoeur."

"Would you marry him in any event?"

"Yes, oh, yes."

"Then I will marry you."

"I have to be honest, Rabbi. I don't think he'll convert."

"If you fill his heart he is already converted."

"Oh, Rabbi," she said.

"I mustn't forget," he said. "Your father left me with a commission to fulfill. I hope you can come to his house at two o'clock next Sunday. Will you be there?"

"Sure," she said. "Can you tell me what it's about?"

"I'm sorry, no. He asked me to say nothing until you were all together."

"Will Bernie be there? He's at law school."

"Yes. I telephoned him and he agreed to fly in."

"It's about the money, isn't it?"

The rabbi smiled and shook his head. "Sunday at two o'clock," he said. "Shall we go and have that glass of wine?"

. . .

After the rabbi left, Rachel watched Ronnie pour the last of the burgundy and then turned to Crevecoeur. "You hear what he said? We're going to be married by the rabbi, because I'm a Jew."

"I suspected you were," said Crevecoeur. "Thanks for telling me."

"I mean it. I like being a Jew. I'm going to stay a Jew."

"I don't know what I am but I'm likely to stay that way. Okay?" said Crevecoeur.

"I want our children to be Jews." She worked up to fierceness. "I promised Laban. At least I would have if I'd had the chance. Is it a deal about the children?"

Crevecoeur grinned. "No deals. Religion has to be earned by lives not yet in being."

"You give me the right to fight for Jewishness?" she said.

"I give you the right to skip every third crack in the sidewalk if you want to."

"It's a deal," she said. "I'll marry you. Let's shake on it."

Ronnie stood up, shook his head and went upstairs. "Ronnie," said Rachel. "Why are you going?" She turned to Crevecoeur. "Did we do anything wrong?"

"You're a worrier," said Crevecoeur. "Haven't you ever seen Ronnie go upstairs before?"

"We've made him feel left out. We've been thinking too much about ourselves."

"When I see him again I'll hold his hand," said Crevecoeur.

Ronnie returned with Rachel's portrait. He propped it against a bale of hay. Rachel looked at it. She had pale green skin, enormous black eyes and an exclamation mark for nose and mouth. She loved it. "I'm taking off," said Ronnie. "I've got myself a deal."

"What do you mean?" asked Rachel.

"I get a free apartment above The Combo for drawing four sketches a night. The customers write their names on pieces of paper and I draw four from a hat. I'm moving tomorrow."

"You can't, Ronnie. Because of me? I won't let you," said Rachel. "I want it to be the same as always. Please, Ronnie."

"Not because of you. I've got a deal."

Rachel pleaded. "This doesn't change anything. We're all good for each other. Give it a chance for just a little while."

Ronnie smiled. "You do carry on," he said, and shook his head. "I've got myself a deal."

Crevecoeur stood up. "You don't have to go," he said. "We're going."

"We?" said Rachel. "Going where?"

"Back to the law. I've been kidding myself out here. I'm a lawyer. That's my profession. You stay, Ronnie. It's a place to paint."

"Charlie," said Rachel, "if you're doing this because of me I'll never forgive you."

"Not because of you," Crevecoeur said. "Because of me."

Rachel ran to him. "Charlie, whatever you want to do is what I want to do. Only that."

"You really pulling out?" said Ronnie.

Crevecoeur nodded.

Ronnie shrugged. "Then I'll stay."

"Good," said Crevecoeur. "It'll be a nice place for us to visit."

"Be my guest," said Ronnie. "It's your house."

"Ronnie," said Rachel, "you want the jeep? Is it all right, Charlie?"

Crevecoeur hesitated. "What do we need with two cars?" he said.

"Will you take it, Ronnie? For old times' sake?" she said.

Ronnie thought hard. "Sure," he said, and added, "Thanks." He looked at them both, turned and walked upstairs.

"Charlie, are you certain it's what you want to do? Go back to the law?"

"I'm sure. It was nice of you to give him the car."

"It was Laban's to begin with, and he never paid him for the picture, remember? It would be impossible out here without a car."

"Ronnie should get paid like that for all his paintings."

"I'll miss him."

Crevecoeur smiled. "More than he will you." Rachel fell silent. She leaned against his arm. "I wonder," said Crevecoeur, "what your father has up his sleeve for Sunday?"

"Laban?" said Rachel. "A joker, what else?"

Once, at college, rummaging with Bernie for a desk lamp in a Goodwill store, Rachel had come across a framed picture of camp girls on horseback. Perhaps fifty of them were lined up abreast. The photograph was six inches high and four feet long. She bought it for two dollars and hung it in her room. Each of the girls, ranging from ten to fifteen years old, had an eager, scrubbed, proud expression, as if willing to bet her future on the permanency of the there-and-then.

Now she recalled the picture as she sat on the floor at Crevecoeur's feet in the house of her dead father, eying her brother, her brother-in-law, Beatrice, Miss Trilby and Rabbi Isaacson with the professional eye of a photographer, focusing through a mental lens, projecting their imminent burst from a common frame of reference. She felt sad that most of these people would soon be strangers and knew she would be sadder if they tried to be anything else. How negative most relationships were and how little sunlight was needed to ruin them. Jackson had been her brother-in-law and with Leah's death he was no longer; Beatrice had been a stepmother and with Laban's death wasn't; Miss Trilby had been Laban's secretary and was no longer. Rabbi Isaacson was there to clean up; when he finished, the house would be spotless and locked, ready for new occupants.

There were residual tears. With her face of soft pink clay,

blanched blue eyelids red, Miss Trilby was a mourner. In a black dress with pearl buttons down the back, Beatrice was a mourner. Laban had moved through the world and hired a claque.

Bernie wore a new, stiff gray flannel suit and a tightly knotted striped tie, with a plaster cast for a face. He might have been a delegate to an international conference, determined to reveal and sign nothing. He made a terrible delegate. Yet he had been her brother and remained her brother and she would never let him go. She smiled at him and he looked away. It didn't matter; sooner or later, when he needed her, she would be ready. She wouldn't make the same mistake twice.

She was afraid to look at Jackson. His hair was mussed and he was unshaven. His clothes looked slept in. Nothing is more painful than a fastidious man who no longer cares about his public appearance.

"I won't keep you wondering," said Rabbi Isaacson. He held a blue-backed document. "Before he died, Laban set up a living trust. I have a copy of it here. Everything he had went into the trust. The Olympic Trust Company is named trustee but Laban asked them not to contact you until I advised you of the contents."

"Are you saying, Rabbi," said Rachel, "that his will meant nothing?"

"That's true. His will means nothing."

Rachel met the rabbi's eyes. "Let me ask you a moral question. If a thief steals something of no value, is she still a thief? I stole Laban's will, Rabbi."

"But she returned it," said Crevecoeur.

"Let me ask you a moral question, Rabbi," said Bernie. "If an angel falls off the head of a pin, is she still an angel?"

"Yes, Rachel," said the rabbi, "she is still a thief. 'But when David saw that his servants whispered together, David perceived that the child was dead: and David said unto his servants, Is the child dead? And they said, He is dead. Then David arose from the earth, and washed, and anointed himself, and changed his apparel; and he came into the house of the Lord, and worshipped: then he came to his own house; and when he required, they set bread before him, and he did eat. Then said his servants unto him, What thing is this that thou hast done? thou didst fast and weep for the child, while it was alive; but when the child was dead, thou didst rise and eat bread. And he said, While the child was yet alive, I fasted and wept: for I said, Who knoweth whether the Lord will not be gracious to me, that the child may live? But now he is dead, wherefore should I fast? Can I bring him back again?' "

There was a silence. "Very good, Rabbi," said Bernie. "The wages of sin is life. Can we please get on with it? We haven't got all day."

"The wages of *life* is life," said the rabbi. He fingered the document. "To summarize: Miss Trilby, you are left twenty-five thousand dollars outright. Mrs. Laban receives fifteen thousand a year for her lifetime. And the children are each given five thousand a year for life. Since Leah is dead her share passes into the residue, as will the other life bequests eventually. I believe it's fair to tell you that the total income of the trust will be perhaps one hundred thousand dollars a year."

"Five thousand a year," said Bernie, working his lips. "Got that, Beatrice? Laban's love was worth five thousand a year." He looked at the rabbi. "And the residue. Who gets that?"

"I'll read it to you." The rabbi turned pages. " 'All the rest, residue and remainder of my property shall be held in trust by my Trustee and the income therefrom shall be paid each year to such person or institution as the Prize Committee, hereinafter defined, shall, by a majority vote on the first of December of each year, select. The decision of the Prize Committee shall be binding on the Trustee and all other persons. In the event no prize is awarded in a given year, the income for said year shall be added to principal. In the event of a tie, duplicate prizes will not be awarded but the Committee will draw lots to select the winner. I can't stand ties. It's better for a nice guy to finish last.

" 'The Prize Committee shall consist of, in the beginning, Rabbi Isaacson acting alone. As each winner is selected he, if he is a person, or the President thereof, if it is an institution, shall be added to the Committee, if he is willing or able to act. His willingness or ability to act shall in no way affect his right to receive the prize. If Rabbi Isaacson dies, or becomes unwilling or unable, for any reason, to act as the Committee before there are any other members, or if any existing member dies, or becomes unwilling or unable to act, and leaves no other members acting, I direct that three persons be chosen to form the Committee in the following manner: my Trustee shall promote a contest based upon the same criteria as the Committee shall use in the selection of a prize winner and shall offer a twenty-five-thousand-dollar award to the person who first sends in the three names ultimately selected. The three persons ultimately selected shall be those who receive the most votes and shall share equally the prize for that year. I offer no salary or other compensation to Committee members. It's not the money, it's the principle of the thing. No person or institution shall win the prize more than once. No Committee member shall receive the prize while serving on the Committee. No Committee member should have less than a long and happy life and God's countenance shining down upon him or her.

" 'What, then, is the prize for? What is left to give one for? We've got prizes for peace, for literature, for science. We've got them for sending in coupons, for being the ten-thousandth person to stand in a line or buy a toothbrush, for giving the date Abraham Lincoln split his first rail. We've got prizes for guessing how much a diamond ring is worth and for defining, in twenty-five words or less, the theory of relativity. We've got prizes for being blind, lame, with a drunken husband and epileptic children. One prize is left and I'm giving it. It happens that my winners will be those who least need it.

" 'Rabbi Isaacson tells me we should restore the joy of religious experience. He says no book has as many words for joy as the Old Testament. I'd buy that if I could but I guess it can't be bought. I've never danced and sung my way through the rabbi's sermons. I know what he means but I don't *feel* what he means so I'll put it the way I feel. I direct the Committee to award the prize on December first of each year to the person or institution, whether belonging to an organized religion or not, that has done the most, in the opinion of a majority of the Committee, to establish the religious experience of joy. My religion is to be joyful. That's it, Rabbi. That's as close as I can get. I've felt good about being alive. I've felt religiously good about being alive. I mean I don't know where my feeling comes from, but I put my money on it anyway and call it God.

" 'Okay, Committee. It's your baby and it's up to you to keep the baby laughing even after he's grown up. I've got no rules and no conditions. Let the prize winners map the terrain. I don't know if the churches, synagogues and mosques have turned God sober but I suspect, given a chance, they still might let Him in for a while to play. Religion is man's imagination at its best. It's not a tragedy.' "

Rabbi Isaacson looked up. "I think that covers it," he said.

Beatrice and Miss Trilby cried in their handkerchiefs. "That wonderful, wonderful man," said Miss Trilby.

Rachel watched Jackson. He was bent over as if his back were broken. She gave him the benefit of the doubt. Maybe it wasn't simply that he was left out in the cold. Maybe he had loved Leah after his fashion but couldn't express it in a way to make it stick. With a brave look at Crevecoeur, she said, "I don't want anything. Let Bernie have my share. I won't take it."

"It's all right, Rachel," said Crevecoeur. "I hope I'm strong enough not to buckle under five thousand a year."

Bernie stood up. He'd taken off his glasses and was wiping them. His pouting eyelids looked naked. "Congratulations, Rabbi. Even from the grave he's laughing at us," he said.

"Certainly he's laughing," said Rabbi Isaacson, with a show of sharpness. "He was a religious man."

ABOUT THE AUTHOR

ALBERT LEBOWITZ

is forty-three years old and lives with his wife and two-year-old son in St. Louis, Missouri. He received a liberal arts degree from Washington University and a law degree from Harvard Law School. During World War II he flew combat duty as a navigator with the 15th Air Force stationed in Italy.

At present Mr. Lebowitz leads a dual existence: he practices law three days a week and during the other four works on his second novel.